HER FIGHT

BOOKS BY EMMA TALLON

HER FIGHT

EMMA TALLON

bookouture

Published by Bookouture in 2022

An imprint of Storyfire Ltd.
Carmelite House
50 Victoria Embankment
London EC4Y 0DZ

www.bookouture.com

ISBN: 978-1-80314-366-8
eBook ISBN: 978-1-80314-365-1

As always, this is for my wonderful babies, Christian and Charlotte.
Everything I ever do is for you.

PROLOGUE

She switched on the small torch and padded barefoot out of the bedroom and down the stairs towards the kitchen. The storm must have knocked out the power, but hopefully if she flicked the fuses, it would come back on. The sound of the rain hammering down on the roof and against the windows comforted her as she made her way through the house. She felt cocooned, as though nestled in the storm's embrace. Though a brighter cocoon would have been preferable.

Reaching the kitchen, she moved to pick up one of the chairs – needing something to stand on to reach the fuse box – but suddenly paused. Faded yellow squares washed across the table before her. She frowned and looked up and out the window to find all the other houses still seemed to be brightly lit. If the storm had taken out the power, the whole street would have been affected.

Something began to prickle at the back of her neck, and she glanced towards the fuse box. The door was hanging open. The prickle turned into a cold alarm that ran down the length of her spine.

As the realisation dawned that there was someone else in

her home, she instinctively turned to run – but barely halfway into her first step, she pulled back with a gasp, dropping her phone with a clatter as she realised she was cornered. She knew then, seeing him there in the doorway, his murderous gaze burning a hole into her, that she wasn't safely cocooned in this storm after all. She was trapped, like an animal in a cage. And the most dangerous predator of all was in there with her.

ONE

The walls of the small white room shone harshly bright and cold under the single fluorescent ceiling light, all the tiny flaws in the paintwork – brushstrokes and chips – showing in unflatteringly high definition. The low buzzing sound from the bulb warred with the sharp ticks coming from the cheap plastic clock that hung high on the wall, encased in a purpose-built metal cage that was screwed to the wall.

Why *was* it screwed to the wall? What exactly did they think people were going to do with a clock? These were the questions Scarlet had often asked herself when she'd been stuck in this room. And she'd been here far too many times this past year.

DI Jennings glared at her from across the table, the frustration in his eyes reminiscent of a tiger whose prey has managed to situate itself just out of reach. 'Where is he?' he demanded through gritted teeth, no longer bothering to try to hide his feelings.

Scarlet stared back icily, her grey-blue eyes hard and unyielding. 'As I told you before, I have no idea.'

'And as *I've* told *you*, I don't believe you. I think you've got him hidden somewhere, with the naïve idea that you might be able to wait this out, keep his head down until the storm blows over. Well I'll tell you something now...' Jennings leaned towards her. 'It will never be over. This storm doesn't pass. I will keep chasing you, hounding you and whatever the hell else I need to do, until I find him. And when I do, you're both going to prison for a very, very, *very* long time.'

Scarlet held his gaze. 'The threats really start to wear thin after a while,' she said coolly. 'How many times have you threatened to put me away now, Jennings, hm?' She raised one dark perfectly arched eyebrow. 'It used to unnerve me, I'll admit. But after a while, it became pathetically apparent that you couldn't put away a tin of beans, let alone me.'

There was a loud thump as Jennings hit his fist hard on the table between them.

Scarlet leaned back in her chair, lifting her chin slightly with a smirk of triumph. 'What's the matter, did I hit a nerve?'

'You cocky little fool. You committed *murder*, Scarlet,' Jennings declared loudly. 'You and I both know it. We had all the evidence, right there in the locker room.' He pointed off to one side. 'And when that went missing and we hit dead ends, I thought it was over, I really did. But this has given me new hope.' A steely look replaced the anger on his face, and the corners of his mouth lifted in a brief smile. 'It's only a matter of time before we find him, and when we do, I can promise you he'll give us all we need to put things right.'

Jennings was talking about her boyfriend, John Richards. Or, rather, her ex-boyfriend. She had to keep reminding herself of that fact, despite the sting it always brought forth. John had been a DI in Jennings's station who had pulled the wool over his eyes and stolen the evidence that would have put Scarlet away for murder. Evidence Jennings had worked hard to get.

John had always been a good policeman with good intentions, but he'd cared too deeply for his criminal girlfriend to let Jennings take her down. He'd saved her when no one else could and gone against his vow to protect and uphold the law he served. They'd had to keep their relationship a secret from that point on. They were two people from very different sides of the track; from different sides of the law. It was an unnatural connection in most people's eyes, but a connection neither of them had been able to ignore. The fire between them had burned too brightly.

They'd hidden it well for a while, but eventually they'd been betrayed and their relationship brought to light. John had had to disappear to keep them both from going down for the mistakes they'd made – her for murder, him for covering it up. Jennings knew the truth, but without John physically there to connect it all, there would remain no evidence of either crime.

Scarlet gave Jennings a look of amusement, hiding the gaping hole of pain she felt whenever she thought of John. 'The mistake you're making is thinking that there's something to give. You've made an assumption that since John and I were together – which, of course, is no crime in itself – he stole some supposed evidence that you claim you had in your locker. But that's all it is. An assumption. You have no proof, and John, should you find him, has nothing to give you. Because it didn't happen.'

Jennings nodded slowly. 'You seem so very confident that you're safe. But let me explain how this is going to go. In *reality*. When we find John, he'll be detained pending investigation. Whether or not he admits it, we have proof you were together and that he was in the station the night the evidence went missing. We have proof that his computer idled for twenty minutes at the exact time the cameras went down around the locker. In fact, in this case, the *absence* of evidence all times together so perfectly that there's no reasonable doubt left in anyone's mind of what happened. That's enough to send him down, whether he admits it or not.'

Jennings leaned back and his gaze roamed her face critically. 'You know, we didn't suspect him at first. He was an exemplary DI. He even helped with the investigation.' Jennings let out a short humourless laugh. 'But, of course, the discovery of your relationship brought everything to light. So he'll be charged – that's a certainty. But then he'll be given a choice and *that's* what you need to be worried about.'

Scarlet felt her stomach constrict, despite her outward confidence, and lifted her chin a little higher in defiance. 'What's this choice then?' she asked drily.

'We don't want him. Not really. He's done a very stupid thing and of course he'll be punished for that. But it's *you* we really want,' Jennings replied. 'He screwed up, but you *murdered* someone. You killed a man in cold blood. *You're* the one I want to see rot behind bars. So we'll give John a choice. He can choose to stay quiet and protect you, but then he'll receive the highest penalty possible and be placed in a max-security prison, in a cell that's nestled right amongst the most dangerous people he's ever put away.'

Scarlet had to work hard at controlling her expression at the cruel glint in Jennings's eye. She knew he meant it. He really would put John in that position. He would create that perfect hell to get what he wanted.

'Or,' Jennings continued, 'he can give us what we need to put *you* away for your crimes and instead he'll receive a suspended sentence. He'll be thrown out of the force of course, but he'll be a free man, safe from harm. He can start again, forget all this.'

Jennings leaned forward once more. 'You might think you've got him under your spell. He might even think he loves you and believes he's a hero. But at the end of the day, even your charms won't be more important to him than his life.'

Scarlet forced a tight smile. 'That's a lovely story, Jennings. That what gets you off to sleep at night?'

Jennings smirked coldly. 'You can quip all you want, but I'm just telling you how it is. Now if you want to confess and save me the time I'm about to waste tracking John down, then I'd say I could probably cut you a deal. You'll do time – there's no way out of that. But a confession would definitely lessen the sentence. And I'd be willing to personally ensure you go somewhere decent, somewhere with good facilities and a more lax approach to visits and small luxuries. Somewhere comfortable, rather than the max-security facility you'll be headed to otherwise.'

He opened his hands and relaxed his expression as he stared at her. 'You'd be wise to consider this. Whether you delay the inevitable or not, you're going down. And if it were me, I'd want my next few years to be a comfortable ride rather than a trip to hell.'

Scarlet shook her head wearily. 'I've told you, there's nothing to tell. John vanished on me the same way he vanished on you. Now, if we're done here, I need to go home.'

'Actually we're not. I have the right to hold you for twenty-four hours, and since you've been here less than two, I'll be keeping you overnight,' Jennings replied.

'What?' Scarlet exclaimed with a frown.

'It'll give you time to think about my offer, then we'll revisit this conversation in the morning.'

He stood up and stared at her coldly, then held down the button on the tape machine. 'Interview paused at 12.43 p.m.'

Releasing it, he gathered up his file. 'I'm not giving up this time, Scarlet. You're going to jail. All that remains to be seen is how long it takes me to get you there and how easy you want to make this on yourself.'

Scarlet stood up and glared at him defiantly. 'That's where you're wrong, Jennings. And the only thing that *really* remains to be seen is how long it's going to take for that to get through your thick head.'

Not waiting for him to answer or escort her, she strode out of the investigation room and down the hall towards the cells.

TWO

Lily gazed out the fourth-storey window across the busy bustling streets of Central London, her brown eyes troubled. Dark clouds gathered ominously in the sky above, mirroring her mood as Scarlet's predicament weighed heavy on her mind. Her shoulders felt tense as she crossed her arms over her chest, her back rigid and her head held proud.

The office she stood in belonged to Robert Cheyney, the family's lawyer – a very clever and very crooked man. He'd been on their payroll for years and had got them out of many a sticky situation over the course of this professional relationship.

Behind her, the hum of office activity grew louder for a moment as the door opened and Robert strode in, red-faced and puffing slightly.

'So sorry I kept you waiting, Lily,' he said cordially as he placed his briefcase on the desk and shrugged off his suit jacket.

Lily shook her head and waved the comment away. 'It's fine – you didn't know I was coming. *I* didn't know I was coming,' she added.

'Take a seat please,' Robert said, gesturing to the chair across the desk.

They both sat, and Lily leaned on one of the hard rolled arms of the overstuffed chair. 'They're keeping her on a twenty-four-hour hold,' she told him, cutting straight to the point. 'She's already been questioned.'

Robert's face fell and he closed his eyes with an almost indistinguishable groan. 'And?'

'All they asked was where John is and she told them she had no idea.'

Robert nodded. 'Tell her not to speak to them again without me.'

'She won't. I think she just wanted to see which way they'd probe before bringing you in.'

'Still, it's dangerous,' he argued.

Lily conceded with a tilt of the head.

Robert scratched his forehead with a thoughtful expression. 'Right. Run me through exactly where we are in real terms, then what the story is. Let's see what we can do with this.'

'We smuggled John to Spain on a boat three weeks ago with enough cash to start over. He took no ID or anything that could link him back here. We're working on getting a new ID to him,' Lily replied.

'So you're still in touch with him?' Robert asked.

Lily shook her head. 'No. We purposely cut all ties, but we left him in good hands, and they're keeping tabs on him.'

'Good.'

The memory of that night flashed across Lily's mind. Scarlet had been heartbroken as she'd said her goodbyes and watched John sail away from her forever. They had been a match made in hell – two people who were absolutely perfect for each other, but who could never be together if they wanted any kind of life. They'd tried. Lord knew they'd tried. But there was nowhere in this world that was safe for them. And, as expected, it had all blown up in their faces.

'The police don't know, or suspect, that he's out of the

country yet,' she continued. 'They think she's hiding him. They've started searching our known businesses and turned up with warrants at our homes this morning.'

'And the houses are clean?' Robert checked.

'Of course,' Lily replied. 'All the legal properties are. Plus, we were expecting this.' She wiped a hand down her face and looked out the window. 'Scarlet said they're keeping her in overnight to make her sweat, then they want to talk to her again in the morning. Make sure you're there and get her home. Can we push for harassment again?'

Robert pulled a face. 'They've got good reason to be doing all they are this time. Later, yes. It's our best shot of ending it down the line, but it's probably wiser to pick our battles and just get her home for now.'

Lily nodded. 'Do that then.'

'The evidence John stole. What did he do with it? Is it likely to resurface?' Robert asked. 'Because if it does, there will be nothing I can do.'

'He gave it to Scarlet and I destroyed it myself. We just have to make sure John isn't found.' She cast her serious gaze back towards Robert. 'Because if he is, Jennings will make him choose between a brutal and conveniently accidental death inside or his freedom if he gives her up. And, honestly, much as he loves her, if it comes down to that, I don't like her chances.'

THREE

Cillian stared up at the brittle concrete balconies either side of the tired alleyway he walked down. Weeds poked up through the cracks of the old path, broken bottles and cigarette butts littering the edges. The sharp acrid odour of urine permeated the air, and the only sounds breaking the otherwise depressing silence were that of a dog barking and a woman screaming expletives in the distance.

This place was a cesspit of junkies, prostitutes and wasters, and was also one of the last places he'd found his sister squatting, back in the days when she'd lived in the chemical clutches of heroin. He couldn't recall the exact number of times he'd pulled her out of places like this, trying to force her to go clean and live her life properly. Or how many times he'd set her up somewhere new, only for her to run right back to the squalid surroundings he'd saved her from. Every time she'd relapsed, it had killed a small piece of his soul. Because he loved his little sister. He'd hated seeing her destroy herself so successfully, time and time again.

But one day everything had changed. His mother's long-term flame, Ray Renshaw, had forced Ruby clean in a brutal manner, locking her in a room and forcing her through cold turkey. He'd threatened certain consequences if she returned to her old ways, and Ruby had come home, defeated. That had been nearly a year ago, and despite all sorts of challenges and obstacles, she'd stayed. She hadn't given up. She'd worked hard and begun to heal, tried every day to forge a better life. She was far from perfect; Cillian held no illusions about that. Ruby was awkward, short-tempered and unpredictable at the best of times. But she was his sister and he believed in her.

The one obstacle that had held her back was her ongoing feud with Scarlet – the two had been natural enemies since childhood. The rest of the family had assumed this would disappear with time, as they were forced to rub down together in the family business. But, if anything, putting them together in such close range had only fuelled the fire. They'd underestimated the animosity that still raged between the cousins until it was too late. They'd traded digs and insults and caused difficulties big and small for each other until it had finally come to a head. Ruby had set Scarlet up, arranging for her and John to be caught together by one of John's team. It was the ultimate betrayal and when things had blown up and the rest of the family hadn't fallen in with Ruby's plans, she'd disappeared again. Cillian had been searching for her ever since.

It wasn't that he didn't think she could fend for herself – it wasn't even so much that he thought she'd slide back into her bad habits, though that was a possibility. It was that Scarlet had finally snapped. Ruby had destroyed her relationship with John, as well as his life, and potentially both their freedom. It was a vicious declaration of war, and Scarlet was done with holding back. She'd sworn that should she find Ruby first, she'd kill her. And for the first time, Lily didn't have the right to stop her. By underworld law, Scarlet had every right to exact her revenge, but Cillian couldn't live with that. Ruby had crossed all lines, but she was still his sister, and he needed to find her before Scarlet did.

He came to the end of the alleyway and paused to look around the squalid estate. He was in the middle of a cluster of flat blocks that surrounded a square of what was now mainly mud but had once been grass. A rusting goalpost stood to one side, the net long gone, and a couple of bikes missing their front wheels lay propped against the railings. Cillian bit down on the toothpick he'd been holding in his mouth and squinted at the door numbers on the front of each building; it had been a while since he'd been here last.

Finding the building he wanted, he cut across the square, aware of several pairs of curious eyes staring at him from behind kitchen curtains.

Entering the building, he made a beeline for the first door on the left, knocking with one hand and covering the peephole with the other. There was a shuffling sound within and then a pause.

'Who is it?' came an uncertain voice.

'I'm looking for a twenty bag,' he replied quietly.

Another pause and then the door began to open. As soon as the latch was off, Cillian pushed his weight against it, sending whoever was behind it flying back into their hallway with a cry. He stormed past the figure on the floor and searched each of the rooms methodically.

Twisting his mouth in frustration when he realised she wasn't there, he stepped back into the hall and rounded on the man who was now trying to stand.

'Where is she?' he demanded, grabbing him by the front of his shirt and slamming him against the wall.

'Who?' the guy asked, staring at him through bleary eyes as if he'd gone mad. 'And what do you think you're doing bursting in here like this?'

Cillian pulled him back and slammed him against the wall

once more, a little harder this time. He felt the almost-healed wound on his back begin to throb from the exertion but ignored it and gritted his teeth. 'I think I'm looking for my sister and you better start answering my questions, or I'm gonna really start getting pissed off. Ruby her name is. Ruby Drew. Red curly hair and a tongue that could cut steel on a cold day. Jogging any memories?'

'N-No,' stuttered the man, realisation beginning to dawn on his face.

Cillian squeezed his gaze. 'Wrong answer, sunshine,' he growled. 'Cause your face just gave you away.' He pulled his fist back into a ball.

'No, wait!' the man cried.

Cillian waited.

'I really don't know where she is, but I do know who you're talking about,' he said quickly. 'Please, I swear.'

Cillian searched the man's face. He seemed to be telling the truth. He felt the hope deflate from his body as he hit yet another dead end. He'd hoped, the same way he had with every other place, that this might have been the one. But it wasn't. She was still out there somewhere.

'What *do* you know?' he asked.

'I only know who she is because she used to score from my partner, but she ain't been here in a long time, honestly.' His voice shook and his frightened gaze remained locked on Cillian's raised fist.

Cillian tightened his grip and pushed his face towards the other man. 'You *sure* that's all you've got to tell me?' he asked in a low, threatening tone.

'Yes, I swear,' the man cried, cowering away from Cillian.

Cillian stared at him for a few long moments, then released him. 'Do you know who I am?'

The man nodded, backing away from him fearfully. 'I do now, yeah,' he replied. 'Listen, he ain't sold her anything, I swear. She ain't been here for ages. And if she comes, we'll send her away, I promise you.'

'No,' Cillian said quickly. 'If she comes here, for any reason at all, you keep her here and don't tell her anything. You get word to Stacey in flat 11B that she's here and to tell me. But Ruby ain't to know, do you understand?' Cillian straightened his suit jacket and watched as the man nodded hurriedly. 'You just keep her busy until I get here.'

'Will do,' he mumbled.

Cillian looked him up and down, feeling the usual wave of disgust he felt when dealing with men like this. Men who had no backbone, who made a living off the suffering of other weak beings around them. He turned to leave.

'You'd better do,' he called back over his shoulder. 'Because if she comes here and you don't, I'll know. And trust me, you don't want to know what'll happen to you then.'

FOUR

Scarlet stared at the one small pane of frosted glass behind the white-painted metal bars then closed her eyes, trying to picture the blue sky she could just about make out beyond. In her mind she added the criss-cross vapour trails of airliners and a bird or two for good measure. She took a deep breath and tried to ignore the stale state of the air in the room. Reaching upwards, she stretched out her back and neck, then ran her hands through her long raven hair, pulling out the knots that had gathered in her fitful sleep.

She shouldn't have been in here today. She *wouldn't* have been, were it not for the sadistic actions of her cousin. As thoughts of Ruby coloured her mind, her mood darkened. When she got out of here she would continue her search, and when she found Ruby, she'd make sure that rotten bitch paid for everything she'd done.

The metal rattle and groan of the door opening sounded behind her, and Scarlet opened her eyes, turning to face whoever had come to take her to the interview room. Her eyebrows lifted slightly in surprise as she recognised the short red hair and pixie face of the woman staring back at her with venom in her eyes.

'Hello, Jenny,' Scarlet said calmy, regarding the woman with cautious interest.

'It's DC Ascough to you,' Ascough shot back, anger flashing across her face.

The corner of Scarlet's mouth twitched up in amusement at the sharp response.

'Come with me,' Ascough continued.

Scarlet walked to the door, and Ascough gripped her arm and propelled her down the hallway. Her grip was tight, pinching Scarlet's skin cruelly, but Scarlet didn't flinch.

Jenny Ascough had been the one who'd discovered Scarlet and John's relationship, thanks to Ruby's vindictive orchestration. The constable had been one of John's team and his friend, but over time her feelings towards him had grown, and it was a poorly kept secret that she'd fallen in love with him. She'd stayed close, waiting and wishing for him to notice and return her adoration. John hadn't been able to tell her he was in love with another, for obvious reasons, and so Ascough had continued believing she had a chance with her enigmatic single boss.

Ruby had found this out and had turned the situation to her advantage, manipulating Ascough and sending her down a path that would serve to destroy them all – even Ascough herself. She hadn't deserved the embarrassment and heartache Ruby had put her through either.

They turned the last corner and Ascough loosened her grip to open the door to the interrogation room.

Scarlet entered the miserable white box of a room that she loathed so much and stifled a sigh, sitting down on the blue plastic chair she'd vacated just fifteen hours before. To her surprise, Ascough didn't leave. Instead, she sat down in the opposite chair.

'Jennings will be a few minutes,' she said, reading Scarlet's expression. 'Which I guess means you and I can have a little talk.'

Jenny Ascough stared at the woman who'd caused her so much heartache, unable to tear her eyes away, and unable to contain the pain and anger her presence incited. Scarlet's pale heart-shaped face, slender figure and long thick hair lent her a vulnerable softness, upon first glance. Perhaps it was what had drawn John in. But there was also a subtle hardness in the set of her jaw and a coldness in her gaze – the only outward signs of the ugly, vicious monster she was on the inside.

'Where is he, Scarlet?' she asked, trying to contain the mixture of feelings that burned through her core. Pain, rage... jealousy.

'I've told Jennings already. I don't know.'

Ascough gritted her teeth. 'You're not on tape. I'm not interviewing you right now. I'm asking as someone who cares about him. As someone who wants to know whether he's still alive and well, or whether he's tied up somewhere in pain and scared, or whether he was just too much of an inconvenience for you to keep around altogether.'

'What?' A look of surprise fleetingly crossed Scarlet's expression. 'You think I've *killed* him?' She let out a short humourless bark of amusement and shook her head. 'Jesus Christ, Ascough... John and I love each other. Or *loved* anyway. I don't know what his feelings are towards me anymore as we haven't spoken for weeks. But mine haven't changed. Whatever you think of me, surely you're smart enough to know I'd never harm him.'

'Love,' Ascough scoffed. 'You don't know the meaning of the word. People like you aren't capable of something like *love*.'

'People like me?' Scarlet asked levelly, her gaze piercing Ascough's. 'Who exactly are *people like me?*'

'Cold-blooded murderers,' Ascough replied scathingly. 'Psychopaths who use their charms on *good* men to lure them onto bad paths, then use them for their own gain until they spit them back out into a world where they no longer have any place – or worse – make them disappear altogether.'

'OK, that's enough,' Scarlet replied, her tone hard as something dangerous flashed across her expression. 'I know you care about John. I know that you love him…'

Those words spoken aloud by Scarlet Drew felt like a dagger straight to Ascough's heart, and she felt her cheeks flush red with a mixture of indignant anger and embarrassment. 'You don't know *anything*,' she shot back.

'I know you love him,' Scarlet repeated strongly. 'And I get it. I love all the same things you do. He's an amazing person and being with him makes you feel special. Makes you feel *seen.*'

Ascough felt a lump rise in her throat and swallowed it down with a frown. 'Don't act like you know anything about how I feel.'

'Whether you like it or not, I *do* know how you feel,' Scarlet continued. 'And for the record, I'm sorry you got hurt, finding out the way you did. I wouldn't wish that on anyone. Ruby shouldn't have set you up like that. It was cruel.'

The way Scarlet was looking at her was too much for Ascough and she glared back across the table. 'I'm not falling for this,' she snapped. 'You might have fooled John with this act, but not me. I know exactly what you are and what you've done.'

She stood up. 'Jennings only cares about putting you away for murder and, believe me, I will *rejoice* the day he does that. But I'm here for John. He was a good man before he met you. He'd worked hard to get where he was, and he had a good life – friends, family. Now, you might have destroyed his career and his ability to be proud of all he's achieved, but I know the deal that Jennings is going to offer him. He has the chance to restart his life, to get back some of what you've taken.'

She looked down at Scarlet in contempt and walked to the door, pausing to look back. 'I'm going to find him,' she promised, her voice shaking with emotion. 'Wherever you have him, if he's still alive, I'm bringing him home. And if he's not, I'll still bring him home, but I'll make sure you suffer in the worst possible ways for the rest of your miserable life.'

FIVE

Lily checked her watch and pursed her lips. Robert had gone to the station over an hour ago so Scarlet should have been out by now.

Suddenly, her phone began to ring in her pocket and she felt the tension leave her shoulders. But as she pulled it out and looked at the screen, she frowned.

She put it to her ear and slowed her walking. 'Alright, Cath?'

'Yeah, I just wanted to check Scar's OK. Did it go alright?' Cath asked, the maternal worry clear in her tone.

Lily hesitated for a moment, not sure how to answer, but was saved as her sister-in-law continued.

'I know she's had to go straight off to work – she texted me to say – but I didn't get a chance to ask her anything. All alright, is it?'

Lily bit her top lip. So Scarlet *was* out. 'Yeah,' she said, deciding that worrying Cath any further was futile. 'All's fine. She'll tell you about it later, no doubt. I've actually gotta go, Cath, but I'll call you later, yeah?'

'OK. Don't work her too hard today. She's probably knackered after another night in those bleeding cells,' Cath grumbled.

''Course. Catch you soon.' Lily ended the call and slipped the phone back in her pocket. She'd figure out what was going on there later.

'Come on,' she called to the young woman just catching up behind her, securing a notebook under her arm. 'Let's get this ball rolling.'

Isla hurried to fall in line next to Lily, and the pair strode up to the boxing club the Drews had recently acquired.

Isla had been an unexpected recent addition to the Drew family firm. They didn't usually take on people in such a close capacity who they hadn't known for many years. In fact, other than George and Andy, two men who'd been loyal to Lily since she'd first started out, there was no one within the close-knit firm who wasn't a blood relation. They had clients and loose colleagues of course, certain people whose skills they called on now and then, but Isla was the first outsider in a very long time who Lily had allowed in.

She'd escaped a bad situation with another firm up in Manchester and had turned up one day, begging for a job. Lily had given her a chance, seeing much of herself in the young woman and trusting her instinct that Isla was genuine. On the off chance these instincts were wrong, she held the threat of being able to return Isla to her old firm at any point over the young woman's head. Isla seemed suitably afraid of her old bosses, the Kings, so this was enough to keep her in line, should the need arise.

So far though, taking on the girl had proven to be an excellent decision. It had only been a few weeks, but Isla had already made herself indispensable. Whatever time, day or night, she was there. Every task, no matter how menial, was taken on with gratitude and completed to a high standard. Finding someone so willing to prove themselves, and already so experienced in the

ways of their world, was no mean feat. She was the proverbial
unicorn of the underworld.

They entered the red-brick building and immediately Lily
was transported to the past. The smell of floor wax and sweat
with the familiar sight of the ring and the pockmarked green-
and-yellow-painted walls covered with pictures of triumphant
boys and men filled her with nostalgia. She'd spent many hours
in here watching Ray fight in their youth and then her sons,
years later.

Back then, the room had been filled with an electric buzz on
fight nights, cheers of support and general camaraderie. The
boxers had jumped around the ring, barely touching the ground
at times they were so nimble, throwing jabs and dodging blows.
And she'd watched, holding her breath with excitement, every
time. That was all such a long time ago now; a different time. A
time before her relationships with each of them had broken
down.

The reminder of the sorry situation going on between them
all brought a lump to her throat and she swallowed it down,
casting her eyes from the dancing echoes of the past and
towards the door of the manager's office.

Jimmy had coached both her boys and had been running
the place for years, so when she walked in, he smiled at her with
the warmth of an old friend. 'Lily, how you doing?' He gestured
to the two chairs on the other side of his desk.

Lily and Isla sat, and Lily crossed her legs, smiling back at
Jimmy before answering. 'Good, and yourself?'

'Better now all that business with Conway's dealt with and
the club is back in safe hands,' he replied.

'Yeah, I bet,' Lily responded.

Just weeks before, the previous owner of the club had been
on the verge of selling it to a local building firm who planned on
tearing it down and building a block of flats. Lily and her twin
sons, Cillian and Connor, had come up with a creative plan to

stop the planning, rendering the site worthless to the builder, then bought it themselves at a significantly lower price.

'This is Isla,' she continued. 'She's working with us now and will be helping me set up the new matches I mentioned to you the other day.'

Jimmy nodded slowly. 'You really want to go this way?' he asked her.

'It's the only way this place can make any real money, Jimmy. You know that.'

Lily held his gaze until he conceded with a reluctant nod of agreement.

'You'll have to be tight on the guest list,' he warned.

'We will. It will be invite only throughout the underworld, any guests of theirs to be vetted beforehand. The only betting vendors will be ours, no private bets allowed, and a no-nonsense security presence,' she reassured him.

There was no *legal* way to turn a decent profit here. Even if they won every match in every paying league, they'd still be broke. But that didn't mean it was a lost cause. There were many young boxers who weren't interested in fighting in the leagues, but plenty of them were still great fighters, and their interest could be piqued for the right price. Illegal fights always paid much more than regulated ones. Lily would throw the events, the boxers would get paid well, the firm would make money from the tickets and the bets, and at the end of each night, they would all come away with a hefty profit.

'How often you going to be doing these nights?' Jimmy asked.

'Once a week, to start. Saturday nights. There's a big buzz right now – the tickets will be snapped up. You know the game, Jimmy. Everyone loves a good fight. After the novelty wears off, we'll drop it to once a fortnight, see how it goes.'

She shifted in her seat, noting the concern still in his eyes.

'It's a good thing for all of us. I'll make sure a decent percentage comes back to you to use on whatever the gym needs.'

'Thanks,' he replied, the word heartfelt. 'This place does need a lot of money spending on it. I don't mean *your* money,' he added quickly. 'You've done enough already. But if doing this means the club benefits, then I guess it's a good thing.'

Lily tilted her head to the side. 'What part do you feel isn't a good thing?'

There was a short silence while Jimmy looked as though he was trying to find the right words.

'Speak freely. I can see it in your face,' Lily said.

'The leagues are regulated,' he said a trifle reluctantly. 'There are standards that have to be met, potential futures that open up with so many wins...' He twisted his mouth to the side for a moment. 'I'm just aware that taking away the structure and the discipline of it all can lead to issues.'

'Well then I hope you'll be there to oversee it and make sure nothing happens,' Lily replied.

Jimmy's face opened up in surprise.

'I'd like you to be involved,' she continued. 'Not everyone can know what we're doing, so I'll be counting on you to help Cillian and Connor pick out the people who are likely to want in, and also to assist on match nights. Make sure rules are followed and so on.'

'Er, OK,' he replied. 'I can do that.'

Lily could see this wasn't something he wanted to do, not really. She'd expected as much. Jimmy had always been aware of the less than legal side to many of the men who came here, and of who Lily was. Of whom Ray had been, when he'd fought here, and many other local faces who'd come and gone over the years. He'd covered for his boys many a time, hidden them, lied for them, provided fake alibis. He'd do anything to protect those who sought sanctuary under this roof, whether they'd done right or wrong. But he'd never partaken in the life himself. He'd always kept things clean, not allowing anyone to tarnish the reputation of the club. But times had changed, and since the Drews had saved the place, he could hardly complain about the ways they wanted to make their money back.

'Isla's going to stay here and sort out some details with you.' Lily stood up and smoothed her black leather pencil skirt before turning to Isla, who'd been watching the exchange silently. 'You know what I have in mind, so get what you can sorted and report to me later. Jimmy...' She turned, and her blood-red lips curled into a smile. 'Always a pleasure.'

'Likewise, Lil,' he replied, standing to walk her to the door. 'Look, I don't want to seem discouraging with this new venture. I just want to make sure nothing bad happens to my boys, that's all.'

'Of course.' Lily paused by the doorway. 'That's a priority for me too. I wouldn't do anything that could result in harm.'

She studied him for a moment then squeezed his arm with a grin as she turned to leave. 'You worry too much, Jimmy. You need a holiday. And who knows, with us looking out for the gym now, maybe you can finally take one too.'

SIX

Lily walked into her house and placed her handbag and keys on the table in the hall, the same way as always, then glanced in the mirror above and studied her face for a moment. Bruise-coloured shadows ringed the underneath of her eyes, reminding her that she'd fallen into the unhealthy routine of getting even less sleep than usual. Not that she could help it. Whenever she lay down, the unsettling situations in her life reared their ugly heads, chasing each other around her mind, and she couldn't switch off. Her family had always been everything to her – she'd lived and breathed for them her whole life. But right now that family was fractured and scattered, and the painful truth was that she had no one to blame for it but herself.

A small noise sounded from down the hallway and she whipped her head around, her senses immediately sharpened. The boys weren't here – she was sure of it. Their cars hadn't been on the drive, and they would have made their presence known when she walked in.

Another noise followed – a sharp clinking sound.

Her heart rose as she realised it could be Ruby. Her daughter had disappeared into thin air in a bid to escape the fallout from what she'd done to Scarlet and John. That had been weeks ago, and no matter how desperately they'd all searched for her, she'd remained unfound. Was it Ruby? Had she come home?

Lily quickly headed towards the door to the large comfortable room that doubled as a study and second lounge. She was sure the noise had come from there.

Pushing open the door, she looked around expectantly. 'Ruby?' The name escaped her lips, filled with hope.

'No. Not Ruby,' came the reply from one of the sofas facing away from her.

Lily's heart sank, and she quickly swallowed her disappointment at the sound of Scarlet's voice, then walked around the sofa until her niece came into view. She was lying down, staring out the window at a large tree beyond and balancing a glass of something on her stomach. On the side table above her head was one of Lily's whisky decanters, now almost half empty, and despite her aunt being in the room, Scarlet made no move to get up. Lily frowned, concerned. This was unusual behaviour for her niece.

She sat down in the armchair adjacent to the sofa and crossed her legs, opening up the box of cigarettes on the side table next to her. She lit one and took a deep drag before speaking.

'If I'd had to bet on which member of this family I'd find in my house half-cut on my best whisky at three o'clock in the afternoon, you'd probably have been the last,' she said casually.

Scarlet tilted her head slightly in acknowledgement but didn't answer, instead continuing her bleak stare out the window. Lily took another drag and blew it back out slowly.

'Your mum would have probably been my first pick,' she continued wryly.

This brought on an amused smile, and a few moments later, Scarlet pulled herself half upright, resting her head back against the sofa as she turned to look at her aunt. 'I just couldn't face everyone today,' she admitted tiredly. 'So I thought I'd hide out here.'

'That's not like you,' Lily replied.

There was a short silence.

'I covered for you with your mum,' she went on.

'Thanks,' Scarlet replied.

'What happened?' Lily asked.

Scarlet shook her head, looking down. 'Nothing we didn't expect. Jennings tried to put the pressure on, but he has no idea where John is. Robert got me out in about ten minutes.' She shrugged. 'Ascough had a little vent.'

Lily's eyebrows rose in surprise. 'I didn't think she was on this? Isn't she a witness or something?'

'She's not on the case officially. Or at least I don't think she is,' Scarlet replied. 'She came in to talk to me off-record. She thinks I killed John.' She laughed, the sound soft and bitter.

Lily's heart went out to her. 'Surely she can't really think that. She might not like it, but she knew you were together.'

'She does. And she reminded me that I've ruined his life and everything he ever worked for,' Scarlet replied, her tone full of sadness.

'Scarlet, you can't do this,' Lily replied with a grim expression. 'John was a grown man who made his own choices. You both knew the risks, and you both chose to go down the path that you did. John didn't blame you, and you can't either.'

She took another drag and then flicked the ash into the ashtray on the table. 'You need to stop letting that woman get in your head. She's hurt and lashing out, but you need to keep it together, now more than ever,' she warned.

Scarlet nodded, staring into the wall ahead. 'I know. I just...' She trailed off, and after a few seconds, her eyes began to fill with angry tears. She blinked them away as best she could, then ran one hand back through her long raven hair, stressed.

'It's just that three weeks ago I lost the man I love, overnight,' she said, hot painful emotion filling her words. 'I had to just send him off to a life of— no, not even a *life*,' she corrected, 'an *existence*, somewhere he doesn't know and didn't want to go, with no real plan. I had to just stand there and watch him go into that... that void of nothingness, after he lost everything. And I couldn't grieve *my* loss, because I had to get back to life and fighting fires every goddamn day, as if nothing has happened. As if I'm OK. As if I haven't just lost him and as if him losing *everything* wasn't the fault of my own family.'

Lily looked away, unable to argue with that. While it hadn't been Scarlet's fault, there was no denying that it had been Ruby's.

'And I was getting on with it,' she continued strongly. 'Hiding it all every day and making sure we're always a step ahead. But you know what? I'm hurt and tired and I'm being dragged back and forth by the police and dodging their fucking tails everywhere I go, and I'm barely holding it together. So Ascough is just one more thing I really don't need. Because she isn't going to stop, Lil.' She rubbed her eyes. 'She's hell-bent on finding John and making me pay for all that's happened. I know I shouldn't let her under my skin, but she still gets there. Because she ain't just some copper. Her fury ain't because I've broken some rule; it's because she genuinely cares about John and wants to right a wrong. And between you and me, there's only so much I can actually disagree with her on.'

Lily felt the pain and exhaustion radiating from her niece, and the maternal part of her wanted to wrap her up in a hug and tell her that everything was going to be OK. But she couldn't do that. Because not only would she be lying, but it would be dangerous to allow Scarlet's wallowing to keep spiralling down this path.

She sat forward and locked onto Scarlet's gaze with a hard look. 'Now you listen to me. You need to snap out of this *now*. I know you're hurting, and you have every right to feel that way. But this ain't a fucking schoolyard, Scarlet. You let your emotions get the better of you and you'll slip. And if you slip, you'll bring yourself and this whole family down. Do you hear me?' Her voice was laced with the quiet, no-nonsense sharpness that everyone in the family knew there was no arguing with.

Scarlet held her gaze and nodded, her face becoming guarded once more.

'Good. If that woman is out to get you, then that's more reason than ever to stand up and see this storm through with a ferocity that matches theirs. They want to crush you, Scarlet. And John hasn't sacrificed all he has for you to be crushed. He did that so you'd survive. *That's* what you need to cling on to now. *That's* what will get you through, if you let it.'

The sound of the front door opening cut their conversation short, and Lily looked over expectantly. Scarlet sniffed and sat upright, rubbing the last lingering traces of emotion from her face and placing the whisky on the table.

Cillian and Connor appeared, and Lily's heart rose as she saw her sons in their family home once more. They hadn't set foot in here for three weeks and she was praying this small move in the right direction was a sign of better things. But as she saw Cillian's cold gaze settle on her, she suddenly wasn't so sure.

SEVEN

Cillian pulled out a toothpick from his pocket and placed it in his mouth as he stepped into the room and sat on one of the chairs furthest away from his mother. Being back here felt bittersweet. This was his home, his anchor, the centre of their family's universe. It was still his home, but where before he felt calm and secure inside these walls, now all he felt was anger and tension. He no longer wanted to be there, in the place their mother had raised them. The place their mother had lied to them.

Connor stayed by the door and leaned against the frame awkwardly, seemingly unwilling to enter the room.

'Alright, Scar?' Cillian nodded to his cousin.

'Questioning go OK?' Connor asked.

'Yeah, nothing major, just the usual questions and a night in their finest suite,' she answered.

There was a short, awkward silence.

'Thanks for coming,' Lily said in a level voice.

Cillian looked away. 'Dan's dealt with. He won't be using his right hand again any time soon,' he said flatly, jumping straight to business. That was why they were here; not because they were family.

Dan was the owner of a takeaway they used as a laundry. He'd had the stupidity to skim off them, not intelligent enough to realise they'd see it missing.

'Good. What does he plan to do now, do you know?' Lily asked.

'He weren't exactly up for chatting after,' Connor replied. 'But Cillian suggested he close up shop and disappear. I think he probably will – it don't really make any money.'

'Keep an eye on it and report back. That place is a health hazard anyway.' Lily stubbed out her cigarette in the ashtray.

Cillian watched her, his turbulent emotions towards her bubbling away just beneath the surface. He missed her. Of course he did. Connor did too. Up until recently, they'd been as close as any family could possibly be. He hadn't been naïve enough to believe that there were no secrets at all between them – he had a few himself – but he'd never in a million years thought his mother would have hidden something as important as their parentage. All these years, Ray had been right there – she'd been *seeing* the man, keeping him close, while lying to all of them about who their father was.

He just couldn't get his head around it all. Their mother's lies, the fact that Ray's blood ran through their veins – Ray, a man they'd always hated. Part of that hatred had been because he was an outsider; an outsider who didn't belong in their circle, yet who hovered close to the edges. They'd been raised to fiercely protect their circle and their family. But now it seemed he had never really been an outsider. He was blood. So where did that leave them all?

'Now you're here, we need to discuss the first fight night,' Lily said.

'What about it?' Cillian asked, rolling the toothpick around in his mouth.

'I need you to take Mickey from the tables over to the club and have a sit-down with Jimmy.'

Lily was talking about one of their croupiers from their illicit gambling nights above their pub. Mickey had always been in the gambling industry and had an uncanny knack of predicting what odds were going to come up in any chosen bookies.

'What do you want out of that exactly?' Cillian asked, though he already had a pretty good idea.

'You and Jimmy know the players, their strengths and weaknesses, who's likely to win against who and why. You need to set up the matches and then work out the best odds with Mickey. He'll oversee the betting on the night. I'll trial him, and if things go well, he can manage the bets on all fight nights going forward,' Lily replied.

Cillian nodded. It was a good move.

'What do you want me to do?' Connor asked.

'I need you to meet with Isla and organise the rest of the event details. She's got a list of what we need to arrange and some of the info you need already, so go and work out how many seats we can fit and where we can set everything up. Tommy's sorting the pop-up bar.' Tommy Harding was the manager of their pub, The Blind Pig. 'You need to work out the invite list. We'll need to extend invites verbally for now, but run it by me before you go out with it.'

Connor nodded. 'Where's Isla now?'

'At the factory,' Lily replied.

'Right. I'll wait in the car.' Connor pushed off the wall and turned down the hallway towards the front door.

'Really?' Lily called. 'Can't you at least stay for coffee?' She sighed frustratedly as her son ignored her.

'What did you expect?' Cillian asked sharply. 'We're here for work. For the business. Other than that, we don't have much to say to you right now.'

'And what if I have something to say to you?' Lily asked, standing up and placing her hands on her hips.

'You had years to say something to us, Mum. But you never did.' Cillian glared at her and followed his brother out of the room, painfully aware of the silence he left behind.

EIGHT

Isla watched Connor's car as it drove away from her down the road, until eventually it turned a corner and disappeared from view. He'd just dropped her off near the hotel she was still staying in on the Roman Road, following the successful completion of all their event-planning tasks for the day. She turned reluctantly towards the hotel entrance, wishing she didn't have to spend another night there bored and alone. But their work was done and Connor had other parts of the business to look after. They worked well together, she and Connor. An efficient team. Too efficient, it would seem, she thought wryly. She'd have to try to slow down whatever they were doing next time.

There was something about Connor she really liked. Not his good looks and charm, though he was doing very well in both departments. It was that his company was just so easy and warm. They had a laugh together, and he made her feel safe, something she hadn't felt for a while.

Her thoughts turned to Calvin, her boss and boyfriend back in Manchester, and her mind clouded. For three years she had been his mistress – the worst-kept secret on the estate where she'd grown up. He and his brother, Jared, had run a successful firm, supplying drugs to nearly half the city and selling knock-off designer goods they produced in a hidden factory. When Calvin's wife, Jazmin – a woman who was feared and revered throughout Manchester in her own right – had finally found out about the relationship and had come after Isla with murderous vengeance, Isla had fled. Jazmin wasn't someone anyone wanted to be on the wrong side of, and Isla knew without doubt that if she hadn't left that night, the woman wouldn't have stopped until she was dead. London was still alien to her and, yes, she was lonely in her small hotel room, but at least she was alive. And hopefully she wouldn't be this lonely for long.

With a sigh, she reached up and tucked a stray wisp of her fine bleached-blonde hair behind her ear and looked up to the moody skies above. The heavens looked ready to open at any moment. She hurried, not wanting to ruin her trainers or soak her clothes. She'd always been careful with her belongings, never having had much money spare. These days she was on the Drews' payroll and earning more money than she'd ever dreamed of earning before, but old habits die hard.

She reached the door to the hotel just as the first few heavy droplets of rain began to colour the pavement and let out a breath of relieved triumph. With an unreturned smile at the bored-looking receptionist, she jogged up the stairs towards her room on the first floor and turned her thoughts back to the fight night. There were logistics still to figure out, and she had a few ideas she needed to write down and put to Lily.

Reaching her room, she decided to start the night off with a hot bath. But as she pushed the door closed behind her, she suddenly realised she wasn't alone. Registering who it was sat in the chair by the window, her eyes and mouth flew open in shock.

'What's the matter, Isla?' the man in the chair asked in a deep menacing voice. 'Aren't you pleased to see me?'

NINE

Calvin King stared across the room at the young woman he'd spent the last few weeks searching for and then watching from a distance. She looked even tinier than usual, all skin and bone and big brown eyes, and he felt the familiar tingle of excitement run through him as they widened with shock. He'd always loved to catch her off guard and play games. It kept things interesting.

Behind her, his brother Jared kicked the door the rest of the way shut, and Isla swung around at the sound before turning her gaze back to Calvin. She walked towards him and her eyes searched his face. His mouth curled up at the sides in a cold smile.

Suddenly Isla's smile matched his, and she wrapped her arms around his shoulders, leaning down to kiss him deeply. He felt the magnetic pull of her as her warm lips crushed into his, and his hands reached up to encircle her small waist.

After a couple of seconds, he pushed her away, holding her still and looking up at her through narrowed, wary eyes. Isla had disappeared on him the night he'd held Jazmin at bay outside her front door; the night Jazmin had found out that Isla was his long-term mistress and had gone there to kill her. He'd told Isla to run that night – but he hadn't meant *disappear*. Yet she had, and he'd heard nothing from her since. He'd had to track her down, though admittedly it hadn't been difficult.

At first he'd been angry, furious that she'd dared run out on him, that she'd dared make such a mockery of him. She was *his*, she belonged to him, personally and professionally, and to disappear like that was disloyal and unacceptable. He was well within his rights to treat her as an enemy and punish her as such. That's what deserters were, after all, in their game. Once you were in, you were in for life – there was no other option.

Yet, as he'd watched her these last few weeks and seen what she'd done, how she'd set this situation up, he'd realised the unique opportunity she'd been busy creating. Despite his fury, he couldn't help but admire this intricate scam she'd been building. And he knew that was what this was; he could see all the signs – he'd been the one to teach her how to put jobs like these together in the first place.

His eyes raked her body, slowly and purposefully. 'I told you to find somewhere local to lie low, and then to contact me,' he said, keeping his tone low and quiet.

Isla touched his face. 'I had to get out of Manchester until it all died down,' she replied, her expression serious. 'You know I did. You know how far Jazmin's reach goes – I wouldn't have been safe anywhere.'

'And when were you planning on coming back?' he asked challengingly.

'When she'd stopped searching and it was safe to return,' Isla replied, holding his gaze. 'She's still got people out there. I know, because I keep my ear to the ground. I've been sat here in this miserable bloody room, waiting for her to quit so I can get back to my life. Back to *you*.' She sighed, looking tired. 'It's not been easy, you know.'

'Jaz will never stop looking for you, Isla,' Calvin replied. 'You're fucking her husband and it's shown her up. She can't stop looking for you or she'll lose face. So you've been waiting for something that'll never happen.'

Isla shook her head with a look of frustration. 'Great. I'm stuck out here for good then, is that what you're telling me?'

'I'm telling you that you should have had more trust in me,' Calvin replied. 'I've always kept you safe before, haven't I?' He raised one eyebrow accusingly. 'I've always looked after you, *provided* for you, haven't I? When your dad got murdered and the council were gonna throw you out on the streets because the flat weren't in your name, who was there?' He tilted his head to one side. 'Who took care of you, set you up, made sure you were OK? Hm?' There was a short silence. 'Well?'

'You,' she said quietly, her gaze softening.

'That's right. *Me.*' He narrowed his gaze at her. 'But yet the moment things got tough, after three years together, instead of showing any loyalty, you stole my roll of cash and ran the fuck away without a word.'

Isla looked down in shame at his reminder of how callous her actions had been after all he'd done for her and all they'd been through. He swallowed hard as his anger rose, and his fists clenched in his lap for a moment as he fought the temptation to beat her to a bloody pulp for the betrayal. Forcing himself to look away, he took a deep breath to calm himself.

'That hurt me, Isla,' he said, wiping his hand across his upper lip.

'I'm sorry,' she said, reaching out and turning his face towards hers.

As their eyes met, he could see that she meant it. The connection between them was still as strong as ever. He wanted her, but Isla *needed* him. She always had done.

Isla trailed her hand down his face and around the back of his neck, slipping down onto his lap and putting her forehead to his. 'I am sorry. I didn't want to leave it this long before we made contact. I just knew Jazmin would be tracking you to get to me. I've missed you every single day.'

'I missed you too,' he admitted, grabbing her to him and holding her fiercely. She was his, and no one, not even his wife, could take her away from him. 'And I'll keep you safe from her, don't worry. We'll figure it out.' Looking up at Jared, he nodded towards the door. 'Go and pack up – we're heading home.'

'No, wait,' Isla said, pulling back and looking up at Jared then back to Calvin. 'We can't leave yet.'

'Why?' He was already pretty sure he knew what she was about to say, but he wanted it to come from her. It would confirm that her loyalties still lay in the right place.

'I've been setting up a job.' The corners of her mouth curled up and her dark eyes sparkled with excitement. 'I haven't just been sitting on my arse all this time, and this wasn't a random location. I found a mark – a *good* one – and got in with them. I've done a recce and been coasting along since, waiting, ready to flip it when I could finally get word to you.'

Calvin leaned back in the chair and nodded slowly, a hint of a smile playing across his face. 'The Drews, right?'

Isla's expression widened into one of surprise. 'You know about it?'

'I know everything, Isla. Did you really think you could set up a scam this big without me noticing?' He exchanged a smirk with Jared. 'She's funny, eh?'

'A proper comedian,' Jared agreed with a low rumbling laugh.

'I've been watching you for a while and I can see what you're doing. To a point anyway. You'll need to fill me in on the rest. Why such a high-profile mark, for a start?' he asked. 'We don't hit people like them usually.'

'No, we don't,' she agreed. 'But that got me thinking, a while back. Why *don't* we?' She kinked one of her eyebrows in question. 'We hit small marks – and they're safe, I know. But they're not huge payloads. We can't hit other firms up north – it's too risky if they find out we've broken the rules that badly. But down here, they don't know us. They don't know our tells, our plays; they don't know who we are at all.' She pushed a strand of her hair back behind her ear. 'I gave them enough truth to allow them to verify me, but not enough to give anything away. And the story was easy enough.'

'Which was?' Calvin asked.

'That I lived as your mistress for the last few years, your wife found out and tried to kill me, and I ran. That much was true enough for them to confirm. Then I added that I'd run away from both of you.' Her hand ran up and down the back of his neck. 'That you were a very bad man who I wanted to escape from and never see again. I was a lost soul with good criminal skills who needed a new home. I was convincing, and it was too good an opportunity for them to resist.'

Calvin looked at her, raising his eyebrows with narrowed eyes. 'Well, I am a very, *very* bad man, Isla Carpenter.'

She grinned and they locked eyes, the tension between them growing. He felt his body respond to her wily ways, and his grip on her waist tightened. He bit his lip and exhaled slowly. That could wait. He and Jared needed to hear the rest.

'What's the prize?' he asked.

'They have a *lot* of cash,' she replied. 'I'm talking six figures, physical, unlaundered money. They have a few businesses, some legit, some not. Laundries here and there. But it's the cash that's interesting and, on top of that, I also heard them talking about some hidden art that's worth mega money. They have small safes dotted around, but there's one big safe I've heard them refer to where they keep most of the cash and the art. I still need to find it, but I have to be careful. I can't exactly ask outright. I'm in, but I'm still proving myself.'

Calvin nodded, his eyes sparkling. 'Sounds like the kind of

money that will let us live like the kings we are – eh, Jared?' He caught his brother's eye and saw the same excitement he felt.

'It does,' Jared agreed with a grin. 'What's the plan though?'

Isla opened her mouth to talk, but Calvin cut her off. She'd done well, but *he* was the one who made the decisions, who laid the plans. Something she clearly needed a reminder on after her little stint out on her own.

'Isla, you'll stay on this and report everything you find back to me each day. Once you discover where this safe is and what we're dealing with, I'll map out the plan, the same way we've always done it,' Calvin said, eying her hard.

She nodded and bowed her head slightly in respectful deference, the reminder hitting the mark.

'We'll hit hard and fast and get out of town quickly. You'll make sure you're with them when we do, so they don't suspect you. As long as they have no idea we're in town or that your story was a cover, they won't think to look in this direction. They'll be left scratching their heads, and you'll stick around to console them until we can move you on without suspicion.'

Isla nodded. 'OK. Will it stay us three, or will we bring the others in?' She looked over to Jared and back to Calvin with a questioning look.

'Just us. The less people involved, the less there is to cover up,' he answered. It was also less people to pay. Big as the payload was, he didn't want to have to share it beyond what was necessary.

He watched her nod once more, obediently. She was still the same Isla; a hustler with a sharp brain and the sly ability to create great opportunity, yet also a young woman with vulnerabilities he'd always been able to manipulate. She was smart and malleable at the same time, a rare creature. She knew who was boss and rarely had the stupidity to question it. Unlike his wife. It was one of the many things he liked about Isla.

Reaching up, he touched her cheek and ran his fingers

across her full mouth, hearing the subtle hitch in her breathing. She looked up into his eyes, and her pupils dilated as she saw the wild desire in his expression. It had been too long since he'd last had her in his bed.

'Jared, I'll meet you back at the hotel,' he said, not breaking his gaze from hers.

Jared made a sound of agreement and tipped his head up in response, then left, shutting the door behind him.

At last, they were alone, and the tension between them became electric. Her breathing turned shallow, and he lifted her off him, standing up and pushing her towards the bed. She didn't resist, allowing him to walk her backward as he stared down at her possessively.

'You know I wasn't sure how this was going to end tonight,' he said in a low voice.

'No?' she asked breathlessly.

'No. I was torn between this and beating the betrayal out of you the way you deserve.' He reached up and grasped her hair in his fist, pulling it sharply.

She uttered a small sound of both pain and pleasure and opened her mouth, holding his gaze in hers.

He bit his lip, bent down and kissed her hungrily, then pushed her back onto the bed.

'Get those jeans off,' he ordered, watching as she did as she was told. 'Stand up.'

She obeyed willingly, and he grabbed her roughly, turning and slamming her hard against the wall. She moaned and panted in anticipation, pushing her body back against him.

'I know you, Isla. I know what you want and what you need,' he murmured, biting into her shoulder. 'And I know you need this as much as I do. Don't you?'

She nodded, too breathless to speak.

He undid his trousers and freed himself, then turned her to face him and hitched one of her legs up over his hip. As her panting grew faster, he reached down and pulled her thong aside. 'Don't you ever disappear on me again.'

'I won't,' she breathed.

With an exultant cry of relief, he thrust into her hard and clutched her to him, moving in an urgent rhythm, claiming her as his once more. 'You're mine, Isla,' he growled into her neck.

'Yes,' she uttered, giving herself to him completely. 'I'm yours.'

'You belong to me.'

Her whimpers of pleasure spurred him on harder and faster, until he lost himself in her entirely.

TEN

Scarlet slammed the car door and looked back as she walked towards the factory, assessing the car park and road beyond. It was becoming harder and harder to move around the city and look after certain parts of the business. Every other day she'd be tailed by the police, and when they weren't tailing her, they were raiding the family's buildings and homes. She was going through a burner phone every few days, unable to trust a number for longer than that. If she'd thought Jennings had been gunning for her before, that was nothing compared to what he was putting her through now.

Reaching the front door, she pushed her long dark hair back over her shoulder and pursed her red lips grimly before she entered the building. She'd actually managed to get a few things done this morning, after slipping out much earlier than usual and dodging whatever tail might have been en route. Her stiletto heels clacked out a sharp rhythm on the hard factory floor, joining the chorus of whirrs and clanks from the heavy machines as she crossed towards the back office. The men and women working their shifts nodded as she passed, and she returned the greeting tiredly.

Lily looked up as Scarlet entered the office and raised her eyebrows in surprise. 'You're up early,' she commented.

'Ditto,' Scarlet replied, taking a seat opposite her aunt.

'Couldn't sleep,' Lily replied, reaching for the lit cigarette that was balanced on the edge of her office ashtray. She took a deep drag and gazed at her niece with a critical expression. 'So what's up?' she asked.

'Nothing much. Figured I'd get out before any plods turned up,' Scarlet replied.

Lily arched an eyebrow. 'You gave them the slip?'

'Yep. If they *had* planned to tail me, that is. Got over to the unit and dropped some goods to the stalls early. With the pressure Jennings is putting on, I'm not sure when any of us will next be able to do it.' She pulled a face and Lily mirrored it. 'There ain't much left, by the way,' Scarlet continued. 'Maybe one more drop.'

They hadn't pulled a truck heist in a while, which meant the stash of stolen gear they fed out through their market stalls on the Roman Road was running very low.

Lily shook her head. 'Even if we could risk it at the moment, which we can't, there ain't a viable route for another few weeks.' She took another drag on her cigarette and looked off into the distance, lost in thought for a few moments. 'They're getting tighter on the roads they use. Most of them are too risky to take.'

'What are we going to do about stock?' Scarlet asked with a slight frown. They made a lot of money from the markets. Stopping or even pausing would cause a considerable dent in their income, not to mention the incomes of their stallholders.

'There's nothing we can do.' Lily's dark-brown eyes moved to meet hers. 'If stock runs out, it runs out. It ain't ideal by any stretch of the imagination, but we can't take more risk than we already are on a job like that. It ain't worth them going away for it.'

Cillian and Connor ran the truck heists and were highly

skilled at pulling them off after years of practice. But only on the routes Lily gave them the green light on. There was always risk on every job, but they were careful to hit at the most remote point, they were in and out quickly, and always made sure to cover their tracks. It was only possible to get away with the number of heists that they'd pulled because the trucks were hit on dead roads in the middle of nowhere. But trucks that were closer to civilisation, on roads with regular traffic or too close to traffic cams, were off limits. As were the newer trucks with better safety technology.

'If it's becoming more difficult overall, maybe we need to start looking at other methods of getting stock,' Scarlet suggested.

'Like?' Lily asked. 'I agree with you, but I can't think of a decent alternative, so if you have an idea I'm all ears.'

Scarlet bit the inside of her cheek as her quick brain worked over the problem. 'The main depot here in England that they all come through once they cross the Channel...'

'Is fitted up to the hilt with the best security systems on the market and a small army of security officers on site in the unlikely event that all of them fail,' Lily informed her, not missing a beat. 'Next?'

Scarlet shifted her weight and crossed her legs as she methodically turned over the options in her mind. 'The Channel crossing is out,' she mused out loud. 'No escape route if something goes wrong on board, and no chance of pulling something off to another boat. We're many things, but pirates ain't one of them.'

'Land pirates perhaps,' Lily replied with a quick grin. 'But no. We're not creatures of the sea.'

Scarlet twisted her mouth to one side, trying to find the angle no one had considered yet. There had to be one.

A thought suddenly occurred to her, but even as it registered, she felt her mood blacken.

'What?' Lily asked sharply. 'What is it?'

Scarlet tilted her head as she weighed it up. 'Remember when Harry Snow wanted to take over the markets?'

'How could I forget,' Lily replied.

'Jasper had made a deal with someone on the mainland at a holding warehouse that a number of the high-street fashion companies used. Someone internal had worked out how to shave off up to something like twenty per cent of their stock in a way that would never show up in their system, even down the line,' Scarlet recalled.

Lily thought it over for a moment then pulled a face. 'We don't know which one, or where it is, or who the contact was. We don't know if that contact is even still there, or, if they are, whether they've already found another partner.' She stubbed her cigarette out in the ashtray. 'We don't have the trucks or the manpower to bring it over, even if we did know all that and could make a deal. And, realistically, even if there was a way of finding out – which I highly doubt, seeing as Jasper's dead and Harry Snow would rather burn alive than give us information we could profit from – we wouldn't be able to trust it. The only people who might be in the know are allies of the Snows. And London has a long memory, Scar.'

Scarlet looked away. Being in their world, especially at the level the Drews were, came with a price. Everyone's price was different, and no one could predict when that invoice would be due. Her initial payment to the underworld had been taken upfront, almost as soon as she'd taken her first step into its shadows. Jasper Snow had murdered her father in the hopes it would weaken their firm, so that he and his father could steal the markets from them without resistance. But they'd underestimated Lily's power, and she'd fought back with a vengeance, protecting what was theirs.

Scarlet had been the one to balance the scales by taking Jasper's life. She'd been unlucky, some would say, to have had to blacken her soul so swiftly. Others would claim that dirtying her hands so early on in her career had been the making of her; that it had cemented her place and removed any question of her strength in a world where strength was everything. She wasn't sure which was true. All she knew was that that night, when she'd killed Jasper, a small sliver of her humanity had died with him. And in its place something colder had grown back. Something harder. Something born of the darkness she'd chosen.

'I'll keep thinking on it. There must be another option out there,' she said, pushing Jasper firmly from her mind.

'Let me know if you think of anything,' Lily replied.

'I picked up the cash from the stallholders while I was there, for the last lot,' Scarlet continued, changing the subject. She opened her handbag and pulled out a smaller canvas bag from within. It bulged at the sides and she opened it up, tipping it towards Lily to show her the thick wadges of cash within.

Lily glanced at it and nodded. 'It'll have to go to Millie's bakery, the record shop and all the laundries between them on that high street. Their usual amount, then split the change evenly between them,' Lily told her. 'With the takeaway out of the loop and our businesses under scrutiny, they're going to have to take the extra weight for a little while.'

'They won't like it,' Scarlet pointed out.

'Tough. We'll make it worth their while,' Lily replied with a hard edge.

The door suddenly opened, slamming back into the wall behind Scarlet, and she jumped, turning with a frown at the abrupt intrusion.

Danny, one of their foremen, entered the room and spoke hurriedly. 'That Jennings is here with a carful. They're parking up now – they'll be inside within a minute.'

Instinctively both Scarlet and Lily's eyes shot to the bag of cash on the desk between them. Scarlet's heart began to thump in her chest. There was no way they could allow Jennings to find them with this much hot cash. With everything else going on, he'd have no problem making a serious case out of it.

'Shit,' Lily cursed, standing up and moving round the desk. She picked up the bag. 'Danny, take this. Go out the back and down the river till you hit the road, then scarper. Wait for my call.'

'Got it.' Not wasting a second, Danny grabbed the bag, shoved it inside his overalls and ran from the room.

Scarlet stood and followed him out, just in time to watch him disappear around the corner that led to the back. Less than a second passed before the front door opened and Jennings marched in with three other officers following behind. She hissed out a long bitter breath as the resentment she felt for the man threatened to spill out but forced herself to stand quietly, trying to calm her racing heart. She prayed he didn't already have anyone round the back. So long as Danny got away, they'd be fine.

Lily appeared by her side, and the two women waited in stony silence for the men to reach them.

'I have a warrant to search these premises,' Jennings barked as he reached them, wasting no time on fake niceties.

'Again?' Lily asked witheringly. 'What is it exactly that you think you might find that you didn't find last time?'

'I don't know, Lily,' he replied, stepping closer with a cold glare. 'But I'm going to keep doing this, circling all your known locations, over and over and *over* again, until I *do* find something. Because we both know eventually I will and, honestly, I don't even mind what it is anymore. There's so much to choose from at this point. The stolen evidence that proves Scarlet killed Snow...'

Jennings pointed a finger in her face without looking round, and she stifled the urge to grab it and snap it off.

'Unlaundered money from your various illegal enterprises, your little black book of all the crooks and their specialties, which I just *know* you have...' He continued reeling off the options in quick succession, his frustrated words booming around the factory. 'John Richards, the DI you lot turned crooked, hiding behind a bucket in the broom cupboard – or maybe John Richards's decomposing *corpse* locked in a fucking freezer – take your pick. I don't particularly care *which* one I find at this point. They all work for me. They all send you lot down. It's like raiding an ice-cream parlour and knowing that whatever flavour you find first is going to taste just as fucking sweet as any of the others,' he spat.

Scarlet watched his red face and the flecks of spittle that flew out of his mouth as he spoke and realised that Jennings was beginning to lose it. He was desperate, flailing around in the dark after so many weeks without one clue or shred of evidence that they'd done anything. She smirked, and a small sound of amusement escaped her lips. His head whipped round, and she saw the naked desperation behind the aggressive mask that was seeing him through the day. She kept smiling and lifted her chin as she studied him.

'Something funny, Scarlet?' he asked.

'Yes, actually,' she replied. She looked him up and down and then turned away from him pointedly. Clearly he hadn't thought to send anyone round the back, otherwise Danny would have been brought back to him by now. They were safe.

'I'm off, Lil.' She caught the return glint of amusement in Lily's eye as she walked towards the door.

'And where do you think you're going?' Jennings demanded.

'Wherever the fuck I want,' she replied calmly without looking back. 'Your warrant's for the factory. Not me.'

Stepping outside, she breathed in the fresher air and raised her face to the sun for a moment, forcing her shoulders to relax. They'd done the hardest bit. They'd made sure there was nothing to find and that there were no trails to pick up. Jennings had nothing and now he was starting to fall apart. Not that they were out of the woods yet – these were still dangerous times and they had to be careful. But it was just a matter of staying vigilant and waiting it out. The force wouldn't allow him the time and money to chase a dead case forever.

She walked back to her car and then slowed as she realised her tyres were flat. Something glinted in the sun, catching her eye, and she bent down towards it with a frown. A small sharp knife stuck out one of the front tyres near the top. Her skin prickled all over in warning and she quickly straightened, turning to scan the area.

The car park and road were silent and still, as was the scrubland to the side of the factory.

She narrowed her gaze, searching for a potential hiding place someone could be watching from, but there weren't many options. It was a wide-open space. Whoever had slashed her tyres and left the small blade embedded in the last was gone.

ELEVEN

Ruby pulled her hood further down over her face and glanced behind her as she crossed the narrow side street. No one was there. No one knew she was back in this area yet.

She hitched the heavy backpack up a bit higher and tightened her grip around the straps. All she currently had in the world was in that backpack, including the money she'd taken from the family safe. She'd tried to think of a better place to store it but in the end had decided to keep it close. She couldn't go to one of the family hideouts – they'd look for her there and find it – and she couldn't exactly try to deposit that much cash in a bank. So nearly two hundred grand in fifty-pound notes were piled at the bottom of the bag, wrapped in her one spare hoodie. She'd left all her nice clothes behind when she'd left, donning her old jeans and trainers. The look helped her blend into the broken fabric of the more neglected estates of this city and become almost invisible.

Her family would have been furious to find the money gone. Not that they should have been. She was part of the family too, and she worked as hard as any of them. That money was just as much hers as it was theirs. And two hundred grand was nothing compared to the rest they still had hidden away. Plus, she planned to put it back in the safe once she returned home. Once her business with Scarlet was over and the right order could be restored. It would be her gesture of good faith. Her proof that she wasn't just there to take. Handing back what was left of the money would be a way of making peace and break the ice, create a starting point for them all to move on from. But for now it would serve as a safety net. Something to fall back on and start over with, should things not go the way she'd planned.

Reaching the end of the next street, she cast her gaze around the open area beyond. It was a small square of patchy grass, surrounded by run-down blocks of flats. She hadn't wanted to come back here really. The last time she'd been here it had been to score heroin, and while the memories of how good it had felt pulled at her heart, she couldn't let herself be tempted. Not now. She had too much to gain by keeping her head clear and her goal in sight. And if she allowed herself to slip, even once, she knew she'd be lost again for good. She breathed out slowly and clenched her fists, pushing the memories away as best she could, then crossed the square with her head bent low.

She'd left London at first, hiding out in random B&Bs in the surrounding countryside where they took cash and didn't ask questions. She'd figured it was best to put some distance between her and the family while they calmed down. Scarlet had made it clear that she intended to kill Ruby for all she'd done, and Ruby had no doubt she meant it.

She wouldn't have had to hide out at all, had her plan not partly backfired. She hadn't just been trying to get John out of the picture; she'd also been trying to get Scarlet sent down. She'd been sure the police would have arrested and charged Scarlet by now. The revelation of Scarlet and John's relationship should have made it as clear as day that John had stolen the evidence that proved Scarlet had murdered Jasper Snow. Ruby had delivered Jennings the whole story on a golden platter. But it hadn't been enough. It seemed that without solid proof, they couldn't do a damn thing, and Scarlet was still free. Which left Ruby in a very bad position.

The normal laws of man didn't apply in the shady world the Drews inhabited. It didn't matter that they were blood or that murder was illegal. In *their* world there was a set of very simple but very rigid laws. One of them being that if another attacks your freedom or life and they *fail*, that person is entitled to consequence-free retaliation. It was a deterrent that stopped their world from falling into total chaos. If one firm wanted to destroy another, they had to make sure it was worth that risk. And if it *was* then they had to make damn sure they succeeded first time.

Ruby had taken the risk and failed. And now Scarlet could unleash her wrath in return, without challenge from anyone. No doubt Ruby's mother and brothers would ask Scarlet to reconsider, from a family viewpoint. But their hands were tied as a firm. They couldn't get involved. The laws were finite, and anyone who broke them was deemed untrustworthy. No firm could survive that.

She reached the door to the flat she'd been heading for and knocked, keeping her head down. After a few seconds, the door was opened by Ali, her old dealer.

'Well, if it ain't Ruby Drew,' he said with a slow chuckle, stepping back to let her in.

She moved indoors quickly, glad to be off the street and away from curious eyes.

'It's been time, girl. How you been?'

'Good,' she lied, peering into his lounge to see if anyone else was there. 'You?'

'Oosh, you can chill – it's just me and Craig.' He gestured

towards his partner as he ambled out of the bedroom. 'Come in. Take a load off.'

Craig shot her an awkward smile. 'I need to pop out,' he said to Ali, slipping his feet into a pair of shoes in the hall. 'I won't be long.'

'Sure, sure,' Ali replied dismissively, pointing Ruby towards the lounge.

Ruby walked through, not taking the bag off her back as she sat on one of the two sofas around the coffee table. A kitchen scale sat in the middle next to a pile of small plastic bags she knew he distributed his heroin with, and the faint smell of weed permeated the air. Nothing had changed. Everything was exactly as she remembered.

She turned away from the table and focused on Ali, who was walking to the kitchenette at the other end of the open-plan room.

'What can I get you?' he asked, his gaze flickering towards the bags on the table.

Ruby swallowed. 'Just a coffee, if there's one going,' she replied.

His eyebrows rose up in surprise, but he nodded and pulled the jar out of one of the cupboards. 'Softest thing you've ever come here for,' he commented with another grin.

'Yeah, well...' She looked away. 'I don't touch the stuff these days.'

'Fair play,' he said, filling the kettle. 'It's never been my bag. Evil stuff. But' – he shrugged – 'it pays the bills. And Craig's expensive.' He rolled his eyes.

Ruby tried to smile at this but couldn't quite make it seem genuine. Her current state of mind was dark and driven, and there was little room left for small talk and niceties.

'So what's going on? What can I do you for?' Ali continued.

Ruby bit her top lip for a few moments. She didn't want to

be here, but if she checked into a hotel nearby, the chances were one of her brothers' watchers would see her. If not Scarlet's. She needed to lie low for just a little while longer, until she'd made it safe to come out of the shadows.

'I need somewhere to stay for a few days,' she said. She watched his expression change to one more serious. 'I have money,' she continued hurriedly. 'It's not a down-and-out situation. I'll pay you for the trouble. I just need to lie low while I sort something out and then I'll be gone.'

Ali let out a long heavy breath. 'I don't know, Ruby. I've got customers that come here...'

'I'll stay out of the way,' she said. 'There's a second bedroom, right? I'll be as quiet as a mouse. You won't even know I'm there.'

Ali ran a hand over his face and twiddled the short hairs on his chin. 'Can I think about it?' he asked. 'I'd need to talk it over with Craig.'

'Sure,' she replied, trying not to sound as impatient as she felt. If it was a solid no, she needed to know sooner rather than later so she could make other arrangements. And seeing as hotels were out, her options were already limited.

'What business you got round here anyway?' Ali asked.

Murdering my cousin, before she gets the chance to do the same to me, she thought. *Removing the cold, spiteful cuckoo in the nest once and for all, so I can finally take back what's mine.*

'Just some personal stuff,' she said.

She'd thought long and hard about what she had to do. She had killed before, just once. But that had been a very different situation. It had been revenge supported by her family and in the end had been as simple as pressing a button. She'd never actually got her hands dirty. It hadn't been something she'd considered before, with Scarlet. Not seriously anyway. But she'd been so set on sending her cousin off to a long miserable life in jail that she hadn't stopped to consider what would happen if she failed. And now that she *had* failed, she'd realised with sobering clarity that this left her with only two choices. Disappear and start again, cutting all ties to everything and everyone she knew, spending the rest of her days hiding and looking over her shoulder, waiting for the day Scarlet finally found her – or deal with it head-on and take Scarlet out, put an end to this lifelong feud and get her life back. The life she should have had from the start. The life Scarlet *took* from her.

There was no third option. There was no going back now, for either of them. It had gone too far. So after debating this for weeks, she'd made her decision. It was time to take her life back.

The kettle came to the boil as Craig walked back in the door. He entered the lounge, took a seat on the other sofa, slouched back and balanced a foot on the other knee.

'I'll have a tea,' he said.

Ali pulled another mug from the cupboard. 'Craig, Ruby here was just wondering if she could crash for a few days. Just while she's sorting something in the area.'

'Oh.' Craig smiled at her politely. 'Sure. I don't see a problem with that.' He shrugged.

'Great,' Ali replied, picking up the three steaming mugs from the side and walking over with them carefully. 'That's sorted then.'

Ruby's brow puckered slightly. That had been easy. She'd assumed Craig would feel reluctant. He didn't really know her after all. Only that she used to be one of Ali's customers.

'Here you go,' Ali said, handing her a mug.

'Thanks,' she muttered, taking it and placing it on the coffee table to cool.

Craig shifted position to face Ali as he sat down next to him. 'So you'll never guess who's back on the block,' he said coyly.

'Who?' Ali asked, taking a sip of his coffee.

'Only Alison Campbell,' he informed him with the knowing grin of someone who'd just imparted the juiciest of gossip.

'No way!' Ali exclaimed, his whole face opening in an expression of thrilled surprise. 'I thought she'd moved away! I ain't seen her around here for, I don't know... at least a year.' He shook his head with a wide grin. 'Huh.'

'Yeah, apparently she hooked up with this really old millionaire geezer, right,' Craig continued excitedly. 'Set herself up for when he popped it and all that. But then it turned out he had a lot more energy than she'd counted on and was a bit kinky, and *then* he kept trying to get her to do it in the woods and that – which she didn't really mind, I mean she's a determined girl. A few leaves and a chilly breeze ain't gonna stand in the way of her and *that* much money.'

'Yeah, there's worse things,' Ali agreed.

'So, she carried on givin' him his jollies in the bushes, but then one day he asked her to wear this outfit, right? And she put it on and it was this weird old flowery dress and these big, like, parachute knickers that were all worn and grey...'

'Right...' Ali frowned.

'And it turns out, they were his *mum's*,' Craig said, dropping the best part of the whole story with a flourish.

'No!' Ali cried, horrified.

'I know, right?' Craig replied. 'I mean there's kinks, and there's just plain fucked up.'

Ali turned to Ruby with wide eyes. 'Oh my days, can you *believe* that?'

But Ruby was watching him through a deeply narrowed gaze. The story was of no interest to her. What *was* of interest was the level of surprise he'd shown at hearing that this old acquaintance was back in the area. Her senses had tingled and she'd thought over his greeting at the door.

'Why weren't you surprised when I arrived?' she asked bluntly, her sharp gaze not moving from his face.

'What do you mean?' he asked, blinking at the abrupt question.

'When you opened the door...' she said slowly. 'You weren't surprised to see me there at all. You just invited me in.' Her brain was whirring as she replayed it in her mind again.

Ali's gaze flicked to Craig, and she looked over towards him. His face had dropped and he'd become very still. Her gaze narrowed further as the suspicions began to mount.

'Where did you go when I got here?' she asked.

'What?' He laughed and looked at Ali. 'I popped to the local shop.' He gave her a look as if she was acting crazy, but she could already see through it.

'What did you get from the shop?' she asked.

'What? What *is* this? I mean...' He made a dismissive sound and rolled his eyes.

'*What*. Did you *get*. From the *shop*?' she asked through gritted teeth, her expression hardening.

He faltered and she shook her head. 'You didn't get anything from the shop, because you didn't go to the shop, did you?'

Guilt flooded through both of their faces, and Ruby stood up abruptly.

'Who did you tell?' she demanded.

'Ruby, look...' Ali began.

'*Who did you tell?*' she yelled, her eyes blazing as her anger swelled from the betrayal.

'One of the girls in another flat. Look, your brother turned up here, and—' Ali started to explain.

'I can't believe this,' Ruby shouted, cutting him off, running her hand up through her wild red curls. She let out a cry of frustration and then bolted for the front door. 'You're gonna fucking regret this,' she called back hotly. '*Really* fucking regret it.'

She ran out of the flat and spun wildly, her eyes darting around. They weren't there yet, but she had no idea how much more time she had. Her heart pounded in her chest, and she bolted down the nearest alleyway. As she sifted through what options she had left, her heart sank to the bottom of her stomach like a stone. There was only one other place she could try tonight. Somewhere she'd hoped never to have to go again.

TWELVE

Scarlet walked into the pub and headed over to Tommy, the man who ran it for them.

'Who's here?' she asked him.

'Cillian's upstairs. Lil was here earlier but went out,' he replied, watching the pint of Guinness he was pulling for one of the customers.

'Thanks.'

She walked across the pub and through the door that led upstairs to the offices and the gambling floor. As the door swung closed behind her, Cillian walked out of her office, his phone to his ear.

'What do you mean?' The demand was angry. 'For fuck's *sake*!' Cillian slammed his free hand into the wall.

Scarlet paused on the stairs, unsure what had caused the outburst.

Ending the call, Cillian closed his eyes for a moment before looking up to the heavens. He hissed out a frustrated breath and Scarlet continued walking up.

Realising he was no longer alone, Cillian stepped back and slipped his phone away.

'Everything OK?' she asked.

Cillian studied her for a moment, his dark-brown eyes guarded. She studied him in return, noting that his chiselled face seemed drawn and his dark stubble was a little longer than usual.

'Everything's fine,' he replied.

'Are you sure?' she asked, concerned. She reached the top of the stairs and stood in front of him. 'Seemed like *something* happened.'

Cillian looked away, his expression grim. 'Nothing that concerns *you*,' he said in a low heavy voice.

Scarlet's eyebrows shot up, but Cillian didn't stick around to continue the conversation. Sidestepping around her, he jogged down the stairs and through the door to the pub.

Scarlet pursed her lips. His response told her more than enough. The call had been about Ruby.

She wandered into her office and sat down behind her desk, slouching back and resting her elbow on the arm of the chair. She put her hand to her mouth and rubbed back and forth as she wondered who'd been on the other end of the phone.

She knew Cillian had been searching for Ruby. They'd argued fiercely about what would happen when she finally reappeared. Scarlet could understand why he wanted to protect her, and she'd told him that. But after all Ruby had done, Scarlet had every right to exact revenge, and she'd told him this too. Ruby had crossed every last line there was to cross and burned every bridge. She had to be stopped, once and for all. From then, Cillian had kept the details of his search private, in the hope he could find his sister first. And Scarlet, in turn, had done the same.

Lily and Connor hadn't joined the argument, keeping their counsel as grave spectators, as she'd known they would. Because it wasn't a black-and-white situation. Whatever happened, there was no outcome that worked in everyone's favour. There was no outcome without consequences. And Scarlet hated Ruby for that almost as much as she hated her for everything else. Even now, in her absence, she was tearing this family apart.

Clearly one of Cillian's trails towards Ruby had run cold. Or perhaps he'd even got close and she'd slipped away. Either way, this served as a stark reminder that Cillian was way ahead of her. She still had nothing on her cousin's whereabouts despite having tried her hardest to find her.

Abandoning her plan to sort the pub's accounts, Scarlet stood up and walked back out of the office and down the stairs.

Tommy looked over as she reappeared in the pub. 'You want the stocktake?' he asked.

'No, I've gotta go,' she said. 'I'll be back later.'

If Cillian was getting close to finding Ruby then Scarlet needed to take things up a notch. Because she absolutely could not let Cillian get to her first.

Twenty minutes later, Scarlet pulled up at the edge of the Eric and Treby Estate and peered up at the fronts of the uniform brown-brick flats. A couple of women stood chatting on one of the walkways that ran the length of the building on each floor. They glanced down when they saw the car then swiftly disappeared inside. Everyone knew who the Drews were here and most chose to stay out of their way.

Scarlet stepped out and straightened her deep-red bodycon dress, pushed her hair over her shoulder and walked determinedly towards the nearest alleyway. Her dark expression matched her mood, and she had no friendly smile for the men hanging around in the entrance today.

As they saw her, one of them pushed off the wall and nodded before disappearing down the alley. She stopped to wait, pulling her phone out to check her emails, knowing the drill. The estate was technically on their turf but they'd never bothered with the inner running of it, already having enough on their hands. Now there was a gang who ruled inside this invisible perimeter, who ran the drugs and other various small enterprises within.

The head of this particular gang was a man known only as Chain, who they had a good working relationship with. To keep this relationship healthy, the Drews publicly respected the rule of gaining his permission to enter. They could ignore it and assert their higher power, but they'd found the more diplomatic approach made Chain more amenable to working with them when they required extra hands.

Soon enough, the man came back and whistled, nodding towards the other end of the alley. She forced a tight smile and passed into the estate beyond.

Chain had a small electrical shop in the centre of the estate from which he conducted most of his business dealings. Upon reaching this, she entered, sending the little bell above the door into a tinkle and pulling her arms in close as she manoeuvred down one of the two narrow aisles towards the desk at the back.

Chain leaned forward over the desk, his large muscular arms crossed in front of him and the gold tooth at the front of his mouth glinting in the light as he met her with a wide grin.

'Scarlet Drew,' he said, rolling her name off his tongue as if tasting it. 'It's been a while. You here to tell me there's a new shipment coming through, eh?' His deep voice rumbled around the small space, his accent a melodic mixture of his Caribbean roots and East London home.

'Actually, no,' she replied. 'We've got issues with stock at the moment.'

Chain pulled a face. 'That ain't good news,' he replied. 'We've been dry a while.'

'I know. We're working on a more consistent solution, but you'll have to be patient. As soon as I have anything, I'll let you know.' She stifled a sigh. Usually the heists they pulled were regular and the problem they faced was having *too much* stock, the excess sold on through Chain's gang.

'Well you didn't come here to buy a laptop charger, so what do you want?' Chain asked, watching her intently.

'Are you going to keep me standing out here or can we sit down?' Scarlet challenged, raising one perfectly arched eyebrow.

Chain smirked and stood up, lifting the counter and stepping back to allow her through. 'Man... I let you in *once* and now you expect the royal treatment every time. This is why I don't keep a woman around,' he joked.

'You don't keep a woman around because you're a player, Chain,' Scarlet said with a short laugh, walking through to the lounge behind the shop, a neat cosy room that was in complete contrast to anything Chain showed to the outside world.

'Blame the game,' he replied, shutting the door behind him. 'Ain't my fault there are so many delights to be tasted in this world. I'm a hungry man.'

Scarlet rolled her eyes and sat in one of the terracotta-coloured armchairs. Chain took a seat opposite her and leaned forward on his thighs, narrowing his gaze as he watched her.

'You know your cousin beat you to me,' he said, cutting to the point.

Scarlet swore under her breath. 'What did he ask of you?'

Chain twisted his full lips to one side for a moment before answering. 'Exactly what you're about to, I imagine.'

'Huh.' Scarlet let out a humourless laugh. 'And what did he tell you about the situation? Do you know what she did?'

'Some. But I got the impression he was holding back. Want to fill me in?'

Scarlet exhaled heavily through her nose and sat back in the chair. 'Ruby and I never got on, that's no secret. She's always been a loose cannon, someone who feels threatened by everyone and everything and, as I'm younger than her, she'd take that out on me when we were kids.' She shrugged. 'I know. Whatever. Kids are kids. But it got more serious when we grew up. You know what she was like before she came back to the fold. You or your men probably dealt to her.'

She paused, and after a moment of reluctance, Chain nodded.

'Ruby only came back because Ray Renshaw forced her through cold turkey and threatened to kill her if she strayed again. She didn't want to be there, but she had no choice. So we were stuck with her. For a time we kept her busy on simple jobs, but she grew resentful and jealous of my position in the firm. Inevitable, I guess.' She clamped her jaw against the wave of resentment that flowed up her body. 'Ruby doesn't understand how life really works, or how hard *I* worked to get to where I am.'

'Or how many pieces of your soul you traded for it,' Chain murmured.

Scarlet nodded. There was no need to hide or sugar-coat things like that here. Chain knew who she was and all she'd done to become that person. They had developed a very frank friendship over the time they'd known each other. Both were aware of how dangerous the other could be, in their different ways, and a mutual respect had been formed between them long ago. More so, she knew, than between him and her cousins. And it was this that made her hold on to the hope she could count on him now.

'I tried to contain the issues. It's never ideal to have a warring firm.' She sighed with a tight look of annoyance. 'But Ruby had other ideas. I was set to go down for a murder, last year. We had an inside copper who removed the evidence from the locker and they had to drop the case.' She looked away as she adjusted the story. The fact she'd dated John was still not common knowledge and never could be. 'Ruby uncovered him to another officer, in the hope it would bring it all to light and I'd go down.'

Chain's eyebrows shot up and he whistled. 'Your cousin didn't mention that.'

'No, I bet he didn't,' Scarlet replied wryly. 'We managed to get our guy out of the picture before they arrested him.'

'Little trip down the Thames?' Chain asked.

'No, of course not,' she answered with a frown. 'We look after our own – you know that. Even bent plods. We set him up to start again elsewhere. We owed him that.' She lifted her chin as the raw wound in her chest burned. She swallowed and focused on the reason she was here. 'We were lucky, getting him away in time. No one went down. But Ruby got very close to getting what she wanted.'

'That's cold,' Chain replied with a disapproving shake of his head.

'It is. But more than that, it's unacceptable. This is *my* world, Chain,' Scarlet said, her tone hard and unyielding. 'I gave up a lot to be here. More than she could ever understand. She's been back for five minutes pushing papers around and then tries to send me down for life because she thinks I'm the only thing in the way of her being *me*.'

'Being you?' Chain repeated.

'She thinks my... *job*, my *role*, was just some empty slot that Lil offered to me. Some position you slip into, like in an office. She doesn't grasp that it never existed. I *am* the position. I created it, built it from nothing. The same way all of us did.' She rubbed her temple. 'But Ruby don't understand work and sacrifice, or even family really. So she tried to destroy me. And I can't let that slide.'

'You want me to help you find her,' Chain said. A statement rather than a question.

Scarlet nodded. 'I'm low on resources as most people are loyal to the firm and Cillian got there first,' she admitted.

'Same way he did here,' Chain countered.

'But you aren't the same as the rest of them.' Scarlet locked her steely gaze onto his. 'Because you and I understand each other in ways other people don't. And I'm hoping we can come to an agreement, where, within my firm, your loyalty lies with me above all others.' She watched him closely and waited.

'That's a big ask,' Chain replied, his expression revealing nothing.

'Not really. No one would ever need to know of that arrangement but us.' She held her breath, willing him to agree. She needed him. She was out of all other decent options.

Chain laced his fingers together and put them to his mouth, silent for a long moment. 'Your cousin only said there had been a falling-out in the family and that you were on the warpath. He asked me to help find her and to report back to him and no one else. I've had watchers out for a week, no sign anywhere so far.'

'And when you do find her?' Scarlet pushed. 'What are you going to do?'

'That depends. When you find her, what are *you* gonna do?' he countered.

Scarlet's grey-blue eyes grew cold. 'Honestly? I don't fully know myself. My gut instinct is to pay her back in the ways the old laws permit me to,' she said. 'I have a right to it. And if I do, you'll be helping me.' It was only fair to give him the truth.

There was another long silence. Scarlet could understand his predicament. She was asking a lot. Chain had always shown loyalty to the Drew firm, but he'd never been asked to split that loyalty and go against one of them in aid of another. Whatever he did, he could potentially lose.

'I'll have to think about this,' he said eventually. 'I have a lot of respect for you, but crossing your cousins ain't something I'd advise anyone to do.'

'And crossing me is?' Scarlet asked.

'I ain't crossing you,' he replied strongly. 'I'm telling you I'll think on it.'

She nodded. That was as far as she was going to get in today's meeting. She knew Chain well enough to know when to stop.

'Well, don't think too long.' Standing up, she straightened her dress and looked down at him with a hard expression. 'Because when I find her, Cillian or not, she'll be getting what she deserves. And I'll remember those who helped me get there faster.'

THIRTEEN

After a week of busy arrangements, hushed invites sent out and RSVPs returned, the Drews' first fight night came around. The gym had been entirely transformed, to the point that if there hadn't still been the photographs and posters from over the years attached to the wall, some people might not have recognised it. Lights had been strategically placed around the room to beam down brightly over the ring, while keeping the audience in a dim softer light, creating just the right atmosphere. Staggered benches surrounded three sides, waiting to be filled with excited spectators. A long pop-up bar had been set up to serve drinks and snacks, and the betting desk sat below a large whiteboard clearly displaying the offered odds.

Lily cast her eye over the room once more, checking that nothing had been forgotten, and the sides of her mouth curled up in just a hint of a smile as she felt excitement bubble in the pit of her stomach. As planned, George and Connor stood watch by the door, and Andy and Cillian were beside the betting table. Their first guests were steadily trickling in, and Isla greeted them with a handout containing all the information for the evening's entertainment. Scarlet hovered nearby, ushering people towards wherever they wanted to go and greeting closer acquaintances with the respect their positions required. She caught Lily's eye with a smile between guests. Everything was running smoothly, for now.

Jimmy stood at the edge of the room watching the gathering crowd with a grim expression. Lily wandered over and stood next to him.

'It's something, isn't it?' she asked, giving him a warm smile.

'It is,' he agreed, his words guarded. 'Never seen the place like this before.'

'Nor has anyone else,' Lily reminded him. 'Which is why it never made any money.'

'True,' he conceded. He glanced at her with a quick return smile. 'I think I'll get a drink.'

'Enjoy,' Lily replied.

She stood there, on the sidelines, for a few more minutes, drinking in the atmosphere. It always excited her, the start of something new. A new venture, a new risk. Seeing something like this succeed gave her a thrill like no other. It was this feeling that had driven her all these years as she'd built their firm from nothing to what it was today. But that thrill also magnified the silent empty space where her brother, Ronan, should have been. He would have loved this.

She looked up to the heavens with a sad smile. 'I hope you're here watching,' she whispered. But as she cast her gaze down, she wondered whether it would be better if he wasn't. He'd have been devastated by the state the family was in right now. Perhaps the fact he wasn't here to see it was a small blessing after all.

Across the room, she saw Cillian's animated smile drop to a look of resentment and he turned to catch her eye. Her attention shot to the doorway, already guessing what had caused his reaction. Her heart rose, and she felt a seed of hope settle in her chest. Had he come? Was it Ray?

She'd respected his need for distance these past weeks, but the silence had been deafening. She'd hoped that he'd cool down enough to talk, to hear her out and try to find a way back from the revelation she'd dropped on them all. But so far there had been nothing. She'd sent him an invite, and although he hadn't sent a reply, she'd held out hope that he might come. It would be a small step forward at least.

A group of four men walked through the doorway, and Lily felt a catch in her throat as Ray came into view. He looked around the gym with a curious expression and then listened intently as Isla reeled off all the information for the night. Lily's eyes roamed over him, drinking him in, and she felt the almost physical pull she'd always felt when Ray was in close proximity. Her heart ached in a bittersweet way as her gaze swept over his handsome, rugged features and down the well-cut suit and crisp white shirt, open at the top to show a hint of the dark hair trailing down his hard, muscular chest. It was said that men aged better than women – another injustice in the already skewed balance between the two sexes, in her opinion – but Ray had aged better than most. She'd missed him terribly these last few weeks. They hadn't been this disconnected for over twenty years.

Ray and his men moved into the room, and Lily nodded to Scarlet, who was watching her for instruction. Scarlet moved forward and greeted Ray as charmingly as she had all their other guests. Lily watched as they talked, and as Ray's gaze swept the room, he finally noticed her. They stared at each other, the tension in the air growing heavy between them. Lily lifted her chin with a small smile in the hope that it might break the ice, but Ray's expression remained hard and unreadable, until eventually he broke away.

Lily swallowed her disappointment, trying not to let it get to her. Ray clearly wasn't going to make this easy for her, but the fact he was here was still a positive sign.

Ray continued to the betting desk, leaning over it to be heard above the noise of the growing crowd, and Lily watched Mickey's eyebrows shoot up in surprise. Mickey said something back to Ray, as if double-checking his instruction, and Ray nodded as one of his men passed him a zipped bag. He pulled out a thick pile of notes and passed them over, and Lily watched the exchange curiously. She couldn't tell exactly how much was there, but it was clearly a considerable sum. Mickey put the money through the counting machine, then scribbled something on a betting slip and handed it over.

Lily waited until Ray and his men left to find their seats before walking over to the betting area. Slipping around the back as Mickey served the next client, she picked up the betting ledger and looked at the lines of coded information inside.

'What did Ray just bet on?' she asked.

'Renshaw? Not someone I'd have put my money on, that's for sure,' he replied, pointing to the entry.

She quickly deciphered the lines and dots they used to record this kind of data. Ray had put a hundred grand down on one single bet. Her eyebrows shot upwards. A grand wouldn't have surprised her, maybe even five, but this was crazy money.

'Who is this?' she asked, pointing at the mark of the fighter.

'McGovern,' Mickey replied. 'He's three to one to win, but the chances of that happening are slim to none. He's up against Dave O'Connell, a seasoned pro. He hasn't lost a single fight this year. He's set to become a big name in the official leagues.'

Jimmy's voice boomed around the room as he spoke into the microphone and announced the first fight. The crowd cheered, and suddenly the room was charged with an electric energy as the fighters made their way into the ring.

George closed the front door, and Cillian made his way to the first row. Connor joined him, and they sat together beside Scarlet and Cath.

Lily glanced once more at the hefty sum in the book and

then towards Ray. He looked to be in good spirits now. The memory of him as a young man fighting in these walls came back to her, and it warmed her heart for a moment. This place had meant a lot to him too, over the years. He'd found solace and guidance within these walls, the same way many others had. He must know that the profit from tonight would benefit this place, and while he might hate *her* right now, clearly he still wanted to help the club.

As the bell rang to start the first round, Lily took her seat beside Cath. Ray and his men were up on one of the higher benches across from her, and while she trained her attention on the fight, she watched him out of the corner of her eye.

Testing jabs swiftly changed to strategic full-force blows as the fighters danced around the ring. The cheers of the crowd grew louder as their moves became faster and sweat began trickling down their faces, and highlighted their bare torsos. Round one came and went, as did rounds two and three, and eventually, as the evening went on, Lily relaxed and let herself be swept up in the fun and excitement.

Connor and Cillian shouted up to their favourites, talking animatedly to each other about each man's odds and fighting habits, and Scarlet watched the proceedings with quiet interest.

'Remember when it was Ronan up there?' Cath asked, leaning into Lily's shoulder to be heard above the noise.

Lily smiled. 'I do. I remember all of them. Ronan, the boys. Ray.'

'Ronan used to scare me silly up there, fighting all those bloody tanks. I used to sit here with my stomach in my mouth, sure that at any moment he wouldn't block well enough or he'd get distracted, and he'd have his face done in by his opponent.'

'But he never did,' Lily reminded her.

'No, he didn't. He could've gone professional, if he'd wanted,' Cath reminisced. 'I was glad he didn't, mind,' she added.

'He always used to say he liked his face too much to go pro. Thank God for his vanity.'

They both laughed, and Lily nudged her sister-in-law with her shoulder. 'He'd have loved this.'

Cath nodded, and they fell silent as the next pair of boxers jumped into the ring.

The night continued and the crowds grew merrier, toasting their wins and drinking away the sting of their losses. All too quickly, they came to the last fight of the night, and everyone cheered with renewed vigour as the fighters appeared beside the ring.

'Look, it's O'Connell,' Cillian said, slapping the back of his hand on Connor's chest to get his attention.

Lily's gaze followed theirs, the name catching her attention. This was who Ray had bet against. He'd placed his money on the other man, McGovern. She glanced over at him through the smoky haze in the air. His gaze was intently trained on the ring.

The bell sounded and the men circled each other, beginning the dance that would eventually end the evening. Cillian and Connor stood up and cheered, and Jimmy – as referee – watched carefully from the sidelines, the way he had all evening. Time ticked on until round one ended, and Lily caught the look of frustration that passed between Cillian and Connor.

'He could have had that,' Connor claimed.

'Must be playing to the crowd,' Cillian remarked. 'Giving them a bit more for their money.' He reached into his pocket and pulled out a toothpick, placing it between his teeth and frowning at the ring.

The second round began, and Lily watched O'Connell carefully. He danced around McGovern, and her eyes narrowed as he missed an obvious opportunity. She was no boxing expert, but she'd watched and supported enough of them over the years to see he was holding back. But why?

Connor whispered something urgently in Cillian's ear, and

the pair fell silent as the match went on. Lily's gaze slid over to Ray. He was watching intently too, his expression unreadable.

'What the fuck?' Lily heard Cillian exclaim loudly, and a collective sound of anticipation arose from the crowd.

Her head whipped around just in time to see O'Connell fall to the ground with a resounding thump. Her eyes widened as Jimmy entered the ring to check the fallen fighter.

'Get up,' Cillian yelled over the roar of the crowd. 'Get the fuck up!'

But seconds later, Jimmy called the fight. It was a knockout. McGovern had won.

The cheers intensified, and a sea of hands flew up in the air as McGovern claimed his win, his smile beaming in elation and disbelief. Even *he* hadn't expected this outcome. Lily looked to the twins, too shocked to say anything as she registered what had just happened. They were both watching O'Connell being taken off, their expressions hard and thoughtful.

A lot of people had taken that bet tonight, the odds being too juicy to ignore. And that had been the point, of course, to get them to spend their money on a man who was unlikely to win. It was how profit was made. It would have been a blow even without Ray's insane bet, but if the rough amount they'd expected to make out with tonight was anywhere near correct, just that one ticket had cost them all their profits and more. *Much* more.

As the possibility that Ray had meant to do this crept into her mind, she blinked it away, shaking her head. He couldn't have. He'd never do that to her – *or* the club. But as she turned to him, he met her eye directly for the first time since he'd arrived and he dropped the emotionless mask. His dark eyes burned into hers with fiery triumph, and it took all her effort to stop herself from physically recoiling. A cold mocking grin crept up his face and he nodded to her slowly, just once.

Long thin fingers of ice reached up from her stomach and

gripped her heart, making it hard for her to draw in her next breath. Lily needed no more confirmation; Ray had set her up for a fall. A large, expensive, public fall. And in doing that, he'd made one thing very clear – the man she loved, who'd always been there, through decades and heartbreak, the good and the bad, was now her enemy.

Ray had just publicly declared war.

FOURTEEN

Lily sat slumped in a chair in the corner of the large empty room upstairs in the pub. Chairs lined the walls, and one trestle table was slotted neatly behind a few of them, giving it the appearance of an unused function room. This was how it looked most of the time. The game tables and various decorative items that adorned the room on gambling nights were all kept off site, in case of inspections. Not that they'd been used at all recently, with Jennings swooping in on a regular basis.

She reached over to the heavy curtain that draped down the window next to her and pulled it aside with one finger, peering out across the empty car park. They'd been careful to leave bogus clues outside of London, keeping Jennings and his team busy for the last few hours.

Dropping the curtain, Lily rubbed her hand over her forehead and down her face, stressed, still reeling from the events of the evening. How could Ray have turned on her like that? Even after everything that had happened lately, they still had decades of history and a deep love and respect that was so ingrained she'd never thought it could change. Clearly she'd been wrong. She took a deep drag of her cigarette.

Scarlet leaned back against the wall beside her, arms folded, expression pinched. Cillian and Connor paced irritably before the man they'd dragged here after the fight. They'd grabbed him from the changing rooms, throwing him in the back of a car with just a few whispered threats. Now he stood upright in the middle of the room as George and Andy each twisted an arm up against his back to keep him still.

'No one's buying it, Dave,' Cillian said, his words hard and cold.

Dave O'Connell made a sound of exasperation. 'There's nothing to buy. I missed my footing and it distracted me for a moment. He caught me off guard.'

'You didn't miss your footing,' Cillian replied. 'We were watching you closer than a fly on shit, because you fucked up way earlier than that. You pulled back from the start of the first round. And I *know* your fighting style, Dave. You ain't pulled back a day in your life.'

Dave shook his head. 'You're seeing things that ain't there, Cillian. I just wasn't myself today, and I'm sorry I lost the match.' He looked over to Lily beseechingly. 'I really am. I know it probably cost ya, but that's the risk of the game. You know that.'

Lily stood up, took another drag on her cigarette and blew it out slowly in his face as she stopped just before him. He coughed and tried to turn his face, but she moved hers closer until she was barely inches away.

'I know the risks of the game, Dave,' she said in a low, dangerous tone. 'But I also know every single way in which this particular game can be manipulated and cheated.' She stepped back, her gaze unmoving. 'I was playing this game, running gambles in the shadows and creating my own rules before you were old enough to wipe your own arse. Of course, when it's your game, it's perfectly natural to create your own rules. Then when you invite people to play, they can choose whether to accept the rules or find a game that suits them better – that's the beauty of it.'

She paced for a moment, taking another drag and eying him side on. He watched her with a carefully guarded expression, silent, as he tried to work out where this was going. The silence was smart. Another great quality wasted on bad decisions. She'd watched him closely since they'd left the gym. So far he'd shown strength, intelligence and a decent backbone wrapped in calculated cautiousness. In any other scenario, she might have considered taking him on. But it was too late for that. Ray had got there first.

'The problem comes when someone walks into another person's game and tries to win by ignoring the rules. By twisting them and cheating.' She narrowed her gaze. 'No one likes a cheater, Dave.'

'No, of course not. I don't either, Lily. Listen, I had a girl-friend who cheated on me once. It killed me, it really did—'

The dull thud of a fist connecting with skin cut him off as Connor stepped forward and punched him in the face. Dave's head snapped to the side from the blow, then rolled back. He shook it off, opening his mouth wide to stretch his face before breathing out slowly.

'It's Ms Drew, to you, cunt,' Connor growled. 'And stop playing fucking games.'

'I ain't playing games, Connor, merely talking about them,' he replied, his tone level and easy.

Lily felt a spark of grudging respect towards the man but pushed it aside. It wouldn't help him to act hard now.

'How much did Ray pay you?' she asked.

Dave looked at her, his watery blue eyes an odd contrast to the rest of his hard leathery face. 'Who's Ray?' he asked.

Lily sighed. 'The thing is, Dave, you don't actually mean

anything to Ray. He singled you out for this job because you were uniquely placed to carry it out. Not because he likes or trusts you. You ain't one of his men, who he'd protect. And he really *didn't* protect you...' She pulled an indifferent expression. 'The moment you went down, he let me know it was him. That was his whole point, you see. To beat me at my own game and then gloat – publicly. To show he could topple my cards by using my own rules against me. The rule that all bets are final, no matter what. The rule that the matches are to be taken seriously, that the fighters are honourable...'

She raised an eyebrow, and he had the grace to look down. She took one last drag on her cigarette then walked over to the ashtray at the side of the room.

'So you see, there's really no reason to protect him,' she said as she stubbed it out. 'You're in deep shit now, whatever you do. Ray saw to that when he showed his winning hand.' She watched as Dave's face drained of its colour, as realisation dawned that he was well and truly screwed. 'He ain't gonna save you. He don't care what happens to you. So exactly how bad things go now is up to you. I want to know exactly what Ray asked of you and how much he paid you.' She eyed him hard. 'And the more time of mine that you waste by lying, the worse your injuries will be.'

Dave's Adam's apple bobbed up and down as he swallowed, his eyes darting between Lily and the twins.

'OK, look... One of his guys approached me a few days ago after the invites went out,' he started.

'How did they know you'd be fighting?' she asked with a frown.

'They didn't. The guy asked me if I'd been signed up. Said he'd been invited and was trying to get a feel of who to put his money on. I told him I was in, figured if he already knew about it that was OK. I knew he wasn't a copper – I've seen him at other underground events,' Dave continued.

'Then what?' Lily pushed.

'Next morning I was out for a jog and a car pulled up. Door opened, Ray leaned out. I mean, I know who he is,' he said, pulling a pained expression. 'I weren't gonna say no. He asked who I was up against and then told me to throw the fight in the second round. I tried to say no—'

'Obviously not hard enough,' Lily snapped sharply, cutting him off.

He met her gaze, and she saw the defeat there. Most men at this stage would begin begging, telling their sob stories about desperation and having no choice. Sometimes it was the truth, often it wasn't. Either way, it made no difference, and clearly Dave knew this.

'How much?' she demanded.

'Twenty grand,' he replied.

Lily's eyebrows shot up. That was a lot of money for pulling something like this. But it was nothing compared to what Ray had taken her for tonight. She shook her head, furious and disgusted with the entire situation.

Stepping forward, she grabbed Dave's face in her hand, digging her long red manicured nails into his cheeks.

'Twenty grand?' she seethed. 'Did it not occur to you at any point that that amount of money for throwing a fight probably meant it was danger money?'

He winced as she squeezed but stayed silent. Her expression contorted as she tried to stay in control of her emotions, and she thrust his face away from her sharply. She took a deep breath in and exhaled slowly.

'He did us out of a lot more than twenty grand tonight,' she shared. 'How much did Mickey say again, Scarlet?'

'According to Mickey, without all this we'd have been around seventy grand up tonight. However *with* Ray's bet and Dave throwing the fight, we ended up about two hundred and fifty grand down,' Scarlet replied from the side of the room.

Lily closed her eyes as the figure hit her, once more, like a brick to the face. There had been a time, the previous year, when they'd had five million *legitimate* pounds in the bank, following a very *illegitimate* con. A chunk of that had gone to John, some had disappeared with Ruby, and the rest they'd invested. Almost a million had gone on buying the boxing club – a money pit that was already sucking more out of them than they'd accounted for. Tonight was supposed to have been the night that all changed; the night the club started producing profit, instead of continually sinking. Instead, Ray's underhand game had lost them nearly everything they had left.

'Quarter of a million pounds you've cost us tonight,' Lily said in a quiet, deadly tone. She looked him up and down. 'Three hundred, if you count the lost profit. What do you have that's worth three hundred grand, Dave O'Connell?' she asked.

He just shook his head.

Lily stared at him coldly. 'Nothing. You don't own a house, no businesses, no contracts...'

'I'll be worth something next year,' he stated. 'I'm set to move up to the professional league. No bullshit, it's all agreed and signed. Next year my fights will be lucrative, and I'll earn that money back in no time.'

'Yeah?' Lily asked calmly.

'Yes. I can pay you back the lot, and as an apology for all this has caused, an extra fifty on top. A cool three fifty,' he promised. 'Think about it.'

Lily laughed silently, her amusement real. Scarlet raised her eyebrow at Dave in disbelief and then shook her head at Lily.

'I don't need money next year, Dave. I need it *now*,' Lily said. 'And I don't do deals with people who've already scammed us. There ain't no second chances with a firm like ours. You cost us a quarter of a million and ruined the first night of our new business venture. You also allowed another firm to make a mockery of us. I don't even know yet what damage that will do to the integrity of the future fight nights.' She turned to Cillian. 'Hands or legs?'

Dave began to panic. 'Please don't do this. There has to be a way we can work this out.'

For the first time since they'd arrived, he tried to pull away from George and Andy – but they were ready for him and twisted his arms tighter. He cried out in pain.

'Ankles,' Cillian replied. 'They'll heal, but his future as a professional boxer is over. Can't fight if he can't dance.'

'Cillian, *please* don't do this!' Dave cried.

Cillian turned and punched him hard in the stomach, winding him. Dave bent over as much as he could with his arms held back.

'You know how much fighting means to me,' he continued in a wheeze.

'I do,' Cillian replied, taking off his jacket. 'Which is why I know how much it's gonna hurt. You knowingly fucked us over. These are the consequences.'

Scarlet's phone rang, and she turned away to take the call.

Lily nodded to Cillian and Connor. 'I'll leave you to deal with it.'

'Ms Drew,' Dave begged. 'Come on, people make mistakes. This is a big one, I know, but I'll do anything...'

'Shit!'

Lily turned at Scarlet's exclamation with a questioning frown.

'I'll be right there.' Scarlet ended the call and picked up her bag. 'Someone's thrown a brick through the window – Mum's in a right state.'

'What?' Lily asked, aghast. 'Who would do that?' Ray's face crept into her mind, but she pushed it away. Bricking windows wasn't his style. 'I'll come with you.'

'Ms Drew, please,' Dave begged again.

She glared at him as she set after Scarlet, her expression hard and unforgiving. 'Save it. It's too late for you. Someone should have taught you a long time ago that when you play with fire, you always get burned.'

FIFTEEN

Scarlet jumped out of the car and scanned the front of the house. There didn't seem to be any windows broken there. As she hurried up the path, Lily right behind her, the front door opened and Cath appeared.

'What happened?' she asked, grasping her mother's arm. 'Are you OK?'

Cath looked drawn, her eyes wide and her skin devoid of the little colour it usually held. Her dark hair was loose around her shoulders, and she hugged an oversized cardigan over her middle tightly.

'I was just heading to bed when I heard glass breaking. I found the brick on the floor. Tried looking out to see who it was but they were already gone,' she said, closing the door behind them as they entered the house.

'Where?' Lily asked.

Cath hesitated and looked at Scarlet. 'Your room.'

Scarlet pulled back in surprise, and her gaze moved to the top of the stairs. 'Right,' she said slowly, the knife in her tyre coming back to mind. 'Don't worry about it, Mum. It's probably just kids.'

'It's not kids,' Lily said.

Scarlet shot her a look of warning, not wanting to worry her mother.

'She needs to know, Scar,' Lily said firmly. 'Forewarned is forearmed, you know that.'

'What's going on?' Cath asked, looking from one to the other.

'Nothing,' Scarlet said strongly.

'*Something*,' Lily said, overriding her. 'We don't know exactly what, but we have some ideas.' She exhaled heavily and ran her hand through her tight blonde curls.

Scarlet sighed sharply, annoyed. Cath was anxious enough already – she didn't need to be worried about people attacking her home.

'What ideas?' Cath asked. 'Scarlet?'

'Come on – I think we all need a drink,' Lily said, walking through to the kitchen.

Scarlet followed her through and took out three wine glasses, placing them on the side. Lily grabbed the wine from the fridge, and Cath sat down on one of the bar stools that lined the large white marble island.

'Are either of you going to actually tell me what's going on?' she asked, accepting a full glass from Lily.

Scarlet walked around the other side of the island and leaned on it, facing her mother and aunt.

'My tyres got slashed the other day at the factory.' She ignored Cath's gasp of shock. 'There was no footage, before you ask. I make a point of parking in the blind spot when I can, to leave less footprints.' Scarlet took a sip of the cold, crisp wine and met her aunt's eyes across the island. They'd avoided this conversation until now, and for good reason. It threw too much light on the elephant in the room.

'Do you know who it was?' Cath asked.

'It's one of two people,' Scarlet replied, turning her gaze

towards her mother and hating the fear she saw behind her eyes. 'It's either Ascough, venting her heartbroken fury—'

'The officer who fancies John?' Cath asked, butting in.

'The officer who *loves* him,' Scarlet corrected. 'She's on a mission to find out what happened and she plans on hounding me until she does. She told me as much. Or... it's Ruby.'

And there it was. She'd said it out loud in front of Lily.

Cath glanced at her worriedly. 'Scar, I'm sure it's not...' she started, trying to placate the situation before it continued.

'You can't be sure of anything where Ruby's concerned, Mum,' Scarlet snapped. 'We all know that.'

There was a long awkward silence and, suddenly, as the three of them sat there – together, yet so disconnected, because of her selfish, vicious cousin – she'd had enough of the pretence. Of the silence. Of how they all skirted around it, as though it was some fragile, breakable subject they couldn't risk going near. It wasn't fragile; it was poisonous. And she was ready to be free of it. She looked upwards for a moment, steeling herself, allowing her anger to escape the carefully welded cage she usually contained it in.

'No one wants to talk about it, but let's be honest, we all *know* it's probably her,' she said bitterly. 'Ruby has gunned for me my *entire* life. And all of you kept brushing it away, assuming it would stop eventually. *It's a phase*, right?' She glared at her mother and at the side of Lily's face as her aunt stared out the window, her expression troubled. 'But it didn't stop. And I'm not sweeping this under the rug anymore. I'm *done* acting like this isn't happening,' she continued with feeling. 'She's broken every boundary, every rule of family *and* firm. She ruined John's life – a man who I *love* and who saved my life. And she *tried* to destroy *me*.'

She shook her head. 'And I'm done accepting that just because she's family. She never treated me like family, so why should I? Ruby is nothing but an enemy to me,' Scarlet spat, all her pent-up frustration spewing out through her words. 'A fucking dangerous one at that, and I won't treat her as anything else ever again.'

Scarlet saw Lily clenching her jaw and shook her head, pushing away from the island. 'I'm sorry, Lil, but she's got it coming, and the fact we share blood ain't gonna protect her anymore.'

'Scarlet,' Cath exclaimed in a horrified whisper.

'No, Mum. I'm done. No one protected me from her, so I'll damn well do it myself.'

With one last glance at Lily, Scarlet walked away, out of the kitchen and up the stairs.

She reached her room, and her shoulders dropped along with her heart. Her cream cotton curtains fluttered gently in the breeze, either side of the broken window. Angry, jagged shards pointed inwards to the gaping hole where the brick had come through. Her mother had clearly picked up the larger pieces of glass from the floor, but the carpet still glittered with all the tiny slivers that had shattered. The brick had been placed on the dressing table. She picked it up and with a sigh sat down on the bed, cradling it in her hands.

It had to have been Ruby. Ascough knew her address, but she doubted she knew her bedroom. Her window was down the side of the house, tucked away from the street. Not an obvious choice for someone taking a chance.

There was a soft knock on the door, and she looked up to see Lily standing there. For a moment, the pair watched each other in silence, then Lily walked in and looked around, surveying the mess. She blew a long breath out through her cheeks and eyed the jagged hole in the window before leaning against the edge of the pane.

Scarlet steeled herself for the argument to come. And there would be one. Whatever had happened, Ruby was Lily's daughter, and family meant more to her than anything. She swallowed and tensed, preparing to stand her ground against the strongest person she had ever known – but her aunt's next words surprised her.

'I should have protected you,' Lily said quietly. 'You were right, no one *did*. And I should have.' She reached out and touched the figurine of a dancing doll that stood on top of Scarlet's drawers. 'I made you a promise, many years ago, when you were just a little girl, that I'd always protect you. That I'd always protect everyone in this family.' She ran a hand down her face, the conversation clearly difficult for her. 'I just didn't ever think I'd have to protect you from each other. But that's no excuse.'

Scarlet stayed silent, not sure what to say.

'What Ruby did to you should never have happened. Maybe if I'd listened to you and kept a closer eye on her, it wouldn't have,' Lily continued. 'That's on me.'

'It's not your fault,' Scarlet replied, shaking her head.

'It is in part,' Lily said. 'Don't skirt it, Scarlet – it's the truth. You deserved better from me.' She exhaled tiredly. 'I can't undo what she's done. I can't excuse it. If she comes home, she'll be fired from the firm with no option to return.'

Scarlet let out a sharp bark of bitter laughter. 'Fired,' she repeated, closing her eyes and shaking her head.

'She burned her bridges,' Lily continued. 'I'll set her up somewhere far away from here and make it clear she must stay away. But you know that I can't offer you more than that. Whatever else she is, she's still my daughter. I grew her in my body; my blood runs through her veins.'

Scarlet sighed. 'I understand that. I do. The same way I know you understand that I have every right to treat her as the enemy she is to me. I have every right to exact revenge after she failed to destroy me. And you have no right to stand in my way. They're old laws, Lil, but, like you taught me' – she lifted her chin – 'they're unbreakable.'

Lily nodded slowly. 'They are. And no, I can't stand in your way. But I won't have to.' She walked to the door and paused, her words filled with quiet confidence. 'You won't kill Ruby, Scarlet. I know you want to, I know you can... but you won't.'

'And why's that?' Scarlet asked.

A ghost of a smile crossed Lily's face. 'Because you're not like her. Ruby never really cared about family, as hard as that is for me to accept.' She bit her bottom lip. 'She took this shot at you because that's never held her back. But you *do* care about family.'

'I told you, Lil. She ain't my family,' Scarlet replied.

'Maybe she's not, but *I* am. Cillian and Connor are,' Lily replied. 'You're a real Drew, Scarlet. Like me, like your dad. Your family mean more to you than anything. Which is why I know deep down, no matter how much you want to do it, you never will. Because you couldn't bear to lose us.'

As Lily's words pierced her heart like a molten sword, Scarlet struggled to hold her gaze steady. Tears stung her eyes, and she clamped her jaw tightly, trying to hold it together. And as Lily slipped out of the room, the hot tears finally fell, burning her cheeks with all the anger and pain inside.

The first tears were followed by a second wave, then another and another, as the last wall of defence she'd been holding up fell. She cried with abandon and for once didn't try to contain it. Because Lily was right. They didn't need to physically stop her from killing Ruby. If she killed her cousin, she'd be killing part of all the people she cared about. All the people she lived for. And the part of them that she killed would be the part that cared about her.

She closed her eyes as the injustice of it all became almost overwhelming. Ruby deserved everything Scarlet wanted to give her. But it could never happen. She was trapped by the very thing she held most dear.

Scarlet cried until the tears ran dry and the fire inside her died back down to the glowing ember of pain that now resided permanently in her soul, and then she sat for a very long time, possibilities running through her mind as she mentally tested each one. She might not be able to kill Ruby, but that didn't mean she couldn't get revenge. There was still a debt to be paid, and she intended on at least collecting some of it.

Eventually, Cath came up the stairs and leaned into the room with a sombre expression. 'I put fresh sheets on the spare bed for you,' she said gently. 'You can't sleep in here tonight.'

For the first time, Scarlet realised she was cold, the broken window letting in the chilly edge of the autumn evening. 'Thanks.'

Cath lingered. 'Do you want to talk about it?'

Scarlet shook her head. 'No.'

She saw the unspoken questions on her mother's face. The worry and stress she'd put there.

'I won't kill her, Mum,' she said, defeated. 'I want to,' she admitted. 'And Lord knows we'd all be better off.' A sharp feeling of resentment stabbed through her as she said the words out loud. She swallowed it down with difficulty. 'I can't promise you I won't hurt her,' she added. 'But I won't kill her.'

Cath bit her top lip as she stared at her daughter, then finally she nodded, accepting her compromise.

'I love you, Scar,' she said gently. 'And I know you're suffering. It's OK if you don't want to talk about it, but I just want you to remember that I'm here. As your mum, as your friend, as whatever you need from me. OK?'

Scarlet tried to return the smile. 'Thanks. Right now, I just need to sleep.'

'OK. I'm heading to bed too. I'll see you in the morning, love.'

'Night, Mum.'

Scarlet took a deep breath, trying to pull herself out of the funk she was mired in. She wasn't sure how she'd exact her revenge just yet, but that was OK. She had to find Ruby first. Clearly she was nearby, and clearly she was back playing her games. But how far would these games go? What did Ruby have planned?

Looking down at the brick in her hands, Scarlet suddenly noticed something etched into the side. She squinted at the rough scrawl.

Tick-tock.

SIXTEEN

Isla looked over her shoulder and pulled up her hoodie as she crossed the road towards the shabby-looking B&B where Calvin and Jared were lying low. It was out of the way in a quiet urban area made up of rows and rows of tired-looking Victorian houses. She took one more paranoid look around before opening the front gate and walking up to the door, eying the cracked, faded paint curling off the windowpane next to her, and the *No Vacancies* sign showing through the murky glass. Clearly, the woman who ran the place didn't care much for cleaning. She waited, knowing Calvin would have seen her coming.

The door opened and she hurried in, following Calvin up to his room.

He frowned. 'You're late,' he said accusingly.

Isla gave him an apologetic smile. 'Sorry, I had to be sure I wasn't followed, so I went the long way.'

Calvin's frown morphed into a smile. 'Good girl.' He pulled her to him. 'I missed you.'

Isla felt the tension leave her shoulders, and she returned the smile. He leaned in and kissed her hard, and she wrapped her arms around him.

On a practical level, Isla knew Calvin was bad for her. Their relationship wasn't healthy or good – it was toxic and dangerous. Calvin's idea of showing love was to control and manipulate and keep people close. But he was also all she knew. Everything about him, his scent, his face, his body – even his violent unpredictability – lured her into a strange sense of familiar security. No matter what logic said, she couldn't control her natural responses to him any more than she could control the wind.

Calvin pulled away and looked into her eyes. 'Come sit down,' he ordered.

Isla took a seat in one of the two chairs around a small table in the bay window. She knew he sat here keeping watch on the road. She idly wondered how he was coping being cooped up in here. Calvin had never done well with being confined. He was a wild creature who needed freedom and space.

She tucked her shoulder-length blonde hair behind one ear and crossed her jean-clad legs as he took the seat opposite.

'I've found the safe and know roughly what's inside,' she said, smiling. 'And it's a great set-up. Possibly anyway. See what you think,' she added carefully, knowing Calvin didn't like her to be too assertive. He needed to be the one to make the decision.

'Let's hear it,' he replied.

'They came into a lot of money last year, several million,' she said, leaning in. 'They tied a lot of it up in various businesses, but they also invested in gold bars and diamonds. Now, these *are* documented as they're above board,' she warned. 'So we'd have to deal with that after.'

Calvin's expression turned to one of calculated interest. She knew exactly what was going through his mind right now. It might not be cash, but it was still an almost ideal situation. Gold bars could be melted and reformed to strip them of their markings and still sell for almost the same value. And the codes on the diamonds could be filed off before the stones were sold through the jewellery quarter in Manchester. Certain jewellers weren't fussy about stolen gems, so long as they couldn't be traced.

'Where's the safe?' Calvin asked.

'*That's* what I found out this morning. I was doing rounds with Connor and he made a detour to collect something. We drove into the countryside to this dirt track in the middle of nowhere. It led to a big old barn behind some trees. Honestly, you'd never know anything was there – it's proper hidden away...' She paused and glanced out the window through the net curtains as someone walked down the road.

'It's alright, it's just the woman from two doors down. She walks that dog about five times a day,' Calvin said, rolling his eyes.

Isla turned back to him. 'So we got there, and he told me to wait in the car and went into the barn. I followed him after a couple of seconds. At first it looked empty, but then he moved some crates and a false floor, and I saw this massive safe sunk into the ground. I couldn't quite see the inside of it, but I caught a glimpse of the gold bar he pulled out and put in a bag,' she shared.

'He didn't see you?' Calvin checked.

'No, 'course not,' she said. 'I got back in the car before he came out.'

'Good,' Calvin said with a nod. 'Then what?'

'Then we came back to the city, dropped it to his mum and finished the rounds. I came here straight after that.'

'What safe was it?' Calvin asked.

They'd had to crack a few safes on various jobs over the years, and Jared had developed a particular skill for doing so. With some of them at least. Each brand had its own weaknesses – some he'd learned everything about and could crack in his sleep, others he had yet to conquer. The rest of them had learned enough to collect the information he needed for potential jobs.

'It's a Chubb Trident,' she informed him. 'The big one. They've sunk it and, if I had to guess, probably bolted it down too. They open it from the top.'

'Key or electronic?' Calvin asked.

'Electronic. Access code pad, not fingerprint,' she replied. 'Which I'm pretty certain was a Paxos.'

'Perfect,' Calvin declared, banging his fist on the table between them, his eyes lighting up. 'No need to steal keys. Jared can get into those in under a minute.'

He looked at her with a smile and a gleam of respect in his eye, and she felt the rush of warmth that always incited. She'd spent years doing anything she could to earn that look. It was bestowed so rarely that it felt like the ultimate reward whenever he finally deemed her worthy.

Calvin glanced out the window. 'We'll need some time to prepare everything. We'll have to go home so Jared can gather equipment and check that the software is still the same on the Paxos. We'll have to sort a vehicle too to transport the haul, get some fake plates made up.'

'OK.' Isla nodded. 'How long?'

Calvin tilted his head as he thought about it. 'I have some business I need to sort out too, which will take a few days. I neglected some things, looking for you.' He turned his stare on her. 'But it seems it was worth it. Ten days. I'll be back in ten days with everything we need, and then all we need to do is work out when's best to strike.' A slow grin crept up his face. 'The Drews won't have a clue what's coming. And when they realise it's happened, we'll be long gone and a hell of a lot richer.'

SEVENTEEN

'Please follow me – your table is right this way.' The waitress smiled at the three of them and hurried off through the busy restaurant towards a vacant table by the window.

Billie shot Cillian a sunny smile and set off after her, Connor falling in a second later. Cillian sighed loudly and followed them, not bothering to hide his disdain. He sat opposite the pair at the cheap-looking wooden table and gave the waitress his drink order.

'Great, I'll get those for you now. Just head up to the carvery when you're ready.' She bustled off.

Cillian glared at Billie across the table. 'This is *not* what I meant when I said I wanted the three of us to have a Sunday roast,' he declared.

'You wanted a Sunday roast – this is a carvery. Three meats to choose from and all the veg you could desire,' Billie replied chirpily, lifting her chin with a wide smile.

'I was hoping *you* might cook one – or that we could cook it together,' he quickly added, seeing her bristle.

'I've told you, Cillian, I ain't doing it,' Billie said, crossing her arms and pursing her lips resolutely. 'You asked me to stand by you through this fall-out with your mum, and though I don't agree with you on it, I have.'

Cillian opened his mouth, but she cut him off again before he could speak.

'No, don't argue, I *have*. I've stood by you, I've stayed out of it and I've kept me mouth shut, just as you asked. And you may have decided we have to boycott the family Sunday lunch these days, but I am *not* signing my own death warrant by taking her place and making you a roast elsewhere. Not this week or any other. If we can't attend the family one, then this is what you get,' she said firmly, nodding towards the carvery. 'Knock yourself out.'

The waitress arrived with their drinks and placed them on the table between them. Holding his gaze with a look of challenge, Billie picked up her glass of wine and took a sip.

Cillian clamped his jaw, frustrated, knowing there was nothing he could say or do to make her budge. She was as stubborn as they came and the only person outside of the family who wasn't afraid to stand up to him. He glared at her and then turned to his brother, who was staring awkwardly at his bottle of beer.

'Did you find Declan?' he asked, changing the subject.

'Yeah.' Connor looked up and nodded. 'Didn't take long – he still goes to the same pub every night.'

'Predictability has its charms,' Cillian said wryly. 'What did he have to say?'

'There's one that should work quite nicely,' Connor replied.

'Yeah? Where is it?' Cillian asked.

'Coming from Bury St Edmunds towards London. He says he can reset the route to send him down Horsecroft Road towards Pinford End. It's a good stretch, nothing but fields and quiet as anything. We pulled one there a couple of years ago, do you remember?'

Cillian frowned. 'Yeah, that was a good spot. Why hasn't Mum picked up on that?'

'Apparently it's a Milford.' Connor shrugged and sat back. 'So Ian didn't bother telling her about it.'

'Ah, I see.'

Ian was their main contact within the large depot most of the mainland trucks came through once they arrived in the UK. Before him, that contact had been Declan. Declan still worked there, but after being investigated for internal issues a few years back, they'd dropped him from their payroll. But Cillian had had enough of their plans being dictated by Lily, so they'd taken him back on themselves on the quiet.

'What's a Milford?' Billie asked, looking from one to the other.

'Milford is a transport company,' Connor explained. 'A few years ago we went to pull a job on one of their trucks and they'd put a random security car behind it. Luckily we had a couple of guys faking a road block half a mile behind, to stop traffic. They saw it and warned us in time.'

'From then on, Mum was too paranoid to let us go for a Milford truck again,' Cillian added.

'Well, that's understandable,' Billie said with a frown. 'Surely you're not thinking of hitting this one?'

Cillian pulled a dismissive expression. 'It was a one-off. A company like that ain't going to waste profit by having security cars follow each and every truck. That one must have been transporting something unusually expensive.'

'But you don't know for sure, right?' Billie challenged.

'Bills, I promise you, there's no way they're all followed by security,' Cillian replied.

'Have you checked? Have you got someone who can check?' she pushed. 'Come on, Cillian, there has to be a reason your mum is so wary of them. All the risks she takes, she wouldn't boycott them for nothing.'

'We don't have a way of checking. We did try, back then, but they're a closed book. French company, very secretive, don't talk to outsiders.' Cillian shrugged and pulled a toothpick out of his pocket. This conversation was starting to annoy him.

'It's an ideal target, Billie,' Connor said, looking at her with an open expression. 'We wouldn't look at it if it wasn't a good set-up.'

Billie pulled the face Cillian knew she always pulled when something was bothering her.

'Why are you so caught up on this?' he asked. 'We've been doing this for years. We could pull this job in our sleep.' He held her gaze sharply. 'Don't lose your balls now, Billie. This is who we are – you know that.'

'I'm not losing my balls, Cillian. Mine are just as big as yours and you know it,' she shot back challengingly, her smile disappearing. 'I know who you are. But I also know who your mum is, and I think you're foolish to allow family issues to cloud your judgement on a potential problem as big as this. You're ignoring the usual precautions just to stick your middle finger up at her, and *that* is downright idiotic.'

They stared at each other over the table, the tension in the air palpable as two such stubborn forces collided. Billie broke away first, shaking her head with a grim expression.

'I'm going to get my food,' she stated, standing up and stalking away with a huff.

Connor raised his eyebrows and dropped them, then took a swig of his beer. 'It's up to you,' he said. 'I think it's a goer, but only if you're up for it.'

''Course I'm up for it,' Cillian replied, pushing Billie's words from his mind. 'When is it?'

'Saturday coming,' Connor replied. 'Pretty late. Should hit that road about ten.'

Cillian nodded. Billie had been the first woman he'd ever met from outside of their world who didn't bat an eyelid at the

things he did for a living. It didn't faze her, the times he kept, or
if he came home with blood on his shirt, or when he asked her to
be his cover. And he had a lot of respect for her because of it.
She was as hard as nails and twice as strong, despite her sweet
appearance. But she didn't know what she was talking about.
And he was sick of everyone assuming that Lily was the only
one in the firm who could make decisions or call the shots.

It had been fine when they were all in it together. When
they'd been a team, a family who'd looked out for each other's
best interests above all else. But his mother's deceit had broken
all that. All his life he'd bought into the lie that Lily lived for her
children. That everything she did, every move she plotted, was
for them. He'd believed they really were behind the scenes with
her, that they knew every secret. But it had all been a façade. In
the end, Lily had turned out to be no more than a selfish liar.
She'd stripped them of their identity, the knowledge of who
they really were, to serve her own needs.

He ran his hand down the beer bottle in front of him and
took a sip before meeting his brother's gaze with a look of quiet
determination.

'We'll pull this job and show the stallholders that we were
able to come through when *she* didn't. And that will be the
starting point for all the future jobs we pull on our own, just the
two of us.' He raised his head. 'Scarlet will stick with her and
they'll be fine. But from this job on, the Drew brothers will be
known as a powerful force in our *own* right, not associated with
her or anyone. We'll build a new empire together. And she'll
finally learn that you really do reap what you sow.'

EIGHTEEN

Jenny Ascough watched as the front door of Lily's house opened and bathed the front garden in light. Two figures came out and although she couldn't see their features from this far away in the dark, she knew exactly who they were. Her gaze narrowed, and she forced down the bubbles of resentment that danced in her stomach with a deep breath. The two women got in the car and backed off the drive as the front door closed. Waiting a few more seconds, she turned the keys in her ignition and followed a little way behind.

She already knew where they were going. They were fairly predictable, the Drew family. At least on a Sunday. There was always a get-together at one of the houses, usually Lily's, where they would stay all day until the evening, and today had been no different. Lily's sons hadn't been for a while, which surprised Ascough, but she didn't care enough to find out why. They weren't her concern. The only person she had time for now was Scarlet.

On the main road, she was surprised to see the pair take a right at the lights rather than left towards their home. She increased her speed slightly, shortening the gap between them to ensure she didn't lose them. A minute later, she realised they were heading towards the hairdressing salon and she backed off again.

'What are you doing here so late on a Sunday?' she muttered as they pulled into the small car park at the back.

She parked down the side road opposite the front, killing the engine and the lights, and watched the dark front of the salon curiously. It was a small building, no offices at the back. She'd scoped out the car park a couple of times, hoping there might be an easy entry point. She'd never actually broken in anywhere before; it went against everything she'd been taught on the force, but the Drews were annoyingly well versed on the tricks the force used and all the red tape and boundaries that restricted them. And so, for the first time in her career, Ascough had decided to cross the line and snoop around their lives in a less-legal capacity. She was convinced that this was the only way she'd find John. But her first tentative attempt to play dirty had come to nothing. The security at the salon had been too good.

A light came on, and she watched through the criss-crossed metal shutter as Scarlet and Cath sat down together behind the reception desk and pulled out the books. They were catching up on paperwork. She sighed in frustration and ran a hand through her short bright-red hair. Right now, John was either dead, his body hidden somewhere they'd hoped would never be found, or he was alive and locked away so that he couldn't reveal Scarlet's secrets. Part of her was certain he *was* dead, but she refused to let herself accept it until it was confirmed. And if he *was* out there, she couldn't let him down. He'd know that she, of all people, wouldn't give up on him, and he'd be counting on that. He'd be counting on her to find him and bring him home.

She closed her eyes as the pressure pressed down on her. Whatever it took, she *had* to find him. Because if he was still alive, he was definitely being held against his will. He hadn't been home since the day he'd disappeared; his belongings still lay exactly where he'd left them. No money had been withdrawn from his bank account. He hadn't been in touch with his father or his friends. Even if he'd been hiding out in the city with one of the Drews' connections, he'd have at least gone out for a walk to the shop or *something* by now, and the network of cameras around the city would have picked him up.

Her first thought had been to try to get into the factory, but she'd given up on that idea after realising the nightwatchman came with a large, aggressive dog. The pub was always busy and, again, the security was top-notch. She had some tech skills, but they weren't good enough to break past a security system. She propped her elbow on the window with a sigh and rested the side of her head on her hand.

The Drews were annoyingly on the ball with security. The only places not done up to the nines with high-tech cameras were their homes. Obviously a deliberate move, to ensure nothing was recorded that could be seized and used against them. The absence of evidence meant they could use the *I was asleep in bed, officer* story, when being questioned about misdemeanours they were most definitely guilty of.

She suddenly sat up. *There was no security on the house.* There was nothing to record *anyone's* comings or goings – including hers. Her heart began to race as an idea formed. Could she do it? Could she find the courage to break into their home?

It took less than a second for her to decide. John needed her. Alive or dead, she needed to find him and bring him home. The police had already searched the place, she knew, but those officers didn't know John the way she did – they'd had a special connection, she and John. Her heart ached as she thought of him, the man she knew, deep in her soul, would have ended up with her had Scarlet not stuck her evil, calculating claws into him first.

She swallowed hard, pushing the wistful thoughts away, and then started the engine, pulling out onto the main road. If there was something to be found there, she knew she'd find it.

Colour tinged her pale greyish skin for the first time in days, and a determined glint shone in her eye as she set off in the direction of Scarlet's house.

Twenty minutes later, Ascough parked a street away from Scarlet's, careful to hide her car from view, and pulled on a pair of gloves. The next time Jennings's team decided to search the place, she didn't want to have to explain why her prints had suddenly appeared.

Getting out, she popped the boot and unzipped an old gym bag, pulling out an oversized black hoodie. She slipped this on, carefully tucking her bright-red hair out of view. Keeping her head low, she pushed her gloved hands into the hoodie's pockets and walked brisky around the corner into Scarlet's road. Her sharp gaze flickered around the neighbours' windows, but there was no one peering out. It was a nice street full of big houses and she felt a spark of jealousy flare through her. She could never afford a place like one of these.

She slowed as she reached the house, checking one last time that she wasn't being observed before ducking down the side path towards the garden. The gate was locked but it only took her a second to jump over it.

The garden was huge and manicured, clearly put together by a professional with no expense spared. She took a moment to give it a look of disgust.

'*Crime doesn't pay*, they said,' she muttered sarcastically. '*Become a police officer*, they said.'

She rattled the handle of a wooden door near the back of

the house, but it didn't budge. Tutting, she continued round to the other side and found a small rectangular window with an even smaller fanlight window on top, and *this* was partially open.

Ascough grinned. 'Bingo.'

She found a bucket near the garden tap, emptied the stagnant water at the bottom, then pushed through the bushes beneath the window. Placing it on the ground, she tested her weight, then, checking her balance, she hooked her hand up through the small gap in the window and pushed the catch. It popped off with no resistance, and she eased her arm in to unlock the larger window below. It took a few seconds, and she had to strain to get the stiff lock to budge from its usual position, but eventually it moved, and with a few huffs and puffs and scrapes to her arm, she just about managed to ease her body awkwardly inside.

As she pulled her legs in, she toppled off the windowsill inside, bounced off the edge of the counter below and landed heavily on the floor. With a loud clatter, a bottle of hand soap and matching moisturiser came down with her and rolled across the tiles of the downstairs bathroom.

Ascough cringed and pulled herself up, hitting the light switch. Nothing had broken and she let out a breath of relief.

She quickly rearranged the bottles on the side, hoping she'd put them back in the right position, then closed the window and turned the light back off. Pulling out her phone she turned on the torch and entered the hallway. This was it. She was inside.

She'd been here once before, with Jennings, when they'd been trying to get Scarlet to slip up about Jasper Snow. Ascough had actually believed her at first. Scarlet had seemed so young and quiet, and Ascough had allowed herself to be momentarily sucked into the illusion of innocence. But she'd soon learned that Scarlet's quietness was deceiving. The woman was deadly.

Using her phone to light her path, she climbed the stairs to the first floor. Any clues linked to John were most likely to be in Scarlet's bedroom.

The upstairs split off in two directions, and after a momentary pause, she veered to the left.

The first room was a study with family pictures and old scribbled drawings pinned to a corkboard above the desk. The next appeared to be a guest room, the third a bathroom, and then a walk-in airing cupboard. Ascough retraced her steps and tried the other side, and as she pushed the door of the first room open, she knew immediately that she'd found the right one. It must have been Scarlet's room since childhood, the wallpaper too young for a woman her age and the shelves filled with a lifetime of memorabilia. The silver velvet sleigh bed and matching armchair in the corner were more Scarlet's current style, Ascough thought, running her hand down the smooth white sheets and onto the grey knitted throw neatly draped over the end.

Had John slept here? she wondered. Her eyes moved up to the pillows. Had he lain here, in this bed, making love to her, not knowing who she really was?

As she pictured John there, under the sheets, naked, an automatic surge of lust mixed with a sharp shot of disgust and pain, and she turned her gaze away, feeling sick.

'Eugh,' she uttered, pressing her fingers into her eyes in an attempt to force the image away.

He'd fallen for Scarlet's charms, her lies, her pretty mask, and now he'd paid the price. If only he'd seen her for what she was. She took in a deep breath and exhaled slowly. He must have been so lonely, she realised, to have been vulnerable enough to fall for someone like Scarlet. Maybe if she'd told him how she felt earlier, and he'd had *her* to turn to, this wouldn't have happened.

Taking another deep breath, she tried to focus on the present. There had to be something in this room.

She looked around, frowning briefly at the boarded-up window before panning slowly across the rest of the room. It was tidy, not much clutter. Not many hiding places.

She started with the drawers, methodically searching each one. Nothing was in there that shouldn't have been. Next she went through the dressing table, rummaging through Scarlet's make-up and her collection of lotions and potions, but there was nothing there either. Kneeling down, Ascough felt under the bed, but there was only a small gap between the frame and the floor, and after running her hands around it, she realised this was a dead end too.

With practised precision, she swept the rest of the room, checking lampshades and stuffed toys, searching for liftable corners of carpet and hidden pockets in the curtains, but there was nothing. The room was clean.

With a sigh, she sat on the bed, frustrated. She was sure there'd be something here. Most killers or kidnappers kept something.

She stared at the drawers for a moment then stood up and walked back over to them. They were flush to the wall but she pulled them forward, and as she ran her hands down the back, she made a sound of triumph.

She pulled out the photo, feeling the Blu-Tack stretch and snap, and squinted at it in the light from her phone. One pale, slender female hand with red manicured nails clasped a bigger tanned hand with small dark hairs trailing up from the wrist. She swallowed hard, recognising the neat nails and the small scar below one of the knuckles. It was their hands, John and Scarlet's.

Turning it over, she felt her heart flip as she recognised his writing. There were just three words.

I love you.

As she stared, each letter branded itself painfully into her soul and she suddenly felt all her emotions rise up until a deep, guttural, furious sound erupted from her mouth. Before she even knew what she was doing, she tore the picture up, ripping viciously, again and again, until all the pieces were scattered like snow on the floor.

When the red haze passed, she blinked in horror down at what she'd done.

'Shit,' she whispered. She kneeled down and began collecting the pieces, pushing them into the pocket of her hoodie. Her cheeks burned as she mentally berated herself for losing it so wildly. She was better than this. She was a police officer, for God's sake.

As she muttered to herself, feeling foolish, the sound of the key in the front door drifted upstairs, and a frisson of pure alarm ran through her like an electric shock. .

Footsteps entered the hallway along with the muffled sound of Scarlet and Cath's voices.

'Oh my God,' Ascough uttered silently, shaking with panic.

Realising she'd frozen, she forced herself to move, grabbing the last few bits of torn photograph and swinging around wildly as she tried to work out where to go. Their voices moved through to the kitchen and she realised in horror that there wasn't a way out – the stairs were in full view of the kitchen.

Creeping out of the room, she edged towards the top of the stairs. She could see the women's shadows in the hallway below, thrown from the light in the kitchen. They were talking about someone from the salon, about how well her training was going. It all sounded so normal, but that didn't help calm Ascough's racing heart in the slightest. These people were criminals – *murderers*. If they found out she was here, that she'd broken into their home, there was no telling the things they would do.

Through all her years in the force, Ascough knew without doubt that this was the most dangerous position she had ever been in. No one knew she was here; she'd covered her tracks too well. There was no backup; no one to save her if the Drews caught her.

Her heart beat harder, and she covered her hand with her mouth, looking around for ideas.

The other side of the hallway loomed next to her. Neither of their bedrooms were that side of the house. Perhaps she could hide in the spare room, wait it out until they were asleep.

'I'm gonna hit the sack,' Scarlet said below.

Ascough pulled back in panic, darting towards the spare room and praying this was the right choice. The doors were all slightly ajar, so she slipped in then pushed it back into position silently.

'OK, love, I'll be up too in a minute,' came Cath's reply.

Ascough heard the sound of shoes being kicked off in the hallway below, and she backed up behind the door, trying to calm her racing heart. Her gaze wandered towards the square of moonlight shining through the window onto the bed, and suddenly she noticed the neatly folded nightie sitting on top. The boarded-up window in Scarlet's room came back to her with sharp clarity, and she stifled a gasp as her quick mind put two and two together. Scarlet must be sleeping here until her window was fixed.

The first stair creaked as Scarlet began to ascend, and ice replaced the blood in Ascough's veins. Her wide gaze turned fearfully back to the door as she realised she was out of options. There was nowhere else to go, and she'd just placed herself right in the path of the devil.

Scarlet rubbed her neck tiredly, pausing to look back at her mother. 'When did you say the glazier was coming?' she asked. She missed her own bed. The spare one was giving her a stiff neck.

'Hopefully tomorrow morning,' Cath called from the kitchen.

'OK. See you in the morning.' A sound came from above and she frowned up into the darkness. 'What was that?'

'What was what?' Cath asked, coming into the hall.

'There was a noise.' Scarlet narrowed her gaze, suddenly alert. 'Did you lock the back door?'

''Course I did. I don't go anywhere without checking the locks – you know that,' Cath responded.

Scarlet's senses tingled, warning her that something was off. There was never smoke without fire.

She flicked on the light switch and mounted the stairs quickly, checking her room first and then her mother's. Moving back across the hall, she glanced into the study, turning towards the airing cupboard with a grim expression as Cath caught her up.

'What kind of noise was it?' her mother asked.

Scarlet paused and her frown deepened. 'Like a tap or a knock on something.'

Cath's worried expression relaxed into one of relief as she rolled her eyes. 'Oh, for the love of Christ, Scarlet,' she scolded. 'You scared the crap out of me for a minute. It's just your window! That bloody board rattles and bangs in the wind. Damn thing keeps me up. You can't hear it your end of the house.'

Scarlet's tension melted away, and she shook her head with sheepish relief. 'Sorry. I'm getting paranoid.'

'That should be *me*, losing it in me old age, not a sharp young thing like *you*,' Cath replied with a tut.

'Oh, stop it, you're not old.' Scarlet rubbed her eyes tiredly. 'OK. That's enough overthinking for today. Let's go to bed.'

She waited until Cath disappeared around the corner and then turned with a sigh to the door of the spare room.

· · ·

A trembling Ascough watched through the thin slit of the not-quite-closed door as Scarlet disappeared into the room she'd slipped out of just moments before. It wasn't the boarded window that had made that noise. As Scarlet had paused on the stairs, Ascough had run across the hall and ensconced herself in the walk-in airing cupboard – but she'd dropped her phone in her haste and it had knocked against a shelf. Horror and terror had torn through her as Scarlet hunted her down, drawing closer by the second. She'd been certain her time was up. The fact she was still here, unfound, was sheer luck.

Removing the shaking hand that had been covering her mouth, she sank to the floor and wrapped her arms around her legs. She'd used all her allocation of luck from the universe today. She doubted she'd be graced with any more. Two hours passed before she felt brave enough to sneak downstairs and make her escape. And as she slipped out of the back door, over the garden fence and into the night where she felt safe, once again, she vowed not to be so careless next time. Because despite her close call, despite the danger she'd found herself in, she was still as determined as ever to find John.

NINETEEN

Ruby hoisted her rucksack further up her back and lingered for a few moments longer in the dank alleyway. Her stomach twisted as she desperately tried to think of anywhere else she could try, but she really had run out of options now. She'd braved a B&B for a bit, but when the landlady had started getting a little too curious, she'd decided it wasn't worth the risk. Not when she was so close. She'd debated sleeping rough – it wouldn't have been the first time – but there were other risks that came with that and it was too dangerous with so much money on her. Not that *this* would be much safer.

Remi Jones was an ex-boyfriend she'd rather forget. She'd rolled with him when she'd been at her worst level of addiction, and the memory of their relationship sickened her now. They'd come together through their shared love for heroin, and together they'd been able to work enough simple cons to keep them wrapped up in its toxic haze on an ongoing basis rather than scavenging alone from hit to hit. She'd moved into his tiny damp flat, and they'd spent their time together drowning in an unhealthy spiral of enablement and addiction.

Theirs was no love story. It was a saga of convenience filled with lies and let-downs that ended when she woke up one day starving and in withdrawal, and found him stealing the last bit of cash she had. She'd begged him to give it back, but he'd laughed in her face, then shoved her and taken it anyway. She'd left that night without saying a word and had never seen him again.

She'd left a lot of people behind her from those years and had burned nearly every bridge on her way out. She'd done a lot of things she wasn't proud of. In fact, back then, she hadn't been that much different to Remi. The reminder of that being another reason she'd rather forget him.

A car came past and the noise roused her from her dark thoughts. She looked up to the sky and eyed the heavy black clouds with a grim expression. Whether she liked it or not, Remi was the only person she had left to try who her brothers didn't know about. And she couldn't put it off any longer.

Cursing under her breath, she pulled up her hood and crossed the road in a determined march. She walked under the archway that separated the rusty iron railings surrounding the cluster of high-rises and followed the old, cracked path through the estate.

Remi's was a ground-floor flat, the front window right beside the front door. The curtain twitched at her quiet knock, and she turned to show him her face. He looked surprised and then disappeared. A second later, the door partially opened, and he peered out with a wary smile.

'Well this is a surprise,' he said, looking her up and down curiously. 'What brings you here?'

Ruby forced a grim smile. 'It's a long story. Can I come in?'

Remi hesitated and glanced back at something. 'I dunno,' he said. 'It's not just me now – my girlfriend Stacey lives here...' He pulled a face.

'Who is it?' came a voice from within.

Remi sighed and opened the door a little wider. 'Just an old friend.'

A skinny, grubby-looking woman stared out at Ruby from the couch. She was slouched back, in just a T-shirt and a greying pair of knickers. Her brassy blonde hair was piled up high on her head, and dark circles ringed her eyes. She frowned, lines creasing her forehead. The lit cigarette in her hand hovered over an ashtray on the seat next to her, and as she swayed, it moved dangerously close to the seat cushion.

'Well, we're busy, old friend,' Stacey said lazily. 'Come back another time.'

Remi went to shut the door, but Ruby shot her hand out to stop it. 'Wait! I can pay you. For your time,' she said grudgingly. She stared at Remi, her eyes pleading for him to let her in.

Remi's face instantly changed to one of interest. 'Alright,' he said guardedly.

Ruby walked in and crossed the room to the only chair that wasn't already occupied or covered in piles of dirty washing and perched on the edge, trying to ignore the stale smell of general neglect that permeated the air.

Remi sat next to Stacey and leaned forward on his knees, watching her closely. 'Got any gear on you?' he asked.

'No, I don't do that anymore,' she said curtly.

Remi shrugged with a forced grin. 'Ahh, well. I was just gonna offer you some of ours, that's all,' he said.

'Course you were, she thought wryly.

Stacey sat silently, watching her with a blank stony expression.

Ruby clutched one hand with her other, uneasily. 'I know it's been a long time—'

'Three years, give or take,' Remi interjected.

Ruby nodded. 'Yeah around that. I'm in the area for a few days and I need somewhere to lie low. Just to sleep. I'd be out of your way all day and evening – I just need somewhere to crash. Somewhere my family won't find me.'

She didn't mind telling Remi that. Despite all else, he had always helped her remain hidden from her family. And he wasn't a gossip. She glanced at Stacey, wondering whether or not the girl could be trusted to do the same.

'How much you offering?' Remi asked.

'Fifty a night,' she replied.

'A hundred,' he pushed, eying her calculatingly.

Ruby exhaled slowly. 'Seventy-five. I'm not going higher.'

He nodded. 'OK. It's just the sofa,' he warned. 'I've got a spare pillow somewhere.'

Ruby cringed internally at the thought of what state that pillow might be in but kept her expression neutral as she nodded. 'Thanks.'

'I'll need the money upfront, each day,' Remi added.

Ruby nodded. 'And you'll keep my presence quiet?' She looked once more towards Stacey.

'She won't tell no one,' he assured her.

'Ain't my business,' Stacey added breezily, finally taking a drag of the almost-burned-out cigarette. 'Long as you're not trouble and your money's good, you're welcome here.' She looked at Ruby's tight red curls. 'Pretty colour that. My mum's was that colour.'

Ruby stood up. 'OK. So I'll leave you guys to it for now and I'll be back tonight. Have you got a spare key?'

'Nah, but one of us will be in. Chuck your bag in the corner, if you like. Save you lugging it around,' Remi suggested.

'No.' Ruby realised she'd said it a little too quickly and tried to soften her tone. 'No, it's OK. It's stuff I need out.' She walked back towards the front door.

'What business you got here anyway?' Remi asked.

Ruby paused, Scarlet's face burning into the walls of her

mind. 'Just sorting out some family stuff I should have dealt with ages ago.'

Looking around at the filth and the mess, the addicts rotting together on the couch as their flesh and their minds wasted away, she saw it suddenly for what it was: a snapshot of her old life. A perfect reminder of how far she had come. A reminder of how far she had yet to go. And getting rid of Scarlet once and for all would only be the beginning.

TWENTY

Lily sat at the desk in her office above the pub and leaned forward on her elbows. She rested her head on her free hand for a second, pushed her wild blonde locks off her face, then took a deep drag on the lit cigarette in other hand. Stressed didn't even begin to cover how she felt right now. There was so much going on and so many fires raging in her world that at times it was all she could do just to keep it together.

Looking at the picture of Ronan on the wall, she pulled a grim expression. 'Could have really used you being here right now,' she said quietly.

The door opened and, to her surprise, Cillian walked in.

'Hi,' she said, sitting up straight. Her heart lifted, the way it always did when one of her children were near. Not that this was often now, with Ruby gone and the boys avoiding her as much as possible. 'Everything OK?' She looked at her watch. It was late and a Tuesday. She'd have expected him to be at home with Billie by now.

Cillian approached the desk and hovered with his hands pushed into the pockets of his suit trousers. 'It's been three days since Ray mugged us off. What are we doing about it?'

Lily exhaled a long breath and sat back in her chair. 'I'm not sure yet,' she said.

'What do you mean you're not sure?' Cillian shot back.

'I mean exactly what I said,' she snapped, her eyes flashing him a warning.

He had the sense to shut his mouth, though his hard gaze didn't leave hers.

'I *know* we need to deal with it. But Ray isn't some wide boy out on a chance, he's *Ray Renshaw*. He's dangerous and powerful, and I'm not sure yet what angle, if any, we have a chance of playing and winning.' She took another drag on her cigarette and blew out the smoke. 'He has more men, more money, more ground, he knows how we think and he's just as cunning as we are. He's the worst possible enemy we could have made.'

'And who's fucking fault was that?' Cillian spat, immediately turning in a small circle and running his hand down the back of his head as he visibly tried to reign himself back in.

Lily bit back the retort that sat on the tip of her tongue and swallowed the sharp sting his words inflicted. There was no point starting another argument right now. But as he turned back, she let her gaze burn into him intensely, letting him know this was the last pass he was going to get tonight.

'We'll deal with it eventually,' she said, her words hard. 'We have no choice but to stand up to him now he's thrown down the gauntlet. But until I can think of a way that doesn't immediately blow up in our faces, we have other issues to focus on. Like getting fighters ready for the next event. Like finding your sister. Like figuring out a better plan to get hold of goods for the markets.'

Cillian's gaze broke away, and she saw a flicker of something in his face for a moment.

'Just tell me when you figure it out. Because I'm done letting that smug cunt get away with shit like this.' He glared at her once more then turned and left, the door slowly closing behind him.

It was ironic how similar he was to the man he hated so much, she thought wryly. Both so stubborn, both so strong. She ground what was left of her cigarette into the ashtray. Both so distant from her now.

She wasn't putting off their retaliation, the way Cillian clearly assumed. She was just as angry and outraged as he was. But it was true what she'd told him: Ray really was the worst possible enemy they could ever have made. His power aside, he was the one person outside their firm who knew *exactly* how she worked. They hid their cards from their opponents, and even their friends, for exactly this reason. Because if things went sideways, they could still strike and take them unaware. But Ray knew all her strategies, all her plays. And that meant that whatever they came up with would have to be out of character.

It would have to be something he wouldn't see coming.

TWENTY-ONE

Jenny Ascough finished her shift and left the station hours later than she should have. They were close to cracking one of their cases, which meant the team would be pulling lates and all-nighters until they finally did. She never used to mind when this happened, but these days she hated it. It used to be John who'd keep their spirits up through the last push on a case, John who made it seem like fun and who would share her chicken chow mein at midnight as they pored over evidence reports looking for something they'd missed. His replacement was efficient enough. But he wasn't John.

The one good thing about leaving so late on a weeknight was that the Tube was almost empty and she was able to collect her thoughts in peace as the train hurtled towards her stop. She jumped off and made the short walk home, pausing only at the fish-and-chip shop to treat herself to something other than her usual microwave meal. Her diet could wait. Tonight her soul needed feeding.

The tantalising smell of salt and vinegar soaking through the paper made her mouth water as she hurried up the stairs and unlocked the door to her one-bedroomed flat.

'Fish, chips and a few episodes of *Friends* tonight, methinks,' she mumbled as she closed the door behind her and kicked off her shoes.

She ditched her handbag in the small square hall and turned into the kitchen, pulling a plate off the draining board and dropping the package of food onto it. As she pulled at the corner of the soggy paper, she suddenly jumped in alarm as she heard a voice behind her. The fish and chips tumbled to the floor as she quickly spun around.

'I see you have a type. Who was this, high school sweetheart?'

Scarlet Drew sat in the armchair behind the door that led from the hallway into the open-plan lounge and kitchen, one leg crossed over the other, and a photo album resting in her lap, which she was casually flicking through, turning the pages with the sharp end of a large kitchen knife.

Ascough's heart raced as she stared, her eyes glued to the knife. 'What are you doing?' she demanded, trying to sound braver than she felt. How did Scarlet know where she lived? Why was she here? Her fear increased, but she tried to stay calm.

Scarlet closed the album and stood up, walking over with the knife pointed towards her and a cold hard look in her eyes. Ascough instinctively cowered against the kitchen cupboards, her mind racing. She was cornered. Her phone was in the hall, and she could see that Scarlet had already removed the other knives that would have been in reach.

'I could have you arrested for this,' she blurted out. 'Do you have any idea how much trouble you'd be in, breaking into an *officer's* house like this?'

'The officer who already broke into *mine* you mean?' Scarlet countered, lifting a dark eyebrow.

'What are you talking about?' Ascough asked, lifting her

chin, but she heard the quiver in her tone. She'd never been good at lying.

'You left a piece of the photo,' Scarlet replied, stopping in front of her and lifting the blade to her neck.

Ascough gasped and tried to pull back, but Scarlet pushed it up harder until it was almost hooked under her jawbone. Her hands moved slowly up into a position of surrender, and her whole body tensed with fear.

'No one else would be looking for something like that photo, let alone be so upset by it they'd rip it up and then try to hide the evidence.' Scarlet pulled a look of mocking disdain. 'Pretty poor work for a police officer.'

'Step back, remove this knife from my neck and get out of my home,' Ascough said, her voice trembling despite her best efforts to sound composed. 'Or I will call this in.'

She knew, as she spoke, that her words were meaningless. If Scarlet wanted to kill her or kidnap her or hurt her, she didn't stand a chance. The woman was one of the most dangerous predators in London.

Scarlet moved her face close to Ascough's, her cold grey-blue eyes piercing into hers, deadly and unreadable. 'You won't be calling anyone. Because if you do, I'll tell them exactly how I came to be here tonight, and *you'll* have to explain our little off-record chat at the station, why you've been stalking my every move, and why you broke into my house and destroyed my property.'

Ascough floundered and her mouth gaped open – as far as it could with the blade still held tightly to her neck – and then with a small sound of fear and defeat, she closed it. She'd thought Scarlet had no idea she was there, watching her, following her around. But it seemed she'd known all along.

'What do you want?' she eventually managed to utter.

Scarlet didn't answer, and Ascough began to shake as the blade bit sharply into her skin and a small trickle of warm blood ran down her neck. A sound of fear escaped her lips, and her panic began to bubble over as she wondered if this was it. If this was where her life ended. She opened her mouth to plead for her safety, but suddenly Scarlet stepped back and pulled the knife away.

Ascough grabbed her neck with one hand and hugged her other arm across her middle defensively, drawing in several deep breaths of relief.

Scarlet picked up a washcloth and carefully cleaned the smear of blood off the blade, studying it before she dropped them both into the sink. Her gaze moved to the mess of food splattered on the floor and then back up to Ascough.

'You aren't as slick as you think,' she said in a dark tone. 'And you're messing with people far more dangerous than you realise. I told you before and I'll tell you again, with a warning to pay attention this time. I don't know where John is. He disappeared and hasn't been in touch since. No one has harmed him, and no one wishes to.' Her icy grey-blue eyes bored into Ascough's. 'There is nothing to be found in my home or anywhere else I go. So you need to back off and leave this alone.'

Ascough swallowed hard. The knife against her throat had terrified her. But even with that fear and that threat hanging over her head, she couldn't abandon John. He meant too much to her. As did balancing the scales of justice, whatever she had to do to achieve that. That was why she'd become a police officer in the first place. To stop evil people like Scarlet Drew ruining lives.

'I can't do that,' she replied quietly, shaking her head.

Scarlet looked at her for a few moments before answering. 'Then as far as I'm concerned, anything that happens to you from now on is down to your own choices. You want to play on our side of the law, Ascough, go ahead. Though I promise you, you do *not* have what it takes to survive. You've had fair warning.'

She turned to leave.

Ascough felt the anger that burned away inside her bubble up and spill out through words that had barely had time to register in her brain before they escaped. 'Is that how it went with John? Did he have *fair warning* of your sick, twisted, fucked-up world?'

Scarlet turned back, the corner of her mouth twitching upwards as a challenging glint flashed in her eye. She looked Ascough up and down and let out a whisper of a laugh. 'You need *help*, Ascough,' she said. 'Professional help.'

'I'm not the one who needs help,' Ascough shot back, incensed.

'No?' Scarlet asked, lifting an eyebrow in question. 'You're stalking the ex-girlfriend of a man you were never romantically involved with, after he rejected you and disappeared, to the point you broke into her house and destroyed a photo of them.'

Ascough felt her cheeks burn red, realising how crazy it all sounded. But it *wasn't* crazy. She was doing this for John. This woman had never loved him. She'd just used him and then got rid of him when her need for him was over.

Scarlet walked to the doorway. 'That was your one and only warning, Ascough. My patience only stretches so far. The law doesn't protect you now you've crossed the line. So if I see you again, things are going to start going very badly for you.'

With a look of disdain, Scarlet walked away, and a second later, the front door closed behind her.

With an exclamation of frustration, grief and anger, Ascough slumped forward and sank to the floor next to her spoiled dinner. Hot tears began to flow unchecked down her cheeks.

What had she started? She couldn't stop now. She *wouldn't*. But how was she going to find John with nothing, still, to go on? And exactly how far would Scarlet go to stop her?

TWENTY-TWO

Cillian pulled up in the car park and glared through the rear-view mirror at the black sedan that pulled into a space a little way behind, facing the gym. Getting out of the car, he yanked his gym bag out from behind his seat, slammed the door and walked into the club, feeling the tension ease slightly as he entered his mental sanctuary. Pausing, he turned towards Jimmy's office instead of the changing room and peered around the half-open door.

'Alright?' Jimmy asked, already behind the desk despite the fact it was only six in the morning.

'Not really,' Cillian answered irately. He looked around the office and spotted what he was looking for. 'Can I use your coffee machine?'

Despite the fact the Drews now owned the boxing club and everything in it, this was Jimmy's office, and after the years of training and mentoring the man had given him, Cillian would always show him the respect he'd earned.

''Course,' Jimmy replied. 'Be my guest.'

'Thanks.' He dropped his bag and walked over to the box of

disposable cups, pulled two out, then promptly turned and left the office.

Ignoring the calls of greeting as he passed the other early-morning regulars, he made his way to the toilets and stopped at the closest urinal. With a smile, he bent down and carefully rubbed the rims of each cup around the bottom of it.

Jimmy looked up with a frown as Cillian returned and turned on the machine. 'What you up to?'

'Oh, you know me, Jimmy,' Cillian said with a cold grin. 'Just being friendly.'

He made two coffees and walked back outside, careful not to spill them, then crossed the road and approached the black sedan. For a few moments they pretended to be busy, looking away as if they had no idea who Cillian was and were there for some other reason than tailing him. Cillian waited by the front wheel, eventually kicking his foot against the door to gain their attention. As they looked around at him, he raised his eyebrows and gave them a grim smile, gesturing for them to roll down the window.

'You quite finished pretending to look for that map, mate?' he asked, sticking his head in and leaning on the car door.

Inside, the two officers visibly deflated.

He laughed. 'Don't worry, boys, it ain't just you. We know all your faces. And your cars.' He grinned again, this time in amusement.

The pair still said nothing, clearly uncomfortable and unsure how to handle the situation.

'Listen, I imagine you're in for a long day, following me around. And don't worry, I ain't got an issue with ya. You're just doing your job and I respect that. A hard-working man is a hard-working man, whatever his game.'

They relaxed slightly, and the one in the passenger seat nodded awkwardly at him. Cillian wondered how terrified they'd be if they could read his true thoughts.

'Anyway. I'm going to get back to my training but thought you boys might fancy a coffee. I'll be in there a while.'

He passed the cups through and, after a moment of hesitation and a shared look of question, they took them.

'Cheers,' the one in the passenger seat said with an awkward expression that was almost a smile.

Cillian watched him take a sip with a wide grin. 'Any time,' he replied sincerely. He tapped the side of the car and walked back to the gym feeling much better than he had a few minutes before.

The place was alive with people training, and as Cillian made his way back to Jimmy's office to pick up his bag, he began mentally running through his workout.

'You done being friendly?' Jimmy asked with a bemused smile as he walked in.

Cillian grinned. 'For now.'

'Who'd you take them for?' Jimmy sat back and watched him with a squeezed gaze.

'The two little piggies sat outside on the road,' Cillian replied, sinking into the chair opposite Jimmy.

'And where did you take those cups before you filled them?' Jimmy asked, his grin beginning to spread as his suspicions grew.

'On a detour through this establishment's fine facilities,' Cillian replied. 'Figured our friends deserved a little extra flavour.'

Jimmy threw his head back and laughed. 'Ahh, Cillian, you're a wrong 'un.'

'So I'm told,' Cillian replied.

'Anyway, how you doing?' Jimmy asked, changing the subject.

'All good. You?'

'No.' Jimmy's keen eyes pierced his. 'I mean really. How you *really* doing? How's that back of yours these days?'

Cillian felt the other man's scrutinous gaze pinning him like a weight and resisted the urge to look away. If he did, Jimmy would know he was lying. That was the thing about Jimmy. Once you were in here, once you were one of his boys, he didn't miss a thing. He felt responsible for you, cared about you, didn't let you carry any kind of burden on your own. Whether you liked it or not.

'It's alright,' he said with a shrug.

'Liar. Let me see it.' Jimmy stood up and walked over.

Cillian bent forward with a sigh of resignation and lifted his T-shirt. Jimmy looked at his back for a moment, then returned to his seat.

'You need some vitamin E cream for that scar,' he said. He opened his mouth to continue, then seemed to decide against it and shut it grimly.

Cillian studied his face. 'You can say it, Jimmy – I ain't that vain. It's just a scar. And it ain't like it's on me boat race.' He reached into his pocket and pulled out a toothpick, placing it between his teeth.

'It ain't neat, no. But I wasn't thinking about that. I was thinking about what you went through to get it,' Jimmy replied.

Immediately, Cillian felt as though his body was being pulled back through a dark vortex, away from this room and Jimmy, back into the bunker. He could feel the coldness of the damp air on his skin, smell the decay and filth on the bed his face was pressed into. And he felt the excruciating pain as the psycho who'd taken him cut deep into his back.

Sitting forward abruptly, Cillian ran his hands down his face, forcing the memory away, bringing himself back. He faked a yawn, masking the sudden action as an attempt to stay awake and liven up.

'How you sleeping?' Jimmy asked.

'Like a fucking baby,' Cillian replied with an edge that would have told most people to stop prying.

Jimmy ignored it, the way he always had. 'Babies tend to wake screaming every half hour, from what I've heard.'

'Look, I'm good, Jimmy. Alright?' Cillian said, raising his eyebrows with a hard stare.

Jimmy shook his head. 'I don't think you are,' he replied. 'You don't want to talk about it right now and that's fine. But if or when you do, my door's open. Don't forget that. Keeping it all in ain't being tough, you know.'

Cillian felt the usual frustration bubble up inside him. No one understood what he'd been through down there. No one ever *could*. They hadn't been there. They hadn't lain there, helpless, being tortured by a man who had less human emotion than a stone. They hadn't had to come to terms with the fact that they were going to die a slow agonising death, cold and alone in a place they'd never be found, and for no good reason.

That was the part that stuck with him the most. Even being murdered by an enemy was better than that. Being killed for revenge, with hot hatred, for what another saw as just cause – at least that mattered to someone. But this had been for nothing. He'd been there to be harvested, to be slaughtered for parts. His killer hadn't even hated him. If he'd succeeded, Cillian's death would have meant nothing. How could he possibly explain how that felt to someone who'd never flirted with hell that way themselves?

'You're getting too soft, Jimmy,' he said, picking up his bag with a sniff. 'I've got training to do.'

Jimmy nodded, retreating gracefully. 'Go on then. I'll catch you later to go over the—'

'Coach!' The door flew open and one of the younger men appeared, wild-eyed and frantic. 'It's Daryl – come quick!'

'What?' Jimmy rounded the desk at lightning pace, following the boy out of the room. 'What's happened?'

Cillian followed, wondering the same. Jimmy began

running across the gym towards a small crowd of people, and he quickly jogged after him.

'Out the way,' Jimmy ordered in a loud, commanding voice. 'Give him some space.'

He fell to his knees and Cillian stopped just behind, looking down at the man convulsing on the floor. As they stood there, with Jimmy shouting instructions to get a pillow and some water, Daryl's body lurched violently forward and vomit spewed from his mouth.

'Help me get him in the recovery position,' Jimmy yelled.

Someone on the other side jumped forward, and they held Daryl on his side as he shook. Cillian dropped and grabbed Daryl's legs, trying to help keep him in position.

'I need to get him to a hospital,' Jimmy said urgently, looking to Cillian. His eyes flicked to the door and he hesitated. 'It'll be quicker than calling an ambulance if I just drive him myself. Help me get him to the car. It's out back.'

'No,' Daryl muttered in a strange gargle. 'Coach...' He trailed off, not able to manage any more.

Jimmy pulled a grim expression. 'It's alright, son. It don't matter what you took – we just need to get you better. I'm gonna hook under your arms, Cillian's gonna grab your legs. Dunston, open the doors. Carl, get my keys from the desk.'

They hoisted the fitting man up between them, carrying him quickly out through the back door. Someone opened the car and they awkwardly shifted Daryl in. Guilt flooded through Cillian as he stepped back. The real reason Jimmy hadn't called an ambulance was to protect *him*. With the police following his every move, they wouldn't hesitate to try to link him to whatever this was.

'Carl, get in the back with him – try to hold him still. You can help me lift him the other end,' Jimmy ordered. 'Cillian, lock up the office.'

Cillian nodded and walked away as Jimmy started the car.

He paused just inside and headed towards the locker room with a grim expression.

'Dan,' he called to one of the men nearby. 'Show me his bag. I need to see something.'

Lily walked through the doors of the gym and made a beeline for Jimmy's office, her heels rapping sharply on the wooden floor. The men around her seemed subdued.

She entered Jimmy's office and saw Cillian in Jimmy's chair, his expression grave as he stared back at her. She took the seat opposite and put her handbag down beside her.

'Tell me,' she said simply.

Cillian placed a bottle of pills on the desk between them. 'These were in his bag.'

'What are they?' she asked, picking up the bottle and turning it over in her hand. There was no label.

'Winstrol, better known as Winnie. It's a type of anabolic steroid, illegal performance enhancer,' he replied. 'He OD'd. He wasn't used to them, didn't know how much to take.'

'What?' Lily exclaimed. 'But Jimmy's so strict on that. And you said he competes. The leagues do drug tests, don't they?'

'The *leagues* do. We don't.' Cillian held her gaze and Lily caught up.

She closed her eyes and rubbed her head. 'He was trying to get ahead for the paid fights. For *our* fights.'

'It's good money – you can see the draw. And he'll be OK. Jimmy called just now – the hospital is sorting him out. But that ain't why I called you,' Cillian said heavily.

'What is it?' Lily asked sharply.

Cillian looked down to the pills still in her hand. 'One of the others was with Daryl when he got this from the dealer – a guy called Tommy Long. He works for Ray.'

Lily felt a sharp stab of something pierce through her at the mention of Ray's name. 'And?' She could see there was more.

'And the deal went down in the Carpenters Arms,' Cillian said.

Lily's eyes widened, and her entire body bristled with anger as he named the pub that sat not a stone's throw from the boxing club. 'Are you fucking serious?' she demanded.

'As a nun on Sunday,' he replied. 'Apparently he's there every day between twelve and two.'

Fury whirled through Lily at the blatant snub. This was *their* turf, *Drew* territory through and through. Ray had never had any foothold here for his drugs – nobody had. She forbade it. They couldn't control everyone of course; there were still deals, small local dealers flying under the radar, but the larger networks were banned from dealing in their pubs. Now and then a dealer from another network would stray by accident, and it was dealt with. But Lily knew this was no accident. Ray was flexing his muscles.

'It could be a mistake,' Cillian offered in a level tone.

'I know you don't believe that,' Lily replied.

'There's only one way to find out.'

Lily hesitated. She didn't want to call Ray – she was too angry. But Cillian was right: they needed to know for sure. Cillian looked pointedly at her handbag and, with an irritated tut, she pulled out her phone.

It rang twice before Ray picked up and then there was silence on the end of the line as he waited for her to speak. Lily gritted her teeth and took a deep breath to try to calm herself before she spoke.

'Tommy Long has been selling on our patch. One of our fighters OD'd on his shit and is currently in hospital. That got anything to do with you?' she asked.

There was a short pause before he answered. 'Tommy's one

of mine, but I don't babysit his route. Or his clients.' His tone was cold and uninterested.

'Well, I'd appreciate it if you could remind him of the boundaries,' she replied in a clipped tone.

'Nah, I don't think so, Lil,' Ray responded. 'I ain't really in the mood for doing you favours anymore. If you've got issues on your patch, that's your problem.'

The phone went dead and Lily's jaw dropped as her anger reached boiling point. She threw the phone across the room with a roar. 'That fucking bastard.'

Cillian looked at the phone in astonishment.

Lily took a couple of deep breaths and sat back in the chair silently for a minute. She was always in control – it was what kept her on top. But Ray was getting under her skin and the feeling wasn't dissipating. She needed to do something.

A plan formed in her mind, and she slowly nodded as she made her decision. 'Cillian, you need to keep your tail busy today and lead them away from here before twelve. Don't come back until after two.'

'What are you gonna do?' he asked.

Lily met his gaze with a look of cold resolution. 'You wanted us to do something about Ray, fight back and make a statement, right? Well, I'm about to do just that.'

TWENTY-THREE

Scarlet pulled the stack of paperwork towards her and began to sort it into piles. Invoices, orders and machine schedules for the factory were soon organised in order of priority, but she barely registered what she was looking at, her head elsewhere.

She'd tossed and turned the night before, thinking about Ascough. And about John. She felt his absence even more now than before. Now, with that photo destroyed, it was like he'd never been here, never been such a big part of her life. It hadn't been much. It wasn't even a picture of his face. It wasn't his warm smile or piercing green eyes, or their lips touching in a kiss. It was just their hands on the grass. It could have been anyone's hands. But it had been *their* hands, and it'd been all she'd had left.

She'd known straight away it was Ascough. No one else would have searched so thoroughly or have such an emotional reaction to that photo.

It had hurt, realising it was gone. The pain had turned to anger, and her thoughts had turned murderous. But she'd forced herself to calm down and had settled on a hard warning. Because despite the pain Ascough had caused, and the royal pain in the arse she'd become lately, Scarlet didn't really want to hurt the woman. Her heart, though misguided, was in the right place. And Scarlet would never forget the public heartbreak Ruby had put her through. Convincing Ascough that John returned her feelings, Ruby had set her up to publicly declare her love for him, making sure the moment was ruined by finding him with Scarlet. It had been a cruel and humiliating heartbreak that no one deserved to suffer.

Still, she hoped the warning had been enough to put Ascough off her pointless crusade. There was nothing for her to find where John was concerned, but if she kept stalking them the way she was, eventually she was sure to see something else damning. And that was the last thing Scarlet needed.

Closing her eyes and stretching her neck, Scarlet picked up the first invoice to log on the system. Where was John now? His face stared back at her in her mind's eye as his boat drifted into the darkness. She swallowed a lump in her throat and opened her spreadsheet. That boat had been set for Spain, somewhere in the south. Had he stayed there? Or had he travelled on through Europe to find somewhere else to make his home?

Another memory jumped forward unbidden. The two of them lying in bed one lazy Sunday morning, enjoying the peace and the luxury of not having to get up for hours. John had asked her where she would pick if they could run away together, anywhere in the world. They'd made a whole list of places, fantasies that would never happen.

She pictured him now, traipsing across the Swiss Alps – his dream location – breathing the fresh air and soaking up the view, and she was suddenly full of fierce hope that this was where he was. He deserved at least that, after all he'd lost.

Her phone rang, breaking through her thoughts, and she answered it quickly. 'Cillian, how you doing?'

'Fine,' he replied curtly. 'You got a tail today?'

'Yeah, why?' she asked.

'Keep them busy – stay away from the boxing club,' he ordered.

'OK.' She frowned. 'What's going on?'

'Mum'll fill you in later.'

The line went dead, and Scarlet put her phone back on the desk with a look of annoyance.

They'd always been close, she and Cillian, but now he barely spoke to her, treating her almost like an enemy. She understood it to a degree. Their loyalties and opinions clashed when it came to Ruby. An invisible line had been drawn, and she was outside of it. But she was still family. And they were still part of the same firm.

For the first time in Scarlet's life, she felt isolated and alone. With her father gone, John gone, the twins pulling away and even Lily keeping up a careful guard until things with Ruby played out, the only person who was still truly close was her mother. But she had to hide the darker shades of her life from Cath, shield and protect her, like they'd always done. There really was no one left with whom she could share her heavier burdens.

The paper she was holding left her grip as she sagged under the weight of her emotional load, gracefully sailing across the desk until it came to a silent stop on the edge. Scarlet stared at it, unsure what the point was in picking it up. What *was* the point? To this paperwork, to the businesses... to anything? Without family or love, what was it all *for*?

The door opened and she jumped, looking up to see one of their machine engineers popping his head in.

'Sorry to disturb, but the belt's snapped on line twelve. I've got an old spare which should see us through the shift but we need another one fitted ASAP,' he said with an apologetic grimace.

'Right. OK.' Scarlet sat upright and straightened the papers in front of her. 'Can you head over to Ripley's? I'll call them now, tell them you're coming.'

'Yeah, 'course. Thanks.' He disappeared with a nod, and the door shut.

Scarlet rubbed her face with her hands and ran her fingers back over her head for a moment. She couldn't do this. She couldn't let herself slide down that spiral of depression. She had to start getting a grip on these thoughts and memories. Because if she didn't, they would eventually destroy her.

'OK,' she breathed, opening the desk drawer and pulling out a small leather address book. She flicked to find the right entry. 'Ripley's, Ripley's...' Reaching the Rs, she ran her finger down the page, pausing as she reached *Ruby*. Her tired eyes hardened to flint and she welcomed the familiar flood of hatred as it refuelled her inner fire. Life might not make much sense right now, but she still had purpose. She still had a debt to collect.

Scarlet couldn't kill Ruby. Her hands were tied by the love she had for her family. But she could still make her cousin pay for her sins in horrible and painful ways. When she was done with her, Ruby's heart would beat on, but her spirit would be broken. And she would finally understand with crystal-clear clarity that her days in London and in their firm were well and truly over.

TWENTY-FOUR

Lily checked the road was clear and then crossed towards the pub on the opposite corner with an air of determination. Connor and Andy fell in behind her, and as she pushed open the door and paused to look around, the chatter inside died down. It wasn't a big pub, just a few tables and one long bar. A couple of the locals who were grabbing a lunchtime pint nodded in respect. Most turned their gazes the other way after seeing the look on Lily's face.

She walked towards the bar, her slow purposeful steps loud in the quiet room, and the barman moved swiftly to meet them. He knew who they were. The pub was under the Drews' protection and in the very heart of their territory.

'What can I get you?' he asked.

'A scumbag on the rocks,' Lily answered, no smile on her face.

The barman nodded. 'I thought that might be what you're after. I've got just the thing...'

A scrawny man with a face too weathered for his years and a pair of sunken, beady eyes slipped off the end barstool and turned towards the door, but as the barman nodded towards him, Connor grabbed him by the neck, halting him in his tracks. The man struggled, but he was weak, and Connor pushed him firmly back towards the stool.

'Take a seat,' he said in a low voice. 'It ain't your time to leave yet.'

Beady eyes flickered between the three of them warily, then the man gave an exaggerated shrug and sat back down. 'Whatever, mate. I'm just 'ere minding my business, wetting the pipe and that, ya know wha'm sayin'?'

'No, I don't,' Lily replied with an icy glare. 'I also don't know what the fuck you think you're doing dealing drugs around here.'

The man threw back his head and laughed almost silently in mocking amusement. 'Don't know what you're talking about, love,' he said with a leery grin that revealed several gaps in his yellow teeth. 'I'm just 'aving a pint. Drugs ain't my game – filthy habit they are. I could probably point you in the direction of one or two dodgy geezers round 'ere who might be doing that sort of thing though. 'Elp you meet your arrest quota. I'm helpful like that.'

It was Lily's turn to laugh, though her amusement was brief. 'It would have been better for you if I *was* a copper,' she said in a dangerous tone. 'However, I'm not. And this really ain't your day.'

She clicked her fingers and Andy pulled him roughly off the bar stool. The man protested loudly as Andy and Connor twisted his arms up behind his back.

'What the fuck, man!' he yelped. 'Lemme go! What's your game?'

'Put him in the car,' Lily ordered. She glared at him hard as they walked. 'And call me *love* again and it'll be the last fucking thing you ever do.'

. . .

Lily watched with cold detachment as Connor and Andy beat the man without mercy. The dull thuds of fists connecting with his head and torso were intertwined with the gargled pleas escaping the dealer's bloody mouth. One sharp crack rang out, which she assumed was a bone breaking somewhere.

They were in a secure area behind the factory. No windows overlooked it, no one could gain access without special permissions and the sounds of the machines inside blocked out the noise.

Connor stepped back for a moment, using his forearm to wipe the sweat from his brow as Andy continued. Connor looked to Lily in question, but she just took another drag on her cigarette, not ready to give him the signal to stop yet. Turning back, he kicked the dealer one more time, the force sending the man sprawling across the ground, then he stopped and gave her a hard look, before walking off to the side.

Lily pursed her lips at his defiance but said nothing. She knew the man had taken more than he deserved. And she knew Connor took no pleasure in doling out the harsh punishment. Usually she'd have stopped them long before now for such a small misdemeanour. But on this occasion there was a bigger reason behind the unusually vicious attack. The underworld was their home, a place where they'd flourished, but it was harsh and unforgiving, and to survive they sometimes had to do some dark things.

She cast a critical gaze over the man. His eyes were swollen shut, and blood poured from his nose and mouth, along with several gashes on his face. They'd stripped him of his jacket and T-shirt, so the injuries they'd inflicted on his body were also starkly visible. As Andy continued beating the man alone, he curled up and his head suddenly lolled to the side.

'Stop.' The word was spoken quietly, but Andy obeyed instantly.

Connor turned to the outdoor tap, washing his hands and

forearms carefully. Splashing his face, he pulled his fingers through his hair and shrugged his shirt and jacket back on over his vest. Andy sat down on a low wall and got his breath back before following suit. The dealer lay still and silent on the ground, having finally passed out. Lily waited for Andy and Connor to collect themselves before she spoke again.

'Wrap him up,' she ordered.

Connor hesitated. 'You're sure you want to do this?'

Lily nodded. 'It's the only way now.'

'It's not the only way.' He looked into her eyes and held her gaze for the first time in weeks.

Lily felt her heart pull towards her son, the youngest by just a few minutes. She'd missed him so much that even this small action affected her.

'What would you do?' she asked. Connor rarely spoke up against her plans.

'Me? I have no sway with Ray. But you do. This is a big statement and he ain't one to back off. You know that.' He regarded her seriously. 'If we throw down like this, we'll be facing serious backlash. But if you speak to him, one on one, offer some kind of treaty...'

Lily shook her head. 'It's too late for that. I know Ray. I know how he works. He's already thrown down with us, Connor. *Twice*. Our bridges are burned. *I* burned them,' she added, casting her gaze away for a moment. 'Which means we're left with only two choices. Either we do nothing as he slowly but surely tears us down. We'll fade away with no dignity, lose face – along with all the businesses we've worked so hard to build.' Her expression twisted into bitter disgust. 'Or we fight back and protect what's ours. And we keep fighting until we either win or lose. It's that simple and that hard.'

Connor closed his mouth and turned away, clearly no more a fan of their options than she was.

Andy stood up and grabbed the sheet Lily had brought to

wrap the dealer in, handing one side to Connor. They kneeled down without another word, wrapping it around the bloodied man on the floor.

Andy hoisted the bundled man up over his shoulder and held his arm out to Connor as he moved to help. 'It's alright, he don't weigh much.'

He walked off, and Connor fell in beside Lily. She glanced at him as they walked. He wasn't angry, like Cillian, more withdrawn. Could she reach him?

'Connor...' She bit her upper lip. 'This fight with Ray, it's my fault and I'm not defending that—'

'It's OK,' he said, cutting her off. 'It's life, right? You never expected this from Ray, I know. Just goes to show the people we love ain't always who we think they are.' He glanced at her, a sadness in his eyes for just a moment before he turned away and unlocked the boot of the car.

Lily swallowed the pain that rose at the double meaning in his words. Connor was right. People let you down. She'd let *them* down. But whether they forgave her or not, she didn't plan on ever letting them down again. She would fight to protect them from every threat until her dying breath. And right now, their biggest threat was Ray.

TWENTY-FIVE

Lily's hands gripped the steering wheel so tightly that her knuckles were almost blue in their whiteness as she steered into Ray's road. She'd refused to let Connor or Andy accompany her. It was too risky – Ray was too unpredictable now. Connor had argued of course. But this was something she had to do alone. Ray would always go for a man before a woman, given the choice – so she didn't plan to give him one. *She* was the head of the firm who he'd waged war on, and she would deliver their retaliation. If there were to be consequences, then he could damn well direct them to her. She no longer really cared what they were, so long as she could protect the rest of her family from him, and fight for what was theirs. She'd worked too hard and for too many years to just lie down and let him take it from her now.

Her love for Ray, mixed with the pain of his turning on her so cruelly, fuelled her rage and fighting spirit to new levels. Never had she felt so wild with fury that she'd run into battle this blindly and with such little care for what came next. But he'd backed her into a corner and *that* had been his mistake.

Because now she had everything to lose, nowhere to go and was ready to unleash hell.

There was no future in this city for a fallen firm. She'd seen it happen before. When a firm as notorious as theirs began to break down at the hands of another, and they didn't retaliate quickly enough, other firms would start to test the opportunity too. Every inch of a falling territory was fair game until it had been won. One enemy would become half a dozen, all looking to expand and climb the ladder. Businesses would be taken, assets stolen – and the people would be next. Members of a crumbling firm would be kidnapped and claimed as conquered, often before disappearing for good. Because claiming that kill added to the infamy of those who took over and kept *their* enemies wary.

She'd lied when she told Connor they had two choices. Because allowing that to happen to their firm – to her *family* – just wasn't an option.

The front gate at the bottom of Ray's drive came into view and a chill trickled down her spine. She clenched her jaw grimly and pulled to a stop beside the keypad. She punched in the numbers and held her breath, praying that he hadn't changed them. A quiet click sounded and she exhaled, waiting for the heavy wrought-iron gates to widen enough to pass through.

Adrenaline coursed through her veins as she swept up the long driveway to the turning circle at the front. It was a stupidly big house for one man to live in. He'd bought it years before, presenting it to her with a plea to marry him. They'd only been back together a year. The twins had been young at the time, still reeling from the man they'd thought was their father abandoning them. Ruby had barely talked for months – possibly the only time in her life she hadn't had a smart answer for everything. When Lily had turned Ray down, he'd raged for a while, unable to understand why. Unable to grasp why she couldn't just live in the moment, without caution, without worry. But that was exactly the problem. Ray loved to throw caution to the wind, and she had three children who relied on her. They needed stability and security, and a home they felt safe in – that would never change.

He'd lived alone here, for all these years. Perhaps if she'd taken the risk and told him then that the boys were his, it would have been different. Or maybe he'd have put her through this punishment back then instead. There was no point wondering now.

She rounded the turning circle, her thumping heart almost in her throat. He was home, she knew. Ray was a creature of habit. He was always home on a Wednesday afternoon, holding meetings with his men. He would have had an alert when she opened the gate, and right about now he would be peering down from the large window above the front door.

She stopped the car and took a deep breath before she stepped out. Ray might have sent his men down to grab her already, but she doubted it. He liked to see how things panned out before jumping in, especially when he'd been taken by surprise.

It took every inch of her energy not to look up to the window as she walked to the boot and popped it open. Gripping the sheets wrapped around the dealer, she yanked him towards her and eased him up onto the lip of the boot. Lily was slight, but she was stronger than she looked, and the skinny dealer didn't weigh much. With another good tug, he fell to the ground with a dull thud, and she yanked the end of the sheet, forcing his body to unroll from it along the ground. Blood covered the white sheet, now underneath him, and his injuries looked even more pronounced as he lay there, inert.

Now she turned to look at Ray, a fiery glint in her furious eyes. As her gaze met his, she saw the shock register.

'You won't pull your dealers off my turf anymore, Ray?' she

yelled. '*Fine*. I'll drop them back to your door myself. But let me tell you now, every single person you send into *my* territory from now on will come back like this. *If* they're lucky.'

Ray's expression turned black as he stared down, his gaze burning into hers. She lifted her chin defiantly. She wasn't afraid of him. She wasn't afraid of anything other than not being strong enough to save her family.

'You want war?' she bellowed, spreading her arms out wide. 'Well, here you are.' Her lip curled bitterly. 'You're about to get it. I've made mistakes and done things you can't forgive, and for that I accepted you turning your back on me. But I will *never* accept you destroying all I've created for my family. The world I built them with blood, sweat and tears – that I *killed* for, that I sold my very *soul* for, time and again.' The words spewed like acid from her mouth. 'I've survived you before, Ray Renshaw, and I'll do it again. But this time, I won't stop at just surviving.'

Her words grew hotter and more passionate with each word. 'Because I swear to you, as God is my witness, if you *ever* hurt my children or pave the way for others to, I will gut you like a fish with my bare *fucking* hands.'

She could feel her whole body shaking as she screamed up at him, knew that she must look and sound like a wild creature, half mad and fully triggered. But she no longer cared. She stepped backward, still holding his furious gaze in hers, and wiped a hand across her mouth.

'And I will watch you die, Ray,' she finished, her voice breaking with a mixture of hatred and pent-up emotion. 'You hurt them and I'll see you dead, if it's the last thing I do.'

Ray watched as Lily got back in her car and started the engine, anger radiating through him like an electric current. He'd always known there was a cold, calculated darkness in Lily. She was a force in her own right, and he knew her hands were almost as dirty as his. But he'd never seen her like this before. So dangerous. So full of loud, challenging vengeance.

'Quick, shut the gate from the office,' said a voice behind him. 'She can't get out if—'

'No,' Ray said strongly. 'Not here. Let her go.' He glared at her tail lights as she drove away and disappeared from view.

'Get him off the drive before anyone sees him,' he barked, gesturing towards the half-dead dealer still lying in a heap. 'Get the doctor out, clean him up and set him up downstairs in the back room.'

'And Lily?' the man asked.

Ray's gaze darkened. 'I'll deal with her myself. Quietly,' he said, his tone resolute. 'One on one. That's the way it started. And that's the way I'll end it.'

TWENTY-SIX

Ruby tucked herself between two bushes growing beside a crumbling brick wall, hiding herself from view as she watched the front of the scrapyard. On the other side of the bush, the wall came to a jagged end and the tall wire fencing that surrounded the perimeter of the yard began. She pulled her jacket around her more snugly and waited for the man she knew would be shuffling up to the gate at any moment. Alan had been running this place for years. Every night at seven he would come out and lock the gate, light his cigarette, take a drag and then walk home for the night. The only days he stayed later were when the Drews called in a favour, which he was handsomely rewarded for.

Like clockwork, Alan appeared, bang on seven o'clock. Ruby shifted her weight from foot to foot impatiently as she waited for him to secure the two gates with the long clanging metal chain and sturdy padlock. As soon as he left, she'd slip out of these bushes and scale down the side to the back, where she could cut through the wire and get in.

Something tickled her cheek and she moved slightly,

assuming it was a leaf. But the tickling continued to move across her face, and she realised with spine-chilling horror that it was a spider. She just about managed to stop the almighty shriek as it made to slip out of her mouth, but she couldn't stop herself leaping in fright as she batted it off and away from her. It scuttled away across the sun-hardened earth, and nausea rolled in her stomach. Her heart pounded painfully, but she forced herself to breathe slowly and stay still. Alan peered over, but after a moment he shrugged and walked off in the direction of his house. Ruby exhaled heavily in relief.

Waiting a few moments more to make sure he was definitely gone, she hurried out of the bush, jumping around and shaking herself off thoroughly. 'Eugh,' she exclaimed with a small shudder. 'I fucking *hate* spiders.' She checked to see that no one was watching then made a beeline for the corner of the fence.

The light tinkling of the guard dogs' collars grew closer as she edged down the side of the lot. They couldn't quite get to her yet – cars and broken machines were piled up between them. But they would catch up with her when she reached a clearing. She pulled a grim expression. Always on the lookout for opportunity, Ruby had made sure to befriend the dogs when Lily had sent her with menial tasks before. She'd brought them treats and spent time fussing over them until they melted like putty whenever she'd come around. You never knew when having access to a place like this could come in handy after all. But it had been a while. She just hoped they remembered her fondly.

The scrapyard was huge, reaching back probably around half a mile or so, if she had to guess. It was a maze of paths and aisles, chaotic walls of various twisted parts organised into some sort of order that somehow made sense to Alan.

The night before, she'd stared up at Remi's tobacco-stained ceiling, unable to sleep, trying to blot out the sound of him grunting away on top of Stacey in the next room. The sound was a sickening reminder that it had been her in there once, before she'd had the sense to get out. And that was when the idea had come to her.

Ruby had been in a painful state of withdrawal the night she'd left Remi. She'd managed to steal a wallet and scored enough heroin to last a couple of days. She'd evened out and then wandered the streets for hours, with no plan and nowhere to go. After hours of walking, she'd ended up here, at the scrapyard. Those were the days before the guard dogs, and she'd sneaked through a hole in the back fence, sleeping rough in a broken-down van for a couple of nights. She'd explored while she was there, looking for anything worth stealing that she could carry. There hadn't been much, but she'd noted certain things that might be of use one day.

Reaching the back corner, Ruby turned and scanned the tall wire fencing, searching for another hole. The old one had been patched up a long time ago, and it seemed no more had been made. She reached into her pocket and pulled out the small set of wire clippers, then dropped down and started working on the bottom row. She grunted and squeezed hard as the metal wire held its ground, time and again, but eventually she made a gap wide enough to crawl under.

Standing up inside, she dusted herself off and looked around. She was blocked in by mountains of small parts, but she eyed the lowest point and decided she could scale it easily enough. She tightened the straps of her backpack then made her slow, careful way up and over the mound. A rusty exhaust broke away as she tested her weight on it halfway up, and she cringed as it crashed loudly to the ground behind her. A sharp woof followed, and a frisson of foreboding ran down her spine. She touched the knife she'd concealed in her waistband, praying she had no cause to use it.

With grim determination, she pushed onwards, trying to

stay calm. The dogs couldn't reach her here or they'd have already arrived.

Scaling the rest of the awkward pile, she peered warily over the top. Two Dobermanns lay patiently on the ground, their ears pricked forward, their beady eyes watching her.

For a few heavy moments, they stared each other out and she willed them to remember her. They hadn't greeted her with the glee they used to, but neither had they bared their teeth and threatened her. One tilted his head to one side and she smiled tentatively, holding out a hand the way she used to. Immediately, both tails began to wag and they woofed excitedly.

She breathed an internal sigh of relief and carefully descended. As she neared them, she pulled out a small bag of meat from her pack. Their excitement increased as she chucked it down, and they gobbled it up in barely a second before turning back and jumping up in an attempt to lick her face.

'OK, OK,' she said, pulling back. 'That's enough. Sit.' She gave the command with the hand signal, and both dogs immediately obeyed. Her shoulders untensed and her heart rate slowed. She was in.

Tentatively, she scratched their ears for a minute then pointed towards the front of the lot. 'Go, lie down,' she ordered. They whined, and she frowned at them. '*Lie down*,' she repeated.

One of them made a quiet huffing sound, then both turned and trotted out of sight.

Not bothering to stay quiet any longer, Ruby made her way through the maze of vehicles and machinery towards an area she'd been particularly fascinated by three years ago. Dodging wheels and doors and crumbling engines, she entered a circular clearing almost totally enclosed by towers of crushed cars at least two stories high. Some were secured by giant metal racks, and across one side there was an industrial catwalk, much like the one in their factory. Grated steel steps led up to it, and the platform above curved out of sight.

Ruby climbed the steps, ignoring the groan of metal as the old catwalk threatened to pull away from its fixtures. The walkway was littered with various small parts, ignored, as the path was barely used. It led to just one thing, hidden away from view in a disused corner. Was it still here? she wondered as she followed the walkway around the curve. Was the set-up the same?

She kicked an old oil can off the catwalk and then suddenly it was right in front of her. Her eyes gleamed and her dark hopes soared as she saw that everything was exactly as she'd remembered. Nothing had changed. It was perfect. An electric thrill ran up her body and buzzed across her skin, and the corners of her mouth lifted into a wide smile. For the first time in a long time she felt truly alive, truly confident that all she had set out to achieve was finally in her grasp.

Lifting her face to the sky, she closed her eyes and breathed in deeply. This was it, the key to the start of her new future. The start of *all* their futures, she corrected, thinking about her family. There were changes ahead, for all of them.

Her past was well and truly behind her. The drugs, the self-destruction – and the cold shadow of her scheming, thieving cousin. Their family – their *true* family, her, her mother and her brothers – would unite as the one strong force they were always destined to be, with no one else to get in the way.

When Uncle Ronan had died, the business became solely Lily's, a firm for *her* family to continue and uphold. Scarlet should have understood her place and bowed out then. She hadn't even wanted to join the firm; she'd been all set to go to university. And she should have gone when she'd had the chance. Because now, after all the problems she'd caused, there was no going back. Now, Ruby was going to get rid of her toxic cousin once and for all. And her plan was so perfect that when they eventually did find Scarlet's body, months if not years down the line, it would look like a terrible tragic accident. And Ruby would be free to soar.

TWENTY-SEVEN

Isla walked into the hairdresser's and smiled at the woman behind the desk. She was on the phone but smiled back warmly and gestured towards the waiting area. Isla perched on the edge of a seat and waited, watching the woman on the phone.

Her name was Cath, she remembered. Scarlet's mum and Lily's sister-in-law. Her dark hair was coiled up in a loose bun, a few strands falling free around her face. She was pretty, with twinkling eyes and laughter lines etched into her skin beside them. Scarlet looked a lot like her, though Scarlet's face was much sharper than Cath's. More like Lily's, she realised, thinking about it.

Cath put the phone down and walked over. 'Alright, love? You meeting one of them here?'

'Yeah, but I'm a bit early. Sorry,' Isla said awkwardly. Everyone was trying to dodge their usual routine at the moment, hoping to evade their police tails. Connor had asked her to meet him here.

'No need for apologies, love,' Cath replied with a dismissive flap of her hand. 'We ain't short on room. You just relax. Fancy a cuppa?'

'Yeah, I'd love one,' Isla replied.

'I'll get the kettle on.' Cath's eyes flicked up to Isla's hair. 'Your roots could do with a top-up,' she commented bluntly.

'Oh. Er, yeah, I know.' Isla laughed nervously, feeling self-conscious.

'Sorry.' Cath laughed. 'I didn't mean to embarrass you – I just thought you might want me to book you in, as you're here.'

'Oh, I see,' Isla replied. 'I usually just use box dyes—'

'*What?*' Cath exclaimed in horror. 'Why on earth you doing that?'

Isla felt her insides begin to squirm. 'Um. I just always have. It's cheap and easy, so—'

'No.' Cath cut her off firmly. 'Darlin' there will be no more box dyes, OK?' She took Isla's arm, guiding her up off the chair and through the salon.

Isla felt a frisson of alarm run through her but followed anyway.

'Sandra?' Cath called over her shoulder as she led Isla to a chair. 'Can I borrow you?'

'Yeah, two secs,' came a voice from the back.

Isla sat down and stared at Cath through the mirror as the older woman pulled her hair out of her ponytail. She cringed as the messy mop flopped over her shoulders.

'Honestly, the box dye is fine,' she tried to argue.

'I'm sure it is, love. And don't get me wrong, I ain't slating them – I've used them myself at times. But you're part of the firm now, which means you get your hair done here,' Cath replied firmly. 'And you don't have to pay for it either.' She smiled.

'Are you sure?' Isla asked, not convinced. 'Lil never mentioned that. Maybe I should check?'

'No need – it's a given,' Cath replied. 'A perk, so to speak, for all loyal members of the firm.'

Isla smiled and her eyes dropped to the reflection of her hands in her lap. The memory of Calvin's hands all over her body, his mouth on hers, flashed through her mind. *Loyalty.* They had no idea how good she was at faking that. At setting up complex jobs and walking away with everything she'd set out to get. It was what she did best. Her marks always underestimated her because she was small and quiet. They thought they could mould her and trust her. They were fools.

A tall, attractive blonde woman walked out of the back and over to them. Cath stepped aside to let her get to Isla's hair.

'Sandra, this is Isla. She's part of the firm as of recently – you might have seen her pop in and out with Lil. Isla, this is Sandra. Also part of the firm but in a bit of a different capacity.' Cath didn't elaborate and Isla didn't ask. 'I'll be booking Isla in, so if you can work out together what she'd like doing, we'll pop it in the diary,' she finished.

Sandra nodded and smiled at Isla. 'Nice to meet you,' she said sunnily. 'So, what we thinking?' She ran her tanned, manicured fingers through Isla's limp hair, and Isla instinctively hid her own gnawed, bare nails in the arms of her hoodie.

'I don't know really. I usually just throw a lighter blonde on and have it cut straight.' She shrugged. 'What would you do with it?' She'd never learned much about hair or beautification when she was growing up. Her dad had raised her as best he could after her mother had died, but his only input into her appearance was to make sure she was clean and that her clothes were practical.

'Well,' Sandra said, running Isla's hair through her hands and moving it around a little. 'I think if we chop in a few layers and shape it around the face, it would really suit you, bring out those cheekbones. Then as it gets longer maybe aim for a full-on wolf cut, which will give you more volume. Then I'd suggest we put highlights through rather than an all over, keeping it light but maybe adding a bit of warmth so it don't wash you out so much. Some caramels perhaps.'

The woman may as well have been explaining the square root of pi for all Isla understood, but she nodded anyway. Sandra clearly knew what she was doing.

The door opened behind them and she clocked Connor coming in through the mirror. 'Oh, I need to go. I'm sorry—' she started.

'No don't worry, Connor can wait,' Sandra said, grabbing a folder from the shelf of the next station along. 'Can't you, Connor?'

Connor walked over to them, smiling broadly at Sandra as she spoke to him. 'Possibly. How are you ladies doing? You having your hair done, Isla?'

'Just chatting about it at the moment,' she answered.

'And then we're booking her in.' Sandra grinned at her in the mirror, laying her hair back neatly over her shoulders.

'Well, you're with the right person, Isla,' Connor said with a winning smile at Sandra. 'Cause Sandra's the best hairdresser in London. Possibly the country. She'd win competitions styling the hair on a coconut, this one.'

'Dear Lord...' Sandra rolled her eyes.

Isla hid a smile. 'I'd better go.' She slipped off the chair and edged towards the exit.

'Twelve sharp, Tuesday,' Cath called. 'That work for you?'

'Oh, er...' Isla froze. Tuesday was when Calvin was likely to get back. 'I can't, got some stuff on. I need to shoot, but rain check?'

'Well, call me when you get a sec, OK?' Cath said.

'Will do,' Isla replied awkwardly, stepping out of the salon into the fresh air.

Connor stepped out behind her and straightened his jacket, giving her a curious look. 'You alright?'

'Yeah, fine. Let's go.' She forced a grin and set off towards his car. Calvin would be back in just five more days, and then they would see this through. It was so close, the reward so much bigger than on any of the jobs she'd pulled before. She just needed to focus on getting through it and not screwing it up. Then perhaps, once it was done, she could finally get back to some normality.

TWENTY-EIGHT

Jenny Ascough stared out the window, so lost in thought she barely registered the swollen purple clouds as they gathered in livid swirls. Slumped back, she chewed the end of an already battered biro and tried to ignore the aching throb behind her eyes as she went over all the information for the thousandth time.

A sharp tap on her desk made her jump, and she spun her chair back towards her laptop. Jennings, the recently promoted DI heading John's case, rested on the edge of her desk, one leg hitched up as he stared over her head.

'Christ, this storm's going to be a big one,' he commented. 'They're sending out weather warnings now.'

'Yeah, I saw,' Ascough replied, wondering why he was there. She wasn't on any of Jennings's current cases, but he knew how much she wanted John found. Perhaps there had been a breakthrough. She bit her bottom lip as her hopes rose.

He turned back to her, his steely grey eyes critically assessing her before he spoke. 'You getting much sleep, Ascough?'

She was surprised by the question. Jennings wasn't exactly

the caring type, or even particularly observant, for someone in their profession.

'Er, yeah, I get enough,' she lied. 'Everything alright, guv?'

He searched her face once more. 'I don't know yet. You tell me.'

Ascough's skin began to prickle in warning. 'What do you mean?' she asked.

'One of my team picked up on you yesterday, following Scarlet Drew,' he said quietly.

Ascough's gaze shot around the office, checking that no one was in hearing range. Her cheeks grew warm and her heart beat harder as she tried to think up a valid excuse, but nothing came to mind that seemed even remotely plausible.

To her surprise, Jennings chuckled slightly. 'You'd never make it as a criminal, you know. Or a poker player,' he added. He looked around the room. 'You know you're not supposed to be near this case,' he said, his tone more serious now.

'I know,' Ascough said, breathing out heavily in defeat and closing her eyes as stress and frustration threatened to overwhelm her once more.

'There's a reason you're not on it,' he continued.

'Case contamination,' she said. 'And I know being there off book could be cause for evidence contamination too. But, guv, there's not going to *be* any evidence. Not for your guys to find. You know that... that...' she stuttered helplessly then trailed off, knowing her argument was doing nothing to help her case.

Jennings tapped out a rhythm with his fingers on her desk as the office around them continued to buzz with life. 'I *should* insist you stop, immediately, for those reasons and more. I should write you up,' he said carefully. 'But I don't think I will.'

She looked up in surprise, and he stared back at her with a serious expression.

'You get seen by anyone – and I mean *anyone* else – and I'll deny all knowledge. I can't protect you, especially on a case like this. Rule-breaking and sneaking around was exactly what caused this mess in the first place.' He tutted and closed his eyes for a moment, shaking his head. 'The irony...' he muttered. 'But here's what I think. I know you won't stop. And I know why. I know your feelings are clouding your usually impeccable judgement about what's right and wrong.'

She opened her mouth to protest that right and wrong had nothing to do with it, but he cut her off.

'I also know that you're right about the Drews. They've learned our methods, they know exactly where we're coming from and the restrictions we're bound by. I want to believe they'll slip up. It's what I keep telling my team, but, like you, I know they won't.' He pulled a grim expression and looked away, the small muscles in his jaw briefly working. 'If you find anything I can use, bring it to me. If it's evidence, I'll replant it; if it's information, I'll stage an anonymous tip.'

Ascough's eyebrows shot up. Jennings was an intolerable bastard at times, but he was a great DI and a staunch stickler for the rules. She'd never known him to even loosen his tie in a hot meeting, let alone support an officer going off book. Realising he was waiting for her response, she quickly nodded.

'Yes, guv,' she breathed. 'I'll keep you updated.'

'Do *not* get caught,' he warned.

He stood up and made to move away, but she called him back. 'Guv? Anything you can share with me, off-record, would help. It's Saturday tomorrow and I'm off duty...'

Jennings leaned down on the desk for a moment. 'We have word there's something happening at the coast, Norfolk way. Some shipment of stolen goods. It was supposed to be last Saturday, but something happened and it got pushed. Hopefully it goes ahead this time. I'm planting my team there early and keeping one car here to follow them out. Scarlet won't be covered until they head out of town.' He gave her a pointed look then turned and walked away.

Ascough felt a small spark of hope reignite. With Jennings feeding her information, she might actually get somewhere. She thought back to Scarlet's cold grey-blue eyes boring into hers in her kitchen, and the knife at her neck. Ascough was dancing in dangerous waters, that was for sure. But so was Scarlet. The only difference between them was that Scarlet hadn't realised it yet.

TWENTY-NINE

'Cath, stop worrying, she'll be there soon. She was just leaving the pub when I spoke to her.' Lily sighed as her sister-in-law carried on. 'Honestly, she's perfectly safe in the car. It's only a short drive, and—' Cath cut her off again and Lily shook her head tiredly. 'Yes, I know the wind took out the bins, but cars are a lot heavier and even if a bin flies *into* her car, it ain't the end of the world... Cath... *Cath!* Christ almighty,' she muttered as Cath talked over her and worked herself up into a frenzy.

Suddenly there was a pause and Lily tilted her head. 'You still there? Oh, Scarlet's home. Right...' Lily rolled her eyes. 'See? She's fine. It's just a storm, Cath. It ain't Armageddon... What?' Her forehead puckered into an irritated frown. 'My bins will be fine, Cath. And, to be honest, if they're not, I don't particularly care. They're plastic tubs, not people. I'll see you tomorrow.' She ended the call with a long, tired sigh. Cath drove her round the bend sometimes.

Pausing at the kitchen window, she stared out at the sky. Torrential rain hammered down in sheets from livid black clouds that hung low and heavy as far as she could see. Lightning flashed brightly across the sky, spreading wide like a contorted spider's web, followed by a deep, deafening rumble.

Lily walked to the fridge and poured a large glass of wine, before returning to the window. The lights were on in every house tonight, everyone home to weather the storm. The big trees lining the street stood their ground, but the bins toppled, one by one, no match for their adversary. She felt restless, stuck inside when there was so much to do. She took a deep drink from the glass, hoping it might soothe the ragged edges of her soul.

It wasn't just that there was work to be done. It wouldn't hurt that much to do a few hours less tonight. But without the distraction that came with it, Lily couldn't avoid the worries that plagued her. Where was Ruby? Was she safe?

They'd all searched for her, these last weeks. They been to every known address, got word out through the communities, offered rewards, sent out watchers, but there'd been no sign. She'd started to worry something awful had happened to her, until Ruby had slashed Scarlet's tyres and thrown that brick through her window. That had given her confidence that her daughter was physically OK at least. That was something.

Lightning shot across the sky once more, the loud crashing thunder following shortly behind. With an uneasy look down the deserted street, Lily pulled the curtains and downed the rest of her wine in one.

It had been two days since she'd struck back at Ray. Since she'd dropped his dealer's beaten and broken body at his front door. It had been a statement and a half, something he couldn't ignore. Something he *wouldn't* ignore. Ray Renshaw hadn't stepped back from a challenge in his life and he wasn't going to start now. She knew that.

It still felt surreal that the man she loved, who'd stood beside her all these years, was now her enemy. A dangerous one at that. She'd put everyone in the family on high alert. Ray could go for any of them in retaliation. But she knew he was most likely to go straight for her. His issue had always been with her.

Placing her empty glass in the sink, Lily turned out the kitchen light then traipsed upstairs to her bedroom to get undressed. As she slipped her cool black satin nightie over her head, she reached for the remote on her bedside table and turned on the wide flatscreen TV on her wall. The news was on, an attractive but severe-looking woman warning everyone that the storm was one of the worst they'd seen in years.

Lily tutted. 'Bloody scaremongers. It's like they've never seen a bit of rain before.'

As she muttered the words, there was a loud crash outside and she peered out the window to see that a branch had fallen and landed on a car beneath, shattering the windscreen. She pulled a face and dropped the curtain.

'Is a bit windy, I suppose,' she added, sitting on the bed and resting back into the mountain of pillows. She stretched out her slim bare legs, crossing them at the ankles, and flicked through the channels until she found a film she quite liked.

Her phone beeped as she settled in for the night and she looked at the screen. It was a text from Billie.

Hey Lil. Just wanted to check in with you with this storm raging. All OK over there? B x

Lily pursed her lips, and her thumb hovered over the keyboard for a moment as she contemplated her response. Of course she was OK. She was Lily Drew. She'd almost typed as much but paused, not wanting to come across too hard. Despite her natural aversion to anyone her boys had dated in the past, she had grown quite fond of Billie and appreciated the girl staying in touch, despite the fact Cillian must be against it.

All fine here. Takes more than a bit of wind and a shower to bother me. Stay safe x

She pressed send and chucked her phone to the side, but just as she started tuning back in, the TV made a small clicking sound and powered off, along with all the lights in the room, plunging her into darkness.

'For God's sake,' she complained.

With a growl of annoyance, she swung her legs over the side of the bed and stood up, waiting a moment for her eyes to become adjusted to the darkness. She grappled along the bed for her phone with a mumbled curse.

Switching the small torch on, she padded barefoot out of the bedroom and down the stairs towards the kitchen. The storm must have knocked out the power, but hopefully if she flicked the fuses it would come back on. The sound of the rain hammering down on the roof and against the windows comforted her as she made her way through the house. She felt cocooned, as though nestled in the storm's embrace. Though a brighter cocoon would have been preferable.

Reaching the kitchen, she moved to pick up one of the chairs – needing something to stand on to reach the fuse box – but suddenly paused. Faded yellow squares washed across the table before her. She frowned and looked up and out the window to find all the other houses still seemed to be brightly lit. If the storm had taken out the power, the whole street would have been affected.

Something began to prickle at the back of her neck, and she glanced towards the fuse box. The door was hanging open. The prickle turned into a cold alarm that ran down the length of her spine.

As the realisation dawned that there was someone else in her home, she instinctively turned to run – but barely halfway into her first step, she pulled back with a gasp, dropping her phone with a clatter as she realised she was cornered. She knew then, seeing him there in the doorway, his murderous gaze burning a hole into her, that she wasn't safely cocooned in this storm after all. She was trapped, like an animal in a cage. And the most dangerous predator of all was in there with her.

THIRTY

Billie read Lily's text and smiled at the casual dismissal of the wildest storm London had seen in over a decade. She glanced out the window of their top-floor flat as lightning flooded the raging sky once more and tucked her fluffy-sock-clad feet underneath her. Cillian walked over with two steaming mugs and handed her one. She took it with a smile and studied the contents pointedly.

'Enough marshmallows?' Cillian asked with an amused grin.

She counted them with narrowed eyes. 'Hmm, just about. I'll allow it,' she teased.

'Big kid,' he muttered good-naturedly, sitting down on the sofa.

He rubbed his eyes, and she studied him over the rim of her mug as she took a sip of the creamy hot chocolate. He was in his pyjamas, like her, using the unexpected night in to relax and unwind. The soft grey cotton T-shirt was taut over his muscular chest, loosening slightly lower down, towards the matching bottoms. His hair was mussed up, now that he wasn't trying to look smart, a look she preferred on him, in truth. He was a handsome devil, whether he tried or not, but despite that, nothing could hide the dark circles under his troubled eyes.

'You look tired,' she observed.

'I *am* tired,' he admitted. 'I'll call it a day after this.' He gestured towards his mug.

Billie's eyebrows shot up. Cillian never went to bed early. She'd long given up waiting for her night-owl partner to come to bed with her at a normal time.

He caught the look of surprise. 'It's gonna be a long one tomorrow night,' he said, sitting forward to grab a toothpick off the coffee table in front of them. He placed it between his teeth and teased it for a moment as he gazed off into the distance. 'That truck's coming in around ten, but it's miles out and we'll be up most of the night clearing up and sorting the goods.'

Billie stiffened. 'The Milford?'

'Yeah.' He gave her a steely look. 'Like I told you,' he said firmly, 'it's a good set-up. And it will help us start pulling away from the main firm.'

Billie attempted to hide her disapproval. She knew there was no point arguing. When it came to Cillian's world, his jobs, the firm, Billie had no say. It was fair enough – she wasn't technically part of their world. She had no right to stick her nose in and try to tell him what to do, any more than he had any right to tell her how to run her business. But she was still worried about him.

Billie loved Cillian dearly, respected him, admired him for his bravery and skill. But she was shrewd enough to have realised early on that Lily called the shots and laid out the plans. Lily was savvy on a whole different level. It was *she* who'd pulled them up the ladder all these years, juggling their wins and their safety in perfect balance. To see Cillian and his brother go after something Lily had warned them was too dangerous left a cold, heavy feeling inside her that she couldn't shake off. And to hear him talk about pulling away from the family firm broke her heart.

'When you say it's miles out, how far as we talking?' she asked.

'Quite far,' he replied, settling back into the sofa. 'It's coming from Bury St Edmunds down towards Pinford End. Tiny place, middle of nowhere. The road's dead at night, no buildings around. Couldn't be better actually.'

She nodded and took another sip of her hot chocolate. 'You'll be careful, right?' she asked, unable to keep it in. Her stomach churned as doubt still niggled, telling her that something was going to go wrong.

'I'm always careful, Billie,' Cillian replied, giving her a sharp look.

She knew that look. He didn't want to have this conversation. He'd told her once that one of the things he liked about her was that she didn't wobble every time he pulled a job, like other girls had.

She forced a smile. 'Good stuff.'

'Actually, I've got a few calls to make to finish setting up for tomorrow,' he said, standing up and walking to the kitchen.

She watched him go, her smile fading as she turned back towards the window. Dark clouds rolled around, the rain hammering down as the storm wreaked havoc, and she stifled a shiver. She'd never believed in bad omens, but as the dark skies mirrored the tempestuous churn of warning inside her, she began to wonder whether they did exist after all.

THIRTY-ONE

Lightning flashed, flooding the dark room with its bright, flickering light, and Ray's dark eyes glittered with cold purpose as he stared at her from the hallway. Neither said a word, and the silence stretched on like a suffocating force between them. But what was there to say? They both knew why he was there. Lily's legs felt frozen, fused to the tiles by icy shackles, but as he took a step towards her, a spark of terror shot through her, triggering her survival instinct and setting her free.

The long kitchen island was between them to one side, but he was too close. There wasn't enough time to run behind and grab one of the knives from the block. Instead, she turned and ran through the archway into the dining room. She briefly considered hiding under the table but quickly dismissed the idea. She'd be cornered.

Darting through the barely used morning room at the back of the house, she prayed he'd follow her rather than backtrack to cut her off. Most of the large sprawling ground floor was open plan, wide archways leading from one area to the next, connecting in the long central hallway like a figure of eight.

Reaching the back of the hallway, she paused, her eyes

darting around in the dark and her body tensed, but he wasn't there. Her heart thumped painfully against the wall of her chest, and a rush of blood pounded in her ears as she tried to work out where he was. She stilled her breathing with difficulty and silently pressed herself against the wall by the stairs. From there she should see him coming and there were several ways to run, but she needed to know where he was before she tried to escape. If she made the wrong choice, it could be fatal.

Thunder crashed through the skies above, and she jumped, already on the very edge of her last nerve. This was bad. *Very* bad. She'd known there would be a comeback from her actions, had known it wouldn't be good, but she'd thought he'd attack her publicly. She'd thought she'd have a chance to fight back. But Ray would have known she'd be expecting that. He knew she'd be prepared. And she had been. People were on alert, and strategic weapons – innocuous items that wouldn't attract attention during any police raids – had been placed through all the offices. But homes were usually off limits, so she hadn't expected this. Which was exactly why he'd chosen this path.

She kicked herself, angry that she'd let her guard down. The storm had provided Ray with the perfect opportunity, and they both knew she didn't stand a chance against him here. Lily had survived and thrived in this cut-throat world all these years because she was ruthless and smart, but at the end of the day, when it came down to physical strength, Ray could overpower her without even trying. She didn't even have a weapon.

'Lily Drew...' The words were stretched out in a low, taunting growl and her head whipped round towards it. 'Running away from me like a scared little mouse.'

He was following her, coming through the dining room if she was gauging it right. She pushed silently off the wall and darted towards the sideboard near the front door. If she could get to the car, she could escape.

'So brave before though, weren't ya, Lil?' he continued in that low, eerie growl.

Her breathing hitched as he drew closer. She reached the sideboard and grappled in the bowl, her eyes widening in horror as she realised it was empty. He'd taken her keys.

She grabbed the door handle and tried to pull it open, but it was locked. She cursed, realising her mistake as the rattling gave away her position. Stifling a sob of dread, she lunged back into the kitchen, knowing if she paused any longer, he'd catch her up. Maybe going back into the kitchen would throw him off. Ray would expect her to go the other way, into the lounge, not to follow him back round.

She darted behind the kitchen island towards the knife block, but the dim sulphuric light from the street light that separated shadow from shadow showed her he'd emptied this too. Her panic rose. There were no *actual* weapons in the house, a precaution they took in case of police raids. She grasped a handful of her tight blonde curls as she turned around, trying to think, searching for *something*.

'What's the matter, Lil? Cat got your tongue?'

Ray was closer now, his taunts coming from the hall.

Abandoning the kitchen, Lily ran back through the dining room, her heart in her mouth. If he caught her before she could arm herself, it was over. He was strong and merciless, a man who lived by even fewer boundaries than she did. And he was driven by hatred now. A hot, deep, painful hatred. She'd seen the strength of it in his eyes. That was the funny thing about love. It could create a deeper hate than anything else on the planet when things turned sour.

'You're very quiet all of a sudden,' he continued in a dark, mocking tone. 'Weren't so quiet the other day, were ya?'

His voice appeared to be moving away. He'd turned into the lounge, as she'd predicted.

Taking the opportunity to move, she carried on through the

morning room, her eyes constantly sweeping for something to defend herself with as her mind searched for a way out. The French doors at the back were locked, the key in her office, but if she could get to the utility room in the corner, there was a door into the garden. That was also locked, and Ray may have removed that key too, but years before, after a series of instances of Ruby losing the key on a bender, she'd hidden a copy on top of the cupboards. Ray didn't know about that.

Reaching the back entrance to the hallway again, she paused, her heart hammering harder than ever as she glanced towards the utility-room door. She was so close. But where was Ray? She strained her ears, wishing he would call out to her again. But there was silence.

She deliberated, looking back over her shoulder. Was he behind her or in front? The silence was harder to bear than the taunts, and her skin prickled as she faltered, unsure. She had to keep going, she told herself firmly – she had to keep moving.

Forcing herself onwards, she crossed the hall quickly and pulled open the utility-room door. For a fraction of a second, she felt thankful that the hinges didn't creak, but as the door swung wider, this feeling was shattered by the sight of Ray lying in wait.

'Leaving so soon?' he growled menacingly.

THIRTY-TWO

Ray launched at her, almost closing the gap between them before Lily jumped back and fled down the hallway. She ran with all her strength, hoping that her smaller frame might be enough to keep her ahead, but there wasn't enough hallway to get up to speed before she had to turn.

As she twisted at the bottom of the stairs, she felt his arm reach over her shoulder and curl around her neck. Instinctively, she pushed herself back into his chest, bent her knees and slipped to the floor to avoid the headlock. Ray wasn't expecting the move and he tumbled awkwardly, hitting the wall with a curse.

Lily rolled away and ran back into the kitchen and behind the island, reaching for the drawers. He couldn't have emptied all of them. Ray was only a beat behind though, hurtling towards her with a roar.

Out of time, Lily grabbed a full cutlery tray and threw it in his face as he lunged towards her. A shower of knives and forks fell to the ground with an ear-splitting clatter, and as she stumbled backward, Lily grabbed everything in reach, launching them at him, one after another. Mugs smashed and fruit flew across the floor, but it made no difference.

Thunder boomed from the skies, and lightning lit up the kitchen, shining on the chaos and hopelessness of the situation, and Lily let out a frustrated cry of fear and rage. He was going to kill her here tonight, no matter what she did. There was no escaping it. She'd always known her days were numbered because of the life she'd chosen, so she'd always been prepared. But despite knowing she couldn't change her fate, she wasn't prepared to stop trying. Because the thought of leaving the twins behind when things between them were so bad, and while Ruby was still lost and alone, was unbearable.

Spurred on by this thought, she ran from him once more, towards the other side of the house. He was close, but as he neared, Lily suddenly realised she had one advantage that could help her. She may not have a weapon, but she knew this house better than he did, especially in the dark.

Adjusting course, she made a beeline for a small pouffe to the side of an armchair and nimbly jumped over it. As she'd hoped, Ray tripped, and she felt a momentary elation as she heard him fall heavily to the ground behind her.

Without stopping, she fled through the next archway, grabbing a heavy crystal whisky decanter off the drinks tray as she passed. In the hallway, she turned and brandished it, ignoring the smash of the stopper as it fell to the hardwood floor. Adrenaline coursed through her as she waited, ready to face him head-on and give him all she'd got, but as the seconds ticked by, she realised something was wrong.

The strong arm that wrapped itself around her neck from behind and pulled tight against her throat made her cry out in shock. She tried to swing the decanter towards Ray's head, but he had already anticipated this and grabbed her wrist, shaking it roughly until she let go. The decanter smashed into pieces, whisky and lumps of crystal skating across the floor in all directions as he yanked her backward off her feet.

She screamed obscenities and clawed at his arm, her nails dragging deep furrows into his skin until he roared out in pain and flung her roughly to the side. Lily skidded across the floor into the wall and quickly clambered to her feet, but Ray was already there. He grabbed her throat, his fingers wrapping around her neck in a vice-like grip, then slammed her hard against the wall, putting his furious face to hers.

'So quick to turn on me, weren't you, Lil?' he snarled, so close she could feel the heat radiating from his skin on hers. His eyes were wild, holding hers with fierce intensity.

'*You* turned on *me*. You started this war, remember?' she hissed with difficulty through gritted teeth.

'Oh, I remember,' Ray replied, his tone quieter now, but just as deadly. 'I remember you keeping my children from me, flaunting them in my face every day of their lives while leaving me to believe they were someone else's.'

'That *isn't* how it was,' she shot back.

'No? Because that's how it feels. I had no choice in the matter, no control. How does it feel to be the one with no control, Lily?' he asked, his grip tightening around her neck.

Lily clamped her jaw. She wasn't going to answer that question and give him the satisfaction of knowing the truth. She waited for his squeeze to tighten. There was no way out of this now. She could beg for mercy, but even if she wasn't too proud to do that, she knew it would fall on deaf ears.

Ray's hand tightened, and she gritted her teeth against the pain, but still he didn't go in for the kill. Did he really want to draw this out? Did he really want to make her suffer for as long as he could?

'If you're gonna kill me, Ray, just fucking kill me,' she spat.

Ray pushed his face up close to hers, and she glared back at him, defiant even in the face of death.

'I'm not going to kill you, Lil,' he said in a deadly voice. 'Not today anyway. I just wanted to show you that I *could*.' With that, he stepped back and let go of her neck.

Lily slumped against the wall, her hands flying to her neck where his hand had been as she pulled in a deep, laboured gulp of air. 'What are you doing?' she asked warily. This didn't make sense.

Ray looked down at her with cold contempt, but there was something else behind his eyes that she couldn't quite place. 'The dealer on your patch wasn't planned,' he said. 'But even if it had been, I'm surprised you took that so far.' There was an edge to his tone as he watched her.

Lily held his gaze. 'That dealer sold Winnie to my fighters. One ended up in hospital.'

Ray's eyebrows lifted briefly, but his surprise quickly faded and the hardness returned to his features. 'That's unfortunate. But it still don't excuse what you did.'

Lily was in a precarious position right now, her throat still throbbing from Ray's grip, her life still just one angry snap away from being over. But she wasn't going to pretend she was sorry. Ray had started this. Ray had stolen from them and humiliated them, tried to initiate the beginning of their downfall.

'What did you expect?' she spat. 'For me to just lie there and take it?' She shook her head. 'I built this firm up for my children, to give them a life, a *future*. And you think I'm going to sit by and watch as *you* tear it down, brick by brick?' She arched an eyebrow. 'You think I care what happens to me? Whether I live or die or suffer, when all I've built for them is on the line?' She glared at him through the darkness, the faces of all she held dear running through her mind. 'I'll cross every single one of your lines time and again, I'll let you strip the flesh from my bones inch by inch as I lie screaming and then dig my grave with my own *fingernails* before I'll let you take *anything* I've built away from my family.' Her voice shook with pent-up rage and emotion as her fear melted away.

Ray loomed over her once more, his eyes glinting dangerously. 'If I wanted you dead, you'd have been dead an hour ago,' he said in a dark tone barely louder than a whisper. 'You deserved this after what you did to my dealer. And you needed a reminder of exactly who I am,' he added. 'I could end you without lifting a finger, Lily Drew. Don't ever forget that again.' He held her stare for a few moments then abruptly pulled away, this time putting more distance between them. 'Consider this war over.'

Lily's heart thumped in her chest as Ray turned the tables again. Was he still playing with her? Was this a game?

'We're not OK, you and me. But I have no interest in tearing down your firm,' he continued.

Lily watched him warily, unsure how to respond, and Ray turned away, walking down the long hallway to the front door. He reached into his pocket, pulling out a selection of keys then dropped them into the key bowl, one by one, save for the last, which he used to unlock the front door.

Pausing as he opened it, he looked out. 'It seems the storm has passed.'

She looked past him to the street outside. While they'd been busy fighting, the rain had stopped, as had the thunder and lightning, leaving just the dark-grey clouds to amble along the sky, their fury spent.

'It seems it has,' she agreed, her gaze resting on the side of his face.

He turned back for a moment, an unreadable look in his eyes. 'Watch yourself.'

Whether it was a threat or a warning, Lily wasn't quite sure. Probably both, she decided, as he walked down the front path and off into the night.

As the house fell silent, Lily walked slowly through to the

kitchen, careful to sidestep the shards of broken crystal and various other debris on the floor, and flipped the switch on the fuse box. The hallway lights flooded the room, highlighting the chaos around her. Cutlery and fruit bowls and smashed china littered the floor. She sat down for a minute and stared at it all, still trying to process what had just happened. Her body ached, her throat throbbed, and her mind whirled.

She'd been so sure Ray was going to kill her. She'd seen it in his eyes. Perhaps that *had* been his initial plan and she'd derailed it somehow. Or perhaps Ray himself hadn't even known which way this was going to go.

Pondering this, Lily made her way upstairs, desperate to lie down and rest her aching bones. But as she reached her bedroom and saw what he'd left there, she realised exactly how precisely Ray had planned this evening out. He'd never intended to kill her at all. He'd just wanted her to believe he did. Every last second of the evening had been controlled and choreographed, from the moment she'd left this bedroom.

Because there in the middle of the bed, clearly placed just after she'd run down to the fuse box, was a neatly stacked pile of money – which she knew without needing to count amounted to exactly two hundred and fifty thousand pounds.

THIRTY-THREE

Scarlet sat back and crossed her slim legs as she contemplated the notes she'd just made on the pad in her hands. Their current laundries wouldn't be able to take the added income from the illegal boxing fights and they had to be careful about sudden increases, especially right now with Jennings watching their every move. Her idea could solve this problem, if Lily was interested.

Above the dull whirring of the machines in the factory beyond her office door, the sharp clack of heels marching across the concrete floor and the murmur of her aunt's urgent tone travelled through. Standing up, Scarlet smoothed down her black knee-length pencil skirt and re-tucked her crimson satin blouse before stepping around the desk. She paused by the door, checking her face in the mirror. She was pale, she noted. More so than usual. She pinched her cheeks in an attempt to give them some colour and ran her gaze critically over the rest of her face and her long dark hair. Hollow circles framed her grey-blue eyes and no smile warmed them. She found it hard to smile these days, as though the muscles required to pull up her face were physically weighed down by her troubles.

With one last grimace at her reflection, she picked up her notes and went through to Lily's office, knocking before entering the room.

Lily sat behind the desk, her usual cigarette in hand as she leaned forward on her elbow towards Isla, who sat in one of the chairs opposite her. Despite the fact it was fairly mild still, she wore a long-sleeved turtleneck with her leather skirt – a look she usually saved for winter. Odd, Scarlet thought.

'Scarlet, do you have the list of who's attending the fight tonight?' Lily asked.

'Yeah, I'll grab it for you in a bit. About eighty per cent of those who came last week are returning. A few extras too.'

She sat down in the vacant seat next to Isla and glanced at the girl. She looked as tired as Scarlet felt – and on edge. Isla had looked on edge a lot recently, she'd noticed. She narrowed her gaze as she studied her for a few moments.

'Ray?' Lily asked.

Scarlet shook her head, returning her attention to Lily. 'No. He's declined this week. Thank God,' she added. 'We certainly can't take another hit like that again.'

'We won't need to,' Lily replied quietly, taking another drag on her cigarette.

Scarlet looked at her with a questioning frown.

Lily exhaled, blowing a long plume of smoke into the air. 'Our issues with Ray are over. I've sorted it.' She dropped her gaze away from Scarlet's.

'How?' Scarlet queried, her frown deepening.

Lily didn't answer straight away; instead, she took another slow drag on her cigarette and sat back in her chair, crossing her free arm across her chest.

What had happened to change this situation so drastically? Scarlet wondered. For the last few days, they'd all been on high alert, well aware that Ray was gunning for them. His fury over Lily hiding the twins from him all these years had been very publicly channelled into attacks on the firm, and after Lily's violent and pointed response, they had all been waiting for the backlash. Right up until last night, Lily had been wound tighter than Scarlet had ever seen her. She'd been *scared*, Scarlet had realised, and *this* was something she'd never seen before. Yet today Lily sat there, cool as a cucumber, telling them it was all sorted out, as if it were no bigger a deal than finding a clerical error in the factory. It didn't make sense.

'Lil? What do you mean you've sorted it?' Scarlet pushed.

Lily ran her hand through her halo of tight blonde curls and sighed heavily. 'I mean just that,' she said. 'Ray came over last night and agreed to a truce. He even brought back the money he swindled out of the fight last week.'

'He came over in the storm?' Scarlet asked in a flat tone. 'To give us our money back and call a truce?'

'Yep.' Lily took another drag and held her gaze.

Scarlet stared back at her, not buying that this was the whole story. Ray was one of the most notoriously vindictive faces in the underworld. And he'd been after blood.

'Yesterday we were watching our backs in case he tried to *kill* us,' she said frankly. 'Surely he didn't just *decide to change his mind*?' She blinked and shook her head with a frown. 'No. Not Ray. Not when it's you. He wanted to seriously punish you, Lil. What did you promise him?'

She saw Lily's stare sharpen.

'I need to know,' she quickly added. 'This may have started between you two, but now it affects all of us – you know that.'

Isla cleared her throat uncomfortably. 'I've got some calls to make; I'll be back in a bit.' She stood up and left the room, shutting the door quietly behind her.

Lily glared at Scarlet from across the desk until Isla had gone, and Scarlet exhaled heavily. Lily was the leader of their firm. Of their family too. She expected and had earned the right to be respected by those she brought in from the next generation. And because of that, Scarlet wouldn't usually push. But she had no choice. Ex-lover of Lily's or not, Ray was a threat to them all.

'I didn't promise Ray anything,' Lily said in a low, hard tone. 'And, no, he isn't someone who just walks away from something like this. He got something he wanted, as did I. And all *you* need to know about that is that it's done with.'

Scarlet held Lily's thunderous glare for a moment, her mind whirling as she tried to work out exactly what that meant. Her gaze flickered down to the long-sleeved, high-necked top Lily was wearing. What was she hiding underneath? The concerned question of whether Lily was alright hovered on the tip of her tongue, but she swallowed it, casting her eyes down with a dutiful nod. She knew when to retreat. Lily wouldn't welcome the further intrusion.

'Well then that's great news,' she said instead, her tone subdued as she decided not to bother faking enthusiasm.

There was a tense silence as Lily stubbed out her cigarette and immediately lit another. She took several drags, clearly trying to settle her irritation, before she spoke again. 'Two hundred and fifty grand,' she said, changing the subject in a clipped tone. 'We need to work out how we're going to launder it.'

'Actually, that's why I came in here,' Scarlet said, grasping the chance to move on. 'I had an idea about how we could launder some of the profits from the fight nights. It might not clean all of it, but it should leave a decent dent.'

'Go on,' Lily said.

'What if we opened a charity, an official registered charity, to raise money for the club? We set it all up, make it official, hold regular fundraisers, which we use for two things. Firstly, to launder the money through the charity. We appoint you as the chairman, me as the head of personnel, Cillian as head of operations, Connor as head of marketing and publicity, Mum as head of fundraising. Jimmy's salary can go through there; George, Andy, Billie, anyone you need or want to payroll, all being paid through an official legal charity from the *not so* legal profits of the fight nights. We make the family salaries ridiculously high – the same way all the rich bastards do in every other charity. And then we plough a certain amount back into the club, which I know you wanted to do anyway. It should shift a lot, and if we take the tax hit our end for those going from cash in hand to payroll, it won't have any negative impact for them. If anything, they'd look more legit and it's not too much of a dent for us. It'd be a win-win, in my opinion.'

Lily raised her eyebrows and pulled a face, seemingly impressed with the idea. 'Charities *are* the biggest scam going,' she mused. She twisted her lips to one side as she considered it. 'You said laundering was the first reason. What's the second?'

The corners of Scarlet's mouth pulled up into a smile. 'To make some connections with the rich and the bored.'

Lily met her gaze with amused interest. 'You want to get in their art cabinets.'

'I do,' Scarlet admitted. 'We made some serious money on that first painting we stole from Grace.'

'Through a fallback plan,' Lily reminded her. 'Using the FBI for their reward money. We can't exactly pull that con twice.'

'No, I know that,' Scarlet replied.

When Scarlet had first joined the firm, she'd come across a unique opportunity, an already stolen Rembrandt painting, hidden in the home of a loathsome man they'd had the misfortune to meet at another charity event. They'd stolen it and the heist went beautifully, but the selling on of the painting did not, and eventually they'd moved to plan B, which was to stage a discovery and hand it in to the FBI for the five-million-dollar reward they had out on it.

'And need I remind you that we still have *another*

painting hidden under the floorboards of the barn, with no fence in place to shift it? The Picasso from the last job,' Lily added.

Unfortunately, the wife of the man they'd stolen the Rembrandt from, Grace, had been a force they hadn't bargained for, and she'd come back at them with a vengeance. She'd burned down their factory and vowed to kill them all. Ruby had been in the factory and barely survived the attack. In return, they'd stolen another of Grace's paintings and got rid of her for good. But the painting, as Lily pointed out, was still sat in storage.

'I'm aware of that too,' Scarlet conceded, 'but I think we could change that.'

'How?' Lily crossed her arms and waited.

'There are art auctions throughout the city all the time. I could start attending them and making connections. I can talk shop all day, and if I can get collectors chatting and move the conversation towards our fundraisers, we could entice them, start building an attendance base of the right people,' Scarlet explained.

Her passion, since she'd been a small child, had been fine art. She'd taken art history at A level, spent hours every weekend in the museums or with her head in a book, learning all there was to know about her favourite artists throughout time.

'That gets us our marks perhaps, but I still don't see how that helps sell anything on,' Lily replied, her forehead puckering.

'OK.' Scarlet painted the picture. 'So we've set up our charity, our fundraisers, and we have as many art-collecting rich people there as I can tempt. As we get to know them, I drop into conversation about our amazing luck in finding that missing Rembrandt in the lock-up, and how we alerted the FBI the way any good citizen would.' She smiled. 'Any straight-laces will be in awe of our incredible luck and thankful that it's been returned to the museum for all to see...'

'And anyone who knew Grace had that painting will subtly call you out,' Lily finished, catching on.

'Exactly,' Scarlet replied. 'She showed it off to her clients to gain their trust – they all knew she had it. But Grace and Harry are dead, Duffy's rotting in jail, and her other men scarpered. No one else around here knows we stole it. She would *never* have let that embarrassment go public. So if we find one of those old clients, we can insinuate that we were close with Grace and make it appear that she sold it to us or was in on the deal. We can't outright lie, as it may come out further down the line, and we need to be able to backtrack and claim miscommunication. But we can insinuate enough to sell the story. Then we can find out who they're using for their black-market art now that Grace is gone and try to set up a meeting.'

In an ideal world they would have been able to sell things like the Rembrandt on themselves, but the harsh reality was that it was out of their league. They didn't have the offshore banking structures to move that kind of money, even if they did have the connections. So they needed to form a partnership with someone who did.

Lily laced her fingers together and pressed them to her mouth. 'It's doable, but we'd have to be extremely careful. One wrong slip of the tongue and we could alienate people or condemn ourselves before we even get a contact.'

Scarlet's heart rose in excitement. Lily was considering it. 'Of course. We'll keep that end of things tight, just you and I when it comes to discussing art with the collectors.'

'It will be solely on you to draw them in,' Lily said. 'Then, yes, we'll keep any meetings and negotiations between the two of us. Then the boys can help us plan and carry out the heists down the line.'

Scarlet nodded. 'Definitely. We'll work as a team, to our strengths, like last time.'

'That's a long way off though,' Lily said quietly. 'Even if it does pan out. Either way, the charity is a good idea as a laundry. Start setting it up; bring the paperwork to me. Contact Robert to help us make sure everything is legally watertight. Once it's set up, we'll look at putting together the first fundraiser. But keep this under your belt for the time being.' Lily glanced at the closed office door, her expression unreadable. 'We have a lot of other things going on right now. Let's deal with all of that first before we start anything new.'

'On that note,' Scarlet said, glancing back at the door that Isla still stood somewhere the other side of and lowering her voice, 'I'm heading up to Manchester shortly, as discussed.'

'Who are you taking?' Lily asked, equally as quietly.

'Andy. Bill delivered the address to me this morning. We should find out exactly who and what we're dealing with in just a few hours,' Scarlet said heavily.

Lily nodded. 'Be careful,' she warned. 'No one can know who you are. Get what we need – *if* you can – and be back here by morning. Got it?'

'Got it,' Scarlet replied.

There was a tentative knock on the door, and they fell silent as Isla popped her head round. 'Calls all done,' she said, assessing them nervously before walking back in. 'All good?'

Scarlet and Lily exchanged a loaded look before Lily turned back to the girl with a smile. 'All good.'

THIRTY-FOUR

A knock sounded at the front door of the flat, and Cillian called through to Billie, 'Get that, will ya?' He zipped up the plain black fleece over the top of the black T-shirt and tracksuit bottoms and stuffed the ski mask and gloves in the pockets. Connor walked into the bedroom a moment later and closed the door behind him.

'Alright?' he asked, shrugging off the casual clothes he'd worn over and reaching for the identical outfit to his brother's that was laid out on the bed.

'Yeah, all good,' Cillian replied.

Connor hopped about on one leg and almost toppled as he wrangled his second leg into the trousers. 'How's Billie? She thawed out about this job yet?'

'Not really,' Cillian replied. 'But she's keeping it to herself now at least.'

Connor pulled a face then folded his clothes neatly and placed them on top of the drawers, before they both walked back into the lounge. Billie sat at the kitchen island looking into her small round make-up mirror as she applied her eyeshadow. She wore a turquoise dress that ruched up at the sides slightly, flattering her hourglass figure and bringing out the bright blue of her eyes.

'You look gorgeous,' Cillian said, walking over and wrapping his arms around her waist. He planted a kiss on her cheek. 'You'll have to wear that again so I can take you out in it.'

'You could take me out tonight if you wanted,' she replied, glancing at him in the mirror. 'I hear there's a great boxing match on.'

'Very funny,' he replied drily, giving her one more kiss before pulling away. 'Just stay away from Mum. As much as you can anyway. She'll still come over and ask you where we are – you know that, right?'

'I do. And I also know what you told me to tell her when she does,' Billie replied with a bored sigh.

'That you haven't seen us all day and don't know where we are,' Cillian confirmed.

'That's the one,' Billie replied brightly.

Cillian eyed her long and hard in the mirror, and she held his gaze with the casual confidence of someone who wasn't afraid of the threat behind his stare.

Eventually she broke away with a soft smile and shook her head. 'Don't worry so much,' she said. 'About me anyway. Just focus on your job, yeah? Get it done and get out. And don't take all night.'

Cillian leaned in and kissed the top of her head, then turned away to pull on his trainers. 'You've swapped the plates?' he asked Connor.

Connor nodded. 'Plates swapped, tools inside, all ready to go.'

'Good stuff.' Cillian pulled his laces tight and thought over their plan for the heist.

The details of the job being so straightforward, they planned to stage a simple breakdown, making sure the old beat-up minivan they used for these jobs took up too much room for the truck to pass. As soon as the driver was out of the cab, they'd hold him up, transfer as many boxes as the minivan would hold, then tie him up and make a getaway, leaving him to be found later on. They'd done it this way a hundred times before, and the road they were pulling the job on couldn't be more ideal. It would be a simple hit, in and out.

'Cillian...' Connor hesitated. 'You're sure about this job, yeah?' he asked.

Cillian stared into the dark-brown eyes of his brother, identical to his own, and saw the flicker of doubt.

'I'm sure,' he said confidently, reaching out and squeezing Connor's shoulder. 'It's a great set-up – you know that. And, honestly, we need this.'

He thought about his mother, and the usual stab of anger shot through him. She'd betrayed them both, put herself first without a care for what it would do to them. Their mother, the person who they'd always relied on to protect and love them unconditionally, had taken one of the most valuable things they had to save her own skin. The key to their most basic level of identity. Finding that out had shown them, in all its ugly light, the truth – that Lily had only ever really cared about herself. It had hurt them deeply, but more than that, it had destroyed their trust in her completely.

'We need to start setting ourselves apart, start sharing the success of the jobs we pull alone, away from the firm. Away from Mum,' Cillian continued. He shook his head. 'There's no point announcing it until we've pulled at least one.'

'Yeah, you're right,' Connor said, standing up. 'Today is the start of a new era.' He glanced at his phone before placing it on the coffee table next to Cillian's, where it would stay until their return. 'And we need to shoot if we're going to get set up in time.'

'True.' Cillian stood up and followed him to the door,

looking back over his shoulder to Billie. 'See you later. Have fun.'

Busy doing her make-up still, she didn't look round. 'See you later.'

He shut the door and pushed his hands into his fleece pockets, focusing on what lay ahead. Connor was right – this was the start of a new era. And he planned to start it off with a bang.

THIRTY-FIVE

'You definitely lost her on the way up?' Lily asked, pressing her hand to the ear that didn't have her mobile against it.

The stands were filling up now for fight night, and the excitement in the room was rising. The chatter and music were making it hard to hear Scarlet on the other end of the line. She ducked into Jimmy's office and pushed the door closed, blocking out some of the noise.

'Good. Keep an eye out though, just in case she reappears.' She paused. 'No, they're still not here. I don't know where the hell they are.' She ran her hand through her curls, stressed. 'We're already two people down, with you and Andy away. I don't know what the hell they're playing at... No, they're ignoring their phones – both of them.' Dark irritation flashed across her face. 'I've gotta go. Let me know when you've got news.'

She ended the call and took a deep breath in, exhaling slowly before walking back into the gym. Everything was set up perfectly, though they'd had to work hard to get it done in time without the boys. The atmosphere was set, the betting stall had a long line of people queueing up to hand over their money, the drinks were flowing and people were ready for a show.

Jimmy sidled up to her, and she shot him a quick smile, not quite able to hide the tension she felt beneath it.

'Everything alright?' he asked.

'Everything is going as it should, so far,' she replied carefully.

'But?' he asked, not fooled.

She pulled a face. 'But my sons are nowhere to be found, and Andy and Scarlet are elsewhere, so there are fewer bodies here to keep things in order, should anything flare up,' she admitted.

'Ah. I see. You think it will?' he asked.

'I think there are people here with big personalities who are betting a lot of money and drinking, and they all live in a world ruled through violence. Everyone here wants to keep this night a polite affair, an escape to forget their troubles and unwind. But there's always a good chance of the wind changing with all of that in the mix,' she answered honestly.

Jimmy pondered this for a moment. 'I'll make a call, ask some of my boys, the ones who know but aren't in this fight, to come in. They can help keep things running smooth. That sound OK?'

'That sounds perfect,' Lily replied, feeling relieved. 'Just let me know who, yeah? And point them to me. I'll pay them for their troubles.'

'They'll be glad of that, no doubt,' Jimmy answered. 'Right, I'll go make the calls.'

He walked off, and Lily crossed the room towards the door. As she neared, Billie entered and made a beeline for the front row, where Cath was currently sat alone. Her hopes lifting, Lily looked past her into the crowd of people behind, but neither of the boys were with her. She sighed, angry. This wasn't OK. These fight nights were big events for the firm and they *knew* she needed them here. Not turning up was unacceptable, and, more than that, it was dangerous.

It was true, what she'd told Jimmy. A room full of drunk, hyped-up faces from throughout the underworld could blow up in an instant, no matter how careful they'd been to not invite enemies to the same events. One accidental slight or one joke taken the wrong way and all hell could break loose. They needed to be able to diffuse things quickly, but she couldn't do that without enough people.

Casting her eye over the room warily, Lily made note of who sat near who, identifying where the possible risks might lie, then melted back against the edge of the room. The best thing she could do was keep watch and catch any potential situation before it happened. She just prayed she was able to do that. Because Lily wasn't sure this particular business could survive another disastrous week. And if the fight nights failed after they'd sunk so much money into the club, financially, they were screwed.

THIRTY-SIX

'This is the place, slow down,' Connor instructed. 'Just round that corner there's a short straight, then another corner surrounded by trees that block the view of the long straight beyond for about half a mile. That'll be the best spot. In the short straight. He won't see us till he rounds that corner, but we'll spot him coming across the fields in the distance before he disappears behind the trees.'

Cillian slowed and turned the corner, pulling to a stop where his brother had instructed. The sky was a clear indigo-black, one thin sliver of the moon visible in the sky and pinpricks of light shining down from the stars.

Connor checked his watch. 'We have about ten minutes, if they're on time.'

'You brought the baby seat, didn't you?' Cillian asked.

''Course,' Connor scoffed. 'This ain't my first rodeo, thank you very much.' He pulled out a cigarette and a lighter, but Cillian grabbed the lighter off him before he could use it. 'Hey!'

'Might not be your first rodeo, but you light that in here and it'll be your last,' he warned. 'You don't have time anyway.'

Connor shook his head and gave his brother a filthy look.

'You know, I really did like you better when you smoked. Before you started planting that stupid, fucking twig in your mouth. Do you even know what you look like?'

'It's a toothpick. And I'm sure you're about to tell me,' Cillian replied, settling in for the rant.

'A scarecrow. A fucking scarecrow is what you look like, OK? I know you think you look all cool and vintage, some throwback to old-school mafia or something with that matchstick sticking out your pie hole—'

'It's a toothpick,' Cillian said again.

'But for the record, you don't. You look like a prat. And you know what, I might smoke, but at least I get rid of the butts. You leave those fucking things – those *torture* mechanisms – everywhere you go. I'm *so* sick of finding them,' Connor blustered, venting his annoyance.

'Well, at least they ain't slowly killing me,' Cillian argued.

'Well, they're slowly killing *me!*' Connor exclaimed loudly. 'They're slowly stabbing me to death, prick by prick, because you can't figure out how to put them in a *fucking* bin!'

Cillian rolled his eyes. 'Now you're just being ridiculous.'

Connor sat back and took a few loud breaths, muttering to himself about not committing murder today.

Cillian ignored him.

'They really will kill you, ya know,' he said once Connor seemed calmer. 'You ever actually looked up what happens to you if you get lung cancer?'

'Oh, will you shut up?' Connor shot back irritably. He undid his seat belt and snatched the lighter back from Cillian. 'I'm getting out and having my damn cigarette. Don't worry, I'll stand upwind so the smoke don't float near your delicate lungs.'

'Good,' Cillian replied.

Connor stepped out of the car and slammed the door, but less than two seconds later, he reopened it and leaned in.

'Changed your mind?' Cillian asked.

'No, the truck's coming,' he replied.

'What?' Cillian sat upright and glanced over his shoulder through the back passenger window. Sure enough, there were headlights steadily moving across the top of the fields in the distance.

'Move the car,' Connor ordered, slamming the door.

Cillian moved it quickly, parking it at an angle near the centre of the road, leaving a gap only big enough for something the size of a Smart car to squeeze through the other side. He pulled the handbrake and got out as Connor opened the boot. Sidestepping out of the way as Connor fixed the jack under the car by the front wheel, Cillian hoisted the spare tyre out and placed it beside his brother, along with the baby seat. He glanced at the dark row of trees. There was no sign of the truck yet. It should drive around the corner any second though, he gauged.

'Go,' Connor said urgently, ready to pretend to be jacking up the car.

Cillian reached into the car and picked up a roll of tape and some rope, then jogged a few metres away before ducking into the overgrown ditch between the road and the neighbouring field. Switching the ski mask and gloves in his pockets with the items in his hands, Cillian put them on hurriedly before ducking low. A thistle poked his thigh and he swore under his breath. He hated being the one in the ditch, but they took it in turns and Connor had done the last one.

Bright-yellow lights suddenly glinted off the back of the minivan, and a second later the truck drove into view. It slowed to a stop just in front of him, and Cillian watched as the driver squinted down at Connor. The low rumble of the idling engine and the sound of the jack being pulled back and forward as slowly as Connor could manage carried on for about a minute and Cillian pulled an expression of frustration under his mask.

'Come on,' he urged under his breath. 'Get out the cab.'

Eventually the driver opened the door and stepped down. 'Hey,' he called in a thick French accent. 'You OK?'

Cillian jumped up onto the road and bolted round the back of the truck. There he paused and peered around the end towards the driver's side. The driver had taken a few steps towards Connor, who continued to work the jack.

'Hey, you hear me? You OK? The baby is OK?'

Cillian ran silently down the truck's side, and then with full force, he kicked the back of the driver's knees, sending him sprawling to the ground. The driver cried out in alarm and pain, and Connor immediately turned and joined Cillian. They grabbed him by the arms before he could get his bearings.

'He's alright, mate, don't worry,' Cillian said as the driver yelled what sounded like a long line of French expletives. 'And you will be too. We just need a few minutes with the back of your truck.'

With deft hands, Cillian wrapped the rope around the driver's wrists behind his back while Connor held the struggling man still.

'Christ, you're a feisty one,' Connor remarked. 'Calm down, for fuck's sake.' He wrapped his arms around the man's torso, turning him awkwardly to face Cillian.

Cillian placed the tape over the man's mouth, careful not to block his nose, and the alarmed cries were instantly muffled. 'That's better,' he said, bending to tie the man's ankles together.

Realising what Cillian had planned, the man quickly raised his leg onto the front of the truck and pushed back hard against Connor, knocking him to the ground and falling heavily on top of him.

'What the fuck!' Connor cried angrily, releasing his grip out of shock.

The driver immediately tried to get away, rolling off Connor and landing on the ground with a thump. Connor quickly made to grab him, as did Cillian, but as they grappled in the dirt, he flung his head back, smashing it into Connor's nose with a sickening crack.

'Jesus Christ!' he yelled, holding his hands to his face and rolling the other way, leaving his brother to deal with the man still thrashing around like a fish on the shore.

Cillian yanked the driver into a standing position, furious that he'd managed to land such a damaging blow on his brother. Out of the corner of his eye, he saw Connor pull his hands away from his ski mask, and in the truck's headlights, he could see they were slick with blood.

Cillian slammed the driver against the front of the truck with force, putting his face close to his. 'We ain't here to hurt you, you fucking idiot,' he yelled. 'All we're gonna do is put you back in your truck and take some of the shit from the back. Don't you get that?' He slammed his hand onto the grille beside the driver's head, hard, glad to see the man flinch in fear. His fear should subdue him.

He glanced over at Connor. 'You alright?'

They'd had drivers fight back before, but not often, and with two on one they were usually overpowered quickly. This was the first time they'd actually sustained some physical damage.

'Let's just get on with this,' Connor answered through gritted teeth. He swore under his breath and started to sit up.

As he said the words, the light around them suddenly changed and increased. Cillian's heart leaped into his mouth, and he moved to look around the side of the truck, pausing for barely half a second before he flung the driver to one side and dived towards his brother.

'Get up! *Move!*' he roared.

The car that had rounded the corner screeched to a halt just feet behind the truck, and both doors opened at the same time Cillian reached Connor. He grabbed his jacket and pulled him upwards off the ground, but the two security guards were already running towards them at full pelt.

'Oi!' one shouted.

'Hey, stop right there!' the other cried.

'*Come on*,' Cillian yelled, dragging the bloodied Connor towards their car.

Lily had been right about the Milford vans. All this time he'd just thought her overcautious, foolish for ignoring the opportunity on a hunch. But she'd been right. And now they were screwed.

Hearing the thuds of heavy footfall draw closer, Cillian's eyes shot down to the jack holding up the front of their car and he made a sudden turn, forcing Connor to go with him. They wouldn't make it off the jack and inside the car in time – the security guards were too close.

'Split up,' he ordered. 'Take them one by one.'

He pushed Connor one way, pointing back up the other side of the truck, then legged it in the other direction down the road. He could hear the man keeping pace behind him, heard as he pushed forward and slowly began to close the gap. Cillian gritted his teeth, and prepared to turn and strike. He could hear his brother already fighting with the other one behind him. He couldn't make out who was winning, but he doubted it was Connor with the blow he'd already taken. He needed to deal with this guy quickly and get back to help him.

'Stop!' the one behind him called out. 'I've got this all on camera and the more you run, the worse it will be for you. Trust me!'

'Not fucking likely,' Cillian growled under his breath.

Without warning, he stopped dead and turned round, surprising the guard who was just a couple of seconds behind. As he started to slow, Cillian pulled back his fist and slammed it into the guard's face. His arms flailed out to the side and he flew backward, hitting the ground hard with a grunt.

Knowing this wouldn't keep him down for long, Cillian turned and raced back to find Connor. The sounds of fighting had settled, which *unsettled* Cillian greatly. What was going on?

'Where are you?' he yelled.

'I'm fucking cuffed,' Connor yelled back from somewhere at the back of the truck.

'Shit,' Cillian exclaimed, his eyes widening in horror.

He glanced over his shoulder and saw the man he'd floored stumbling to his feet. This was the worst situation they'd ever been in, and he faltered, panicking, unsure what to do. His instincts were pulling him towards Connor, and despite the fact he'd stopped running, his feet were slowly still leading him in that direction. But Connor was caught, and the guy behind him had started catching up.

'Shit, shit, shit,' he groaned, putting both hands on his head in despair. For the first time since they'd fallen out, he wished to the deepest depths of his soul that his mother was here to tell him what do to.

'Get out of here, Benny,' Connor shouted. A name they used when they didn't want to give away the other's identity.

'Shut up, you,' came another gruff voice.

'They ain't seen you,' Connor continued, ignoring this. 'Just get out, *now*! Get the hell out of here!'

But Cillian's head was already shaking in response. He couldn't leave Connor. Not now. Not ever. They were two halves of one whole, and if one of them fell then they would fall together.

'No,' he called back. 'No.' He sped up, no idea what he was going to do when he reached Connor. He couldn't even see him yet – the truck was still in the way.

'Get *out*, Benny!' the words were stronger this time. An order. A demand. A warning cry filled with deep fear for the safety of a sibling. 'I mean it! Now!'

But Cillian was there, and as he passed the end of the truck, he could see his brother standing on the other side, on the verge, his hands cuffed and his ski mask removed, misery and failure written all over his bloody face.

Connor shook his head in despair. 'Fucking run,' he begged, his voice quiet and broken as his pleas fell on deaf ears.

The guard standing beside Connor tensed and shifted his body into a defensive position that was all too familiar to Cillian. The guy was a boxer, or had been, perhaps in his earlier years. The man glanced back at Connor with a growled warning not to move then started to edge slowly towards Cillian between the front of the security car and the back of the truck, and as the bright beam of the headlights lit up his features, Cillian could see the grim, hardened expression on his weathered face.

He thought about running. He thought about charging the man in front of him and running as fast as he could with Connor down the road. But then he saw the body cam on the guard's stab vest and the second one in the security car. Connor's mask had been removed – his face would be all over the footage.

The footsteps behind grew louder still, and in that instant he knew they were done. There was no way out of this.

He met his brother's eyes across the car between them as all hope died. Their time was up. After all the years they'd spent running the East End, pulling cons and heists – so daring, some of them, that the underworld would talk about them for years – their downfall had come. And it had come for one simple reason. They had strayed from the most basic rule their mother had dinned into them since they were twelve years old. The rule of risk versus reward. She'd warned them that ignoring it would result in being burned. She'd warned them too that ego and overconfidence was the enemy of success in their game. And she'd been right about all of it.

It was oddly poetic really, he thought, as all of this flew through his mind in less than a second – in less than one stride of the men rushing towards him. They'd pulled this job to spite the person who'd given them this life. To turn from her and leave the firm she'd built for them, to leave her with no one but Scarlet to carry on the family legacy she held so dear. And now that would be the exact outcome. She'd be left alone without them, only they wouldn't ride off into the sunset to carve their new path in the underworld, as planned. They'd be riding straight to jail and towards a long stretch behind bars.

Another second passed as Cillian processed this, another beat of his heavy heart and another beat of a foot hitting the ground as the guards closed in. An aching pang of regret shot through him at the terrible mistakes they'd made. At the mistakes *he'd* made. He'd been the one to drive this, not Connor. But Connor would pay for it just the same. Guilt flooded through his soul with a crippling strength as he saw the desolation in his twin's eyes. He thought about Lily and Billie. This would kill them both, Lily especially. He'd let them down. He'd let them all down and now he couldn't take it back.

Dropping his gaze from his brother's, Cillian bowed his head and raised his hands into the air in surrender.

THIRTY-SEVEN

'No!' Connor cried. 'What are you doing?'

'Shut up,' the man still edging towards Cillian spat. He paused as Cillian lifted his hands, straightening up out of his previously aggressive pose and narrowing his gaze at him warily. 'Giving up are ya?' he asked, his tone suspicious.

The guard behind finally reached Cillian and grabbed him roughly, pulling one arm down as he fumbled in his vest for his cuffs. 'About fucking time,' this one added grumpily.

'Here, use these,' the guard in front said, pulling a set of bar cuffs from his inside pocket and holding them out.

The deep chugging of the truck's idling engine and the softer purr of the security car still filled the air, but something about it suddenly changed.

Cillian glanced towards the truck. Had the driver got out of his binds and put it into gear? He'd last seen him near the front grille, his mouth taped and his arms behind him as he watched them all wide-eyed.

The noise grew louder, and the guard standing between the two vehicles looked up at the truck too, a small frown of concern appearing.

As another bright set of lights washed across the truck doors they were all staring at, Cillian's head turned just in time to see the car round the corner. It slowed for a split second, as though it was going to stop, then suddenly it sped up, tyres screeching furiously on the tarmac as it charged forward.

Just as shocked as the rest of them, Cillian stumbled sideways, trying to get out of its path. He was still in the middle of the road, and much as prison wasn't his idea of fun, it was still preferable to being run over.

The guard behind him quickly darted out of the way too. Connor just stared from his place on the verge, as did the guard standing between the security car and the truck, his arm still outstretched, holding the bar cuffs.

By the time any of them realised that the car wasn't trying to get past them, that it was aiming straight for the security car and still gathering speed, it was too late for him to move out of its path. With a yelp of horror, he tried to dive, but the big black Mercedes hit, slamming the security car forward and crushing him between its crumpling bonnet and the undercarriage of the truck.

The sickening crunch of metal on metal and the sound of the three vehicles impacting resounded through the air and then faded to a terrifying silence. The two cars themselves weren't in too bad a state, the bonnets damaged and lights smashed, but otherwise intact. The man now crushed between the car and the bottom of the truck, however, wasn't as lucky. He was slumped forward over the wrecked bonnet of his car, face down, blood splattered all around him. He didn't move or make a sound, clearly dead.

As Cillian stared, in shock, the doors to the car opened and his head whipped round. It took a moment to register what was happening, and to recognise the dresses beneath the two black ski masks that matched his.

'Stop right there,' the guard behind him yelled, finding his voice and trying to take hold of the situation. 'Take those masks off and stand back over there,' he demanded, pointing towards Connor. He grabbed Cillian's arm again, attempting to slap on the handcuffs he'd finally managed to locate, but Cillian pushed him away, watching in awe as Lily marched towards them, her fury evident in her every step, even with the mask on.

'I don't think so, sunshine,' she growled, raising her arm and pointing her revolver at the guard's head.

Immediately, the guard's attitude changed, and he clambered back, almost falling over as he raised his arms in the air. 'Please, look, there's no need for that. I'm just going to back off over here, I didn't see a thing, it was a hit and run, I'll tell them nothing,' he babbled.

Cillian breathed a sigh of relief as Lily reached his side, more thrilled than he'd ever been before in his life to see her. Billie had walked over to Connor, he noted, and was handing him a second gun. Connor checked the barrel before marching off down the side of the truck.

'You OK?' Lily asked. 'What happened to your brother?' Her tone was all business, the way Cillian knew it would be until they were all out of danger and all evidence had been cleared up. It was how she worked. The shit would hit the fan later.

'Driver nutted his nose – he'll live,' he replied.

'How many?' Lily demanded.

'Just these two and the driver. Connor's rounding him up now.'

Lily walked closer to the guard she had her gun trained on and gestured to the ground. 'On your knees. Hands behind your head.'

He began to cry, snivelling and shaking as he did as he was told. 'Please,' he whined. 'I have a family.'

'Yeah, don't we all,' Lily said heavily, her tone edged with accusation as she glared at Cillian. 'Camera. Give it to me,' she barked at the guard, nodding to the body cam on his chest.

'I-I-I...' he stuttered.

'I-I-I don't have all fucking day,' she shouted. 'Camera. *Now.*'

With shaking hands, he unclipped it and handed it to Cillian as Connor reappeared with the driver. He'd had the sense to put his ski mask back on before going after him, so the driver still hadn't seen his face. The guard on the ground *had* seen Connor's face, Cillian thought suddenly, but only briefly and from a distance over the road. It was covered in blood too, from his smashed nose, which should mean the guard wouldn't be able to recall much detail, if any at all.

Connor dumped the driver beside the guard and they leaned together, terrified. Billie walked over and stood beside them silently.

'Go with him to the heist vehicle,' Lily ordered Billie, gesturing to Connor. 'You'll have to drive; we'll deal with his cuffs later. Drive to the south-side barn. He'll direct you. Go straight there, *do not* stop, not for any reason. Do not speed. If you're pulled or catch a tail, stay quiet and follow his lead. Go *now.*'

Billie nodded. Connor handed Lily the gun then led the way to their car. Lily handed Cillian the gun.

'Get the body cam off the other one and rip the main cam and the video storage box out the dash. *Quickly.*'

Cillian hurried off and did as she asked, feeling a devastating wave of guilt wash over him as he moved the other guard's body to get to his camera. He'd never meant for anyone to die. It was supposed to be a straight heist. The man was in his late sixties. This was probably a part-time job, an easy little number to add a bit extra to his pension. He pulled the camera out of the dead man's vest and turned away to the car, feeling a heaviness settle in his chest.

'That everything?' Lily asked as he returned.

'Yeah. All clean,' he replied, holding it out for her to see.

'You got any more rope?'

'No, but I have tape.' He pulled the roll of thick tape out of his pocket and Lily glanced at it before looking back at the guard and then to the handcuffs that had been dropped to the ground.

'Tape his mouth,' she ordered. 'Then cuff him to the side of the truck. Make sure you throw the keys.'

Cillian handed Lily the cameras then grabbed the guard by his vest and yanked him onto his feet.

'Please, oh God, just let me go,' he begged.

'Shut up,' Cillian replied. 'You'll be fine.' He dragged the terrified man over to the truck and cuffed him securely.

'Hurry up – we've been here too long,' Lily warned, an edge to her tone.

Satisfied that the guard was secure, Cillian returned to the driver and pulled him out of the middle of the road, propping him against the wheel of the security car. The driver glared at him, anger in his eyes, but he didn't try to move as Cillian wound the tape tightly around his ankles, Lily's gun still trained on his head.

Cillian finished with the tape then rocked back onto his haunches and stood up, looking down at him with a critical eye. The man was trussed up to the nines. 'He won't move from there,' he confirmed.

'Get in the car,' Lily ordered. She pulled back, lowering her weapon and turning towards the driver's side of her ruined Mercedes.

Cillian jogged around and slipped into the passenger seat, closing the door in silence as Lily restarted the engine. Neither of the headlights came on, and as she reversed, the ear-splitting sound of crashed metal parting made him cringe.

Without even flinching, Lily pulled out onto the road and

moved gently past the two bound men and the mess of the crash, then picked up speed as they left it all behind them. Cillian looked back over his shoulder, still in shock at how close they had been to being sent down tonight. Shocked too, at the price they'd had to pay to get away. The image of the older guard slumped over the hood of the security car came back into his mind and he closed his eyes, trying to force it away.

Turning back, he took a deep breath and glanced sideways at Lily. 'Mum... I'm...'

'Don't,' she demanded through gritted teeth. 'Just don't. I still need to get us across country to the barn without being pulled, and then I need to get this car fixed before anyone notices it's gone or starts asking questions.'

'They won't know it's us. We took the cameras—'

'They *might*,' she shot back. 'There's no footage, no, but your brother's *face* was uncovered. They saw the *car*. If that guard manages to give any detail on either, they may well come asking.' She ripped the ski mask off her face angrily now that they were out of sight, and Cillian could see the fear and fury she was trying hard to contain.

'He won't,' he replied, taking off his own mask. 'He didn't really see Connor; he'd only just come over to me when you hit the security car. It was the other guard who saw him properly, and—' He closed his mouth. He didn't need to tell her why that wasn't a problem anymore.

'You'd better pray you're right,' Lily replied. 'But for now, until I get us back to the barn and out of immediate danger – *if* I can even do that – I don't want to hear another word. I need to focus. But believe you me, when we get to the barn, we will be having a very long conversation indeed.'

THIRTY-EIGHT

Lily gripped the steering wheel tightly as she turned another corner, trying to stop her hands from shaking. Adrenaline coursed through her tense body as she prayed to God they got through the next two roads without meeting another car. They'd been lucky so far, but they weren't there yet.

The south-side barn was the nearest safe place they had to the location of the twins' almighty fuck-up. It would provide enough shelter for her to pause and work out what the hell they thought they were doing, and to hide the car until it could be fixed.

When Billie had come to her earlier that evening and asked to talk privately, this had been the last thing she'd expected. Billie had known something wasn't right; her instincts on point as usual. When Lily had heard what they'd gone to do, her blood had turned to ice. She'd *told* them, time and again, that the Milfords were often followed. They were a complete no go, a potential first-class ticket straight to prison. So why on earth had they done it?

As her blood pressure rose and her frustrated fury threatened to spill over, she took a couple of deep slow breaths.

Cillian had wisely stayed silent since her last order, one small mercy at least. She didn't think she'd be able to stop herself exploding at him if he said even one word right now.

She'd been terrified from the moment Billie had told her, but the second she'd turned that corner and saw them, her two precious sons, being cuffed by those security guards, her heart had leaped into her mouth. She'd slowed, stunned, unable to believe that the worst really had happened. She'd seen that guard's arm outstretched towards Cillian. She'd thought it was a gun in his hand. And then her natural instinct to protect them had taken over. She barely remembered pressing her foot down on the accelerator, or even making that decision. She remembered Billie's voice, her panic as she kept asking Lily what she was doing. But all she cared about was saving her sons, nothing else. Not herself, not Billie, not the car. Nothing but them.

She'd felt remorse pierce right through her when she'd realised it wasn't a gun. When she'd realised she'd killed him. She also knew in that moment that she would do it again, to save her children. But she was so angry that she'd had to. If they'd just listened, if they'd just had one ounce of the sense she'd tried to hammer into them over the years, that man would still be alive. And she wouldn't have his blood on her hands.

Turning the final corner, the metal gate at the start of the track that led to their barn came into view. Connor had left it open, knowing she would be right behind him. Relief flooded through her at the sign that he'd arrived here without issue. She was relieved that *they* had made it too, without being seen. The last thing they needed was a witness. She turned into the lane and crawled down the hill towards the barn.

The minivan was parked up on the side, and Billie was perched on the edge of the passenger seat, her feet on the ground and her head in her hands as she leaned forward on her thighs. The girl was no doubt traumatised after what had happened tonight, Lily thought as she pulled up and cut the engine. Tonight's events would take their toll on all of them, but Billie wasn't used to their world, wasn't used to being faced with the sort of things she'd faced tonight. Lily didn't hold this against her; the girl was strong and her loyalties lay in the right place. She hadn't hesitated when Lily had handed her the gun and asked her to come with her. And anyone prepared to go as far as she was to save her sons had more than earned her respect.

Cillian got out and walked over to Billie, crouching in front of her and lifting her head so he could see her face. Lily looked away, allowing them a few seconds before getting out herself.

'In the barn. Now,' she ordered in a low, furious voice.

For once, both did exactly as she'd asked without question. She followed them, Billie falling in behind.

Inside, Lily turned on the weak battery-powered lamp that hung from the middle rafter. It swung slightly and shone across the space, highlighting their four faces just enough so they could make out each other's expressions. The barn was empty at the moment, other than a few boxes along one wall that housed generic equipment they sometimes needed for jobs, and Lily paced back and forth between them and the door.

'Why?' she finally managed, all her anger and hurt and fear and frustration filling the one simple word.

Cillian looked down and rubbed his neck, and Connor opened his mouth but no words came out. She made a sound of disbelief and wiped her hand down her face.

'I told you *never* to go for a Milford. What little we knew about them was that they send security cars after a load of their trucks. You *knew* this,' she said, her voice getting louder and angrier with each word. 'What were you *thinking*?' She looked at them, from one to the other, her heart breaking as she thought about how close they'd been to being locked up.

'If Billie hadn't told me, if she hadn't known what you were doing was *that fucking stupid*, you'd be on your way to prison right now. On your way towards a fucking life sentence,' she yelled. She put her hand to her mouth for a moment. 'Don't you realise that?' Her voice broke. 'Did it really all just go in one ear and out the other, all these years? Robbery in this country has a maximum sentence of *life imprisonment*. And for *you*, for the Drew twins, two members of a firm the police have spent years and God only knows how much of their budget trying to put behind bars, they'd go all out. They would throw the fucking book at you!'

'It was stupid,' Cillian finally said. 'We thought you'd just told us that, because...' He trailed off and shrugged.

Lily stared at him, her eyes widening. 'That I told you that because *what*?' she asked. 'Because I didn't want the extra money? Because I have some other secret family hidden away that I send to those jobs? Do you even hear yourself?' she spat. 'What possible reason could I ever have to warn you off a job like this other than to protect you? Christ!'

Tears sprang to her eyes as her hurt and frustration boiled over, and she turned away, trying – and failing – to blink them away. They fell down her cheeks, and she wiped them angrily with her hand. Turning back, she stalked a couple of paces towards them, her finger pointed at them in accusation.

'Everything I have *ever* done in this life, since the day you were born, has been for *you*. And you may not want to acknowledge that right now, because you're angry with me, but it's the truth. Every late night, every fight to get to the next level, every piece of my *soul* that I sold to create this firm has been for *you*, for *your* future,' she cried.

'And I have *protected* you, for your entire life.' Her voice wobbled, and the tears began to fall again, but this time she didn't try to hide them. 'I protected you as children, from monsters under the bed and from truths that could hurt you. *Including* Ray,' she added, raising her arms helplessly then dropping them in defeat. 'I protected you as you grew, from enemies and outsiders, from the police, from suffering the same struggles as I did.'

Her heart ached, and she shook her head; all the pain and anger flooded out. 'I have protected you with every ounce of strength and power I have. You have no *idea* the things I have done, the risks I have taken.' She grasped her hair in her fists for a moment. 'I had to leave the fight tonight – you remember that, right? The fight? Our very new, very volatile venture that needed *all of us* there?' She was screeching at them now like a madwoman, but she no longer cared. Tears flowed freely, and for the first time in years, she let the mask drop and allowed them to see everything behind it.

'I left that fight to whatever chaos it turns into, tooled up and drove like a *lunatic* out of London to get to you, because you are more important to me than any part of the business. You're more important than the fourteen years I'd have got for possession if I'd been pulled with those guns. You're more important to me than my ability to breathe. And *then* I find you already cuffed, outnumbered, your face out and on camera, Connor.' She sobbed and looked up to the heavens, turning in a circle as she tried to find the words that would make them understand.

'I killed that man tonight.' She rubbed her face, pressing her cool fingers onto her aching eyelids for a moment before dropping them. 'And I'd do it again,' she admitted defeatedly. 'I would kill, or crush, or shoot, or torture *anyone* if it meant saving you from ruining your lives. Because I am still here protecting you, every single day. And I always will be. Even when you hate me. Even on days like this when what I have to protect you from is yourselves.'

Cillian watched in shock as she crumpled before him, defeated, and her furious, heartbroken words finally hit home. Guilt flooded through every inch of his body, and shame washed over him. Seeing her like this, hearing her voice the things he should never have even questioned, was a hard and overdue wake-up call. He felt as if a bucket of ice-cold water had been thrown over his face, and the red haze he'd been lost in since he'd found out about his true parentage dissipated. He could finally see her clearly again. Without Lily, they would be nowhere. And today, especially, they'd have been done for.

It had hurt, finding out about Ray. It had been a shock that she could have kept something that big from them, and it had thrown them sideways. He still couldn't understand it. But, despite that, he realised now that they should have had enough faith in her to listen and try to work through it.

He closed his eyes with a deep internal groan. What had they done?

Opening them again, he looked to Connor and saw the same shock and realisation and horror in his face. They held each other's gaze for a long, awful moment and then turned back to their mother. Cillian stepped forward and reached out towards her with his hand, the few metres between them feeling like an ocean.

'Mum...' His voice was subdued and tentative. 'I'm so sorry.' He uttered the simple words and sighed, shaking his head.

Lily looked over to him, surprise in her miserable eyes at the unexpected apology.

'We were stupid tonight. I know. And I can't lie, we meant to hurt you by doing it.' He watched her flinch as though he'd punched her in the face and it took all his courage to not break eye contact. 'We felt betrayed by you, when we found out about Ray, that you'd kept that from us all these years and *lied*. And we felt...' He floundered, not sure how to put it into words. 'I don't know, just, a lot of things. And we're still figuring that out.'

'Hiding that from you wasn't—' Lily began.

But Cillian cut her off. 'Please, let me speak.' He rubbed his eyes, stressed. 'We were angry with you and we blamed you. We still do. It wasn't OK to keep that from us. Maybe as kids there were reasons, but we ain't been kids for a long time. Even if you didn't want to tell *him*, *we* had a right to know.' He eyed her now openly. If they were going to have this out, it *all* had to come out. And she had to own her part the way they would own theirs.

'He's right, Mum,' Connor said, moving to stand beside him. 'There was no reason you couldn't have told *us* when we got older. So we knew who we were, where we came from.' He exhaled through his nose unhappily and looked away.

Lily's eyes welled up, and her lip wobbled before she bit down on it hard. She nodded, working to contain herself before she replied. 'Maybe that's true. Maybe I should have sat you down once you grew up. But I knew how much you hated Ray and I didn't want to add that to your burdens for no reason.' She shrugged. 'If it hadn't been for you needing that blood, Cillian, there would never have been any reason to cause you that pain.'

'But life *is* pain, Mum,' Cillian responded. 'You say you've always tried to protect us from things like pain, but that's part of life. And this pain should have been part of *our* life. That wasn't your decision to make, past a certain point.'

Lily nodded and closed her eyes, her forehead creasing into a line of grief as they finally had the conversation they should have had weeks ago. 'You're right. You're right...' She paced a few steps and ran her hands over her face. 'You've grown into two such strong, capable men. Men I am so proud of. But I still see you as those two little boys scraping your knees and climbing trees. And it's hard sometimes to stop shielding you the way you needed me to back then.' She looked away with a sigh, looking ten years older suddenly.

'But you're right. I should have told you, and I'm sorry. I'm sorry that I've caused you both pain. I never meant to hurt you. And I didn't mean to bubble-wrap you either. You *are* adults, and you are entitled to make your own decisions. For the record, that's it. I've never kept anything else from you. And if you have any questions about what happened with Ray back then, I'll answer them truthfully.'

She took a deep breath and stepped closer towards them. 'But this has to stop. You can hate me all you want, you can blame me and pull away, but stupid moves like tonight *must* stop. I'll always protect you, but this was a fucking close shave. You nearly destroyed your lives tonight. *All* our lives. We still ain't even out of the woods yet, and we won't be until the search dies down and the evidence on my car is removed. So, just, no more of this, alright? You got it?' She pulled herself up to full height and sniffed, her hard mask falling back into place as she regained control.

Cillian saw the proud tilt of her chin and the composure that must have cost her a lot to fake and shook his head. 'Nah,' he said. 'It's not alright.'

'*What?*' The exclamation came in sync from both Lily and Billie, who he'd forgotten was still hovering quietly at the back of the room.

'Are you serious?' continued Lily. 'After all—'

'No more stupid moves,' he said, cutting her off and lifting his hands in surrender. He closed the gap between them. 'I promise. I mean the rest. I don't hate you. *We* don't hate you.' He glanced back at Connor. 'This has gone on long enough and has clearly cost us all too much. No more.'

He reached down and wrapped his mother in a hug, amazed as he always was at how small she was in his arms.

After a second, she relaxed and hugged him back fiercely.

'We love you, Mum,' he said quietly.

Connor came over and wrapped his arms around them both, squeezing them in a bear-like grip, and the three of them stayed locked in their healing embrace for some time.

'We do love you, Mum,' he added after a while. 'Though

I'm not really sure you can claim you bubble-wrapped us as kids. You had us picking locks at twelve.'

The words weren't magical and they didn't undo all the pain. But the corners of Lily's mouth rose in amusement for a moment, and Cillian squeezed a little tighter. And just like that, the darkness between them finally started to slip away.

THIRTY-NINE

The rich meaty smell of the minted lamb joint roasting in the oven filled the downstairs of the house as Lily set out an array of vegetables on the side. It seemed lighter in her large, open-plan kitchen today, sunny and warm somehow, and she knew this was because her boys were back. Sunday lunch had always been the most important part of the week for her. It was the coming together of family, no matter what, to just be together. The last few weeks without the boys hadn't been the same.

Today though, they'd come, Billie in tow, and were in the lounge chatting away as though they'd never left. The three of them still had a way to go, she knew. But they were here. And that was all that mattered.

Cath passed Billie a glass of wine over the counter, then another to Lily and then poured her own before putting the bottle back in the fridge and picking out a pinny from the kitchen drawer.

'You sure you don't need any help?' Billie asked again, taking a sip of the crisp white wine.

'No, we've got it covered,' Lily replied, passing a chopping board to Cath. 'It's just these last few bits.'

She gifted her a small smile and Billie returned it.

Cath took a sip of her wine and stared out the kitchen window, her forehead knotting into a frown. 'Where's your car?'

Lily's eyes flickered to meet Billie's for a moment then moved back to the freshly chopped carrots in front of her. 'Oh, it's at the factory.'

'But you weren't at the factory last night. Or is that where you went when you disappeared? *You* disappeared too, come to think of it,' Cath said, turning to Billie with a suspicious gaze. 'What were you two up to?'

Lily's hand paused. 'Listen, if anyone asks where we were last night…'

'I know, *not* at the illegal boxing night that absolutely doesn't exist,' Cath replied.

'Yes,' Lily said slowly. 'But also, we three were here having a girls' night in. We watched *Pretty Woman* and drank a load of wine. You stayed over.'

'Oh, right, alibi time,' Cath said with a sigh. 'Where were you really?'

'Doesn't matter,' Lily replied. 'It's just in case.'

''Course it is,' Cath said drily, pursing her lips.

Billie stood up, looking over to the lounge. 'Think I'll just check on Cillian.'

Cath glared at Lily accusingly once Billie had left the room. 'So what did you do?'

'Nothing,' Lily replied evenly. 'Can you do the courgette in strips? I'm going to grill them.'

'With that garlic-soy marinade?' Cath asked.

'Yep,' Lily replied.

'Want me to make it?'

'Yep.'

'You don't need an alibi for nothing.' Cath turned and pulled the ingredients she needed out of the cupboard. 'Where's the rice vinegar?'

'Top left. There's likely no need for it, but just in case,' Lily replied.

'I don't believe you. You're nearly out of sesame wok oil.'

'I know – it's on the list.'

'You know I don't believe you, or you know you need the oil?' Cath asked.

Lily looked towards the hall at the sound of the front door. Two seconds later, Scarlet walked in, her long dark hair tousled by the wind.

'Hey, sorry I'm late – traffic was murder,' she said, sitting on the stool Billie had just vacated.

Saved by the bell, Lily thought wryly. 'Good to see you,' she said. 'And you're not late – I haven't even put the veggies in yet.'

'Hello, love,' Cath said warmly. 'Where've you been? You didn't say in your note.'

'Manchester,' Scarlet replied, hopping back off the stool and walking to the cupboard.

'See, Lil? That's how you answer that question,' Cath stated sarcastically. 'With an actual answer. It's not that hard.' She gave Lily a pointed stare and then got back to slicing the courgettes. 'Have fun, did you, love?'

Scarlet picked out a wine glass and filled it with the rest of the bottle in the fridge. 'After a fashion,' she replied.

Lily studied her face. 'Did everything go OK?'

Scarlet nodded. 'It did. It went exactly to plan, in fact. We got everything we need.'

Lily smiled. 'Perfect.'

'I'm assuming I don't want to know,' Cath said in a clipped tone.

'You assume correctly,' Lily replied, picking up her glass.

'Whatever.' Cath untied her pinny and dropped it dramatically on the side. 'I'm popping out to the car to grab something – in case you need me for another blind alibi in the next two minutes,' she said scathingly.

'Cath, I told you, it's nothing. Just covering the bases,' Lily called after her, trying to placate her sister-in-law. She could have told her, but she couldn't be bothered to explain the whole story right now, and Cath's reactions would be too much to deal with. Lily just wanted to enjoy their first Sunday lunch back together as a family.

The TV on the wall behind Scarlet had been on quietly in the background as they cooked and a familiar image caught her eye. She'd been about to chop another carrot, but her hand paused as she listened to the newscaster report on the heist gone wrong and the man killed. Remorse shot through her as they named him and talked of his wife and young grandchildren. She swallowed and tilted her head as she listened, slowly chopping the carrots as she pretended to focus on them.

Scarlet watched her with a frown then turned towards the screen. At times her niece was too sharp, Lily thought with a flutter of annoyance.

'What's going on?' Cath asked as she walked in and followed their gazes to the TV, but Lily barely heard her.

As the item came to a close and the woman moved on to what the police had so far, Lily held her breath.

'... Police say they are looking for a black car, possibly a Mercedes, with a damaged front, and four suspects, two male, two female – and they ask for any member of the public who may have information to step forward. Nina Korowski reports...'

Lily blew out slowly as the news moved on. There had been no detail on them whatsoever, no witness sketch, no markers the guard picked up on that they'd missed, nothing. So long as she got that car cleaned up and back here soon, they should be in the clear. It had already been picked up this morning by the mechanic they used for this sort of thing, and he'd told her he'd have it back within a day or so.

Feeling the tension begin to lift from her shoulders, she

turned towards Cath to ask how the marinade was going but her words were halted by her sister-in-law's accusing glare.

'Car's at the factory, is it?'

Ruby peered through the leaves that hung from the low branches of the tree down the road, her dark eyes full of hate as she watched them all through the large front windows. Her mother and Aunt Cath were in the kitchen, wine in their hands, sorting out the food for the big Sunday lunch. And Scarlet was with them. Scarlet the *usurper*. Scarlet the bitch who sat in *her* kitchen, with *her* family, while Ruby had to wait this dance out in the cold.

Her cousin had been so very clever in turning the family against her. Oh, Ruby hadn't helped herself at first. She knew that. She'd not always been easy, disappearing off into drug dens and making bad choices. But she'd put that behind her when she'd come back, and she'd worked hard to create a fresh start. Her family had been behind her, thrilled that she was ready to take her rightful place beside them. But Scarlet had worked against her from the beginning, belittling her, trying to keep her down, trying to force her out.

With one last glare, Ruby turned and walked away. She would be back here soon, but it wasn't yet time. The scales still needed balancing, and she was nearly ready to do what needed to be done. Scarlet had asked for what was coming; she deserved it. And once Ruby was done cleansing her family of that poisonous leech, she would bring in a whole new era. An era without Scarlet. An era with Ruby by her mother and brothers' side. An era where she finally showed both her family and the rest of the underworld exactly what she was made of.

FORTY

Running down the stairs, Scarlet's eyes swept the hallway for her handbag. She'd overslept, having indulged in too many drinks the evening before. Lily had been in a celebratory mood with the twins back, and the wine had flowed with abandon.

Her eyes lingered on the large, framed picture of their family in pride of place on the wall, the same way they did every morning. She'd been seventeen when they'd done that photo shoot. There she sat between her parents as they leaned towards her with smiles on their faces, no idea they had barely a year left before Ronan would be taken from them.

'Miss you, Dad,' she whispered under her breath before carrying on to the kitchen.

Cath was leaning over the breakfast bar with a grim look and a greenish tinge to her skin as she stared into her coffee.

'Jesus, you look terrible,' Scarlet remarked, trying to hide a grin of amusement as she recalled hoisting her mother inside the night before while she'd bellowed out the words to ABBA's 'Dancing Queen' for the whole street to hear.

'Well thank you very much,' Cath replied witheringly. 'Kick a dog while she's down, why don't ya...'

Scarlet let out a low chuckle. 'I did try and tell you not to open that last bottle.'

'You should have just hidden *all* the wine from me at that point,' Cath groaned.

'It wasn't wine,' Scarlet replied wryly. 'It was vodka.'

'*Vodka?*' Cath exclaimed. She shook her head and raised her eyebrows. 'I don't even remember drinking vodka.'

'I didn't think you would.' Scarlet pulled open the medicine drawer and found the paracetamol. 'Here.' She placed them in front of her mother. 'Take some of these and go back to bed. It's quiet at the salon – Sandra can open up and I'll head over in a bit. Take the day off.'

'Are you sure?' Cath twisted her face into a look of guilty wistfulness. 'I can still go in if you need me.'

'No, honestly, don't worry. I'll call you later and bring us home a Chinese, yeah?'

'Alright, if you're really sure,' Cath said uncertainly.

'I am.' Scarlet grabbed a banana from the fruit bowl and picked up her keys. 'See you later.'

From a glance out through the upstairs windows, it appeared that there were no police cars waiting for her this morning, which was a refreshing change. It meant she could actually get on with some of the less-legal business that was piling up, waiting for attention.

She closed the front door behind her then tripped lightly down the steps to the car and almost got in before something on the bonnet caught her eye.

With a frown, she walked around the door to take a closer look. Two words had been sprayed into the sleek black paint-work, with shaving foam she presumed, by the way it had corroded the shine.

Tick-tock.

Scarlet scanned the street, wondering whether Ruby was

still there. Whether she was watching for her reaction. But there was no movement.

She clenched her jaw and seethed as Ruby's attempts to get to her started to work. It wasn't the actions themselves that particularly bothered her – they were stupid and spineless; it was the fact that her cousin was coming so close and then hiding out of sight. Out of reach. She was taunting her, while all Scarlet dreamed of was catching the bitch. But that was the difference between them. Ruby had always hidden behind walls built from vicious deceit, lashing out from a distance like a coward. Scarlet dealt with things head-on. But she couldn't deal with her if she couldn't find her.

Slamming the door of her car shut, she stalked back to the house and opened the door.

'I'm taking your car today,' she called through as she exchanged her keys with her mother's.

'OK, love,' Cath called back, her voice still thick with hangover.

Scarlet closed the door for the second time and headed for the other car on their drive, pulling her phone out of her bag as she slid into the driver's seat. She dialled a number and started the car as she waited for it to connect.

'Where are you? We need to talk. I need to accelerate the plan...'

Pulling up on the side of the backstreet she'd been instructed to go to, she peered through the window at the large run-down housing estate in front of her. High-rise concrete buildings were nestled together, shadowing the thin walkways between. Washing hung out to dry off some of the balconies, and others were bare, their windows boarded up against squatters. Graffiti and damp stains covered the drab grey walls, and Scarlet knew, instinctively, that this was definitely one of Ruby's hiding places. It had all the right markers.

The passenger door opened and Chain slipped in beside her, his muscular frame and thick padded black jacket filling the small space. He looked sideways at her appraisingly, his dark-brown eyes narrowed. 'So why the rush, Scarlet Drew?'

'I'm done playing her games,' Scarlet replied with a hard edge, her jaw set as tightly as her expression. 'She needs dealing with. What have you got for me? Why are we here?'

Chain leaned back on the headrest and stared down towards the estate. 'My boys have spotted her a couple of times around here,' he replied. 'They've been hanging around as much as they can, but there's only so close we can get. It's not our turf – we can't just walk in.'

Scarlet nodded. This estate was outside their jurisdiction too, by just a couple of streets. Ruby had chosen well, if she *was* in there.

'They ain't caught her leaving yet, only coming back. She enters through that archway usually late at night. She moves fast too. You wouldn't catch her if you tried to wait her out and follow her in. This is the closest cover. By the time you get across after her, she could be anywhere.'

'So we need to catch her coming out then,' Scarlet replied.

'We've tried. I think she leaves another way. And it's a big estate, could be anywhere.'

Scarlet exhaled heavily through her nose in frustration. Her eyes flickered up over the tops of the high-rise flats and back down to the gate ahead of them. 'It's like the Eric and Treby – a rabbit warren. She knows we can't go in en masse, and that if I go in alone, I'll have no clue where to start.'

'I wouldn't advise it either,' Chain muttered, glancing at her smart clothes.

'No,' Scarlet agreed. She'd stick out like a sore thumb.

'You chose me then,' she said, changing the subject.

'What?'

'Cillian asked you to report to him before I did,' she reminded him.

'What makes you think I haven't?' Chain asked.

'You haven't,' she stated confidently.

Chain let out a short, sharp chuckle then looked at her with a serious expression. 'I expect that to stay between us.'

'Of course,' Scarlet agreed. 'I protect my people.'

'Yeah? Who protects you?' he asked.

The question stirred up an old memory.

'Aunt Lily takes care of you all, remember?' Lily had said. They were sat on the stairs and she was just a little girl, cuddled under Lily's arm. 'I'll never let anyone hurt you. Any of you. You're safe, I promise.'

'Who looks after you, Aunt Lily?' she'd asked, afraid. 'What if someone comes to hurt you?'

'I don't need anybody to look after me. I'm very strong, my love. No one can hurt me.'

'Well, then I want to be like you when I grow up, Aunt Lily,' she'd replied. 'I want to be strong so no one can hurt me either. Not ever.'

The memory faded and she looked over at him. 'I protect myself,' she replied firmly.

He held her stare for a few moments, until Scarlet broke away and pulled a thick envelope out of her bag. She opened it and pulled out a wad of cash, handing it to him. He slipped it inside his jacket.

'Keep me updated. I need to find her. Soon.' Her grey-blue eyes clouded over as she stared back at the estate. 'I have everything in place. It's time Ruby was taught the lessons she should have learned a long time ago.'

FORTY-ONE

Jenny Ascough watched Scarlet drive away with a deep frown. What on earth was going on with the Drews right now?

She'd seen Ruby, in the early hours of that morning, spraying Scarlet's car. It had seemed a bizarre thing to do, even by their standards. Ruby's appearance had triggered her unresolved anger, and the hot, uncomfortable sense of injustice that came with it. It had been the first time she'd seen the woman who'd been the root cause of the chain of events leading to John's disappearance, and it had thrown her at first. She wanted, so much, to confront her. To ask Ruby why she had played with them all the way she had, why she'd used her like a pawn. Why she'd used Ascough's tender feelings towards John as if they were cards in a game, there to be played and displayed in a losing hand, for her own gain.

Ruby had set her up to find Scarlet and John, knowing full well once she found out the truth she'd do the right thing and report it. But she'd also set her up for embarrassment and heartbreak. And it had been the hardest pill Ascough had ever had to swallow. How could anyone do that to another person? She'd asked herself that question so many times – and so badly wanted to ask Ruby. But she knew there was no point. There would be no resolution from it. So she didn't confront her. But she did follow her.

She'd almost let Ruby go, intent on waiting for Scarlet, as planned, but she'd been too curious. Abandoning the car she'd swapped with a friend for hers – an extra precaution she'd taken after discovering Scarlet clearly knew hers – she'd followed Ruby on foot, almost losing her a couple of times. But eventually she'd ended up here. Ascough had deliberated about following her into the estate; it was fairly notorious for gang activity. In the end, she'd decided against it and had made her way back towards Scarlet, pondering the strange events of the morning.

She'd been surprised when Scarlet had ended up back here, in the same spot she'd watched Ruby from herself. And her interest grew when the other man had joined her in the car. She recognised his face vaguely from past police files. She couldn't quite place his name, but she knew she'd seen him before. Perhaps he had something to do with John's disappearance. Perhaps he and Scarlet had killed John together.

A shiver ran down her spine, and she put the car into gear, pulling away from the dark, depressing estate. As she turned the corner, her phone rang. She looked at the caller ID and answered, putting it on loudspeaker.

'Guv,' she said in greeting.

'Ascough, how are things? Good weekend?' Jennings asked. His tone was light, but they both knew what he was really asking.

'It was OK,' she replied. 'I followed that lead we talked about on Saturday but nothing came of it. And Sunday was pretty quiet.'

'And this morning?' he asked.

Ascough opened her mouth to tell him about the strange behaviour between Scarlet and Ruby, and about the man she'd seen in the car, but something made her hesitate. She narrowed her gaze at the road ahead as she thought it all over. She didn't want to drip-feed Jennings a load of unimportant rubbish, for fear he'd lose interest when she finally did find something of use.

'Nothing of note,' she said eventually. 'I'd better go – I need to get home to change for my shift and I'm driving.'

'OK. We'll catch up soon,' Jennings replied with a note of disappointment.

'Yes, guv. Thanks, guv.' Ascough ended the call and bit her lip.

Something big was heating up between Scarlet and Ruby, but what? And who was that guy with Scarlet in the car?

FORTY-TWO

Isla walked out of the run-down hotel she'd been staying in and glanced both ways down the street before jumping in the waiting car before her. It wasn't a market day, so she hadn't had to walk to meet Connor for once.

Connor blinked and smiled with a look of slight surprise. 'You look different,' he remarked.

'Yeah, well, you know...' She shrugged. 'I'm getting more settled around here now, so I started getting some more permanent clothes and things, rather than living out of my backpack.'

'Yeah?' He looked at her for a moment. 'Well. That's great.'

He set off down the road, and she put her belt on, tucking her freshly styled hair behind one ear.

'It suits ya,' he continued as they turned the corner.

Isla smiled at the compliment. She'd gone shopping the day before, sick of her old jeans and hoodies, of cheap clothes designed for comfort and practicality. Since coming to London and being around the Drews, she couldn't help but feel the vast differences in the way they styled themselves. She couldn't pull off the kind of heels Scarlet and Lily wore, or the skin-tight dresses they were forever encased in. She doubted she'd even have the confidence to put one of those on. But she found herself wanting to make more of an effort, in her own way. So she'd purchased two pairs of smart black skinny jeans and a pair of moderately high-heeled black boots. She'd bought a couple of satin blouses and a few other smart flattering tops, and then she'd gone to a cosmetics shop and let the assistant teach her how to apply her make-up. It had been a long day and so much to take in, but the assistant had been kind and taught her the basics, selling her items which, once applied, gave her a natural look still. Improved but not drastically changed.

She'd picked out a cherry-red satin blouse this morning to add to her new jeans and boots, and had spent an age doing her face, carefully applying the soft bronzer to her cheeks and reapplying the eyeliner three times before it sat right. She'd finished off her new look with a nude lip gloss and a pair of small gold hooped earrings. And now she felt like a million pounds.

The only thing that could have improved her mood was if the job ahead of her was already over. Calvin and Jared were set to come back tomorrow, and the following day they would be carrying out their plan. Her nerves were on edge just thinking about it. What if something went wrong? What if someone saw through the façade and figured out she was a fraud too early? Her stomach flipped over, knots forming within as she stared through the windscreen.

'You alright?' Connor asked, glancing at her.

She immediately smoothed the worry from her face, plastering on a bright smile. 'Yeah, fine. What's up first today? Am I with Lil?'

As she didn't drive, it seemed to have fallen to Connor to pick her up and drop her to wherever Lily wanted her each day. Mostly it was with her, sometimes not.

'Actually you're with me for a bit first,' he replied. 'I need to drop some of the cash off to our laundries. It's already in the back.'

Isla twisted around. She could just make out the brown packages within a gym bag in the footwell where it wasn't quite fully zipped up.

'OK.' There was a lot of cash in that bag. Easily over a hundred grand. Nothing compared to what they had in the safe though, she knew. She glanced at Connor. 'So where are we taking it?'

'Some can go through the pub, some to the salon and the rest through a chain of small takeaways and shops that we run through. You can come with me, get acquainted with how we do this. At some point, we might need you to do the run on your own,' Connor replied, turning down the road in the direction she knew the pub was. 'Then you'll go to the factory and help Mum with some stuff there.'

Isla nodded. 'The money, that's not all the takings from the fight,' she said, working it out in her head. 'There was that extra from the week before too, with Ray…'

'It's too much to put through all at once,' Connor explained. 'The rest has been taken out to one of our safes, one off-radar.'

She glanced at him, her quick mind working over what that meant. 'The one at the barn?'

He shot her a sharp look. 'Maybe. It don't matter for now. What matters is that it's secure. Scarlet's apparently working on a plan to clean it and syphon it back to us, as our current laundries can't take any more.'

'Why do you clean so much anyway? Can't you just use the cash?' Isla asked, curious.

Connor laughed, amused. 'If it was a few quid, sure, we'd get away with it. But the businesses have grown, there's too many big numbers coming in. And we get collared and looked into too often to risk it.'

'What's Scarlet's new plan then?' Isla probed.

'I'm not sure. Mum just mentioned we'd have a meeting

about it soon and that it was a good idea. I don't really care what it is, to be honest, so long as it works,' he said.

'Yeah, 'course,' Isla replied absently.

Two hundred and fifty grand in cash was a lot of money to be added to a safe like that.

A lot of money indeed.

FORTY-THREE

Ruby wearily shrugged her backpack higher up her back, silently cursing the fact she couldn't put the bulky bag of money still shoved in the bottom in a bank or a safe somewhere. It was a heavy load to carry around all the time. But it wasn't safe anywhere but with her, especially while she was staying on Remi's couch.

Still, she was close now, to the end goal. She'd clocked the men that the gang leader from the Eric and Treby had sent out to look for her. They were far from their own turf here, and it was unusual. She'd realised they were likely working for her family in some respect, but she'd wanted to find out who before she gave too much away. Knowing that even her mother didn't have the reach or the manpower to come in and search all the flats here, she'd let them see her, then dived into the estate on the opposite side to where Remi's flat was situated. They'd set up camp there, and she'd given them a second glimpse, and a third, waiting to see who would come when they had enough to report back. Eventually the big boss turned up. And with him had come Scarlet.

This had been what she wanted to know. Who he was

working for. Whose side he was on. And now that she knew, she could use it to her advantage. Scarlet wouldn't want them to deal with her, Ruby knew. Scarlet was predictable. She'd want to face her herself, alone, without anyone's help. Less witnesses for her to worry about telling Lily. Which was perfect for Ruby. She needed Scarlet isolated. All she needed to do now was get her to the scrapyard. But timing was everything. She had to make sure her cousin was going to be available to come at her minion's call, once Ruby let them see her disappear into the scrapyard, make sure she wasn't tied up elsewhere. She was close now. It would all come together over the next few days. She just had to have patience.

Reaching Remi's front door, she knocked and waited to be let in. His face appeared briefly at the window, and as she stepped inside, she could see the signs of withdrawal starting to set in. His gaunt face was more drawn and he hovered, tensely bouncing on the heels of his feet as though standing still was painful. Stacey appeared to be in much the same condition on the other side of the room.

'You got the money for staying here?' Remi snapped.

Ruby nodded, casting her eyes away carefully. 'Here.' She pulled the notes she'd already counted out while safely locked in a coffee shop's bathroom down the road. 'That's for the next three nights.'

Stacey's eyebrows lifted in surprise as she dashed forward to take half of it from Remi, who'd already snatched it out of Ruby's hands. 'Why three?' she asked bluntly, pushing the money down her bra and slipping a foot into one of her dirty trainers by the door.

'I don't think I'll need to stay past then,' Ruby replied. 'I'll be out of your hair. Maybe even before – I'm not sure exactly yet.'

Stacey stopped putting her shoes on and locked eyes with Remi. The look they shared was clear. Neither liked the sound of losing the daily income that had started to support their habit.

'Well, let's not be hasty,' Remi said. 'Where are you going after that?'

'Home,' Ruby said shortly.

Stacey licked her lips and placed herself in front of the door. 'Well that's nice, ain't it?' she said in a low tone that sent a shiver of warning down Ruby's spine. 'Going home. What you been doing here anyway? Eh? I've been wondering actually – where's all this money been coming from?'

'Right, get out of my way,' Ruby snapped, trying to move towards the door.

'I'm just asking,' Stacey replied, blocking Ruby's path. 'Just seems a bit odd really. Is it in your bag?' She lifted an eyebrow.

Ruby felt her heart start to hammer against her chest. If they got hold of this bag and found out how much money was in it, there would be nothing in the world that would stop them from taking it. Two hundred grand – or close to that, after what she'd used for her general expenses – was a lot of money for anyone, but for junkies like them, it would be worth killing for.

'Get out of my way, Stacey,' she said in a low growl, trying to hide her fear. She couldn't let them have it. It was her family's money, the money she needed to give back to them, to show them how genuine she was about working for the good of the whole family and not just herself. If she came home empty-handed, how could she explain that? They'd never believe it had been stolen – they'd assume she'd screwed them over and lied.

The flicker of Stacey's eyes gave away Remi's lunge just early enough for Ruby to duck sideways. She hadn't survived on the streets for all those years without gaining some skills. His hand grabbed at the bag, but she pulled it away and swivelled quickly, shooting a well-aimed kick at the back of his knees. Not expecting her reflexes to be that good, he was caught by surprise and fell heavily to the floor with a cry of anger.

Ruby tensed into a half crouch, trying to keep her eyes on both of them, the exit still blocked by Stacey. Luckily, the girl seemed too stunned to move just yet, but Remi was quick to rise. Acting on instinct, Ruby kicked his groin hard before he could fully stand, and he immediately fell back to the floor with a cry of agony.

He curled up, cradling his privates and screamed out at Stacey, 'Get her, you dumb bitch! What are you waiting for?'

Stacey looked at him and then to Ruby, her wide eyes narrowing with a look of determination.

When she sprang forward, Ruby dived towards her too, head-on, and for a moment they grappled as Stacey tried her hardest to throw Ruby down and twist her sideways to get to the bag. The bag was an extra weight that Ruby had to account for, but even so, she quickly realised she was stronger than Stacey. Like most people who lived only for the next high, she'd neglected herself to the point of emaciation and had no real strength past her desperate will to get to the bag.

Ruby pushed the girl back with all her strength, and Stacey slammed against the door hard, but as she bounced off it, she lurched towards Ruby like a feral cat. Ruby grabbed hold of her hair and yanked her sideways, and she flew across the room, hitting the sofa with a scream of pain and a trail of expletives exploding from her mouth.

Remi was now on his knees, still clutching his privates but with a determined venom in his eyes, and Ruby knew that he was desperate enough for the money that he'd fight through that pain if she stayed even a second longer. She grasped the handle and flung the door open, running outside without pausing to shut it. She ran as fast as she could down the dark narrow footpath, not caring which way she was going, knowing only that she had to put distance between them before either could start chasing after her.

She ran until her legs hurt and her lungs felt as if they could burst. She ran until there was nothing left in her to give. And then finally, in a back alley far away from the place she'd started, she fell into a crouch with her bag against the wall and cried.

FORTY-FOUR

After a long day of hiding out in crowds and basements of coffee shops, Ruby was back in her least-favourite bush, watching the front of the scrapyard. Alan had locked up and was outside lighting his after-work cigarette, and any moment now he would walk away, leaving the coast clear for Ruby to sneak to the back and enter by her hand-made personal entrance.

Alan looked at his watch, took another couple of puffs on his cigarette and then ambled off in the direction of his house. She waited a minute and then slipped down the side and made a beeline for the back. She was tired now, aching from lack of sleep and all the worry, her clothes rumpled and slightly ripe due to the infrequency of being able to wash them, and all she longed for was a clean, comfortable bed. But she couldn't have that. Not yet. For now, she'd have to camp out in the scrapyard. There was nowhere else to go yet. Not until her plan was carried out in full.

She ducked through the hole she'd made at the bottom of the wire fencing and climbed over the scrapheap beyond. Dusting herself off at the bottom, she hoisted her backpack into a better position and looked around with a frown. The dogs weren't there to greet her. Perhaps they weren't as interested today. They knew her scent, knew she was no threat to the place. There was probably something more interesting at the front. A passer-by or cocky squirrel.

As she rounded the first two-storey-high pile of cars and parts, she froze, her eyes widening in shock. Alan, who she'd seen lock up and go home just minutes before, was finishing his cigarette, leaning back on the hood of a half-crumpled car. She thought about running but realised there was little point.

'I wondered when you'd be coming back,' he said casually, appraising her as he took his last puff and then ground out the cigarette butt on the ground. 'Didn't take me long to find where you'd come in last time.'

Ruby watched him warily. 'Have you told anyone I was here?'

He knew who she was, and he most likely knew the whole family was looking for her. Lily used the scrapyard for many various reasons.

'No.' Alan tilted his head to the side, studying her. 'Ain't my place to meddle in family affairs. But I do want to know what you're doing here. Just sleeping rough, or you up to something else? And I want the *truth*,' he warned.

Ruby debated whether to believe him. He could have already called Lily or one of the others, and they could be on their way here right now. But his face was relaxed and open, a seriousness behind his eyes. And he was well known for keeping out of other people's affairs. It was why Lily had trusted him all these years.

'Sleeping rough,' she answered. 'I don't want my family knowing where I am right now.' She watched for his reaction carefully.

Alan nodded, holding her gaze. 'Fair enough.' He sniffed and looked across the end of the large stacked-up yard. 'It's dangerous on the higher piles – don't go clambering about,' he warned. 'Unless you want a house-height of pure metal falling on your head.'

'I won't,' Ruby said, her hopes rising.

'I won't tell anyone you're here, but if you get yourself caught, that's your issue. I'll deny ever seeing you. Your family are regular customers and I don't want to upset that,' he continued.

'Fair enough,' Ruby replied.

'Also, you should know, your mum's car's being dropped here in the morning – early. She'll be in to pick it up before opening,' he told her, in his open, level way. 'It needed some private work done.'

Ruby's heart thumped against the wall of her chest a little harder. She hadn't seen Lily for so long. Had her mum missed her? Was she worried like she used to be when Ruby disappeared, or was she too busy with Scarlet to think about her?

'OK,' she said with a shrug that did nothing to hide her tension. 'I'll stay out the way.'

Alan studied her for a moment and then gave her a grim half-smile. 'Right. Follow me.' He pushed off the car he'd been leaning on and walked around to another section of the yard.

Ruby trailed after him, hoping she'd made the right choice in trusting the man. Her instincts told her she had, but being so close to her goal made her nervous of anything that could throw a spanner in the works.

Alan stopped in front of an old lorry cab. Its wheels were bent at an odd angle, but otherwise it seemed to be fairly intact. He gestured towards it. 'Doors are unlocked and there's three seats in good nick. Should be space enough for you to lie down across them. There's a couple of old blankets up there and a pillow. Can't say it'll be that comfortable, but it'll keep you out of any bad weather at least.'

'Oh.' Ruby was taken aback, totally thrown by the kind gesture. It had been the last thing she'd expected tonight, and a lump of emotion formed in her throat. She swallowed hard and pushed her wild red curls back off her face. 'Thanks,' she managed, her tone softer than it had been for a long time.

Alan shrugged. 'Saw you before. Figured you might just need a hand to get back on your feet. It ain't forever, mind. You need to sort yourself out. But for short-term, as a stopover, knock yourself out.'

'I appreciate it,' Ruby replied sincerely.

'Just remember, I ain't seen ya,' he reminded her with a stern look. He turned around and began to make his way back towards the entrance. 'I'm letting the dogs out now, so they'll be back to say hello. I gather you've already made friends out of them.'

The corners of Ruby's mouth lifted in amusement at the defeat in his tone. She turned back to the cab, climbed the high steps up and got in, smiling a wide, genuine smile when she saw the clean pillow and the two woollen blankets folded neatly on one of the chairs. She closed the door and shrugged off her backpack, slipping it into the footwell. There was a full-looking plastic bag down there, and she tentatively peered in. Inside was a large bottle of water, a multipack of crisps and some chocolate bars. She raised her eyebrows in surprise and then grabbed one of the chocolate bars, unwrapping it quickly and taking a big hungry bite.

She'd been lucky tonight. Alan's reaction to her breaking and entering had been unexpected. For a moment, Ruby felt a flicker of guilt for what he would have to go through once she'd carried out her plan. He'd been so kind to her, despite wanting nothing more than to stay out of their business. And all he'd asked in return was her silence, so that he could continue living his life in peace. But when Ruby was done, he certainly wouldn't be enjoying any peace. He'd have a body on his hands and a whole lot of secrets to keep if he didn't want to get entangled in it all. He'd probably feel responsible somehow too.

Responsible for letting Ruby in, for not telling Lily that he'd seen her. For leaving such a dangerous area the way it was. Good people like him usually did.

But that flicker of guilt died away as quickly as it had risen. She didn't really care what happened to Alan or how her actions impacted on his life. He wasn't anyone important. And if he was weak enough to feel bad about it all, that was *his* problem.

Pulling one of the blankets around her shoulders, Ruby opened one of the packets of crisps and pushed the man who'd bought them for her out of her mind. She didn't care about Alan. She didn't care about anyone. The only things Ruby cared about were getting even with the bitch who'd been such a stain on her life and finally taking back what was rightfully hers.

FORTY-FIVE

Cillian pulled the car to a stop by the front gates of the scrapyard and peered out as Alan, the man who ran it, ambled forward to open the gate. 'You sure you don't want me to hang about?' he asked.

'No, you get home – get some more sleep. You had a late one last night and I don't need you until this afternoon,' Lily replied, casting her eyes over his tired face.

She reached across and held his cheek for a moment, the way she used to when he was a boy. He laughed and pushed her hand away, not unkindly.

'Alright, I know, you missed me. But I ain't going anywhere – you don't need to be soppy every five minutes,' he teased.

'Soppy?' she asked, raising her eyebrows at him. 'You just had something on your face, I'll have you know. I was just saving you the embarrassment of being seen like that out in public.' She sniffed and tilted her chin up pointedly as she told the lie she knew he wouldn't buy for a second. 'And who said I missed you anyway?'

Cillian grinned, his handsome face lighting up in a devilish way as he chuckled.

'Whatever, fine, I missed you,' she admitted with a small grin. 'But only because you're funny. I missed the entertainment, that was all.'

''Course it was,' Cillian replied, still chuckling.

Lily squeezed his arm before opening her door. 'Only joking,' she said as she got out. 'You ain't that funny.' She winked at him then shut the door and walked through the gate that Alan held open for her. Her smile lingered, as did the warmth in her heart at the light banter she'd just shared with her son. It was something she'd always taken for granted before, these everyday interactions. Now, she cherished every one of them. She'd felt lost without her children. She still felt lost without Ruby. She still had scouts out looking for her, but she already knew they wouldn't find her. When Ruby didn't want to be found, she knew exactly how to disappear. Lily had learned that many years ago. It wouldn't ever stop her looking though.

'Alright?' Alan said in greeting, closing the gate behind her.

'Good thanks, Alan. You?' she asked politely.

They walked across the open area at the front of the yard then turned past the first stack of broken cars, out of sight of the entrance.

'All fine here,' he replied. 'Dave dropped it off this morning. All fixed, good as new.'

They turned another corner into a clearing, and Lily cast her eyes over the sleek black Mercedes parked in the middle. All evidence of the crash had been removed, the bonnet, grille and lights all in perfect condition, as though nothing had ever happened.

'I gave him the cash you left – he said there were no additional costs, so you're all square,' Alan informed her.

'Thanks,' Lily replied with a smile. 'That's perfect.' She ran her hand across the grille and took a closer look.

'So, how's the family?' Alan asked.

'They're OK,' Lily replied. 'Most of them anyway. Still no sign of Ruby.' Lily had spread the word throughout their world, to all their contacts, Alan being one of them.

'I'm sure she'll turn up,' Alan replied in his easy way. 'I'm sure she'll miss her family and home too much to stay away for long.'

Lily shot him a small smile that didn't quite reach her eyes. 'It's not quite that simple this time.'

Alan had known their family for many years and had seen Lily's stress rise and fall away as Ruby had come and gone, all the many times she had before. It was only natural he'd assume she'd come home once the drama was over. But that couldn't happen, not this time. This time when she found Ruby, she would have to relocate her outside of their home city. Lily would always be in her life, helping her, supporting and loving her – nothing on this earth could ever change that – but Ruby could no longer return home. She'd gone too far this time. Setting her up with a fresh start a few miles away was the only way of allowing everyone to move forward in peace, *including* Ruby.

'When it comes to family, it's as simple or as complicated as you make it,' Alan offered, looking directly at her with his clear wise eyes.

Lily looked away. 'I agree,' she said heavily. 'And, unfortunately, Ruby complicated it as much as one person possibly could. So she won't be coming home this time. But I do need to find her as soon as possible, to sort some things out. So if you see her, or you hear anything, come straight to me. Not Scarlet,' she warned sharply. 'That's important. *Me.*'

Alan nodded and handed her the keys. 'Will do.'

Lily opened the door and slipped into the driver's seat, then turned on the engine. The Mercedes roared to life and then settled to a smooth purr as it idled. She waited for Alan to move out of the way then pulled it carefully around the corner and through the front gates with a sigh of relief. The car was fixed, there was no evidence of any damage and no paper trail connected to the work. They hadn't had any knocks on the door yet about the heist, but now, even if they did, without a damaged car, they should all be in the clear.

With that out of the way, she could now focus on more pressing matters. And, unfortunately, for people like them, there were always more pressing matters.

Ruby watched her mother pull away through a gap in the stacked crushed cars that made up the wall separating the clearing from the rest of the yard, fire burning in her chest. She wasn't sure what she'd expected Lily to say when she'd settled in here to watch, but hearing her mother tell Alan that she wouldn't be welcome at home had hit her like a spear through the stomach. Stating that, out loud and so calmly, confirmed exactly where Lily's loyalties lay. With *Scarlet*. That snake had wormed her way in so deep that now, when things between them had come to a head, her own mother was taking Scarlet's side. Even now, after all that had happened, Lily still couldn't see her little cousin for who she really was. For *what* she really was – a conniving, wheedling, game-playing thief.

Turning away, Ruby slunk off towards the lorry cab she'd slept in the night before. It wasn't Lily's fault, she told herself. Scarlet was clever, good at masking the ugliness within. And when she was gone, Ruby would forgive Lily her mistakes. She would forgive her for putting her niece before her own daughter and for forgetting what was important in life. Oh yes. Ruby would show them all just how forgiving she was. And then she'd use their shame against them, to make sure they never allowed anything to come between her and her rightful dues ever again.

FORTY-SIX

Isla walked up the stairs towards her hotel room and shrugged the bag of food shopping up onto her arm so she could pull the key from her handbag. It was a new handbag to go with her new look. It was nothing flashy, just a small black leather crossover off the market, but it made her feel smart. She'd walked around with it imagining herself as an important businesswoman going about her day, rather than just Isla, the scruffy girl from the estate with nothing going for her. It was a silly game, really, but it was fun.

She unlocked the door and pushed it open with her leg as she shifted the heavy bag back into her hand. Walking through, she didn't expect the door to slam so quickly behind her, being used to it creaking lazily back on its hinges, and she jumped with a start. As the deep chuckle sounded from behind her, she knew before looking round that he'd been waiting behind the door for her to arrive.

'Did that scare ya, did it, little Isla?' Calvin asked, amused.

She turned with a grin and a swift exhale, putting her hand to her chest. 'I didn't expect you for another couple of hours,' she replied, reaching up to him.

He pushed her back, and his face creased into a dark frown as his eyes raked her up and down. 'What the hell do you look like?'

Isla felt colour flood to her cheeks, feeling crestfallen at his reaction to her new look. She tucked her loose hair behind one ear nervously. 'Don't you like it?' she asked. 'I thought I'd smarten myself up a bit.' She was wearing her new black jeans with a white crossover top that she'd thought quite flattering.

'Why've you put all that shit on your face?' he demanded, grabbing her chin roughly. He turned her face from side to side. 'You look like an idiot,' he declared. 'Like you're trying to imitate the posh slags we're stealing from. What's the *matter* with you?' He curled his lip. 'You look like you're playing dress-up in a whorehouse. I bet they've been laughing their arses off at you, prancing round looking like that. Wash that shit off your face and put your own clothes back on. Go on.' He shoved her towards the bathroom. '*Now.*'

Isla hurried into the bathroom and shut the door as the tears started to pour silently down her face. Shame washed over her as Calvin's words echoed in her head. What had she been thinking? He was right – of *course* she looked like an idiot. But still, his reaction hurt.

Her confidence in tatters, she scrubbed the make-up off her face, hot tears mixing with the cool water she splashed up over the sink. Patting her skin dry, she stared into the mirror at the reddened, miserable face before her.

She reached for the bobble she'd left on the side, quickly pulled the hair she'd so carefully styled that morning into a ponytail and took out the gold hoop earrings. Immediately, the old Isla appeared, the barefaced girl from the estate, and she cast her eyes away, feeling like a fool. She'd been naïve and stupid, waltzing round the way she had, allowing a few new clothes and some face paint to make her feel like she was something else.

Had they been laughing at her? Maybe they had been. Suddenly, she felt horrified and embarrassed by the possibility, and she tutted at herself in annoyance before sniffing and wiping away the last of her tears.

'You're such an idiot, Isla,' she muttered, glaring at herself in the mirror.

'What's taking so long?' Calvin's voice boomed through from the bedroom.

'Just getting changed,' she called back.

Pinching her cheeks, she quickly slipped out of her top and kicked her boots off before shimmying the trousers down her legs. Luckily, she had some of her old clothes hanging on the back of the bathroom door – her old blue jeans and a hoodie – so she shrugged these on.

Opening the door she shuffled through, and joined Calvin at the table in the bay window. She sat down and looked out, trying not to look as embarrassed and miserable as she felt.

'That's better,' he spat. 'Can finally see your face again. If I wanted a dolled-up trollop, I'd be with one, but I'm with *you*. I like you natural, looking like yourself,' he said, gesturing towards what she had on. 'I don't want to see that again, you hear me?'

Isla nodded and forced a small smile.

'Where'd you get the money for it all anyway?' he asked, suspicion creeping into his tone.

Isla shrugged. 'You know they've been paying me. It's how I've been living,' she said.

'Splashing out on a whole new wardrobe and frivolities like that stuff is more than just *living*, Isla,' he replied, his tone changing to a calmer, more calculating tone. One she knew all too well. 'How much they giving you exactly?'

Isla's heart dropped. She'd wondered when this was going to come up. He'd never let her keep more than a small amount of cash back in Manchester. 'It changes all the time,' she lied. 'Not sure what to expect one week to the next.'

'Clearly it's far too much, whatever the amount,' he said. 'And *you* clearly can't be trusted to look after it properly. Where is it?'

Isla turned to look at him now, her gaze level. 'I can, Calvin,' she said carefully. 'I won't buy anything stupid again. But I need it – to live off.'

'You *don't* need it, Isla, because after tonight, we're going back home to Manchester.'

Isla stared at him and raised her eyebrows. He stared back at her, but after a moment, his expression softened slightly, and he gave her a crooked smile.

He put his arms out to the side in an open-armed shrug before dropping them back in his lap. 'I know, I know. You ain't got somewhere to go back to yet. And I've had a think about that.'

'Good, because I really didn't fancy my chances on the street,' she said with a small laugh.

'You've impressed me, putting this job together. It's much bigger than anything we've pulled before, and we'll have some decent money in our pockets for a change once we've shifted it all on. You're so much more now than just the scared little girl I picked up off the floor.' His eyes roamed over her. 'So here's what I'm gonna do. When we get back, I'll tell Jazmin it's over and that I'm moving out.'

Isla's eyebrows shot up in disbelief. Over the few years since they'd started seeing each other, Calvin hadn't once offered her this. He'd been brutally honest about where she stood in his priorities, and it had always been below his wife, so this was entirely new.

'Really?' she asked, unable to stop the shock colouring her tone.

Calvin had married Jazmin several years before he'd taken an interest in Isla. Jazmin's father had been in business with Calvin's, two crooks running the city's drugs together in their heyday, so to disrespect her was unacceptable, Calvin had told Isla. The fathers had eventually handed the reins over and retired, and so Calvin, Jared and Jazmin were equal partners in the drugs game, and in their later venture of making and selling knock-off products, which had been where Isla had worked for them.

'Really,' Calvin answered. 'She's a pain in the arse and keeps too tight a hold on things. We've been trying to push her out for a while; separating should speed things up on that front.'

Isla felt doubtful. She'd met Jazmin – the woman was the fiercest human being she'd ever met. She wouldn't let go of her own business that easily, no matter what Calvin and Jared did.

'We'll set up somewhere nice, and once we've shifted her out, Jared and I can run things our way. And you can stay at home and enjoy being my main woman for a change. I think you've earned that. And I've certainly earned the fucking peace,' Calvin continued.

Isla processed this, not sure what to say.

'Well go on then, smile,' he said. 'You've finally got what you wanted.'

And so she smiled and reached over to take his hand. 'It's in my bag, all of it,' she said, pointing to the handbag she'd discarded on the floor by the food shopping. She knew him better than to think he'd forgotten about the money she still had in her possession.

'Good girl.' Calvin walked over to her handbag and opened it, rifling through all her previously cherished new belongings until he found her cash. He pulled this out and flung the bag into the corner, its contents rattling out across the floor.

Isla stared back out the window. He could take her cash if

he wanted. It wasn't anything new. And it was nothing compared to the rewards that tonight would bring. Right now, that was all that mattered. That this job went perfectly and nothing – absolutely nothing – got in their way.

FORTY-SEVEN

The weighted bag rocked back and forth as Cillian slammed his fists into it, over and over again. His core muscles burned as he pushed himself, working hard as always to keep his physical condition in top form. He enjoyed the burn of these workouts, knowing the pain was for good cause, but as his wound twitched and a sharp, stabbing pain shot through it, he immediately stepped back, wiping the sweat from his forehead with his arm.

He sniffed and walked back to the bench, pulling off his gloves. The wound ached now, the warning that he was pushing too far throbbing through it. With a sigh, he sat down and waited for the pain to subside. A shadow fell across the floor in front of him and he looked up into the concerned face of David Higgs, one of the coaches.

'You alright?' David asked.

'Yeah, just been pushing it a bit hard,' Cillian replied, shrugging it off.

'Let me take a look.'

He gestured towards Cillian's back, and Cillian twisted, lifting his T-shirt. David leaned down to inspect the raw red scarring and placed his hand over it for a moment.

'It's hot. You need to put a cool pack on it and park your training for the day, alright? See how you feel tomorrow.'

'Will do,' Cillian conceded. The coach was right – he needed to be careful. After the butchery Joe had performed before the surgeons at the hospital had patched him up, he had to be careful not to re-open anything internally.

David clapped him on the shoulder, and a look of mutual agreement passed between them before he walked off.

Cillian watched him go back to the ring. He was a good man, David Higgs. And someone Cillian had grossly misread just a couple of months before. When people had started disappearing from the club, he'd mistaken the man's quiet protection towards his son as him hiding a dark, murderous secret and had been sure he was the person they'd been looking for. Cillian had never seen the true culprit coming until it was too late. Until he'd woken up on a filthy operating table in the darkest corner of a forgotten war bunker.

He'd made his peace with David after getting out of hospital, apologising for reading him so wrongly and for the beating David had suffered at the hands of his brother when they'd come searching for him. And, to his credit, David had accepted it with grace, holding no resentment towards him. Cillian had a lot of respect for him for that.

Chucking his gloves and bandages into his gym bag, he took a swig from his water bottle and made his way towards the exit. The plus side of finishing early was that he now had more time to get back to Billie and grab some breakfast with her before he set off to meet Lily. He pulled out his phone and sent her a quick text.

Picking up breakfast from that place you like. What do you fancy? Should be about twenty mins. X

He slipped his phone into his pocket and walked out into

the morning sunshine. Things between him and Billie had shifted after the heist. They'd argued – their first proper explosive argument since they'd met – when they'd got home that night. And the explosions had mainly been from Billie. He'd held his own at first but then fell quiet and allowed her to rant, realising, as she let out all of her fear and frustrations, that whether he liked it or not, she was right.

It had been hard to take, knowing she didn't hold him up on a pedestal the way all the others had, believing him to be all-knowing. His ego was bruised, and part of him felt a crushing disappointment. But during her rant, Billie had reminded him that he wasn't with her because she was like all the others. He was with her because she was straight and direct with him, because she took no shit and because she accepted him for who he was – *all* of him. And that included his shortcomings. She had asked him then whether he wanted to be with someone who only saw his perfect surface, or someone who saw every ugly fault underneath and loved all of him anyway.

That had really thrown him. His ego had deflated. It wasn't a battle of wills, or an attempt to pull him down – it was pure concern born out of love. After all, he wouldn't have even been here had she not gone against him and told Lily what they'd planned. It had been hard to swallow his pride, but he'd backed down and told her she was right. And when she demanded that in future he needed to take her opinions into account, even when it came to his work, he had agreed. Since then, to his surprise, they had become even closer.

Turning the corner towards the back car park, Cillian didn't see the men surrounding his car until it was too late to turn back. He stopped and eyed the man leaning against the door warily.

'What do *you* want?' he asked, his tone showing exactly how unwelcome this visit was.

Ray walked towards him. 'To talk to you. That's all,' he said.

'Well, I ain't got time to talk,' Cillian replied.

Ray was standing between him and his car, three of his men fanned out to the sides, so Cillian stayed where he was, aware that from here he could dive backward to escape the situation if needed. He was too outnumbered to risk cutting off his only exit, especially as he had no idea what Ray wanted.

Ray was a tricky person to predict at the best of times. Were they enemies at the moment or not? Ray had returned the money he'd scammed from the fight night, but Lily had made a bold move with that dealer. That would have been embarrassing for Ray. Was that dealt with, or was this the beginning of a retaliation?

'I only need a few minutes of your time,' Ray pushed.

Cillian narrowed his gaze and glanced over to the other men. 'Why are the rest of the boy band here?' he asked. 'Need them to hold your hand? I ain't carrying.' He raised his arms to the side in an exaggerated move.

Ray exhaled, and one side of his mouth lifted in amusement. 'If I'd thought you were carrying, I'd have guns on you already,' he replied. 'And they ain't here for this – we've just stopped off en route to a meeting.' He clicked his fingers and tilted his head towards his car.

The three men walked off and got in, leaving Ray and Cillian alone.

Ray cast his gaze into the distance and shifted his weight awkwardly. 'You talking to ya mother yet?'

'That ain't your business,' Cillian responded sharply. 'But despite that, yeah, we're good. So you can stop circling like a vulture looking for weakness.'

The muscles in Ray's jaw twitched as he bit back whatever retort had been ready to slip out. 'Good,' he said. 'She needs you.'

'What would you know about what my mum needs?' Cillian asked, moving one step closer to Ray with a frown, all caution gone as his natural defensiveness kicked in. 'You dropped her like a hot fucking stone the minute you found out about us then punished her by going after our business. You've made her life hell.'

'Well I guess that makes two of us then, eh?' Ray shot back in his low, gravelly voice. 'Or three, I should say. The pair of ya threw your toys out the pram too, from what I hear. Freezing her out and treating her like crap. She's your mother, and a *good* one – one who's gone way beyond the normal lengths for you lot. You shouldn't take that for granted.' A warning hardness flashed through his eyes, and for a moment, the two men stared each other out.

'So you do care then?' Cillian eventually said.

Ray shook his head and looked away for a moment, his expression unreadable. 'Care – *love* – ain't never been the problem between me and your mum.' He bit his top lip. 'Hold on to your Billie, Cillian. Something that works that easily between two people ain't always so easy to find.'

'What is that supposed to mean?' Cillian asked, annoyed with himself for getting drawn in even as he asked it.

Ray shook his head again. 'It don't matter. Listen, I'm glad you're back talking to your mum – she does really need you. You lot are all she's ever really cared about. But she ain't what I'm here to discuss.'

'Then what *are* you here to discuss? Because I've got places to be,' Cillian snapped.

Painful flashbacks of the worst day of Cillian's life began to play out in his head, seeing Ray standing there. Ray had been the one to suggest he put himself in the line of fire to draw out the man at the root of all the boxing-club disappearances. Ray had also been the one to pull him out, along with Connor. The one to save him and get him to hospital. The one who gave him the blood he needed to survive. He felt it now, running through his veins like a poison. A poison that kept his heart beating. A poison that caused him no actual harm and was no real poison at all, other than in his thoughts. He knew this rationally. But it was hard to change his feelings towards Ray after decades of free-flowing natural aversion, of making sure Ray stayed an outsider.

Ray wiped a hand across his chin and shifted his weight onto his other foot. 'I know we haven't always seen eye to eye. And I'm not proposing we sit around campfires singing kumbaya,' he added in a defensive tone. 'But with all that's happened, there are some things we need to talk about.'

Cillian shook his head, his defences closing up tightly. 'Nah. There really ain't.'

'Cillian—'

'No, I'm serious.' Cillian cut off Ray's attempts to continue. 'We've gone twenty-eight years without needing to talk, and we can go twenty-eight more, no problem.' He shrugged his gym bag up on his shoulder and walked around Ray towards his car. 'Carry on with your life, Ray, and we'll do the same. We don't need or want nothing from you.'

'Yeah?' Ray challenged, turning to face him. 'You needed my blood not too long ago.'

Cillian clenched his jaw and swivelled round with a flare of anger. 'Want it back, do ya?' he snapped. 'Fucking take it – go on.'

He marched forward until he was right in front of Ray, arms outstretched and a dark challenge in his eyes as he stared at the man who'd fathered him. He knew his reaction was pointless and stupid, but he couldn't stop himself. Ray had hit a nerve. He didn't want to be beholden to him for anything, but this was the one thing he couldn't escape.

Ray stared him out, the fierceness in the older man's eyes reminding Cillian exactly who he was provoking. But even that didn't calm down the fire Ray's words had ignited.

'Don't be fucking stupid,' Ray growled. 'I don't want

anything from you.'

Cillian stepped back, containing his feelings with great difficulty. 'Clearly you do or we wouldn't be here.'

Ray wiped a hand across his chin and paced a couple of steps to the side, his actions serving to diffuse the tension that had gathered through their exchange. 'What are your plans for the future?' he asked.

The swift subject change caught Cillian by surprise and he frowned. 'What, you want my five-year plan?' he asked sarcastically. 'Hate to break it to ya, but we pretty much plan job to job, and focus only on the next mark, same way you do.'

'Five years, ten... What will you be doing then? Same sort of thing you do now, I imagine. Where is there for you to move up in your mum's firm?' Ray asked, watching him carefully.

Cillian let out a loud, sharp bark of surprised laughter and shook his head in disbelief. 'You are unreal. You're seriously trying to *recruit* me? Trying to steal me from my own firm? For what? So I can join your league of goons?' he asked, looking towards Ray's car in disgust. 'Fuck you, Ray. No amount of your blood could buy that.'

Having heard enough, Cillian turned and walked back towards his car.

'I ain't trying to *recruit* you, Cillian. I'm—'

'Save it,' Cillian shot back, cutting him off. He got into the car and threw his gym bag onto the back seat.

Ray muttered expletives under his breath as Cillian started the engine and backed out of his space. He turned the car and let his window down as he crawled past Ray towards the exit.

'Don't come here again. I ain't interested. Ever. My loyalty lies with my firm, and my only family are Billie and the people I grew up with. That's it. And no amount of DNA is ever gonna change that.'

He closed the window and swept out of the car park, leaving Ray behind without a second look back.

FORTY-EIGHT

Scarlet paced her office as Lily relayed instructions to her down the phone. 'Got it. Yeah, I think it's still in the storage room off the casino area. Let me check – hold on.'

She opened her door and walked through to the open space they used for their secret casino nights. The sharp taps of her heels on the hardwood floor echoed around the room as she made her way to a small door at the end. It creaked loudly as she opened it, and she made a mental note to buy some WD40 to ease the hinges.

'Yeah, it's here. If you all head over, we can grab some chairs and go over the plan before we leave for the...' She trailed off as something caught her eye through the voile curtains hanging over one of the large sash windows.

'Oh for the love of God... Scrap that. Jennings is here with a team – they're going to raid the pub. Is there anything here I don't know about?' She paused as Lily answered. 'OK, good. If I don't contact you within an hour, they've pulled me in. Which means you'll have to go through with it without me.'

Two squad cars pulled up, blocking her car in. She seethed, knowing full well they'd done that on purpose.

'I know,' she continued, answering Lily's concerned comments. 'But if that's the case, you'll just have to deliver the surprise without me. I'll call you when I can.'

She ended the call, watching Jennings lead the suited-up team to the front door, then turned and marched out of the room to meet him. He reached the bottom of the stairs as she reached the top, and they glared at each other in mutual hatred for a moment before he ascended to her floor.

She waited as he clicked his fingers towards the offices and the door to the room she'd just left, the men and women who'd followed him up branching off to cover each area. She could hear someone downstairs demanding that the few customers who'd come in for a peaceful drink leave the premises immediately and for Tommy to hand over the key to the drinks cellar.

Jennings brandished a piece of paper and thrust it towards Scarlet with a look of contempt. 'Here's the warrant. I'm sure by now you know the drill,' he said curtly.

She didn't take it, keeping her arms firmly folded. 'And I'm sure by now you know you'll find nothing and this will be a waste of police time and money,' she shot back, lifting her chin as she stared at him coldly.

Jennings pulled the paper back in an irritated motion. 'I'll leave it on your desk. Which one's yours?' he asked with a mocking smile.

'That one,' Scarlet said, nodding towards her open door. 'The one with John Richards hiding in the footwell.'

'Hilarious,' he said witheringly.

'What's hilarious is the fact you continue with this pointless harassment,' Scarlet replied. 'How much exactly *have* you spent now on trying to frame us?'

'We both know you don't need to be framed, Scarlet,' he replied. 'We just need the evidence. And we'll continue doing this until we find it.'

'Oh, I don't think you will,' she replied. 'The thing is – and

I'd wager it's probably something you hate about the body you work for – but the police force is just a business, like any other. They have budgets and goals, and pie charts to show the powers that be the correlation between spend and achievement.'

She stepped closer, watching his pale watery eyes as they filled up with hatred. 'You've followed us for weeks, begged for warrant after warrant to raid our premises, with nothing but the same baseless suspicions each and every time. Even *I* know it must be getting harder to get them passed, when each time you go back with nothing to show.' She raised one eyebrow and watched his weathered cheeks darken as she hit her mark.

Jennings's lip curled up, and he turned into the large room they used for the gambling nights. There was noise coming from the open cupboard Scarlet had been in just minutes before as someone in there searched through the cheap, plain pieces of furniture they kept there for various practical uses.

'You've done this space up nicely, haven't you?' he remarked, ignoring all she'd said.

Scarlet walked in after him, her arms still folded, and looked around with a small smile. 'We certainly did,' she replied.

'And what exactly do you do with it?' he asked, walking around the edges and inspecting the windowsills and the stack of smaller chairs they kept in the corner.

'Oh, you know, sit in the middle and talk about our feelings mostly,' she said with jovial sarcasm.

He turned to look at her and waited for a proper answer.

She laughed under her breath. 'We hire it out for private events. Parties, weddings, corporate functions.'

Jennings held her gaze for a moment, and she could see the cogs working overtime as he tried to figure out what they really did here. But with nothing to point him in the right direction, he ended up at a loss.

'My lawyer already has one complaint of harassment filed against you, from before. You remember that, I'm sure.'

Jennings began to breathe heavily through his nose as he glared at her. 'Yes, I do indeed remember that little game. It even worked, at the time, I'll give you that. But it all got shown up for the hot air it was the moment it came to light that your boyfriend, John, stole the evidence that linked you to the murder of Jasper Snow out of the locker.'

'Except that didn't happen,' Scarlet shot back. 'Yet another tale you and the girl he turned down dreamed up between you.'

She stalked a little closer, stopping at a safe distance from the seething man. 'You have no evidence – the story is circumstantial at best. Which means that *this*' – she gestured around her – 'is harassment, for the second time.'

'Where is he, Scarlet?' Jennings asked, the frustration he felt poured into his words.

'I have no idea. Literally no clue,' she replied honestly. 'But going back to my point, this continued disruption to our lives, our businesses, our homes, the cars you have following our every move is wearing very, *very* thin.'

She watched him register where she was going, saw the miniscule shake of his head and the way he closed his eyes tightly for half a second longer than would pass for a blink, and she knew that *he* knew she'd got him.

'My lawyer is putting the new and improved harassment complaint together as we speak, including all the pictures and dates and times and notes we've kept. The details too of Ascough's little one-woman mission. Did you know she'd broken into my house?'

She raised an eyebrow in question and saw the fleeting look of surprise in his pause before he rounded back in her defence.

'DC Ascough is an upstanding officer and would never go against the laws she upholds,' he declared. 'But, that aside, she's not part of my team on this case. So any claims you have against her are of no relation to ones you believe you may have against me.'

Scarlet had planned not to involve Jenny Ascough at first, out of pity for the other woman. Whatever else was going on, Scarlet understood exactly how painful her heartache was, first-hand. But despite her empathy towards Ascough, she had warned her to stay away and the woman hadn't listened. Scarlet had had to work harder than ever to throw her off these last few days, and her understanding only reached so far. Ascough would have to be forced to abandon her crusade the hard way.

'Well, we'll see what your legal team have to say about that. It certainly doesn't look good, considering her history with this whole situation. Robert will be logging the complaint later today, along with the threat of taking you to court if nothing is done about the situation.' Her expression turned cold, and her grey-blue eyes pierced straight through him. 'So I imagine we'll be seeing a lot less of each other very soon.'

'PC Dawes,' Jennings called to the man still rooting around in her storage cupboard. 'Make sure you conduct a very thorough search. These people have more skeletons than a grave-yard. I'm sure we'll be able to uncover something here today. Check their drinks licence too.'

Scarlet smiled, a dark and genuinely amused smile. He couldn't be more wrong. But that was the thing detectives like him never understood. Professional firms like theirs – the ones worth a damn anyway – kept their legal fronts as clean as a whistle if there was any chance of them being scrutinised. It was what kept them one step ahead, what kept them in the game, thriving through the dark streets of the underworld. There wouldn't even be a receipt out of date order in this place.

'Knock yourself out,' she said. 'I'll leave you to it. Oh, and don't worry about moving your cars to unblock mine – it's a short walk to the factory and I'm in the mood for some fresh air. There's a bit of an odd smell in here, don't you think? Kind of like pork, but when it's on the turn. You know what I mean? Like it's gone well past its sell-by date.'

She eyed him with a steely, challenging gaze for a moment then turned away, not looking back as she dropped her cold parting words. 'Do help yourself to a drink downstairs, won't you? You can raise a toast to your professional funeral. Because after the shame of failing at this so many times and the legal shitshow that's about to begin, that really is all that's ahead of you now.'

FORTY-NINE

Isla sat in the back of the car, next to the bag with all the equipment Calvin and Jared had brought back with them to open the safe. They chattered away with each other in the front, seemingly relaxed and both in good moods as they drew ever closer to the barn where the Drews housed their excess cash and most valuable assets. She went over the plan again in her head, over and over, until it was almost a mantra, using this to keep herself calm. This wasn't her first job, and it would be far from her last, but the cool calmness she usually possessed when she got into work mode eluded her tonight. For the first time, she couldn't shake off the feeling that something was going to go wrong.

Perhaps it was because this was a new city, and a new type of mark. Perhaps it was that there was so much more at stake than the other jobs she'd been involved with. She'd never had so much to lose before. If this went sideways, it wasn't a case of just scarpering and lying low until a disgruntled but average member of society gave up chasing them, or until the police gave up trying to work out which estate reprobate had tried to break in somewhere. This time, the people involved were dangerous, and if things didn't go to plan, she could lose every-thing, her life included.

Calvin turned and appraised her, his eyes meeting hers in the darkness. 'What's wrong?' he asked.

Jared fell silent and glanced at her in the rear-view mirror.

She forced herself to relax and shook off the concern with a small smile. 'Nothing. I'm good. Just tired.'

'Well, you won't have to worry about that no more. Not after tonight,' Calvin said, turning back round. 'You won't be running around at anyone's beck and call, tiring yourself out all the time.'

She nodded. 'Yeah, I know.'

Jared slowed the car and glanced at the map on the screen of the phone in the holder beside him. 'Says it's around here somewhere,' he said. 'Where's the entrance?'

Isla leaned forward and craned her neck between them, peering down the road. 'It's up ahead,' she said, squinting as she tried to make out where the gate was. 'Keep going – it's a bit further.'

Jared drove on, and the car fell into a tense silence.

Eventually, the tufty grass on the verge fell away and she spotted the curve of the dirt track.

'There.' She pointed.

The car turned, and the yellowy beam of the headlights swept over the wooden gate that was set back between the bordering fields on either side. Jared stopped the car, and Calvin turned to her with a pointed look.

'Oh, right.' Isla unbuckled her seat belt and got out of the car. She pushed the gate open quickly then jogged back, knowing it would only annoy them if she took too much time.

Slipping into the back, she barely had time to lift her feet off the ground before Jared drove forward. She swallowed and tried to ignore the warning pounding that had begun in her chest as they wound their way down to the barn.

'This is it, Jared,' Calvin said, excitement in his tone. 'This is the big one.'

'Mate, I have big plans for the cash from this,' Jared replied with a low rumbling chuckle. 'Big fucking plans. I got ideas for a whole new branch of the business.'

'Yeah? Well, count me in, bruv. Whatever you wanna do, we'll go in together, fifty-fifty, same as this job. Same as everything going forward, once we've pushed Jaz out,' Calvin replied, clapping his hand on Jared's shoulder.

Fifty-fifty. Isla turned the words over in her head bitterly. She'd been the one to bring the idea to the table, to scope out the details and lead them to it. And neither of them had thought to even include her in the split.

Jared sniffed. 'I dunno how easy that'll be, man,' he said. 'I know she's your missus and you think you can force it, but she's more clever than she lets on, you know.'

'She ain't as clever as she thinks,' Calvin replied with a sneer. 'Don't get me wrong, we'll have to pay her off, but she's a dumb bitch. We can convince her it's worth a fraction, chuck her enough that she thinks she's doing alright and tell her to piss off out the area.'

Hiding her expression, Isla moved her gaze out of the window to the empty fields beyond. Jazmin was anything but stupid, and underestimating her was like underestimating the distance between your bare arm and a pissed-off python. But she wasn't about to share that opinion.

'What about Sunny?' Jared asked.

This Isla listened to with interest. Sunny was Jazmin's father. He was retired, the same as Calvin and Jared's dad, but he was still a force to be reckoned with.

'I'll spin it to him that she was wrecking the business, that she couldn't handle it. I'll make a show of taking care of her, like it's in her best interest,' Calvin replied.

They pulled to a stop beside the barn, and the brothers

immediately got out of the car. Grabbing the bag next to her, Isla joined them and stared up at the large wooden structure. Under the moonlight, the wood shone silvery grey, all the warmth sapped away by the darkness. The wind rustled through the long grass nearby, and Isla shivered.

This was it. They were here. They really were about to do this. Her heart pumped with adrenaline as she followed them to the double wooden doors.

'Isla, pass me a torch,' Calvin ordered.

She did as he'd asked and peered with wide eyes into the barn as they pulled one door back and walked in. A stack of hay bales stood to one side of the door, and she pointed to the other end.

'There,' she said breathlessly. 'Under that single bale by the tractor. It's under there.'

They shone the torch in the direction she'd pointed and started to make their way over. After a moment of hesitation, Isla began to follow, but before the brothers reached the bale, the loud bang of the wooden door slamming shut behind them echoed around the space, and the barn was suddenly flooded with light.

Jumping at the unexpected sound, Isla turned around, and as she registered who was before her, her eyes widened with horror. Her heart dropped like a frozen stone into the pit of her stomach, the contents of which threatened to reappear as her eyes swept over the Drews, all there together in force, and then locked with the person she feared most in the world.

But the tall, hard-faced woman stared past her to Calvin, pure venom in her eyes.

'Hello, husband,' she hissed. 'Surprised to see me?'

FIFTY

Isla's throat constricted, and she suddenly felt as if she couldn't breathe. This couldn't be happening, she thought. It had to be a bad dream.

There was a short silence, and she glanced behind her at the King brothers. They were both tensed in a defensive position, their eyes flickering across the group of people before them.

'Jaz,' Calvin said carefully. 'What you doing here?'

Isla's attention moved back towards Jazmin, deep fear gripping at her heart. The last time she'd seen her, the woman had been trying to beat down her door to kill her. Now she smiled – a wide, terrifying smile. The smile of a predator who knows its prey has nowhere to run.

'I'm here with my new business partners.' She gestured towards the Drews, her long blood-red nails glistening under the floodlight they'd turned on.

Isla looked to Lily, whose cold eyes were trained on the interaction between Jazmin and Calvin. 'Lil?' she breathed.

'Isla, come here,' Calvin ordered from behind her.

Lily smiled at this command with a dark, knowing expression. 'Why would she do that?' she asked him, stepping forward to stand beside Jazmin. 'She's not with *you*. She's one of us.'

Calvin made a disrespectful snorting sound, still trying to appear unbothered by the fact he was clearly in a very bad position. 'She ain't with you, you stupid bint,' he declared. 'She's the one who's tried to rob ya.'

Isla watched Connor and Cillian's faces darken as Calvin insulted Lily. Calvin would pay extra for that comment, she knew.

Calvin shrugged and held his arms out. 'Look, I didn't even know this was her plan till just now. But ya know...' He shrugged. 'I was here, figured I should see what she's up to. Clearly a mistake to trespass on your property, and I can see that now. We'd never have come with her had we known she planned to steal your shit.'

Isla's face opened up into an expression of deep shock, her fear momentarily forgotten. She turned to him in amazement. '*That's* how you plan to get out of this?' she asked. 'By throwing *me* under the bus.' She shook her head and let out a humourless laugh. 'I'm not even sure why I'm surprised. I should have seen that coming.'

'Oh, Isla, you wouldn't see a fucking bus coming down a one-way street,' Calvin responded.

He turned to the sea of faces still staring at him. 'She's dumb, I have to admit. It's why I came, to see what she was up to, make sure she was OK. I just can't believe she was planning something this underhand. Honestly, take her,' he offered. 'Do what you need to do. I can't defend her for this; I can't even look at her knowing what she was about to do.'

Suddenly, out of nowhere, a deep bubbling laugh rumbled up from Isla's core and spilled out of her mouth, and she put her hands to her head as she let it all out. She laughed and laughed, the manic sound filling the space around them and up to the rafters as the rest of them watched in silence. Eventually, she stopped and sighed out a deep breath, placing her hands on her hips.

Lily looked at her, the corner of her mouth twitching up in amusement. 'Feel better?' she asked.

Isla smiled at her. 'You know what, I really do,' she said with feeling. 'I think that was the icing on the cake.'

'What are you on about?' Calvin demanded.

Isla walked over to stand with Scarlet, Connor and Cillian, making sure to give Jazmin a wide berth. She didn't understand that part yet and she was still completely terrified to see her here, but she trusted in the Drews enough to wait and find out what was going on with that later.

'Isla actually *is* with us,' Lily said in the discomforting calm tone she reserved for moments she was at her most dangerous. 'But you're right about one thing. This *was* her plan. Mostly anyway.'

Jazmin's deadly grin widened, and she wandered off to the hay bales she and the Drews had been hidden behind, taking a seat on one of them. She glanced sideways at Isla, who was still watching her uneasily.

The King brothers were now trying to skirt slowly around to the side of the barn, clearly trying to figure their way out of the trap they'd walked into.

'Look, whatever business you have with her, she's yours,' Calvin said. 'We want no truck with you, alright? So keep her and we'll get out of your hair.'

'I don't think so,' Cillian said, moving forward and pulling a gun out of his pocket. He pointed it at Calvin's head and cocked the trigger.

'Whoa, easy, mate. No need for that,' Jared said, ducking behind his brother.

'You're right, there's no need for this yet. You're not leaving this world that easily,' Cillian replied in a steely tone.

Scarlet moved forward next, standing beside Cillian as she

glared at them both. 'We don't like thieves. Or at least thieves that target one of their own. Because there's a code of conduct in this way of life, isn't there? You don't try to steal from another firm, unless you're ready to take them on and overthrow them for everything they've got. It's war or nothing here. It's the only way to ensure order is kept and chaos doesn't take over. Surely it can't be that different up in Manchester, can it?' She turned her question towards Jazmin.

'No,' Jazmin replied. 'We live by the same code up there when it comes to black-market business.'

'That's what I thought,' Scarlet replied.

'Jaz, please,' Calvin begged. 'You're my fucking *wife*.'

'Yeah?' she asked, seemingly amused. 'So why you here with *her*?'

Jazmin pointed to Isla, and a fresh chill washed through her body. She swallowed and edged closer to Connor, glad he was beside her. Sensing her distress, he reached out and subtly squeezed her arm in a gesture of support.

'She's *nothing*,' Calvin wheedled. 'Just a stupid girl I was trying to help get back on her feet, that's all. I felt I owed her that.'

'Owed me?' Isla spat. She moved closer, staying carefully behind the line of Drews, where Calvin couldn't reach her, and stared at him with open contempt. The memories of all the abuse he'd subjected her to over the last few years flooded through her head and merged into one huge tidal wave of pain.

'Yeah,' she uttered in a deep guttural sound full of that pain as it swirled, refusing to be locked back up. 'Yeah, you owe me alright. But not *this*. You owe me my life back. You owe me every day that you took from me, from the moment I lost my dad at eighteen.' She clamped her jaw shut for a moment as the memory of that time threatened her strength. 'You owe me the rights to my body, my self-esteem, my self-worth.'

'Hark at this... Do you hear yourself?' Calvin spat. 'Jaz, she's a lying cunt. She was a fucking slag when I met her, begging for it, didn't take no for an answer. And I was an idiot, probably drunk when it started. I can't even remember it – it was that blurred for me—'

'*Shut up,*' Isla screamed, her body shaking with the injustice of his words. She'd been a virgin when he'd raped her. A scared vulnerable girl he'd taken and systematically abused every day since.

Connor moved towards Calvin, angered, but Lily stilled him with her arm. Isla put her hands to her cheeks and swallowed, calming herself down as best she could. Lily was giving her a unique gift. The gift of being able to say everything she had ever wanted to say to her abuser. And she was going to use it.

'I never led you on. I never *wanted* you. I was a kid who'd just been left alone in the world and who was *lost*. I was a kid who'd never had a boyfriend, had never been with a man, had never had the courage to even try to talk to a boy I liked.' Tears clouded her vision, and they dropped onto her cheeks before rolling off her face. 'And you took advantage of that.'

'Jaz, you don't believe this bollocks...' Calvin said, looking towards his wife with pleading eyes.

'A few days ago I probably wouldn't have been interested in her version of events, no,' Jazmin said in a bored drawl. 'But then I met my new mate Scarlet here. And we had a very long talk. And I learned a lot.' She pulled a face, wrinkling her nose. 'And now – yeah – I actually do believe that bollocks. I mean, she ain't the first, is she? At some point, when girls all start to tell the same tale, you've got to wonder why.'

Isla looked over to Jazmin, thrown by the surprising source of support. Jazmin met her gaze and exhaled slowly, not exactly smiling but not shooting murderous daggers at her either.

Spurred on by this, Isla held her head a little higher as she turned back to Calvin. 'You took everything from me before I even had a chance in life.'

'I gave you everything,' he shot back, glaring at her. 'You had nothing. You were just another fucking hood rat with no hope and no future. I sorted you out a flat, bought you furniture, fed you, clothed you and looked after you – and *this* is how you repay me? Making out you were somehow abused.'

'I worked my arse off in your hooky factory, night and day, and you gave me lower wages than *anyone* so that I couldn't afford to look after myself. So I was *forced* to accept your help. I couldn't afford to pay bills and buy food in the same month with the little cash you allowed me,' Isla shot back heatedly. 'You made me reliant on you, then used me any way you wanted. And we *both* know that, don't we?' She lifted an eyebrow. 'If you weren't screwing me whenever it took your fancy, you were beating the shit out of me to make yourself feel better after a bad day,' she reminded him. 'And if you felt like amusing your-self, you'd play games with my head to make sure I lived in fear. But you know what, I should probably thank you for that. At least partially.' She gave him a crooked half-smile, the action not reaching her eyes. 'Because I learned a lot.'

Calvin had opened his mouth to defend himself, but as she delivered that last line, he paused and narrowed his gaze.

'I learned how to deceive someone and play them right into the position I need them in. Like tonight.' Her brown eyes met his. 'When you found me, I thought all my nightmares had come true. I fed you that lie off the cuff, that I was scoping out this firm. It wasn't planned – I was just jabbering on in the hope you might buy it and go easy on me, and you actually *did* buy it, *really quickly*.' She raised her eyebrows in mocking disdain. 'I mean, I thought it would take more, but I've come to realise that you have a habit of underestimating people.'

Lily silently took Cillian's gun, keeping it trained on Calvin as she murmured some instruction. He tapped Scarlet and the pair walked around the back of the haystacks. They reappeared a moment later with a thick roll of tape and some thin rope.

'I went straight to Lily after you left that day and told her you were here. I told her what I'd said, and how you had jumped at the chance to steal from them,' Isla explained. 'And then I asked for her help in getting rid of you for good, so that I could live my life freely. At first I meant maybe hiding me – or sending you off on a wild goose chase. But she was pretty pissed off that you'd jumped at the chance to steal from them. Apparently they don't take lightly to that around here. So then I suggested playing this all out right up to this very point. And she agreed.' Isla glanced at Jazmin. Her involvement was the only part she hadn't known about.

'You set me up,' he growled.

'You set yourself up,' Isla replied. 'I just laid the bait. And I only did that to save myself from being dragged back to the hellish existence you kept me in before. Or worse perhaps. I've no idea what you had planned.'

'More pain than you can possibly imagine,' he spat furiously. 'And I can fucking promise you you'll find out exactly how much, when I get out of here.'

'You aren't getting out of here,' Isla said calmly. And to her surprise, she actually felt as calm as she sounded. She'd expected this part to be hard. She'd never condemned a man to death before. But she was strangely fine with it. More than fine in fact.

'No one even knows you're here, remember? If your men knew you were here, that might be a problem. But they don't. You said yourself that no one else was to know about this job. Less people to have to split it with, remember?' She watched the realisation dawn. 'No one even knows you're in London. You'll disappear with no trail, and nothing will lead to me.'

'It's true,' Jazmin confirmed as Calvin opened his mouth to

argue. 'I checked before I left. No one has a clue where you two are.'

'Listen, I ain't never done all that to you, Isla,' Jared piped up, carefully moving away from his brother. 'We ain't the same person, yeah? I ain't him. He ain't nothing to me now.'

'You back-stabbing bastard,' Calvin shouted at him, enraged.

'You guarded the door though, didn't you,' Isla replied, looking back at Jared. 'Every time he beat me or raped me. You laughed about it, played along with his games. And you've done your fair share of those same bad things to other girls. I've heard you boast about it. You're the King brothers. The ones who own the estate, who treat all the people within like their own personal supply of whatever you need at the time.'

'You *are* a matching pair of cunts,' Jazmin agreed wryly. 'But that isn't the only reason you're not walking out of here today. You see, business is business, boys. And I just don't think our partnership is working out anymore.' She pulled an expression of mock sadness and shrugged.

'Jaz, I swear, you need to get me out of this and I'll make it worth your while,' Calvin begged urgently.

'Cillian.' Lily nodded towards Jared. 'Secure that one first. And *you*,' she said to Jared, 'you move one muscle and I'll shoot your brother.'

Cillian walked over to Jared and grabbed his wrists, but Jared panicked. He took one last look at Calvin as blind fear took over his face and made his decision.

'Fuck this,' he cried before twisting out of Cillian's grip and trying to bolt for the door.

Two things followed his unwise move simultaneously. Cillian thrust out his foot, tripping the man up so that he sprawled forward and hit the ground with a dull, painful thud, and the resounding echo of a bullet being let off resounded through the barn.

As Jared registered this and looked up at the smoke rising from Lily's gun, Calvin fell to the floor with a high-pitched scream of shock and agony. Isla's eyes widened to the point she felt they might pop out, and her mouth dropped as she saw the blood begin to gush out of the wound on Calvin's thigh.

Lily turned her gun towards Jared, her hand as steady as ever as she cocked the trigger once more. 'Your brother's leg was the last warning I'll give you. The next shot will be between your eyes. Now hold out your fucking hands and do as you're damn well told.'

FIFTY-ONE

Scarlet walked over to Lily as Connor and Cillian finished securing the King brothers to two wooden chairs, placing them back-to-back and binding them together so neither could move. Jared still squirmed, his cries muffled by the thick tape covering his mouth, but Calvin sat stock-still, his eyes the only indicator of his fury and fear.

'Are you going to tell her?' Scarlet asked quietly, her gaze slipping towards the young woman sitting almost in a trance as she watched the twins work.

Jazmin stood silently on the other side of the bound men, her head held high as she stared at her husband with cold triumph.

'I thought about it,' Lily replied, equally as quietly. 'Technically, it's the right thing to do. But she's fragile. Only just beginning to rebuild. And I don't think she'd be able to live with it. I think she'd blame herself, and I can't see that there's anything good to be gained from her knowing.'

Scarlet nodded. Since Isla had come into their lives and Lily had taken a chance on her, they'd been quietly looking into her. At first, they'd only asked Bill Hanlon – a friend they'd used many times over the years to gather information that no one else was skilled enough to get – to confirm the story Isla had given them. But when he came back with snippets of more disturbing information, they'd asked him to delve deeper.

After a few weeks of gathering small pieces of the overall puzzle, Bill had uncovered the full story of what had happened to Isla's father, a man called Ben. He'd disappeared one day, when she'd been just eighteen, and the story the brothers had fed to her and everyone else around them was that a rival firm was suspected of murdering him. They'd spread the news far and wide until it had become fact in people's minds. But there had been one person who'd known the truth. Someone who shared that truth with a few people in whispers, unimpressed by the turn of events. And that truth was that Calvin and Jared had killed the man themselves.

According to Bill's source, they'd embarked on a bender, drinking and snorting cocaine for two days straight before calling a late-night meeting with two of their men. Ben had been one of them. He'd worked for the firm since before the brothers took over and had been close with their father. Annoyed by the fact they'd dragged him out so late while still too inebriated to discuss business, he'd stood up to leave, snapping at them to call him back when they were sober. Things had turned nasty very quickly, the brothers taking offence in their drugged-up, drunken state.

Jared had told him to remember his place, but Calvin, not happy with the simple warning, had begun making lewd comments about his daughter, Isla, in an attempt to goad him, a punishment for the imagined slight. Ben had stood his ground, warning Calvin not to even think about going near his daughter. Taking this as a challenge, Calvin had stated a new intention to ruin Ben's precious daughter and make her his side piece. When Ben roared back that this would happen only over his dead body, Calvin had called his bluff, stabbing him repeatedly until he no longer drew breath.

They'd hidden the murder from everyone, along with the body, swiftly realising their mistake when they'd sobered up. Ben had been a respected member of their firm, someone who'd earned their place long before the brothers took over. But despite realising their mistake, the brothers felt no real remorse, and to add insult to injury, Calvin had quietly gone on and carried out his threats, taking Isla and turning her into his own personal toy.

Scarlet watched Isla as she pushed her hair back behind her ears before hugging her middle in a subconscious gesture of defence. She'd been through so much at the hands of that heartless psycho. But Lily was right – all the truth would bring her now was heartache. Because despite the fact it was no one's fault but Calvin's, if Isla knew the argument that led to Ben's death had been about her, she would only blame herself. It was kinder to leave her in the dark.

She left Lily's side and walked over to Jazmin, stopping beside the tall, strikingly handsome woman. 'You all good?' she asked carefully. 'Feeling OK?'

She still hadn't got the full measure of the other woman yet, and under normal circumstances, they would never have dreamed of bringing someone they'd known so briefly into such a dark and deadly situation. But these weren't normal circumstances, and the benefit of her involvement had been worth the risk.

The risk itself wasn't that she'd publicise these events or become a threat to their freedom. Jazmin was just as much involved as they were, and she wouldn't damn herself. The risk was that now it was all really happening, she might change her mind. Calvin was her husband, and she must have loved him once. Was there still an ember glowing deep down in her heart that could reignite as they reached the point of no return?

There was a lot to lose if so. Because Jazmin was here for more than one reason.

'I've never felt better,' Jazmin replied, her tone resolute. 'You've saved me a lot of hassle here today.'

Curling her lip in a strange expression that was half smile and half disgust, she threw daggers at Calvin. 'Didn't think I'd heard the stupid ideas you bragged about carrying out one day all round our area, did ya?' she asked him. 'Nah, you thought they were all too scared to tell me. People did keep their mouths shut when it came to your whoring, I'll give you that. Well, up until someone let slip about *that* one anyway,' she corrected, pointing at Isla.

Isla turned red and tensed.

'Then they *all* came flooding out, so many of them, all previously hidden by my men, to save my feelings.' She laughed then, a deep guttural laugh. '*Feelings*. For you!' She laughed again. 'That's the funniest part. Or maybe the fact you assumed that silence was out of respect for you was the funniest part. I'm not sure. One of the two.'

She grinned, touching her long dark-red nails to her chin, just below her matching lips. 'Thing is, that wasn't actually the case, my dear, ignorant, self-absorbed husband. My men – *my* men,' she repeated, driving it home, 'were never loyal to you. Those who worked for *my* father, for *my* side of the firm, have always been loyal to me. They hid your women for the sake of my peace, but they weren't gonna ignore your talk of pushing me out and taking over my side of the business. I've known for weeks that you've been whinging and wishing and considering making a plan. I mean, you didn't even actually *have* a plan.' She screwed up her face and looked at him in disdain. 'You went round mouthing off and didn't even have a follow through. Pretty stupid, even by your standards.'

Calvin seethed, breathing in and out heavily through his nose as he glared at his wife with deep hatred. Cillian and

Connor wandered back towards Lily, waiting patiently for further instruction.

'I'll be honest, I wasn't actually sure how I was going to oust you first, before you got a chance to give it a go,' Jazmin continued, pulling an awkward face at him. 'The firm is so intertwined, and I couldn't figure a way to deal with you without your men knowing it was me. You're always so careful to let them know what you're doing and keeping them close. So when Scarlet here came to me with an offer to get rid of you both today, while your men are totally in the dark about where you are, I couldn't refuse.' She smiled at Scarlet, then turned back to Calvin.

'I checked it all first of course, asking them where you were. No one had a clue. They even seemed worried, which was great, because I pretended I was too. Wifely concern and all that. They're off scouring Manchester now, certain one of the other gangs has taken you. We'll probably end up with a couple of fights on our hands as they go around accusing people. But your disappearance will fade to an abandoned mystery in time, and I'll bravely pull myself together and run the businesses single-handedly, going forward.'

Calvin growled something from underneath the tape over his mouth.

'What was that, love?' Jazmin asked with mock concern. 'I can't quite make you out.' Her face creased into a grin, and she chuckled in amusement at her own joke.

'Don't worry – things are in good hands. I've actually just agreed a great new deal for the knock-offs,' she told him. 'With the Drews, in fact. We've become their new supplier. It's great for the business, really takes that side of things up a notch, branching out with inter-city deals like this.'

She paused and took a deep breath in, letting it out slowly as her eyes moved over Calvin one last time. 'I married you for the business, you know. Thought you'd be easier to control that way, rather than as just a business partner. I shouldn't have wasted my time. Goodbye, Calvin. I'd say it was fun, but...' She shrugged.

It had been Scarlet's idea. Their markets were still in desperate need of stock, and as yet they hadn't come up with a viable alternative to the heists. She'd wondered, at first, whether the skills Isla had picked up on the Kings' production line could be put into practice here. She'd put the idea to Lily, to use Isla to head up their own operation. But to do that they needed time, and trustworthy production workers, and a space somewhere hidden that it could all be set up. There were more variables than Lily liked and they'd dismissed the idea, but as they did, another potential opportunity had dawned on Scarlet.

The King brothers were going to be out of the picture soon enough, and the reports from Bill had highlighted the feud that was brewing between them and Calvin's wife. Scarlet had persuaded Lily to let her arrange a meeting with Jazmin, initially to discuss the supply deal as though there was nothing else going on. From there, she'd agreed with Lily that she'd carefully feel the situation out, and should there have been no opening for more, she'd have left it at that. However, the further opportunity she'd hoped for *had* come up – Jazmin had been very upfront in their discussions that she would be the only point of contact, telling Scarlet that she planned to be taking the business forward with no partners.

When that green light had flicked on, Scarlet had laid out the offer she *really* wanted. They would take Calvin and Jared off Jazmin's hands and ensure they were never found, leaving Jazmin free to run her business with zero comeback. In return, they wanted a steady supply of the goods they'd been bartering for at half the price they'd previously agreed, for a duration of five years. It cut Jazmin's profit drastically, to a point no businesswoman would usually be happy to agree, but what they were offering had been too good to refuse.

After barely a few seconds of hesitation, she had agreed, with the caveat that they allowed her to be there to watch them die.

That had been when Scarlet had shared Isla's story. There had been a tense moment where Scarlet had thought things were going to take a drastic turn. Jazmin accused them of trying to screw her over, of scamming payment for something they already planned to do, but Scarlet had held her ground. She'd told Jazmin that they had no plans to kill the brothers for what they'd done to Isla, only to punish through light torture before sending them back home with a warning never to return. Killing them was an offer on the table for *her*. It was a lie – the brothers had already sealed their fate with the Drews, but it had been enough to calm Jazmin down.

Jazmin had heard Scarlet out as she revealed the truth behind Calvin's toxic obsession with Isla, and it had been the first time she'd seen something soften behind the fierce woman's eyes. Her acceptance of the truth was the only reason Scarlet had allowed her to come tonight. Isla was safe from her now. Isla was safe from *all* of them.

Jazmin walked across the room to sit back on one of the hay bales, and Scarlet moved with her, aware that Isla was still unaware of all this – and still terrified of the woman. But they hadn't wanted to tell her and risk spooking her before she'd played her part.

She reached Isla and tugged her arm. 'Come with me.'

They walked over to the two men bound together and moved to face Calvin. Picking up on Scarlet's intentions, Cillian picked up a hammer from the array of tools they'd piled to one side and handed it to Scarlet. She offered it to Isla.

'You don't have to take this,' she said, 'but you can if you want to. And now is the time. There won't be another opportunity.'

Isla stared down at it and then up to Calvin, her mouth

pursed as she thought it over. Eventually, she shook her head, meeting his eyes with hers.

'No. I'm better than you,' she said quietly. 'You robbed me of everything you could, and I'll never understand why. But the one thing you can never take is that. That I'm *better* than you, in every way that counts. You'll die tonight, and I'll celebrate that,' she said, a sad smile curving up her face. 'Because this world is better off without you. Both of you. But I won't inflict pain on you while you're vulnerable and can't escape.' A steeliness flashed through her eyes. 'That was *your* thing. And I'm not like you.'

She walked away, and Scarlet's mouth turned upwards in a ghost of a smile. Isla was stronger than she'd thought.

As Isla left, Jazmin stood up and marched towards Scarlet, grabbing the hammer out of her hand. Scarlet tensed, unsure what was going on, and Cillian's arm shot out, pushing her back, but there was no need. Jazmin wasn't turning on them – she was just grasping an opportunity with both hands.

She lifted the hammer high over her head and slammed it down into the region between Calvin's thighs, stepping back to assess her handiwork with gleaming eyes as he released a blood-curdling high-pitched scream of agony, through the tape. He bucked in the chair, shaking and twisting as his screams went on and on, but the binds were too strong, and with the brothers' combined weight, back to back on the chairs, they didn't move.

Jazmin pointed the hammer at Isla. '*That* was for you,' she stated before turning back to her husband with venom in her eyes. '*This*' – she raised the hammer again and slammed it down once more, this time in the open bloody wound on his thigh – 'is for *me*.'

The screams reached even higher, and then after a sudden moment of eerie silence where Calvin looked as though he might pass out, he roused once more and they continued.

'I think that's enough,' Scarlet said to Cillian after Jazmin wiped the handle of the hammer on her jacket and handed it back with a smirk.

Cillian looked over to Lily with an upwards tilt of his chin. Lily nodded and handed her gun to Connor before glancing at Isla and shooting Scarlet a meaningful look.

Scarlet dropped away from the centre of activity and made a beeline for Isla. 'Come on,' she said. 'Let's go outside and get some air.'

'It's happening now?' Isla asked.

Scarlet nodded. 'We can stay if you'd rather.'

She shook her head. 'No. I've had enough of him for one lifetime.'

They walked through the barn, and Scarlet pulled the wooden door closed behind them. Isla breathed in deeply and closed her eyes for a moment, flinching only slightly when the first shot sounded, not moving at all at the second.

Scarlet squeezed her arm, and Isla opened her eyes. 'I'm OK. Really,' she insisted. 'Actually, I'm *great*. For the first time since I can remember, I feel free. I feel...' She searched for the word. 'Peace.'

Scarlet nodded. 'Well, I don't know how much peace I can promise you, being part of this firm,' she said wryly. 'But you *are* part of this firm. And we look after our own. So the one thing I *can* promise you is that you will never have to deal with someone hurting you like that ever again. Because you're one of us now, Isla Carpenter. For better or for worse, you run with the Drews.'

FIFTY-TWO

Lily laced her fingers together and placed them on the plain wooden trestle table she sat at the head of in the gambling room of the pub. Scarlet sat to her side, along with Isla, Cillian faced her from the other end, and Connor and Jazmin completed the circle.

'Now that we're all here, we need to discuss what will happen going forward with the goods we'll be buying from Jazmin,' she said, casting her eyes around the table. 'We will no longer be pulling any heists on the trucks.' She paused as her gaze met Cillian's and he cast his down to the table. 'It's too dangerous. This past weekend aside, the risks are getting higher all round. So going forward, we'll no longer be pushing stolen goods through our market stalls; instead, we'll be selling knock-offs. Jazmin has some great lines already going which we'll buy into straight away, and we'll be looking at working with her on other types of designs we know our customers go crazy for.'

This had been one of the additional benefits Lily had brought to the table after Scarlet had succeeded in bringing Jazmin to London. Scarlet had made a good deal – a great one, in fact – but Lily had worked with people like Jazmin for many years and knew the likely pitfalls ahead. The prize of having Calvin and Jared removed from her life was more than worth the drastic drop in profit at first, but after a time, the shine of that end of the deal would wear off. They had to be careful to make sure they continued adding other benefits to the arrangement, to keep Jazmin in check. And one thing they could offer her was their expertise in what designer goods sold quickly and in high quantities. Lily had promised to continue sharing that information and had offered to assist with the set-up of new lines.

'Isla.' Lily turned to the girl, who was watching and listening intently. 'You will be our go-between, dealing with the logistics of getting the stock from Manchester to London, going back and forth, handling any issues that arise and keeping myself and Jazmin up to date with everything.'

Isla's eyes momentarily widened and flickered towards Jazmin, but she quickly tried to hide her feelings and nodded seriously. 'Anything you need,' she said, with a slight undertone of doubt.

'Hey,' Jazmin called to her across the table. 'They're gone. Their reign is over. This is a new start. And as far as I'm concerned, you've got a clean slate.' She leaned back in her chair.

'OK,' Isla replied with a nod. 'Sounds good.'

'Then that's settled,' Lily said, turning to Jazmin. 'Tommy, the man behind the bar downstairs, has a bag with your first payment in. Isla will be in touch about the first shipment next week, and you can organise that between you. It's been good doing business with you.' She offered the woman a tight smile.

Jazmin chuckled and looked around the table. 'Guess that's my cue.' She stood up. 'I'll be seeing ya then.'

They all waited for her to leave and listened for the creak of the downstairs door before Lily continued.

'Now that's sorted, I want to just cover a couple of things

while we're all together. The fight nights.' She looked around at them, raising her eyebrows at her sons. 'There was a small kick-off after I left at the weekend to find you two. A misunderstanding over a misheard comment, from what I gather. Without me, you two, Scarlet or Andy there, it could have turned very nasty. But luckily, as we were so low on men, Jimmy had the forethought to pull in some of the off-duty boxers to help out. They proved themselves to be very handy, sorting it all out quickly before it escalated. We were lucky,' she warned, an edge to her tone. 'But it also showed up some candidates to potentially help out on the regular going forward. Cillian, I want you to find out who they were from Jimmy and size them up. Because I don't know about you, but I've been painfully aware lately that the size of our firm is our biggest vulnerability.'

'What do you mean?' Connor asked with a frown.

Cillian tilted his head and waited, his expression unreadable.

She reached into her handbag and pulled out her cigarettes, lighting one and taking a deep drag before continuing. 'We're not the biggest firm in London, and we've never wanted to be.' She blew out her smoke into the air. 'We've always been happy with our corner of the city, and why not? It's a decent-sized turf and we've done well from it. So I'm not suggesting we start moving the fences and argue with the neighbours – but we need more men.'

She watched their expressions. Cillian was wary, the twist of his mouth indicating he wasn't sure. But he was silent, waiting as usual to hear what else she had to say before he decided what to think. Scarlet's face was more open, neutral as she considered the idea, but one eyebrow slightly hitched in interest.

Connor stared back with a deep frown. 'What's wrong with the people we've got?' he asked defensively.

'Nothing,' Lily replied. 'But a few years ago, when we had roughly the same amount of people we do now, we sat somewhere in the middle of things.'

Isla stood up and nipped to the window to grab an ashtray. Lily smiled her thanks as she placed it in front of her and retook her seat.

'There were the Tylers, at the top of the tree,' she continued, 'then the Greeks in the north and Ray's firm in the south, a few branches down.'

Something dark flickered across Cillian's face, and Lily looked away, choosing not to address it. This wasn't the time.

'They were bigger than us, but not by too much.' She flicked her ash into the ashtray, feeling the weight of her worries settle on her shoulders like a thick cape. 'We always sat in the middle somewhere, along with the Italians, the Jamaicans, the Jews, a few others... And those below us were so much smaller, their businesses so unscalable, that we didn't even need to think about them most of the time. But things have changed.'

She eyed them seriously, her slim face drawn. 'All those firms have been steadily growing, and we're now outnumbered by those we used to sit beside. And the small insignificant firms we paid no mind to before are starting to catch us up. We're falling down the tree, and while, yes, our businesses make good money and we thrive here – if we don't evolve with the rest of the underworld, we *will* be taken over. It's that simple. It's the law of the jungle – I've taught you that lesson many times. Weaker beings are always devoured by stronger predators. And we are *all* predators in this line of work.'

She took another deep drag on her cigarette, her mind going back to the night of the storm and the look in Ray's eyes in the flash of lightning as he'd held her by the neck against the wall. Lily had never been afraid of being alone, and she still wasn't now. But that night had brought home to her the fact that they were vulnerable as a small firm on such a lucrative turf. They needed more protection. And there was a level of protection in numbers.

'So, Cillian, size up Jimmy's boys, see who wants this kind of life. See whether they've got what it takes.' She held his gaze until he nodded.

'And, Scarlet.' She turned to her niece. 'Start putting together some plans for that charity idea of yours. We have too much money lying around, and it needs to be shifted.'

'First-world problems at their finest,' Connor said with a grin.

'Jail-time problems if it's uncovered by the police before we clean it,' she reminded him sternly. 'Money like ours comes with risk and responsibility – you know that.'

Connor held his hands up in mock defeat.

'We need to stick together now, more than ever,' Lily said, looking around. 'Things are changing, and we need to keep up and stay alert. There needs to be no more hidden agendas or reservations between us.' Her gaze lingered on Scarlet for a moment. 'And any issues need to be dealt with as a family.'

Cillian stifled a yawn, and Lily stubbed out her cigarette. The boys had been up all night digging deep graves behind the barn to bury the King brothers in. They were bone-weary now.

'Boys, head home, take today off and come back in the morning. Scarlet, take Isla and divvy up the things that need actioning today. I'm meeting with Bill in an hour to see if he can keep watch over Jazmin for the time being, then I'll head back to the factory.' She stood up and slipped her handbag over her shoulder. 'You can never be too careful with a new business partner.'

The others all stood too, and her gaze slipped down Isla's body with a frown. 'Isla...' She stepped aside, waiting for the others to move out towards the door. 'What happened to your new clothes?'

The girl was back in her old hoodie and jeans, the confidence she'd recently developed subdued once more, and it concerned her. Had the brutality of last night sent her backward? Was she suddenly not sure about the people she'd thrown her lot in with? The last thing Lily wanted was for Isla to only be here out of fear. Fear had a way of developing into all sorts of problems, like a cancer that spread and grew until it couldn't be cured.

'Oh, yeah...' Isla laughed awkwardly, looking away. 'I know I looked a bit stupid in them.'

Lily frowned. 'Who told you that?'

Isla's cheeks flooded crimson, and she pushed her hair behind her ear, not meeting Lily's eye. 'No one – I just caught myself in a mirror.'

Lily pursed her lips, seeing straight through the lie and shrewdly guessing what had happened. 'Was this mirror called Calvin, by any chance?' She raised an eyebrow and waited for Isla to look at her.

'Listen, Isla, I know after all you've been through it must be hard to break old habits, like letting that bastard's words affect you. And it will take time. But I know you're smart enough to see that if he told you that, it wasn't the truth. He would have said that because he hated seeing you look so confident and happy and attractive.'

Isla hung her head, but Lily reached out and lifted her chin with her finger.

'No, listen to me,' she said. 'I'm serious. That's what bullies do, Isla, all of them. They keep their victims in the dark, insecure and unaware of their strengths, so they can continue to treat them like muck and get away with it. It's standard playbook bollocks.'

She looked into the younger girl's eyes, willing her to pull through the damage Calvin had caused. 'I thought you looked very nice in your new clothes and with your hair and your face done. But it doesn't matter what I think, or what he thinks, or what the next person you pass in the street thinks – what matters is what *you* think. And maybe I'm wrong, but I thought I saw you feeling confident and proud in your new look. And that *confidence* was what looked *really* good on you.'

Isla nodded in reply, looking thoughtful, and Lily squeezed her shoulder, leading her towards the door.

'There's hope for you yet,' she said as they walked.

Her words were for Isla, but her thoughts travelled off towards another young woman, and her heart weighed heavier once more. There was hope for Ruby too, if she would let herself be found. She didn't care what Ruby had done in the past anymore – her anger at the girl's actions had long faded. All she wanted now was to find her lost, wayward daughter and pull her in tight, before helping her start anew somewhere safe. Somewhere good. But as the days and the weeks went on, her hope was beginning to crumble, and she couldn't shake the dark feeling that she might never get the chance.

FIFTY-THREE

Scarlet slammed the door to her car and tiredly turned towards the house. It had been a long day after the events of the night before. She'd barely had four hours' sleep after they'd finished clearing the scene, and now all she wanted was to rest.

The porch lights were on, lighting her way in the dark, and she could see her mother through the kitchen window wiggling her hips in time to something on the radio as she filled two large lasagne dishes. She smiled. One would go in their fridge and one would be for Lily, she knew. Her mouth watered as Cath opened the oven and pulled out another dish that was clearly meant for their dinner tonight, steam rising as she placed it on a rack to cool.

As she took her first step up the path, a car screeched to a halt behind her and she turned. The driver's window slid down and Chain's face peered out at her. 'Get in,' he said in a low voice. 'We found her, but we ain't sure how long she'll be there.'

Scarlet's heart rate picked up as she heard the news she'd been waiting for all these weeks. Looking wistfully at her mother once more through the window, and all the welcoming sights of home that beckoned to her aching bones, she bit her lip and turned away, back into the darkness.

'I need my car,' she replied quietly. 'And I need to stop somewhere first. Follow me and then lead me there?'

Chain nodded, and a few seconds later she drove back out of the street, Cath none the wiser to the fact she'd even been there.

Crawling to a stop behind Chain, Scarlet peered out at the large scrapyard. It looked dauntingly eerie at night, the tall piles of cars forming jagged grey walls in the poor light from the moon, long shadows reaching out across the space in between. The front was open enough, but once you delved further in, the place was a maze, she remembered. It was hard enough not to get lost in the daylight, but navigating it at night would be near-on impossible. Then again, she realised, that was probably why Ruby was hiding out there.

Chain left his car and came to lean on the front of hers. He lit a cigarette, the glowing ember from the cherry at the end bright in the otherwise almost total darkness. Scarlet stepped out and joined him, staring at the entrance.

'Nathan saw her go in about an hour ago,' he said quietly. 'She didn't see him.'

'Where did she get in?' Scarlet asked.

'Somewhere near the back. Hole in the fence. He didn't go in after her, but she hasn't come out either.'

'Where is he now?' She cast her gaze across the sleepy industrial area. No one worked here at night, and there were no houses for the next few streets.

'Gone, now that I'm here. He's done his job,' Chain told her.

'As have you,' Scarlet added. 'I've got the money in the car...'

'Later,' Chain said, cutting her off. 'Let's get this done.'

Scarlet's eyebrows shot up. She hadn't expected him to stay.

She didn't particularly want him to either. There were things that needed to be said that were too private and personal for his ears.

'That's OK, I've got it from here,' she said.

'Yeah?' he asked, nodding across the road. 'You wanna go in there alone? You sure?'

She eyed the dark, creepy scrapyard in front of her and then the tall, broad man beside her. The oversized hoodie couldn't hide the well-earned muscles beneath, and for a moment she wavered in her decision. His cap hung low over his eyes and she couldn't see them in the darkness, but she caught his full lips parting into a grin as he caught her assessing him.

Turning away, she pursed her lips, ignoring his deep rumbling chuckle. 'I'm sure,' she said firmly.

This was her fight, no one else's. She hadn't come unprepared and, besides, Ruby wasn't even expecting her. She should be able to catch her off guard. Hopefully not too far in.

She walked back to her car and reached for the bag she'd detoured to pick up. She'd stashed all she needed for this moment a long time ago. Pulling out a pair of trainers, she kicked off her heels into the back footwell and slipped them on.

Chain watched as she pulled out her gun and checked it was still loaded. 'So it's that kind of reunion then.'

She shook her head. 'No. Much as I wish it was, I promised Lil I wouldn't.' She clenched her teeth as a stab of frustration speared through her. She had never lusted for someone's blood the way she did for Ruby's, but she knew she couldn't do it. She sniffed, chucked the bag back in and slammed the door. 'This is just to get her to the car and cuffed to the door.'

Chain pulled a face and nodded slowly. 'If you want to go alone, it ain't my business. But I'll wait here till you're out.'

'Please yourself. Your money's in the dash if you get a better offer,' she said, walking away from him, her head already on the task ahead.

She crossed the road, all the pain and anger and injustice she'd felt over the last few months – over all the years of her life – swirling into a hurricane of emotional adrenaline inside. Ruby had been a toxic disease in their family for too long, and no matter what happened tonight, Scarlet was going to make sure that disease was cured once and for all. She might not be able to kill her, but she was going to make sure Ruby left their city so broken that she never wanted to return. And the rest of them could finally live their lives in peace.

With her mind on the gap in the back fence, Scarlet almost passed the front gate without looking at it, but the nagging sense that something was off caused her to pause. She tried for a second to place what it was, having learned many years before never to ignore her instincts, and then it came to her. There were no dogs. Her forehead creased into a frown, and she cast her eyes slowly around the front of the yard. Alan always kept dogs. They never left the inside of the fence.

Stepping forward, her eyes moved to the handles in the middle of the gate. The chain was hanging loose from one side, the padlock open. Her head shot up, her senses alert now, as she searched for Ruby. This wasn't a coincidence – this was a trap, she realised, her quick brain working it out. Ruby had let herself be seen to lure her here. She should have known just from that. Ruby was a master at staying hidden.

Slowly, she pushed the gate open, cringing as the hinges complained in a loud whining creak. And as she slipped in, she saw her, or rather the silhouette of her, in the moonlight, standing at the other end of the open space at the front, just before the yawning emptiness where the darkness stretched on into the maze beyond.

After no more than a second, Ruby turned and disappeared, her footsteps echoing off into the darkness.

FIFTY-FOUR

Scarlet gritted her teeth and moved forward into the dark, eerie scrapyard, speeding up to a jog in an attempt to catch up with her cousin. Ruby's footsteps still pounded up ahead, growing duller as she ran deeper in and increased the distance between them.

She slowed as the footsteps fell silent, silencing her breaths and pulling back into the shadows. Her grip tightened around the cold metal gun and she drew comfort from the fact she knew Ruby wouldn't have anything as efficient.

'How's my life treating you, Scarlet?' Ruby called, her snide remark coming from somewhere further in.

Gauging the distance between them, Scarlet moved out of the shadows and silently pushed forward in a half crouch, keeping to the edges, her gun pointed ahead.

The bitter taunts continued. 'You calling her Mum yet?'

Scarlet entered a clearing, and once more Ruby's outline came into view on the other side. She paused and glared, though it was too dark for either to see the other's face at this distance.

'The life I've carved is my own,' she shot back. 'The only

person who's fucked up the chances in your life is *you*. I haven't ever needed to steal any part of *your* life. But you stole a big part of mine, didn't you?' Her voice quivered under the weight of the emotion in her words.

'What are you talking about, Scarlet, eh?' came the retort across the clearing. 'Your pig boyfriend?'

'His name is John, as you damn well know,' Scarlet snapped, her anger intensifying as Ruby added insult to injury. She shook as it coursed freely through her body, looking for a release.

'His name was John and he was a man. A *good* man. Someone who valued love and loyalty above everything, and you ruined his life,' she shouted. 'You took away the future he'd worked so hard to build in the force, you took away *our* future together and you made it *impossible* for him to stay in his own home, around his own *people*, his *family*, his *friends*.'

Hot, angry tears fell down her cheeks, but she ignored them. 'He's out there now, somewhere in this big cold world – where I'll never even get to know – trying to start over with nothing and no one.' She shook her head, her grief for all they'd each lost almost overwhelming her for a moment. 'You had no right to destroy him like that. He's a *person*, Ruby, a decent one, and you took everything he held dear. You ruined his life – and mine,' she added. 'And for *what*?'

A cruel, mocking laugh rumbled through the air. 'Good,' Ruby shot back. 'I'm glad I ruined something for you. You deserve it. And for what, you ask? *Revenge*, you stupid, poisonous bitch. Revenge for all you've done and as a taster of all I've got in store for you. 'Cause I ain't stopping at just that. I'm taking *everything* from you, the way I should have a long time ago.'

Scarlet shook her head. 'No. I don't deserve it. And *he* didn't deserve it. He deserved all the love and success in the world. All the happiness we could have shared down the line.'

Fresh tears fell as the deep wound in her heart ripped back open with full force. 'But that ain't something a self-serving psychopath like you could ever possibly understand.'

'Oh, don't worry, Scarlet,' Ruby replied in a low, derisive tone. 'I'm sure wherever he is now, he's found all that happiness and success again with some other girl. He's probably chilling in some hot villa somewhere, balls deep in a local waitress he met at lunchtime.'

'Shut up,' Scarlet snapped. 'You have no idea who you're talking about.'

John's piercing green eyes stared back at her in her mind, his love shining through them. Ruby didn't understand what they'd had.

Her cousin laughed, assuming she'd hit the mark, not realising it was the disrespect to John's character that bothered Scarlet rather than the picture she'd painted. But how could she realise? She'd never loved anyone in her life – she had no idea what really mattered to people.

Raising the gun, Scarlet stepped forward into the clearing, allowing Ruby to get a clearer view of the weapon. 'This is loaded,' she said flatly. 'And I would love you to give me an excuse to fire it right between your eyes. So I'll say this just once... Put your hands in the air and walk past me, back out of this yard, *now*. We're getting in my car and going for a drive, you and me.'

Ruby let out a sound of amusement. 'I don't think so,' she said resolutely. And with that she dived sideways behind the next wall of cars, too quickly for Scarlet to stop her.

Jenny Ascough watched from behind the boot of an old Vauxhall as Scarlet ran after her cousin, reeling from the conversation she'd just heard. Transfixed, she moved to follow them, barely even registering what she was doing.

In a bid to be more covert as she followed Scarlet's move-
ments, she had fixed a small magnetic tracker, no larger than a
penny, underneath her car a couple of days before. It sent a
signal to Ascough's phone, and she'd been watching, since then,
from more of a distance. It was a highly illegal and risky thing to
do, and something she only had the guts to keep up short-term –
if it were found, she could face serious consequences. But she'd
been getting desperate, imagining John's time running out as he
sat in some dark, dismal place under Scarlet's cruel grasp.

Except now, after hearing all Scarlet had just said to Ruby,
out here where she thought she was alone, her guard fully down
and her emotions pouring out through her words, that imagined
reality had just become impossible. All this time, Scarlet had
been telling the truth. Not about all of it of course, but certainly
about her feelings for John and her ignorance of his
whereabouts.

Ascough's hope both lifted and crashed at the same time as
she trailed after them, unable to pull herself away. She'd come
too far now to just walk away. She needed answers. And something told her if she kept listening tonight, she might just get
them.

FIFTY-FIVE

Chain stared at the front of the scrapyard from his position just inside an alleyway running between two small industrial units across the road and exhaled heavily through his nose. Scarlet had made it clear that she didn't need his help and, even if she hadn't, she wasn't his problem. She wasn't part of his crew; whatever business she had here was her own. This was nothing more than a transaction – Ruby's location, for money.

But despite that, he couldn't help but hesitate when the other woman turned up. Who was she? What did she have to do with any of this? Something had pulled at his core as the woman had caught sight of the open gate and slunk in after Scarlet. She wasn't a friend – he could tell that much from how cautiously she'd checked out Scarlet's car before she'd realised it was empty. She hadn't wanted to be seen.

He wiped a hand down his face, muttering again under his breath about how this wasn't his problem, then looked up and down the street with a heavy sigh. Despite everything, he couldn't stop the nagging pull of concern in his chest for the girl. She'd got under his skin over this last year. The naïve, skinny girl with the piercing eyes her cousin had first brought to his shop had turned into a fiercely strong, sharp, deadly woman who he couldn't help but respect, and who'd stirred up something inside him that he couldn't quite place. Her quietness as she soared through the grittiest levels of their world and her natural presence, which needed no volume despite her physical slightness, had transfixed him.

Not that he would ever voice that though. Neither she nor anyone else could ever know he was so entranced by the woman despite his best attempts not to be. And not that it made any difference to the fact she wasn't his problem. He didn't need extra problems – he had enough of his own.

He eyed the gate, mashing his lips together in a grim expression. It had been a few minutes since the woman had entered, and there was no sign of anyone now. He should leave, he told himself. His job was done – he should take the money Scarlet had left him in the glovebox and get back to his life.

But instead, he growled with annoyance and shoved his hands deep into the pockets of his hoodie as he gave up on the internal fight.

'Fuck it,' he muttered, crossing the road. He'd just make sure she was OK. Watch from a distance, check she was alright, and then leave. He definitely wouldn't get any more involved than that.

FIFTY-SIX

Ruby ran down the side of the next wall of vehicles, turning only to check that Scarlet was still behind her. The gun flashed in the moonlight as she tried to keep up, and Ruby smiled coldly. She was faster than Scarlet – a simple edge, but the only one she needed now.

Reaching another corner, she dived sideways into the next clearing, speeding up to cross it as she neared her destination.

She ran up the grated metal, ignoring the unsteady shake of the structure under her feet, reaching the top just as Scarlet ran into view.

'Stop right there,' Scarlet yelled as she slowly walked across the open space, careful to keep her eyes and her gun steadily trained on her cousin.

Ruby stood still and lifted her hands in the air once more then smiled, knowing Scarlet still couldn't see her face in the darkness, the expression almost manic as the excitement inside her bubbled higher. They were so close now. One more strategic step to go and Scarlet's reign was over. Scarlet's whole *life* was over once she followed Ruby up these stairs. And she *would* follow her, Ruby knew without doubt.

Scarlet's most prominent weakness, which Ruby had taken advantage of her entire life, was that she was predictable. Predictable to Ruby at least. It had always been easy for her to manipulate Scarlet's emotional responses to her, to pull her into whatever trap she'd set. A whole lifetime of baiting her verbally and physically, big set-ups designed to hurt her or short jabs when Ruby was simply bored – even after all these years, Scarlet still hadn't worked it out and evolved. And that would be her undoing. In just minutes there would be nothing left but the memory of her. Even her body wouldn't be found for a while. It was so simple and so elegant, this plan, that Ruby wasn't sure she'd ever created anything else so perfectly beautiful.

She took a slow step back, taking the chance to position herself properly while Scarlet was still too far away to see the small movement in the dark.

'This is it, Ruby,' Scarlet called. 'Come down the stairs and I won't shoot you.'

'Hmm, not sure I really believe that,' Ruby replied.

'If I wanted you dead, I'd have shot you already,' Scarlet snapped.

'Oh, I *know* you want me dead. Don't lie, cousin,' Ruby replied with a tone of dismissive disbelief. 'I think we're past all that now, don't you?'

There was a short silence before Scarlet replied. 'I did want you dead,' she admitted, her tone more controlled than before. 'I wanted it more than anything. Part of me always will. But I love my family too much. And though I hate you with every cell in my body, you share the same blood as the rest of us. And killing you means killing a part of them. So I can't,' she said, her voice falling flat with resignation. 'Don't get me wrong, I plan to pay you back for all you've done. And you will *never* be welcome back into our lives, but your life is something I won't take.'

Ruby laughed, shaking her head. 'You talk such big talk for

someone who won't be left with any say,' she said, narrowing her eyes with fresh loathing as she stared down at her. 'I'm going to destroy everything you ever cared about, once you're gone, in the hope you continue to suffer as you look up from hell.'

It was Scarlet's turn to laugh, a short bitter bark. 'More words, Ruby. Never any action behind them, is there?'

She moved closer again, and Ruby watched her carefully. Once Scarlet got close enough, it would be time to move on to the last stage of the plan.

'Slashed tyres, bricks through windows... The car bonnet was irritating, I'll give you that. But that's all you are. An irritant,' Scarlet said sharply.

'Irritants can cause a lot of damage,' Ruby taunted, her dark smile still in place as she counted down her cousin's steps. *So close*, she thought with glee.

'Oh, I know,' Scarlet conceded with a nod. 'You proved that point more than enough times over the years.' Her voice grew harder. 'Come down, Ruby. I'm tired of these games. I can still shoot you without killing you, and my patience is wearing fucking thin now.'

Scarlet reached the jagged piece of door that stuck out from a rusty crushed truck, the point Ruby had decided was close enough, and she laughed. 'I don't think so, bitch. You'll have to fucking catch me first.'

She dived around the corner that she knew Scarlet couldn't see yet, the unusual curve of the catwalk hidden as it wrapped around the other side of this wall of cars, and the shot that her cousin let off with a cry of rage flew safely past her into a pile of junk beyond.

Ruby followed the curve around, so familiar with it now that the darkness didn't faze her as she ducked under stray metal bars and dodged sideways to avoid wing mirrors that stuck out further than the rest. She heard Scarlet behind her, running up the stairs and following as fast as she could on the unfamiliar and hazardous pathway so high off the ground.

Scarlet swore loudly as she hit something, and the sound served only to add to the warmth Ruby felt inside as she rounded the final sharp corner and stopped. This was it. Her eyes gleamed as she backed into her hiding place, waiting for Scarlet to pass.

If she was lucky, Scarlet would miss the round, purposeful gap in the catwalk just ahead and would assume it connected to the other side. It was dark – there was a good chance it might happen. But if not, if she saw it in time and stopped, Ruby was tucked away just a couple of feet behind – in the perfect position to dive out and shove her forward.

The twelve-foot-tall barrel-shaped tank below wasn't visible from up here, but it was two-thirds full, with all the oil that had been drained from the engines of the vehicles that had been crushed and made up the walls of the jagged, chaotic maze they were in. There was a lid that lay over it usually, for safety, but Ruby had removed it. Oil was much harder to tread than water, and there was no way out of the tank once inside. It was a horrible way to die really. But that was another reason she liked it so much.

Scarlet's steps drew closer, and Ruby crouched, ready to send her to meet her maker.

Ascough ducked behind a car, having found another way around the side of the clearing Scarlet had slowed in as she pointed her gun up towards Ruby. From where she'd come out, behind Ruby and ahead of Scarlet, she could see the hidden walkway winding around the back – and could see what Ruby was planning. Or partly at least. She watched her step back in line with the path and listened to the conversation between them play out before Ruby set off again at a sprint.

The gunshot made her jump, and she stopped herself crying out just in time, clapping a hand over her mouth. Scarlet ran up after Ruby, and Ascough moved silently ahead of them below, cutting across to where she thought the catwalk joined up on the other side.

But Ruby suddenly stopped and disappeared from view, and Ascough frowned, peering up at the place she'd just stood. Something clattered behind her, and she whipped her head around, all her senses alert. She peered into the darkness and waited a few beats, but nothing else came.

Shaking off the spook, she cast her eyes back up and moved to get a better look. As she did, Scarlet came back into view, hurrying as fast as she could manage around the dangerous obstacles sticking out across her path, towards where Ruby had been, her gun still outstretched.

Ascough's gaze flickered forward; she was still confused as to where Ruby had gone, and she realised for the first time that there was a wide gap in the walkway. She looked down, and her eyes widened in horror as she saw the tank underneath. Scarlet was headed straight for it.

She opened her mouth but then hesitated. Scarlet would see it – of course she would. Wouldn't she?

Her hand moved up to her forehead as she weighed up the risk of Scarlet not seeing it against the risk to her own safety if they knew she was here. Biting her lip, she continued to watch, unable to tear her eyes away.

Scarlet neared the edge of the gap, and for a moment Ascough stopped breathing as she almost missed it, but she saw it just in time, abruptly pulling to a stop just one step away from the edge. Her arms flew up in surprise, the gun in her hand forgotten for a moment, and Ascough blew out a breath of relief.

That relief was short-lived though, as she caught sight of Ruby once more. Stepping out of the shadows behind her, Ruby lunged towards Scarlet, her hands outstretched and every ounce of her weight thrown forward.

'Scarlet, watch out!' Ascough screamed up to her.

Time seemed to slow as instinct forced her out into the open. Scarlet's head turned at the unexpected warning, and her body tensed in instant defence. Ruby's course was set, no energy held back to change it, but as her body soared towards Scarlet, Scarlet twisted and pulled herself back to one side.

Ruby tried to twist too, clutching at the air as she missed her cousin by inches, but she had thrown herself forward with too much force to stop, and, as she contorted helplessly in the air, her body hurtled backward off the edge of the catwalk and down into the tank below.

FIFTY-SEVEN

Scarlet fell against the bars on the edge of the catwalk, her weight causing it to wobble dangerously for a few moments, and she clutched the top bar to steady herself, watching with surprise and horror as Ruby flew past her and off the edge. Their gazes locked as Ruby twisted and tried to grab her, and she saw the fanatical fury and murder in her cousin's eyes before she fell out of view.

Scarlet dropped her gun with a clatter and scrambled towards the edge in shock. Below, there was some sort of giant vat, filled with a dark liquid she couldn't place. Ruby's head bobbed up, her tight curls plastered to her head with whatever the substance was, and as the smell suddenly registered, she realised it was some sort of vehicle oil.

Dropping onto her stomach, she reached over the edge towards her cousin. 'Grab my hands,' she shouted.

Ruby spluttered and coughed, her head disappearing again under the oil. She reappeared a second later, one hand darting upwards towards Scarlet's as the other flailed helplessly.

'Ruby, *grab my hand*,' Scarlet yelled again, more urgently

this time. 'Come on,' she pressed, reaching as far as her muscles allowed.

Ruby's fingers grazed hers, but she bobbed back down, and Scarlet looked out for whoever had called up the warning. Ascough stood below, staring up at the situation in horror.

'Get up here,' she called to her. '*Now*, Jenny. Help me get her out.'

Ascough ran off towards the stairs, and Scarlet's eyes caught another movement coming from the other side of the clearing. 'Chain, up here – help me!'

She pushed herself further over the edge as Ruby's head bobbed up again, spluttering as she dragged in another gulp of air. The oil was too thick and her clothes too heavy, Scarlet realised. She was being dragged down.

'Reach for me,' she begged. 'Come *on*, Ruby, just *reach*.'

The sound of two pairs of feet drew nearer, and the catwalk shook with their weight, but Scarlet didn't dare turn away for a moment.

Ruby pushed up in a stronger attempt, and for a moment, their hands connected. Scarlet squeezed, trying desperately to maintain a grip, but the oil was too slick, and Ruby's hands slipped away. She tried again, and once more she grasped her cousin's fingers, but she still fell back and under the oil.

Ascough and Chain reached her, and Ascough dropped down by her side. 'Where is she?' she asked in panic. 'What shall I do?'

'Chain,' Scarlet called back, 'grab my legs and ease me over – I need to get closer.'

He kneeled down and wrapped his thick arms around her legs just above her knees and pushed her forward. Scarlet held the edge as they moved and then closed her eyes as she let go, forcing herself to trust in his grip. Ruby had been under for longer this time, and Scarlet felt fear take hold of her heart, despite all that had happened and the hatred they'd shared their whole life.

When her head came up this time, she could see Ruby had given all the fight she had left, and as her cousin's arm rose weakly out of the oil, she knew it was her last chance to save her.

With grim determination, she grasped Ruby's wrist with both hands, screaming at her to hold on as she squeezed with all her strength and tried to pull her up. But the oil was unrelenting, dragging her back into its depths, and as Ruby's hand fell limp and disappeared for the final time, a cold shock settled over her.

Ruby was gone.

FIFTY-EIGHT

Ascough folded the last of her jumpers and placed it in the suitcase laid out on her bed. She looked around at her small flat, a place she'd once looked at as her home, as an extension of who she was, and felt nothing. It wasn't her home. It wasn't part of her. It was just a collection of walls broken up by doorways and windows, designed to protect whoever was in it from the elements. It didn't mean anything more.

It had been only two days since she'd left that scrapyard, the fear of God having been laid into her by the man she now knew to be Chain, a gang leader with a very dark history and a penchant for inflicting pain. She'd found him in the files, after seeing him before, and she knew from reading those that he and Scarlet together was the most dangerous recipe for destruction possible.

Scarlet had been less aggressive towards her as they left the scrapyard that night, still in shock, as they'd all been. Not that she was sure this mattered. Scarlet didn't need to raise her voice to be threatening. She'd calmly pointed out that Ascough needed to keep what had happened here to herself, for her own safety as much as anyone else's. Ascough was tied up in this mess as deeply as Scarlet and Chain were. More, in fact, considering she'd have to explain how she was even there in the first place. It would be the end of her career for sure, and possibly her freedom, paired with the harassment case she was already a part of.

Ascough had sat up for the rest of the night, not able to sleep, thinking hard about all that had happened lately and about how far she was from the person she used to be. Before she'd found out about John, she'd had her head screwed on. She'd been happy and on a good path with her career, enjoying her life and sleeping peacefully at night.

But now she was a mess. She'd spent the last few weeks stalking a stranger for reasons that weren't even really there. She'd allowed her mind to be twisted with hatred and paranoia, clinging on to it like a lifeline to distract herself from her heartbreak. And on top of that, she'd crossed lines she never thought she would even consider before now. She'd been horrified when John had betrayed the laws he upheld, but she had ended up doing exactly the same thing.

John wasn't coming back, that much was clear. He was gone, and even Scarlet didn't know where he was. There was nothing left for her here. It was time to move on and start anew, leaving all this darkness and pain behind her with the Drews. She wanted nothing to do with them anymore. She never wanted to set eyes on them or this area of London ever again. It had cost her too much of herself.

She'd resigned the day before, stating only that she needed to move closer to home and would take whatever job came up there. Now she was no longer part of this station, her part of the Drews' harassment claim would likely be dropped and she would be able to put that behind her too, in time.

Staring blankly at the wall, she unloaded all the emotional

baggage she'd been carrying and mentally left it behind her. It wouldn't really be that easy, she knew. But she had to try.

Zipping up her last suitcase, she dragged it onto its wheels, placed her key on the bedside table and left the flat, and her life here, for good.

EPILOGUE

Scarlet pushed through the front door of the small, cluttered electrical shop, and the bell above it tinkled. She walked down one of the two narrow aisles towards the desk at the back, her expression grave as she waited for Chain to appear from the door behind it.

He walked through, his broad frame filling the doorway, before he leaned down over the counter on his crossed arms, his expression unreadable.

'I was wondering when you'd turn up,' he said.

Scarlet nodded, no smile lifting her face as she chose not to bother hiding how she felt. There was no point.

'Listen, don't sweat it. I know what you're gonna ask and it suits me just fine. I wasn't there. I don't know anything. I don't *wanna* know anything, to be honest,' he said, addressing the issue head-on.

Scarlet nodded again, this time in acceptance. 'Good. Keep that up. In return, I'll protect you and keep you out of it, if my involvement somehow ever comes up. I hope it won't of course,' she added with a wry expression. 'But if it does.'

'All agreed then,' Chain confirmed.

Scarlet turned to leave then paused and looked back. 'Why did you come in after me?' she asked.

Chain shrugged. 'I saw that woman come after you. I thought I'd just check it out.'

Scarlet studied him for a few seconds. 'Thanks,' she said, the word quiet but full of sincerity. 'You're a good man.'

He laughed at this, the action not reaching his eyes as they watched her. 'Oh, Scarlet... I promise you I'm anything but that.'

The corners of her mouth flickered up almost into a smile. 'I meant good to have around. We all know this life kills the goodness in all of us.'

Turning away, she exited the shop and pushed her hands into the pockets of her jacket as she walked back to her car.

Nothing had really changed in the last two days. No one else knew that Ruby was dead. Lily still watched the horizon for her, Cillian still searched, Connor still waited for one of them to be successful. From a clinical perspective, their collective futures looked brighter than ever, even though they didn't know one of the main reasons why yet. Ruby was gone. She no longer posed all the many threats she would have, down the line. There were no more loose cannons in their ranks or hiding somewhere ready to pounce and cause chaos.

Their businesses were thriving, new ventures were unfolding, and neither Jennings nor any of his team had been sighted since their lawyer had hit back. She hadn't been bluffing when she'd told him how things were likely to go. It didn't matter that he was right – he had no proof. And he'd chased ghosts for too long. Budgets were still budgets, and the police force was already suffering cuts and squeezes.

She reached her car, unlocked it and slipped in, feeling the burden of all she had to now carry with her weighing heavily on her slim shoulders. Ruby's body would be found eventually. Once the tank was full and was taken wherever it went to be emptied, she would still be there at the bottom. It would likely be passed as an unfortunate accident. Someone who broke in to find a place to sleep and who ended up tripping into the tank in the dark. But she would be identified, and Lily and the twins would have to face the heartbreak of losing her – of losing someone they loved dearly, despite all she had put them through. And this Scarlet wasn't looking forward to. Because she knew, despite the fact she had tried to save her, had tried with all her strength, that she would carry that guilt around with her forever. The guilt of being part of what had caused those she loved that unbearable loss and pain.

Holding her head high, she carefully adjusted her expression, hiding all her secrets within, and pulled out onto the road. Life, for the rest of them at least, went on. And there was, as ever, so much to do to make sure the Drew firm remained on top.

Connor stepped out of his building and started to cross the residential car park, coming to an abrupt halt as a car suddenly swung in front of him and stopped barely a foot away.

'What the fuck!' he exclaimed, about to have a go at whoever was inside. But as the door opened, he just rolled his eyes. 'What do *you* want?' he asked rudely.

'To talk to you,' Ray replied.

'No thanks,' Connor replied with a note of sarcasm, stepping sideways as he tried to get around him.

Ray got out and blocked his path. 'Ten minutes. I just want to put *one* thing to you, an offer for you to think over.'

Connor tutted. 'What offer?' he snapped. 'I'm late for something, so tell me quickly here, so I can tell you to fuck off now and get on with my day.'

'Doing what, running errands for your mum or running errands for your brother?' Ray asked, raising his eyebrows.

'Listen here, you cunt—' Connor shot back to that comment.

But Ray cut him off. 'No, *you* listen,' he growled, leaning forward into Connor's angry face. 'I ain't saying that to insult you, but you know it's the truth.' He tilted his head to one side and raised an eyebrow, holding Connor's gaze.

Connor stepped back, still furious but quiet now.

'You don't want to know me as a parent, and that's fine. But there's an opportunity here that both of you seem to have missed,' Ray stated. 'You're loyal to your mum and I would *never* try to undermine that. But the firm she's built up for you is small and there's three of you who'll take over down the line. There's always one natural leader who becomes the head and leads. Not three.'

Ray stared at him intently, and Connor frowned as he turned over this concept in his head.

'Our firms have always been friends. This recent spat aside,' he added. 'And they could be more than that one day. Especially with two brothers heading them up.'

'What are you saying?' Connor asked, totally thrown.

'*Ten* minutes,' Ray pressed again. 'Just hear me out, and then I'll leave you to think it over. That's all I'm asking.'

Connor looked over to his car, clenching the keys in his hand and biting his lip as he warred with his loyalties and the deep curiosity to find out more.

'Ten minutes,' he said eventually in a hard tone. He turned back towards his building. 'Follow me.'

A LETTER FROM EMMA

Dear readers,

Well, here we are again. Book twelve... It feels surreal that this is really book twelve. What did you think of this one? As always, I read every review online and read every comment on my page, as your opinions mean a lot to me. So please do let me know what you liked, who you hated, what you're looking forward to finding out. If you would like to hear more about the series, sign up here. Your email address won't be shared and you can unsubscribe at any time.

www.bookouture.com/emma-tallon

It was harder than I thought, writing Scarlet and Ruby's final dance. Ruby is such a complex character, and over the previous four books, several sides of her came out. At times you all hated her. And at other times I know many of you rooted for her, willing her to succeed as she tried so hard to be good. Even I rooted for her. But that's the thing about bad characters – about bad people. No one is ever one hundred per cent bad. Even the worst people have their good moments. That doesn't always redeem them though, and I think in this case there was no other way things could have ended. In the end, Ruby drove herself off the road. All her years of self-destructive behaviour finally caught up with her.

I'm looking forward to starting the next instalment in this

series. So many questions left to answer. So many new problems to uncover. In fact, I'd better leave you now and get started!

Thanks for reading and I'll see you all again soon.

With love,

Emma X

facebook.com/emmatallonofficial

twitter.com/EmmaEsj

instagram.com/my.author.life

ACKNOWLEDGEMENTS

Firstly, thank *you*. Yes, you. The person reading this. Without you and everyone else who reads my books, I wouldn't be able to do this. You make it possible, and I appreciate you more than you know.

A heartfelt thanks also to my fabulous editor and friend, Helen, who so brilliantly helps me mould my chaotic first drafts into the finished stories you see. Helen, you're an awesome person. We make a great team, and I'm so grateful for everything you do.

I'd like to add a special thank you to another editor who has worked on my previous eleven books, Jon Appleton. Jon, you've been with me from the beginning, and every time I get close to copy-edits, I've always greatly looked forward to them. This is my twelfth novel and the first I've done without you. I've missed our banter and all the lovely comments you've shared over the years. But I'm thankful to have had you for so long. Until our paths cross again, my friend, good luck and I wish you nothing but greatness.

My last thank you is reserved for two particularly wonderful author friends, Casey Kelleher and Victoria Jenkins. You've seen me through many a mental writing breakdown, every panic, every plot hole, every problem I can't solve. You've cheered me on when I've limped towards a deadline with nothing left to give. You've buddied up for writing sprints when motivation ghosts me. And I honestly could not do this without you. You're my tribe, and I love you to bits.